Rachel Gillian North is a 32 year old Local Government Officer who has always lived in Devon. Her parents bought her first pony when she was 11 years old and this developed into a lifetime passion for all things equine. Rachel now has two young American Quarter Horses who live at her rural home near Widdon Down.

She wrote her first 'book' when she was 7, and 'A Horse Called Ambition' is her first full length novel.

A HORSE CALLED AMBITION

RACHEL GILLIAN NORTH

Indigo Dreams Publishing

First Edition: A Horse called Ambition

First published in Great Britain in 2013 by:
Indigo Dreams Publishing Ltd
24 Forest Houses
Cookworthy Moor
Halwill
Beaworthy
EX21 5UU

www.indigodreams.co.uk

ISBN 978-1-909357-35-8

A CIP record for this book is available from the British Library.

Designed and typeset in Minion Pro by Indigo Dreams.
Cover design by Indigo Dreams, artwork supplied by K Taran-Tula & R G North
Printed and bound in Great Britain by Imprint Academic, Exeter
Papers used by Indigo Dreams are recyclable products made from wood grown in sustainable forests following the guidance of the Forest Stewardship Council

Because their love affirms us
we can find a way to be at one amid chaos.
Because their choices are made vicariously
we learn to play God.
Love's ambition will always be
to reach new heights,
to put their needs before our own.
We will never tire of our endless journey
to understand them better.

R.G. North, 2013

‘For Ziggy, for everything …’

Gratitude in abundance to all four of my wonderful parents, Gill and Mike, and Rob and Alison, for their support with the book, and being so proud of me despite the fact that I am rather odd! Spencer, Liz and Beccy – your helpful comments and unyielding faith in the book allowed me to persevere where I might have given up.

To Ronnie and Dawn of Indigo Dreams for their support and for giving a first time author and an untested genre a chance, I can't begin to express my gratitude. Thank you both so much. Lynn, I will never forget the things you have taught me, your attention to detail is superhuman.

And finally my heartfelt thanks go to Janet and to K, for loving me, just the way I am.

A HORSE CALLED AMBITION

Barefoot Forward!

Hope you like it!

Love

Rachel xx

Chapter one

Patience is a virtue.

Jules shifted uncomfortably in the saddle. Taut features gave away her nerves. Luckily her horse, Romeo, was calm.

'So, why the long face?' Maurice chuckled at his own joke and rested a tweed clad elbow on Romeo's chestnut withers.

Jules gently nudged Romeo with booted heels, asking the horse to move away from the old farmer. It was good of him to drive the horse lorry to the cross country event, but his total density to her fear and the importance of the day made her all the more fractious.

Romeo was on terrific form, the 16 hand high Irish bred hunter took everything in his loose stride. As Jules began to warm the horse up, she was comforted for a moment by the familiar rhythm of his wide grounded canter. She wished they would call her number so that she could get it over and done with.

Nerves had always been her downfall when it came to competing.

A formidable presence in the legal world, the twenty-nine-year-old solicitor, 'Juliette Walker' was the picture of confidence in suits. All that changed when she donned her cross country shirt. Jules could go from clearing fences with clockwork perfection, to a mane gripping, knee rattling mess. It only took a single exuberant toss of Romeo's perfectly level head to make her to fall apart.

She had purchased Romeo three years ago. Jules' understanding of consumer law meant the horse had undergone every pre-purchase check possible. After two veterinary inspections, a test ride by a local dressage instructor and no less than seven visits to the seller's yard by Jules herself, she still wasn't convinced. In the end she had gone on what she called gut instinct. She smiled as she recalled a discussion with her friends on the subject, where she had had to agree that for someone called Juliette, the purchase of a horse called Romeo must be fate, even if it was a little corny.

Jules shortened her reins and glanced self-consciously down to make sure her hands were level. She held her breath and aimed Romeo at the low practice fence, only exhaling once they were safely over.

'One more then iss' you lover!' Maurice called from outside the practice ring, Devonshire twang sounding out across the busy field.

The knot in Jules' stomach tightened uncomfortably and she walked Romeo towards the collecting ring, falling in line behind a waiting bay mare and her infuriatingly confident looking rider.

Twenty miles east, Rosie Hall glanced at her watch, fingers pulling impatiently at a lock of her long brown windblown hair as she stood in the gateway of the field.

She glanced up across the sloping green sea to the two stables and adjoining storage area, just in time to see Harry's ample white hindquarters disappearing through the open door into the hay barn.

'Little bugger,' she shouted but smiled in spite of cursing. Harry got away with most things, mainly because he was good natured and sensible, but also because at his age, he had earned the right. He would be in there, munching away at a bale and probably making a mess but he couldn't hurt himself and she had other things on her mind.

'Yeah, because standing here waiting is so important,' Rosie rolled her eyes as she spoke. The horsebox should have arrived at 1pm and it was now half past. Had he loaded? Had they broken down? Was there traffic? As Rosie waited for the arrival of her new horse, she thought about the day her parents had purchased Harry.

He had been the perfect first horse, a wise but exuberant twelve-year-old. Now he was twenty-five and nearing a well-earned retirement. The proud and sturdy Welsh Cob had taught her so much over the years, not just about riding and the various competitive disciplines they had dabbled in, but also about responsibility, about having an entity that could not survive without you; selflessness, financial balance, love.

As a teenager she did her best to keep up with the latest trends. Somehow though, Harry's need for a new winter rug or another vet's bill had always seen her with only a foot in fashion, and a social life among non-horsey friends which was intermittent and compromised. In her early twenties she had pubbed and clubbed, often with a man in tow, but Harry always brought her back down to earth. Now at twenty-eight, of all Rosie's bad decisions, only a handful related to Harry. He looked and behaved almost exactly as he had always done. The only telltale sign that he was getting older came from the gradual whitening of his once dappled grey coat and the slight dip in his broad back.

Rosie realised she would be unlikely to cope when she lost Harry. It was his mortality which had led to this moment, awaiting arrival of a four-year-old gelding.

She rested her elbows on the gate, cupped her face in her hands and gazed proudly at the stables. Her stables.

There would be no more livery yards, farms or riding schools for her and her boy now. Not since she and her husband Matt had purchased Orchard Cottage with its two bedrooms, double garage and most importantly, 3 acres of paddock.

Rosie and Matt completed construction of the stables and hay barn just a week ago. They had worked so hard on the project since they had arrived at the cottage in the spring that they had totally neglected any plans they might have had for the cottage itself. Harry's comfort was more important. The rather primitive dwelling still had no shower and the decor ranged between 1970s chic, and pretty shabby.

Rosie and Matt had been saving and working towards a place with land for Harry almost since they met. The Cottage was undeniably remote. The nearest village of Monkerswell was 3 miles east and it was a 24 mile commute to the City of Exeter where Rosie worked. But the first time they had seen the Cottage they had known it would be home. Rosie didn't see the flaking paint which fluttered from the window frames, or the cracks which scarred the render, she only saw the positives.

Matt had sufficient space to indulge his passion for tinkering with fast cars and Rosie had Harry, just a glance out of the bedroom window at last.

Rosie popped a tab of chewing gum into her dainty rosebud mouth wishing she had a hair band and a cigarette. Nine months of cold turkey and she still missed a fag as much as the first day, especially at tense times like these, nervously awaiting a new beginning. Thank goodness for Matt, he was ever forgiving, dealing with her moods, her whims and her impatience. Most of all though he embraced Harry, even loved him. He understood her devotion completely, rather than some of her former boyfriends who had put up with her horse at best and been jealous at worst.

'Wish Jules was afforded the same,' Rosie said quietly. She scowled when she thought of Tristan, her friend's selfish and petulant partner. He knew she and Gill hadn't been able to make it to the Horse Trials at the Equestrian College. His refusal to accompany Jules left an already nervy rider alone on her big day.

Rosie glanced at her watch and wondered if Jules and Romeo

had made it safely round the solid cross country course of impossibly high wooden fences, banks and drops. She glanced at her mobile which was stuffed in the top of her welly boot and hoped Jules remembered to call when she had finished.

'Where is the bloody lorry?'

Meanwhile, in Suffolk, Gill Newman marched towards the Steward's office to declare her entries for the 1st, 3rd and 5th race.

Dubai Day at Newmarket Race Course was the most important day of the year in the Arabian Horse Racing calendar.

The hot September sunshine meant the meet was well attended. Most of the Arabian scene elite were milling around in expensive suits and Ascot was rivalled for its hat reputation by the array of well-dressed women.

Gill studied her form book and was thankful of her decision to keep one of the less experienced horses she had in training safely at home. Although Marilliam's Immortal Mist had indeed qualified for the prestigious event, Gill felt confident in her decision to persuade the mare's owner that next year she would be ready and this year, she was not.

Gill stood in the queue outside the office, impatient to get back to her three runners. She blushed and nervously tucked shoulder length blond hair behind a delicate ear when she noticed an on-course bookmaker throwing an amorous glance in her direction. At forty-two, she had the look of a woman ten years younger. Her figure, kept trim by the daily grind of running a medium sized training yard, showed no sign of the daughter she had seventeen years ago. She was often admired, but Gill had no time for relationships.

After what seemed like an age she finally reached the front of the queue.

She set off at a jog back to the stable area to check that Khaleb's Ambition was nearly ready for the first race. The twelve-year-old chestnut mare, whose stable name was Amber, wuffled a welcome through fluttering nostrils as Gill approached.

Kelly, the groom, popped her head over the stable door to greet her boss. As Kelly let herself out of the mare's stable, she was already giving Gill the lowdown on the mental and physical conditions of the horses.

'Amber is just fine, totally relaxed as usual. I've plaited her mane and polished her hooves so she's a shoe in for best turned out in the parade ring!'

Gill smiled. At all Arab race meetings a prize was given to the groom of the most well-presented horse and Kelly was proud of herself in usually picking up the £20 prize money and the title, 'Best Turned Out'.

Amber was Gill's own horse; the horse that started the ball rolling. When Gill learned about Arabian Racing, she knew she had found Amber's forte. The mare hid raw speed and power underneath an easy, calm exterior.

'Rocky is not doing so well,' Kelly continued. 'He still hasn't cooled off after hotting up in the lorry and he's pacing his stable like he's demented.' Gill's smile faded as she turned towards the large chestnut's stable. Rock Farm's Fury rolled a white eye at Gill as he tossed his head and turned away from the stable door to conduct another unruly circuit of the small loose box.

The stallion belonged to an Arabian breeder, who was racing Rocky in the hope the horse would make a name for himself and be worth more at stud. He was a handful at home and on the course. All who cared for him bore bruises. Gill couldn't help secretly liking him because he was just playful really. When he snatched at your arm with gleaming teeth and waited for your retaliation, he was merely instigating a game.

Gill felt sorry for stallions. Apart from the highlight of covering a mare they were largely kept in isolation to avoid them injuring other horses. They missed out on the social elements of a being part of a herd. If Rocky was able to win his race today he would, at last, be triumphantly retired to the owner's stud and would be their problem again.

'And Monty?' Gill asked, glancing with a smile at the perfectly formed black horse.

'Monty is Monty,' Kelly laughed, 'completely transfixed by everything but keeping his manners, as always.'

Monday's Eclipse, or Monty, was eagerly watching the activity around the racecourse stables. Hazel eyes set deep in an elegant head greedily absorbed the pre-race bustle. Monty's owner was very influential in Arabian horse world. Gill still felt his being placed with her for training was a test by the large terrifying woman. If she failed, the good reputation her business so desperately needed, would not be gained. If she succeeded, she could find herself with more of Norah Ranger's horses. Gill wasn't sure whether the pressure would turn her into a nervous wreck, but the bank manager would certainly ease a little of the financial pressure if the business got its head above water.

'Okay, Kel, let's get Amber's bridle on, first race in twenty!'

'Easy boy, easy easy,' Jules attempted a soothing murmur, which was really for her own benefit.

Romeo was jumping the course in his usual workmanlike manner; ears locked forward, always looking for the next fence. He tucked even white socks neatly up under his chestnut chest, making each jump seem effortless. He could have done it on his own.

As they neared the home run, Jules all but shut her eyes for a drop jump over a log and down into a lake. Romeo's hooves met the water, soaking her white jodhpurs and dampening the ebony plait which flowed from her hard hat and Jules finally began to relax.

Soon she was balancing her curvaceous form up over the chestnut's withers, urging him on for the ascent out of the water. The horse felt her exhilaration and upped his tempo for the remaining jumps, which they cleared as team. Jules' earlier nerves seemed to have been imagined as she crossed the finish line, muddied and laughing. She hugged her horse's neck and even insisted the waiting Maurice pat him. Romeo outwardly beamed at his reward.

With the course safely completed, Jules travelled home happily in the horsebox, passing the time chattering to Maurice and leaping up to check on Romeo, who was swaying calmly in the back.

Later that evening when Jules had finished feeling Romeo's legs for any heat and waited until he had eaten and probably half digested his evening feed, she had one last hug with the most important male in her life. She sighed happily, not minding the darkness as she made the short walk from Maurice's farm where she rented a stable, to the village where she lived with Tristan. Another important man in her life, but his idea of looking after Jules was rather different.

'Hi, Sweetie! Jules kicked off her boots at the back door of the terraced cottage and was not surprised when she didn't get a reply. She burst through the kitchen into the front room.

'Guess what?'

'Yes?' The dark-eyed and burly estate agent sat cross-legged on the couch. A lump of cannabis resin sat on a tatty piece of cling film on the coffee table in front of him, beside an overflowing ashtray and half a mug of cold tea. Although he was only in his early thirties his general demeanour was one of exhaustion and contempt for a cruel world.

'Well – my wonderful horse won us this!' Jules whipped a yellow rosette out from behind her back and stood grinning on the faux sheepskin rug. Tristan noted the colour of the rosette and barely hid his schoolmaster like disapproval.

'So you didn't win then?'

'Well no, but the competition included professional riders and horses. When you consider Romeo and I worked for this alone, we did very well to be placed at all. 3rd really is pretty good!' Jules' lip quivered and she beamed at her lover, green eyes pleading for some praise.

'Extra food for the horsey then.'

Jules leapt onto his lap for a congratulatory cuddle, taking the remark as the most positive she was likely to get.

As she lay with her head on his chest, he curled his finger gently under her chin and lifted her face. She melted as he gazed down at her and kissed her nose.

'Tea, baby?' he purred at the adoring Jules.

Jules climbed from his lap and headed back to the kitchen to put the kettle on, knowing it was a request, not an offer.

Rosie crept from the house, up the field and towards the stables in moonlight. She tiptoed over the concrete yard in front of the buildings. The horses were at the very top of their paddock, she went to the corner of the end stable and peeked around it. Two pairs of eyes stared back at her, ears pricked towards the intruder.

'Scuppered!' Rosie laughed and walked towards the horses. She had been hoping to spy on Harry and the new arrival, but they had been, as horses almost always were, one step ahead of her.

The youngster eyed her warily as she moved towards him.

It had taken him nearly an hour to leave the horse box that afternoon. When the breeder's assistant lowered the ramp his wide eyes and rigid legged stance suggested that although he had been fairly happy to get into the box, now that he was in a strange new place without his old pals, he was rather more reluctant to leave it.

After it became apparent that gentle coaxing and even a rope around his rump was not enough to persuade him to disembark, Rosie had suggested they leave him totally alone.

They went into the cottage to sort out the finances and passport transfer which would make the four-year-old, American

Quarter Horse officially hers.

A few coffees and a few thousand pounds later, Shiny Red River was still in the same spot at the back of the box. Perfectly calm, but not going anywhere. They had tried leading a whinnying Harry into the box and back out again, but even the reassuring and inquisitive older horse could not tempt Red out into his new field. Much to Rosie's disappointment, the breeder's tight schedule had made a hands-on approach necessary and he had been half shoved down the ramp and out of the box. Sweat had darkened his purple liver chestnut coat, illuminating the scattering of white hairs which ran along his back and down over his huge powerful quarters. As soon as his head collar was removed, he trotted away into the paddock, glad to be free of human hands.

Now, Red was wary and the building of trust would take longer. Even in the milky glow of a shining half-moon, Rosie could read the fear in his eyes. She longed to dash over to him and hug him, but she knew in his frightened state he would only endure her affection at best and injure her at worst. Instead she turned her back to him and rubbed Harry's white face, talking softly to her old friend.

Without looking, she knew the youngster would be watching her passive welcoming body language, longing to step forward and investigate. Taking care not to look at Red, she ran her hands over Harry's neck and withers, then his more sensitive stomach and legs. As Harry stood still, resting a hind hoof and enjoying her caress, he unwittingly showed Red that Rosie was trustworthy – an integral part of his new group.

Red watched eagerly and began to step forward. Harry stretched his neck out to its full extent, ears flat back with a look in his eye that said 'one more step mate'. He would not bully the young horse, but he had best not overstep the mark!

Rosie mixed the evening feeds for her two horses. She fed Harry first with his usual mixture of wetted and softened pony nuts which were easier on his old teeth. Twenty feet from Harry's usual feeding spot, she placed a soft rubber bucket and stood back to allow the youngster to greedily gobble down his chaff. Without making eye contact she sat on the grass and quietly hummed, while Red ate, further confirming her intention to do him no harm. When they had both finished, she kissed Harry good night and spoke softly to Red from a distance, before going back inside.

Matt was waiting with a glass of wine and a warm seat on the sofa.

'How is he?'

'Going to be a while before he trusts me, but we'll get there.'

She snuggled up to Matt and hoped she was right. Not only was Red largely unhandled, he was also an unbroken four-year-old and she knew the window for easy training that a very young horse afforded, had long passed.

Gill and Kelly finally neared the end of their long journey home. The horse box trundled off the motorway and began winding through the country lanes that led to the village of Stoke Rewe. They talked over the day and planned strategies for the coming races.

'I think Amber has had enough you know,' said Gill.

'Why? She was just perfect today?' Kelly shone with happiness as she recalled the horse crossing the finish line in the Mare's Championship Race. Two lengths in front of her tired competitors, Amber headed to the winners enclosure looking just as fresh as she had on the way to the start.

'She was perfect, bless her. She could run forever. But I feel like her whole career has been building up to this day and she did it, you know? She is the champion mare. She came through for me, bless her dear heart. It makes me think. Too many more races and her age will start to show, why not go out on the biggest high possible for an Arab?!'

'But what will you do with her, she's too young to retire from doing anything at all?'

'Well I thought I might speak to Norah—'

'Oh! Kelly cut her off with a shriek. 'You're going to put her in foal to Monday's Eclipse? What a beautiful baby!'

'Well, let's see what Norah says!'

It had been a good day, all in all, Amber's win, Monty's gallant photo finish second. The only downside was Rocky's lazy amble in to fifth place. Now his owner wanted him to continue to race until he got a win, so Gill wouldn't be rid of the menace yet.

Gill had wanted to throttle the jockey when he told the downhearted owner that Rocky's problem was lack of concentration and that blinkers in training may help him stay focused. Gill thought Rocky's problem was, in fact, that he just had no desire to win. He was cheeky and excitable and loved mares. To come first in a race just wasn't that important to him and while the potential for speed was great, he had no real desire to break a sweat just because some human was telling him to run.

Gill gently negotiated the box round the last sharp bend and the security lighting of Newman's Arabians threw light on her home.

Home, sweet home, a white rendered cottage stood to the right of the driveway, which led to a large American style horse barn, complete with 12 boxes and an open plan feed and storage area. Gently sloping pasture divided into acre paddocks surrounded the house and outbuildings, encased at the boundaries by thick Devon hedgerows.

They pulled closer to the barn; Gill was filled with apprehension as she looked into the floodlit area.

The loose box doors were wide open. She killed the engine. Kelly heard the hooves first.

'They're out!'

They stared at each other in disbelief. Three precious

racehorses in training, Tom, a prize stallion at stud and three beloved ponies stabled with Gill at livery, were somewhere in the darkness. More worryingly, they were all together.

As they jumped down from the cab, another worrying sound startled them.

'MUM!'

Gill ran out of the flood light and into the first paddock.

'Charlie?' Gill bellowed, 'Charlotte!' Gill's voice was high with fear. She prayed for her eyes to adjust.

Gill heard the teenager's pounding footsteps and Charlie came into view. They hurled themselves at each other and Gill held her daughter tightly before stepping back and addressing her with renewed urgency.

'What happened, Charlie?'

'They … oh … Mum the horses!'

'Honey, please, what's happened?'

'I was in the house, watching TV, when I heard galloping past the window.'

'Okay. It's okay.' Gill turned back to a stunned Kelly. 'Unload them,' she gestured towards the box, 'get them in their stables, then come and help me.' Gill grasped Charlie's hand. 'Come on.'

But Charlie held back, tears streaming from her face.

'Tom kicked Pebbles right in front of me. He can't walk properly.'

Gill took a split second to process the information.

'Right. Back to the house, call your Uncle Mike. Call Mrs Sanders. No, don't call Mrs Sanders yet, let's see how Tom is. You'd better get Bob here. The number is in the blue book in the office.'

Gill tried not to think too hard about the last instruction. Bob, the vet, had to be called now to give him chance to get there as quickly as possible in case there were any serious injuries, but Gill knew the resulting bill would probably cost her Amber's winnings.

What choice did she have? A Stallion loose with three valuable mares and the livery ponies, which were entrusted to her care? Pebbles the gelding kicked? She grabbed head collars from the gate of the second paddock and braved herself for an exhausting night.

A week later, the three friends sat around the kitchen table at Orchard Cottage.

Rosie poured them each a glass of wine and for a moment they sat in silence.

'I just don't understand. Who would do that and why?' Jules shook her head. She sipped and savoured her wine, conscious she was driving and it would be her only glass.

'Gill, do you think it could have been Alex?' Rosie asked.

'Oh no, he wouldn't have the energy to get off his fat backside and run round opening gates!' Gill laughed, in spite of herself, at the notion of her overweight ex-husband sneaking around her paddocks late at night. 'We're pretty much all right now. He doesn't pay nearly enough attention to our daughter, but I have long since given up on that.'

Gill was still dealing with the aftermath of the break-in. She should have had two runners at Taunton today. She'd had to withdraw them and pay the wasted entry fees herself, because although Tom, the stallion, had been fine after his moonlit adventure, care of the other horses had prevented her from riding Monty and maintaining his peak racing fitness. As for the mares, Tom had bruised one of them badly with his amorous advances and the owner had been in agreement to give Marilliam's Immortal Mist two weeks rest.

'How is Pebbles now?' Rosie stood up to stir the chilli con carne which was bubbling on the hob.

'Very swollen, still not flexing his hind leg properly. Bob said another few inches and his hock joint would have been fractured. Tom's aim must have been out. Sally is being very good about it.

She has been keeping Pebbles with me for five years now. The little girl who bounced around on her pony is becoming a woman for sure.' Gill paused for a long pull at her ruby red glass before continuing.

'They are all suspicious, the racing owners, the livery owners. I can't blame them though, I don't know who did it, or if they will come back. Knowing my luck Norah will pull Monty next.' Gill stood up, frustrated. 'Low-life's ... If I got my hands on them ...'

Gill moved over to the window. Jules and Rosie looked at each other. Rosie was the first to attempt to say something reassuring.

'Gill, you have paid for all those extra security lights and the police have promised to drive by?'

'Yeah, and they are hardly going to come back are they?' Jules piped up and then regretted speaking.

'I just wish I knew who did it.'

Gill gazed out of the window at the dimly lit orchard which flagged the cottage, giving it its name. 'At least they didn't let the brood mares out.'

Gill had a collection of brood mares who were temporarily residing at Newmans waiting to be covered by one of the Stallions. Starfighter, stable named Tom, was truly a selective breeding accomplishment. His champion sire had been a star of the racing world in Dubai itself and his mother was a tall French bred mare who had taken the European circuit by storm.

Tom was stunning. With an average racing form in the UK, his looks and pedigree alone were enough to earn him early retirement at the age of seven. He now enjoyed a more leisurely career which involved regular sex and large feeds. A bright bay with a sleek little head, he had huge black eyes and a neat compact muzzle. Tiny diamond shaped ears were countered by a tail which pointed skywards whenever he moved. Mrs Sanders lived in France and was happy to leave the generation of his progeny to Gill, who handled the payments and mare selection as well as the actual covering.

Not all the brood mares at Newmans were there to be covered by Tom, however, and some of them still had shoes on. Their release by the intruder could have led to serious kick wounds and in spring there could have been foals coming out Starfighter when they should have been Monday's Eclipse. As it was, the three racing mares that had been on the midnight rampage would have to be scanned next week to make sure they were not in foal, and any terminations paid for at Gill's expense. Gill was holding off advising the owners of the mares that this was a possibility in the hope that all would be well.

The vet's bill, wasted entry fees and extra livery free of charge for the brood mares while Tom rested, was crippling Gill.

'I didn't go to bed at all that night; it took us two hours to get them all back in to their stables. They wound each other up so much, they weren't in the mood to be caught. Bob didn't leave until four in the morning, dealing with poor Pebbles. Jasper, Carol's old horse, was showing signs of colic until lunchtime the next day. He wasn't sweating or rolling as such, but he definitely had bellyache. Sally's other horse Ryan has got windgalls on his fetlocks the size of peaches. That's what I don't get, whoever did it must have known horses well enough to realise that letting them all out together like that would cause mayhem? It's the suffering of the animals that makes me mad.'

Gill swung away from the window, aware that she sounded like a stuck record and changed the subject.

'So, Rosiekins, how's this youngster of yours?'

Later that night, as Jules drove home towards Kysford, she fought the tears with a loud radio and some tuneless singing.

She had known before she went that the conversation would mainly revolve around Gill's misfortune the week before and Rosie's new arrival, but she had still hoped for a window to share her own week from hell.

After her successful day at the hunter trial last Saturday, Sunday had been spent doing approximately bugger all, as usual. Trying to get Tristan to leave the house and share in any normal couple activities was a battle she regularly lost. For the most part he refused to join her at the farm to see Romeo. He also refused to join her when she visited her parents. Dinner parties with friends were rare and only occurred as a result of her agreement to do something disproportionate for Tristan in return.

Not only did he never want to socialise, he also punished her for going without him.

Monday evening after work he had refused to eat the food she prepared, saying he had gone off the idea of eating, after goading her into cooking.

She spent Tuesday evening not talking to him, after the usual row about his refusal to partake of any housework whatsoever. Wednesday, he had gone to visit his pot dealer and had not returned until the early hours, spaced out and wide awake.

Thursday she made a real effort to be nice. To be a good girl. He had refused her when she tried to take him to bed. Another knock to her confidence.

She had thrown an embarrassing and hysterical crying fit, the frustration of the week too much for her. She picked at Tristan like a scab until he reacted, chasing her up the stairs and pinning her to the bed by her wrists. Even as he hissed into her ear, his head pushing hers into the bed clothes, telling that she was a mental case and if she didn't shut up he would gag her, she prayed the violence would turn to sex, silencing her desperation for affection.

He still hadn't spoken to her. Friday evening he had passed out at about seven. This morning he left for rugby before she had woken up. She had toyed with the idea of going to watch the match. That usually made him happy. She hadn't gone though and she regretted it now as she neared her home, knowing he would probably be back by now. If they had lost the match, he would be unbearably moody.

'My princess is home!'

Jules was picked up and swept over the threshold, before she had a chance to recover the key from the lock.

Tristan kissed her, tender and sweet, as he held her in the hallway. He took her hand and led her into the lounge. He collapsed onto the sofa and raised his arm, beckoning her to sit beside him. Still wary, she began taking her coat off.

'We won today. Your boyfriend scored the winning try!'

'Well done. That's great.' The penny dropped and Jules realised the reason for his good mood. He had a habit of totally ignoring previous arguments if he wanted her attention. Behaving as though the preceding days had not been the war at home was a pretty normal trick, their relationship roller-coastered between breathtakingly good and ear-splittingly bad. Somehow, it always seemed to end up being Jules' fault when things went wrong.

Had it not been for his laziness, his persuasive and assertive manner would have made him a fortune in houses. Unfortunately, his weakness for cannabis saw him lacking in drive and determination.

Jules sighed and decided to take the going when it was good. She sat beside him and allowed herself to be cuddled.

'Off you go to the kitchen!' He grinned at her.

'Oh, Tristan, you can make your own dinner, I've had mine at Rosie's.'

'Go on, into the kitchen, my little princess.' He continued to grin, as Jules stared at him in disbelief. 'There's a present for you.'

'What? The oven?' Tristan laughed at Jules' scepticism and even she managed a grin at her own joke. He slid his hand underneath her and hoisted her from the sofa whilst he remained sat down.

Jules tentatively walked to the kitchen, expecting him to tell her that now she was up she could cook.

As she opened the door she heard a skitter of claws on the tiles. Stepping forward, she peered under the breakfast bar. There sat a tiny Border collie puppy. He looked terrified and she quickly dropped to her knees to ease his fear. He was almost entirely black, apart from a jagged white blaze which ran from his short nose up over the dome of his head.

'There there, little one,' Jules spoke softly to the puppy. He looked up at her with pleading eyes, desperate for some kind of solace in an unfamiliar world without his mother. He couldn't have been more than eight weeks old. Jules felt weak with compassion when she noticed the puddle beneath him. For another ten minutes she sat still, speaking slowly to the little animal, until eventually, gingerly, he walked over to her. Gently, Jules picked him up and held him in her arms. The puppy tucked his head under her chin and whimpered as he exhaled.

It wasn't until Jules heard Tristan come into the kitchen that she realised she was clinging to the dog with tears streaming down her face.

Jules had lost her childhood friend, a collie named Billy, at sixteen. The tragic event had marked the beginning of an incredibly painful journey into adulthood. Jules had vowed then she would never have another dog of her own, unable to allow herself to bear that kind of loss a second time. That was up until this moment, when she couldn't bring herself to put the puppy down for fear of cutting short the tidal wave of love sweeping over her.

Red-faced, Jules turned her tear filled eyes on Tristan and managed to find a small and rusty voice.

'Thank you. Thank you so much.'

Chapter two

Rosie adored Sundays. She woke early, leaving Matt to snore into the bed clothes. Walking through the kitchen she purposely ignored the dishes and wine glasses from the night before. Un-brushed brown hair bounced around her, as she headed down the path that led through the orchard and into the field.

A week after his arrival, Red was fitting nicely into the family. Rosie lifted the latch on the gate and Red let out a shrill greeting through his pert nostrils. He left Harry where they had been grazing side by side, to lope down the field towards her.

Harry wuffled a welcome in Rosie's general direction before walking directly to the stable block. He knew that was where he was fed, and at his time of life he wasn't about to waste energy dashing down the field to greet Rosie, only to have to walk back up again for his breakfast!

Rosie gently stroked Red's cheek. He rewarded her by lowering his head in acceptance and allowing his ears to be caressed. In just one week Red had gone from mistrust to adoration. Rosie was shocked by the speed at which he had come to allow her touch and accept her presence. She was delighted at his enthusiastic greetings.

Rosie mixed their breakfasts in the small tack and feed room which adjoined the two stables, she wondered if it was too early to begin some serious training with Red. She knew their bond was not nearly strong enough for her to attempt to get on his back yet, there was a lot of groundwork to do before that could happen, but she decided it wouldn't hurt to give him a little example of what was to come.

She fed the horses and set about creating a schooling area on the level part of the field to the side of the stables. She used fencing wire and plastic posts to create a 40 foot square enclosure. When she had finished, she decided to give the horses some digestion time while she made some breakfast for herself and Matt.

'See you in a bit, guys!' she called to the horses as she jogged back down the field towards the house. Red, who had finished his own breakfast, was sideling up to Harry, hoping for some left-over's. The young horse watched in amazement as Rosie disappeared through the Orchard and back into the house. He had never had so much attention and while he was coming to like it, Rosie still confused him entirely!

Matt stood by the open fridge door in black boxer shorts, blonde hair tousled. He used his left toe to scratch the back of his sun bronzed right calf. Rosie whistled at him as she kicked off her wellies. She slapped his bottom as she passed him and sighed happily. She ignored the gurgling pipes as she used the kitchen tap to fill the kettle. They knew they would need a plumber to service the old spring fed system eventually, but while the water kept coming, the expense didn't seem justified.

They'd had a fantastic first summer at the cottage, despite the rain in July and August. Now the September sun was showing no signs of retreating. However warm it stayed, Rosie knew she only had a short time to get working on Red before the nights drew in and her job confined her during daylight hours.

'How are they?'

'Red came cantering down to greet me again!'

'Great. Umm … Rosie?' Matt turned from the fridge and smiled grimly.

'I know that voice, what is it?' Rosie stood eyeing her husband, hands on hips.

'Your mum phoned.'

'Oh no.' Rosie's glorious day fell around her feet as the kettle began to boil. 'What did she want?'

'She didn't say. I said you were seeing to the horses and you would call her back.'

'Well,' Rosie slammed the tea bag canister down onto the work surface, 'she'll be waiting a long time!'

'Come on Rosie, you haven't spoken to her since July. And the way you two left things ... You really should speak to her.'

'Yeah, well she really should have been honest.' Rosie began packing the dishwasher ferociously.

'Steady girl, you're going to break stuff.' Matt wound his arms round her waist and pulled her gently away from the appliance, 'If you've decided not call her why are you still angry?'

'Because now I have guilt to add to being infuriated and I didn't need it today. Today was going to be about Red.'

'I know, honey.' Matt eased her head towards his chest and stroked her hair.

'Look this is stupid, you're right, there's no point in being wound up. You finish packing the dishwasher and I'll make us some pancakes for brekkie.' Rosie forced a smile and kept it there, as she fetched eggs, milk and lemon from the open fridge.

By the time she was flipping pancakes she started to genuinely relax again. Her mother could still knot up her backbone with one phone call. But Rosie had learnt to accept those feelings a long time ago and she wasn't about to give her mother back the power she had wielded all those years, just like that.

Matt and Rosie had visited Rosie's mother at her home in Kent on their way back from a weekend in London that summer. It was an obligatory visit performed out of duty.

It was uncomfortable from the moment they arrived, but when her mother had casually dropped a bombshell about Rosie's father, Rosie had lost it.

In less dramatic circumstances, the outpouring of feelings Rosie had unleashed would have been a valuable step forward for both of them. As it was, any therapeutic benefit to Rosie's brutal honesty was lost in the enormity of the news. Her mother had lied about Rosie's father, her own father – and let her grow up living that lie.

While Rosie and Matt ate their breakfast, they planned the day ahead. Matt was going to watch the stock car racing at the local circuit in the afternoon and, after some gentle goading, Rosie allowed herself to be persuaded to go with him once she had finished her training session with Red. Matt was planning to buy a car to race himself and he wanted to get a feel for the track and his competitors.

An hour later, Rosie sat on Harry's bare back in the makeshift schooling area. As they trotted in a fluid circle, she did her best not to laugh at the watching youngster.

Red stood on the outside of the school, desperate to be in the action, but frightened of the plastic fencing.

She eased Harry up and allowed him to walk at his own pace. He seemed to be enjoying his little ride and she was happy to give Red something to think about – watching a master at work. Harry was too old for school really and tight turns played havoc with his ageing joints.

She halted him and slid down from his back. Harry stood perfectly still and waited while Rosie gently slipped a head collar on Red and drew back the tape to form a gateway into the school. She unclipped the lead rope from the head collar and left Red loose at the entrance. She walked back to the waiting Harry and hopped back onto him. She turned Harry around so that they had their backs to Red. Then, she prepared herself to be patient and waited.

Sooner than she had expected, she heard Red approach. He recognised that Harry turning away from him was an inviting gesture and took it as his cue to enter the school. When Red had had his fill of sniffing Rosie's knee where it rested on Harry's shoulder, she gently clipped the lead rope on and rubbed his forehead. With an almost imperceptible cue, Rosie asked Harry to walk slowly forward.

Red had done well in learning to be led by Rosie on the ground so far but stood still, confused, when he felt the rope strain from her hand now. Using the same pressure and release technique she had taught Red to lead with from the ground, Rosie gently increased the pressure on the rope without looking at him. As Red took a step forward, he was rewarded by an instant slackening of the tension. Rosie eased Harry on and the three of them completed a circuit of the school.

She dismounted, taking care not to make Red jump. After removing Harry's bridle and allowing him to move off, she made a fuss of the young horse.

Rosie had never been trained to move the way she did around horses, so sensitive to subtle gestures. Her parents bought Harry for her after just a few lessons at a local riding school. Even as a child, there was more heart in her riding than the constant reminders to put her heels down and keep her toes in would have afforded alone. She loved to read up on Natural Horsemanship, enlightened and excited every time a Renowned Horsemanship Practitioner published another gem of wisdom.

She didn't religiously follow any specific methodology though. She took from what she read only what made sense to her and worked with her horse. Mostly, her calm inviting manner and knack for viewing the world through equine eyes came naturally.

Rosie was still beaming from her ride and Red's acceptance as she breezed back into the house. After a quick lunch she went with Matt to the stock car races, her mother gone from her mind completely, for now.

'Gillian, stop talking. It's a bad trainer that has no rivals and you are on the up. It doesn't have to be a coincidence that the same day your little mare wins the Champions title, someone vandalises your yard.'

Gill politely pretended to mull this theory over. The truth was, it had already crossed her mind, but she had dismissed it as unlikely. Arabian race meets, although increasing in popularity, were not yet televised and she just couldn't believe that someone had witnessed Amber's triumph and immediately set off for a 250 mile journey to Devon, just to let some horses out?

Gill was more concerned at the moment that since Norah Ranger, her most influential owner, had arrived; she had not mentioned Monty.

The terrifying woman had called ahead of visiting Gill, something she rarely did, preferring to turn up unannounced to check on her horse. She had not specified a reason for her visit. Norah was hardly the kind of woman with the time or inclination to pop over for a girly chat.

Gill sipped tea, noticing her hand was shaking slightly she quickly set the cup back down and folded her arms. She was glad she had put in the small area of patio and invested in some good solid wood garden furniture. She would have been at home on a grubby plastic chair in the barn with the horses, but had acknowledged the need to have somewhere more elegant for entertaining owners.

'Well the main thing is, everyone has recovered and none of the mares are in foal. The scans came back yesterday.'

Gill raised her eyes skyward to thank some higher being for not destroying her business.

'Lovely spot here, Gillian,' said Norah, and she tipped the last of her tea into her wide naturally downturned mouth, short wiry red hair swept back by afternoon breeze. 'Right then.' Norah stood up abruptly and strode towards the horse barn; Gill leapt up to skitter after her. 'I want to see Monday's Eclipse before I go.'

'Oh, Monty ... er ... Monday's Eclipse is out in the paddock at the moment.'

Norah stopped walking and raised her eyebrows.

'-But it's almost time for him to come in, so I'll just go and get him,' she said.

'Send your girl for him, I want to see Starfighter.'

Gill grinned an apology at the red-faced Kelly who had been cleaning tack in the yard. Kelly threw her sponge into the bucket of warm water and stomped towards the paddocks. Kelly was not used to being referred to as 'girl', or sent anywhere.

'Well, he certainly appears as good as they say.'

Norah let herself into the bay stallion's stable. She bent over to run her hand down Tom's foreleg and Gill prayed he wouldn't bite her large behind.

'Want to see him move?' Gill's eyes sparkled at the prospect of turning Tom loose in the sand school and allowing him to show off.

'Not today thank you, Gillian,' said Norah, she looked at her watch, 'might want to send one of my mares over to him. Right, must go.' With that Norah strode out of the barn towards her car.

Again Gill found herself running to catch up.

'But you wanted to see Monty?'

'Monday's Eclipse. Not today. I will phone you about my mare.' With that, Norah heaved herself into a brand new Range Rover and rocketed away down the drive.

Gill waved before thrusting her hands into the pockets of her jeans. She shook her head as she stepped back into the barn. Kelly was leading Monty into his stable.

'Where's the troll gone?' Kelly was not smiling.

'She left. Said she had to go. To be honest, I don't think she was that interested in seeing Monty, she just wanted to get a look at Tom.'

'Well she is bloody rude.'

'I know, I know, Kel, I am sorry. But people like Norah are our bread and butter.'

Kelly laughed. 'Did you see that suit she was wearing? I have never seen a woman look less feminine in white!'

Gill had to laugh as she took a body brush over Monty's velvet coat.

'Did you speak to her about Amber?'

'Damn,' Gill cursed. She had been so worried that Norah was going to pull Monty from the yard, she had clean forgotten to negotiate his stud fee for Amber.

Rosie hated Mondays.

She had recently negotiated working four days a week instead of five. Although a three-day weekend was magical, if anything, the Monday morning blues were worse.

She sat at her desk, trying to get stuck in to work. She had already killed half-an-hour going through her emails.

Rosie was intrigued by an email from Jules, saying that she had a surprise and inviting Rosie and Gill over that evening. She had been relieved when she read the ps. which said that Tristan would be at rugby practice and they would have the house to themselves. It wasn't that she disliked him, not openly anyway, but he was so awkward and insensitive. She hoped her friend was not going to announce that she was pregnant.

Rosie decided to make herself a coffee and vowed to get down to some serious work, as soon as she had had a caffeine boost. She had worked for Housing at the City Council for nine years. Her main role was to interview people who had found themselves with nowhere to live and then determine whether the council had a legal duty to house them. If they did have a duty, she then became a caseworker, finding temporary and later, permanent accommodation.

Rosie would like to say that she always allocated people to housing based on their needs. Did they need support? Did they have drug issues? Were they escaping domestic violence? Unfortunately, in reality, because places at specialist facilities were at a premium, people sometimes ended up wherever there was a room.

'Rosie love, phone,' called the woman at the desk next to hers, just as she was exiting the open plan office.

'Arggh!' Rosie exclaimed. 'Thanks, Val.' Rosie rolled her eyes at Val as she walked back to answer her phone. Val Laughed

'White, two sugars?'

'Val, you're a diamond.' Rosie sat down again and took a deep breath in preparation for the mouthful of a greeting all staff were obliged to reel off when answering the phone.

'Good morning, Housing Advice—,' she was cut off mid-spiel by a familiar and unwanted voice.

'Rosie, it's me.'

'I am at work, actually.' Rosie fiddled with the phone cable, twisting the plastic coated wire around her short strong fingers.

'Well you won't answer your phone at home, so what choice did I have?'

'Let me see … Not calling?'

'I thought you were old enough to handle this more maturely.'

Rosie tried to stop her hackles rising. More maturely? The sound of her mother pausing to inhale a cigarette tipped her over the edge.

'You can't force me to deal with this because you don't think I should be upset. If you feel guilty it's because you should feel guilty.' She slammed the phone down and fled the office, thankfully reaching the staff kitchen without bumping into anyone in the corridor.

Val looked up from spooning coffee into mugs. Seeing Rosie's flushed face, she gently moved her friend aside to shut the door, so they wouldn't be disturbed.

'Now, it's been a long time since a client upset you, so what the hell has happened?'

Rosie wasn't ready to speak. She hadn't talked to anyone about the trauma her mother had casually inflicted on her three months before, except Matt, who had been there at the time.

'Gimme a minute.'

Val added milk and hot water to the mugs, as she waited for Rosie to compose herself.

For the first time since the incident, Rosie began to relay the uncomfortable truth. Telling someone else made it feel frighteningly real. When she'd finished, she felt as drained as the empty mug she held, and Val was left far short of being able to dish out her usual brand of tough love.

Later that evening, Rosie commended herself on getting through the day. The phone call from her mother had dragged the festering truth she hadn't dealt with, back into the forefront of her mind. She had been blissfully able to shut things out since she had returned from her mother's in July, until now.

She had allowed herself a sob in the privacy of the paddock. With Matt working late and with Harry's strong white shoulder to cry on, it was hard to hold things in.

Once the horses were done, Rosie negotiated the narrow lanes back towards civilisation again. She turned up her stereo and tried to look forward to seeing Jules.

Rosie reached the market town of Honiton and fought the urge to stop at the local services to buy some tobacco. Orchard Cottage nestled in the beautiful and remote Flackdown Hills. The

24 mile commute to Exeter was a bind, but justified. Gill's yard was situated just outside of Exeter and it made sense for Rosie to drive and pick her up, in order to get to Jules' cottage in the Teign Valley to the south-west of the city.

Rosie reached the village of Stoke Rewe in good time, made her way over the level crossing and headed up the private lane to Newmans. As she pulled into the yard, Gill dashed out of the barn and headed towards the house shouting, 'Just coming!'

It was typical of Gill to still be bedding down the horses when she should have been in her smart clothes and ready to go out. Rosie wound down the window and greeted Kelly, who was soaking haynets ready for the stable kept horses to come in for the night.

Rosie chatted to Gill's right-hand woman while she waited. Kelly was devoted to her job and to Gill. She lived in the village and had turned up at Gill's yard almost a year ago, announcing that she'd just finished school and all she wanted to do with her life was work with horses.

Rosie asked Kelly how her course was going. Kelly talked enthusiastically about the latest module of her equine studies course, something her mother and Gill had jointly insisted on.

Finally, Gill came shooting out of the house, draped in a classic black shawl over unusually clean Levis. She always managed to look like a film star, despite buying all of her clothes in local charity shops.

Gill folded her slender legs into the car, fastening her seatbelt and kissing her friend's cheek in one fluid movement.

'So, what do you reckon then? Think she's pregnant?' Gillian cackled as Rosie turned the car around to descend back down the drive.

'That's the first thing I thought of,' Rosie laughed, as she changed gear. 'Seriously though, Gill, I hope not. I know. The last thing we want is for her to be chained to that odd ball for all eternity.'

As they passed the house, Rosie spotted Charlotte through the upstairs window. She waved up to her friend's daughter, but the teenager pretended to ignore the passing car, gazing nonchalantly into the middle distance.

'Bye-bye, darling, see you later!' Gill shouted loudly out of the open car window, beaming and waving, evoking a scowl from Charlie who promptly turned away. 'Best way to deal with a teenager Rosie. Be bright and happy and totally oblivious to the fact that they think everything in the world is crap and boring and depressing! She's got the hump because I asked Mike to come over this evening. I know she's seventeen but after the break-in, I just don't feel comfortable leaving her at night.'

'I thought she loved Mike?'

'Unfortunately her fascination with my brother ended when she came out of long socks.'

The women arrived in Kysford and parked outside Jules' cottage. They hadn't managed to get out of the car before Jules was at the front door, smiling and hurrying them inside.

'Come in ladies. Wine? Coffee?'

Rosie and Gill asked for coffees and sat down on the white leather sofas. Jules served the drinks, but didn't sit down.

'The niceties can wait! I'm going to get him!'

Rosie and Gill raised their eyebrows at one another when Jules rushed out the room.

'Must have been one of those concealed pregnancies!!' hissed Gill.

'Maybe it's a new man in her life!'

'And she brought us round to meet him while Tristan was out playing rugby – get our opinion before she ditches him?'

Rosie stifled giggles as Jules came back.

Walking beside Jules on a baby-blue lead was the most adorable scrap of a puppy Rosie had ever seen. She immediately dropped onto the floor to welcome the little black creature and was rewarded with enthusiastic licking.

'Oh, Jules, he is so sweet,' Gill smiled, but stayed on the sofa.

'He was a surprise from Tristan, waiting for me when I got home from Rosie's on Saturday night!'

'Have you named him yet?' Rosie had become a climbing frame for the little dog who had instantly decided she was as wonderful as she thought he was.

'Yep.' Jules bit her lip. 'Ziggy. What do you think?'

'It's just perfect, isn't it Ziggy? Yes it is, yes it is!' Rosie cuddled the excited puppy as he clambered around her neck.

As soon as Jules sat down, Ziggy used Rosie as a launch pad to propel himself onto Jules' lap. He flopped down across her knees, exhausted from his visitors already.

'What is it, Gill?' Jules could see the older woman wasn't hiding how she felt very convincingly.

'Sorry darling, I really want to be delighted for you, I do. It just worries me a bit that's all, ever since I met you, you've said you never wanted another dog, losing your last one was too painful?'

Jules shook her head, waiting for Gill to get to the point.

'If Tristan surprised you with him, did you really have a chance to decide if you wanted him?'

'I never thought I would want another dog, but when I came home and he was in the kitchen, it felt right,' said Jules. She laid her hand on the puppy's head and he sighed contentedly.

'But he didn't let you make the decision, you must have told him about what happened with Billy?'

'Well, yes of course he knew! But he must have seen something I never would have seen – that I was ready for another dog.'

'Jules, Billy was run over right in front of you! You said yourself you were traumatised forever. I think he should have discussed it with you; it's something you decide together as a couple, to get a dog? Be different if he had come home with the idea, but not the actual puppy?'

'Come on, girls!' Rosie jumped in, sensing the temper about to flare in Gill.

'You've never liked him have you?' Jules said defensively. Both women ignored Rosie.

'No, actually.' Gill exhaled and her unchecked opinion flowed. 'You can't tell me some of the things you've told me about the way he treats you and his depressing drug addiction and expect me to think he's a jolly nice chap!'

'Things have changed since we got Ziggy – he's cut down on pot,' Jules retorted, her temper soaring.

Rosie got to her feet, uncomfortable, trying to think of something to say.

'Oh right, in the two days since you got a dog, your whole relationship suddenly has firm foundations?' Gill threw her hands in the air.

'Yes actually.' Jules stood up to take Ziggy to the kitchen.

'Gill, will you shut up? What's got into you?' Rosie demanded when Jules had left the room.

'Oh he just pisses me off. He treats her like crap and then comes home with a puppy without discussing it with her, knowing they both work full-time, hey presto she thinks he's the perfect man!'

'Actually Gill, I spoke to a partner at the firm today and I can work from home two days a week and Maurice is going to look after him the other days!'

Jules stood in the doorway. She winced inwardly at the thought of Maurice feeding her precious pup lard and other muck and getting him covered in cow crap, but she didn't share her misgivings with Gill, who sat, arms folded and eyes questioning, ready for further debate.

But Jules wasn't in the mood.

'Well, I have lots to do so …' Jules gestured towards the door. Rosie headed towards the hallway, pausing as she passed Jules.

'It was lovely to meet him, thanks.' She leant in to kiss her friend's taut cheek.

Gill stayed where she was. She looked Jules square in the eye for a few more seconds before getting up. She walked past Jules without saying goodbye, leaving Rosie to wave as they drove away.

'You and your mouth.' It was Rosie's turn to go on the offensive as they wound through the dark lanes towards Newmans. 'Why couldn't you just say, 'lovely puppy Jules' and keep how you feel about him to yourself? We've all kissed frogs, Gill, Jules needs to make her own mistakes.'

'He reminds me of Alex.'

Rosie was stunned for a moment; she pictured Gill's ex-husband, flirtatious, outgoing and the life of any party – the exact opposite of Tristan.

'I know. They hardly seem similar. It's the control thing though. The way he seems to have this hold over her, the way she loves him, it's dangerous. He's controlling in the worst way, he's one step ahead so she never questions him too much.

'This puppy feels like another nail in the coffin. She's too desperate to please him. Someone like Jules should be adored without having to try.'

'So it's kind of nearly as bad as if she had been pregnant?'

'Got it in one.'

Jules paced the living room, trying to cool down. Gill had gone too far this time and she felt completely justified in suggesting her friends leave early. She could hear Ziggy scratching at the kitchen door, trying to get to her, but she needed to calm down first.

'Who does she think she is?'

Jules jumped when she heard the key in the lock and rushed

to greet Tristan as he came in.

'Not now babe, bad practice session.' Tristan refuted her embrace with one hand and headed up the stairs to the bedroom. She headed into the kitchen to lay down Ziggy's newspaper for the night, determined not to allow the thought that was circling in her head to come to the surface. The thought that Gill, crass as her approach had been, was right.

Rosie woke up on Friday morning and remained in bed, cocooned in the duvet.

Matt had already left for work. The working week had passed in a blur with a number of late finishes, so she felt perfectly justified in letting the horses wait an extra ten minutes while she woke up slowly.

She had not called Jules or Gill since Monday night's argument, having decided it was best to let the air clear. She wondered if either of them had bitten the bullet and phoned the other. She could see both sides of the argument and she would usually have forced reconciliation by now, but she was emotionally drained of late.

Matt kept trying to talk to her about her mother, but Rosie didn't want to deal with that either.

The doorbell rang and Rosie had to leave the warmth of her bed to struggle her way into jeans. She pulled a jumper over her bare breasts as she ran through the kitchen and into the timber porch.

'Morning, Mrs Hall.' Terry, the postman smiled at Rosie's dishevelled appearance. Rosie smiled and waited for Terry to hand her what she assumed must be a recorded delivery letter. She would normally have been chattier, but conscious of her lack of bra she just wanted to get away as quickly as possible.

Terry handed her a clipboard and stood aside to reveal a huge box.

'Oh, it's come!'

All inhibitions forgotten Rosie dashed barefoot into the chilly morning air to look at her package.

'Steady on there!' The postman laughed at her childlike delight.

Rosie traced her finger over the customs and excise duty stamp. She signed for the package and said goodbye to Terry. She quickly finished dressing and headed back outside equipped with scissors.

She carefully peeled back layers of bubble wrap, to reveal her most recent and deliberated eBay purchase.

'Oh, wow!' Rosie heaved the brand new black leather Western saddle aloft, admiring the ornate tooling across the seat. She set the saddle down and continued to dig through the packaging until she found the matching bridle.

Red's first set of tack.

Rosie carried the saddle and bridle to a waiting rack and peg in the tack room. She stood back, amused by the contrast between Harry's neat general purpose English tack and Red's enormous Western apparel. Rosie had only had a few Western lessons and briefly wondered whether it was sensible to try and back a horse using unfamiliar tack and a new discipline, but dismissed the thoughts as semantics.

She fed the horses and decided to have her own breakfast before she showed Red his new work clothes. If his initiation to saddle went well today she could be riding him within the next few weeks!

Rosie was contemplating a naughty but delicious croissant with butter and syrup as she breezed back into the cottage.

'You shouldn't leave the door unlocked you know.'

Rosie's heart propelled itself up her oesophagus and threatened to leap out of her mouth.

'Blimey, Dad!' Rosie cried. 'What are you doing here?'

'Well, your mum called me.'

'Oh.' Rosie met the gaze of the man she had grown up calling Dad and almost regretted her use of the word to greet him.

Jimmy saw the awkwardness in her eyes and stepped forward to embrace her. 'I've put the kettle on love. Let's sit down.'

Rosie perched on the edge of the sofa waiting for coffee, her mind blank.

'Do you remember the summer when I had a lot of work on? I had to stay in the city for a while?' Jimmy set a mug in front of her.

'I was … fourteen? I hadn't had Harry very long. You said the commute back to Kent would have been too much, so you were staying near the office. You didn't come back for a month.'

'I'm sorry. That was when your mum told me. She'd had quite a few whiskeys and got nasty. She just blurted it out.'

Although Jimmy had known for 16 years, Rosie saw there was still disbelief in his eyes; it was the same disbelief she felt.

'Why did you come back, I mean, if that was why you left then, what made you come back to her?'

'I didn't come back to her, I came back to you, you silly sod.' Jimmy smiled at Rosie, the beautiful girl he would always love more than anything else. 'I held you the day you were born, I listened out for your first words, drove you to school. I adored you. I couldn't just leave you in that house with her.'

Rosie remained silent. Her mother's alcohol problem had been present since she could remember.

The older Rosie got and the more she learned about life, the more she understood about her childhood. She and Jimmy had always been close, he'd shielded her from her mother's problem as best he could, and when she was older, they had picked up the pieces together, united against the common enemy in their lives – fire-water. Soon after Rosie found a cheap house share with some girlfriends and left home, Jimmy finally divorced Selina.

Selina had once been a vivacious and successful woman. Features editor for a small publishing house by day, she maintained her position in charge of a woman's magazine for a good few years after the drink had taken hold. A glass in the kitchen after work inevitably became a bottle on the floor and eventually her job hit the deck with her.

'I knew I came second to the baby you didn't have. I used to think, she's got me, why does she need another child? You were the reason I coped, the reason I understood it wasn't because I was inadequate.' Rosie looked over at Jimmy, meeting his soft blue eyes for the first time since he had arrived.

'When she found out we couldn't have any more children she started changing. Rosie, it was nothing to do with you. Part of the problem was she didn't want you to be an only child.' Jimmy's face changed. 'The way you suffered was unforgivable. She looks like a strong woman, but she is weak and consumed with her own sense of failure.' Jimmy moved from the chair to join Rosie on the sofa. 'But we know all this, love. We've been through it a million times.'

'You were always so open and honest with me. Why didn't you ever tell me about not being my real father?'

'You already had one rubbish parent, you didn't need another.'

Finally the tears came and Rosie clung to Jimmy, to Dad. As he held her in familiar arms that had always held her, she felt an overwhelming gratitude. For a man who had lived a lie.

'You are my real father.'

Chapter three

Monday morning came too quickly for Jules.

'Unfortunately, Jules, this is going to mean a lot more work.'

Jules smoothed the skirt of her new suit where it wrinkled, wishing she had bought a bigger size. She sat firmly between sizes 12 and 14, but always bought the 12, believing it would force her to shed a few pounds.

'No problem.' She smiled up at the partner of Hodges & Grath, who gave her a cringe worthy thumbs-up before marching back to his office. She had always known becoming a solicitor would mean putting the hours in. Had it not been autumn, David Barker's words would have instilled more dread in her, but she couldn't ride Romeo much in the winter anyway, with the short days and inevitable rain. Now that she had been given a go-ahead to work from home, she was confident she could cope with Ziggy.

Before she got started on the abnormally large and high profile case file she had just been given, she nipped up and closed her office door to make a phone call.

'Maurice? How is he?'

'Oh, 'ello Julie.'

Jules winced, he would insist on calling her Julie.

'We've just 'ad a bit o' lunch and then we are goin' out to check on the cows.'

'Well, that sounds lovely.' She hoped Ziggy's lunch had been the puppy food Maurice seemed to be using far too slowly and not more food from his own plate. 'You will call me if there is anything wrong, won't you? And I will still be there to see to Romeo and collect him at 6pm.'

'All right then, Julie!' Maurice slammed the phone down after the jovial phrase, which also appeared to have meant goodbye.

Jules was bleary-eyed by the time she finished reading the file. She popped the last piece of a large bar of chocolate into her generous and shapely mouth and downed the last of a somewhat stagnant mug of tea. Glancing up at the clock on her pc screen, she realised she was late to meet Tristan for lunch.

They worked in the same district of Exeter, a leafy avenue of grand Georgian buildings, with the odd modern monstrosity thrown in. The majority, old and new, housed white-collar workers.

She trotted up the High Street and her heart sank when she realised Tristan was not at their usual meeting place, outside Chaucers Restaurant. She called his mobile. Switched off. She wasn't sure what pissed her off most, the fact that he had not waited more than five minutes for her? No, she decided, she was most pissed off because she knew in her heart he probably had never come. He would be racing home in his sports car, to smoke pot in the ten minutes he would have before he had to turn around and drive back to work.

Jules headed around the corner to the shopping centre and tried to exhaust her fury with some retail therapy, but her heart wasn't in it. As hard as she tried, the anger soon turned, as it always did, to pain. Jules mourned the love he didn't show her.

By the time she returned to the office, her resolve was set. She would give him an ultimatum, her or the cannabis. As much as she adored him, she was sensible, and she knew her life couldn't continue like this.

She thought back to when they met, over two years ago. The death of a mutual friend brought them together. It was a strange and unromantic love story. She was low and alone and he was impressive, strong and obviously smitten with her in an exquisitely shy and endearing way. Unfortunately the cannabis use he had initially portrayed as a Saturday night thing was increasing rapidly and turning him into something very different from the man she fell in love with.

Later that same Monday, Rosie took full advantage of the flexible working hours which a local government job afforded. She sprang up from her chair as soon as the clock said 4pm. She had no more appointments and wanted to get home as quickly as she could.

Her dad, Jimmy, had booked himself and his partner, Crystal, into a local hotel. But, after he and Rosie had spent Friday together going over the re-written past, Rosie insisted they both stay at the cottage. The four of them had spent a wonderful weekend together, on Saturday they lounged in the garden, relaxing and catching up on each other's news. On Sunday morning they went to watch Matt enter his first stock car race. He came in mid-field. The vehicle he had lovingly been working on in every spare minute was woefully dented and ravaged. He emerged from behind the steering wheel grinning and exhilarated, already talking about the modifications he needed to make to the V6 engine of the four-year-old Vauxhall. If Rosie hadn't been so concerned for his safety, she would have shared more readily in his joy.

In the afternoon Jimmy and Matt worked on the car together

while she took Crystal for a gentle ride on Harry.

Tonight was their last night, Crystal had to get back to work and Jimmy had a meeting regarding one of his many investments. Since selling the estate agents business in Covent Garden, in order to retire, he had invested in a number of small companies. He was largely a silent partner, but expected concise progress updates and offered advice where he could. Tomorrow he was meeting with the director of a cycle courier firm which was beginning to turn a healthy profit, success fuelled by the London congestion charges.

Rosie arrived home to a big hug from Jimmy and heard about their day, exploring the Flackdown Hills that surrounded the cottage.

After feeding and grooming Red and Harry, she returned to the house to find Crystal had started dinner and Jimmy mending one of the dining chairs, which had recently shed a leg. She sat at the kitchen table chatting to Crystal about the best way to achieve a moist sponge cake and for the first time since she'd found out Jimmy was not her father, it felt like she still had a family.

Crystal was a Trading Standards officer in the borough of Kensington in London, so she and Rosie automatically had working for a local authority in common. She was ten years younger than Jimmy, a lithe and radiant blonde. It was not hard to see why he had fallen for her.

As the four of them dined on Crystal's mozzarella bake and the evening blossomed into a good memory for the future, Rosie wished it could be enough. Even as she sat opposite Jimmy, she couldn't stop wondering who her biological father was.

Jules, on the other hand, was having a far less wholesome evening. After seeing to Romeo and collecting Ziggy from

Maurice, she had returned to a wasted Tristan, a messy house and a headache.

'Where were you today, we were supposed to have lunch?'

'Are you starting?'

'Tristan you are completely smashed. I thought you were going to cut down?' Jules longed to tell him about the new high profile case she was working on and how Ziggy had greeted her at the farm. She longed for him be interested.

'Get off my case.' He lazily reached forward for his joint, which had been resting in the ashtray. He ignored Ziggy, who was nudging at his hand.

'At least speak to the bloody dog, Tris'

'I will re-phrase then, babe – FUCK OFF!'

She recognised his temper was about to flare and quickly shut Ziggy in the kitchen. She walked back into the living room, not satisfied. Angry, determined.

'You don't have to shout at me you know?'

'It's the only way I can get you to leave me alone.'

'What is so great about pot that makes you want to be bad tempered and useless?'

'Get me a beer.'

'What?'

'Beer first. Talking later.'

Jules stormed into the kitchen and fetched a can of beer from the fridge. She handed it to him.

'Having a smoke numbs me. Sometimes I need to be numb.' He opened the beer and relished the hiss as the ring pull released. He drank half of the can in one go. He looked up at the waiting Jules.

'What? The rugby is on now.' He gestured for her to leave the room.

'Is that it? That's your explanation for spending most of your salary on that shit!'

'You're like a child, aren't you babe?'

'Gill was right about you,' Jules muttered, and instantly regretted it as Tristan showed the whites of his eyes.

'What's that bitch been saying?'

'Tristan, you really are pathetic.' Jules rushed towards the door. She heard him coming towards her, just in time to turn and face him, but not to shield herself. He caught hold of her plaited hair at the root and dragged her up towards his 6 feet height, so she had to stand on her toes. She grasped her head trying to yank her hair away from him, crying out with pain.

'Don't talk to your fucking friends about me. You don't even know me, they certainly don't fucking know me.' He let go of her so quickly she fell to her knees. Instantly, tears spilled over and ran down her face, unchecked.

'Tristan, we've been together for two years, why don't I know you?'

'You want to know me? You really want to know me?' He grabbed her wrist and pulled her over to sit on the couch; he re-lit the same joint and took a long drag, inhaling it for so long, when he breathed out, the smoke was all but invisible.

'Yes.' She reached her hand towards him. 'I do.' Jules stopped crying. Despite his assault, she was ready to listen, sensing a doorway in emotions opening up at last.

Tristan leant forward, initiating an eye contact she did not dare to break.

'When I was a boy, I didn't have a home like you. I was never in one place long enough to fit in. I couldn't make any friends because we were always moving to the next city and it got hard to keep saying goodbye, so I stopped trying'

Jules knew his English father and Dutch mother had travelled all over the world for most of Tristan's life. His mother was a financial adviser who had a small number of inconceivably rich clients and had travelled to wherever they needed her. It was only in the last few years, since his mother's retirement, that his parents had settled back in Holland.

Jules had learnt most of what she knew about his upbringing from his mother and was taken aback by Tristan's sudden openness. He rarely talked about his childhood and it was usually like getting blood from a stone. Sensing she could easily irritate him into clamming up, she stayed quiet and waited for him to continue. She reached over and took a minimal pull at the loaded and hot joint. She barely inhaled and passed it back to him, hoping to show camaraderie in a way he would appreciate, without getting stoned herself.

'I don't remember my childhood as awful, but I was always lonely. Until I came to the UK to live with my Gran, but then she left me. After Gran died, I worked for a trader in Norwich; he had a few interests, including a nightclub. Social life went with the job. There were so many drugs flying around, I was spaced out most of the time. I stopped feeling lonely though; I finally felt like I had a place I could call home, I was part of something so cool. It was a lot of fun. Good times.'

He paused and finished the can of beer. Jules instantly leapt up to get him another.

'My boss was hiding the profits. Hid a whole other identity, from the tax man and his business partner. I used to manage all the off-the-record parties, then I would score a wrap of speed and come back get to high in the offices above the VIP room. Got seriously addicted. One night the police turned up, looking for my boss. I managed to hide the drugs, but they found my boss and he lost everything. I had no job and no home. I knew I had to get my act together. That's when I came to Exeter for a fresh start and discovered pot. It's not as good as coke or speed, but it stopped me from taking the hard stuff and I got a career at last. You know the rest.'

Jules nodded. She had bumped into Tristan at a wine bar opening soon after someone they both knew had been given a month to live. Tristan had been shy but charming and such a gentleman. He was attentive when she broke her heart over Freddie's brain tumour after a few too many champagnes.

In the early days, he made the pot he smoked seem like a social thing. It was only after they had lived together for a while, in the house she funded the deposit for, that she realised he couldn't live without it.

'I'm sorry.' She all but crept towards him and he allowed her to slide onto his lap. She held him tightly and was surprised when he held her back.

Later in bed Jules sobbed quietly while Tristan slept deeply beside her. She didn't understand drug addiction. She tried to push the feelings of rejection down inside her and vowed to help him, to love him. She even comforted herself with the notion that she could cure him with her love. But, above all, Jules felt helpless with the realisation that she couldn't give him the ultimatum she had planned to.

Gill smoothed her trouser suit and tucked her hair behind her ears. She couldn't get used to being all dressed up.

She had decided to hold an Open Afternoon at Newmans. It was Norah's suggestion, to invite potential owners to come and see the yard and facilities and to generally have their ego's stroked. Although it was autumn and the next racing season in April felt like an age away, a prospective race horse would need to start training straight after Christmas – now was the time to secure new business.

Charlie had relished the opportunity to get involved in something social, which wasn't altogether to do with horses and had turned Gill's usually straight bob style into ringlets earlier that morning. Now Charlie was positively dancing around Gill's guests, topping up their champagne and replenishing the nibbles which the caterer had delivered. In a bright purple dress with her long dark hair loose and natural, Gill thought how beautiful her daughter looked, even if the dress was eye-poppingly short.

It was a mild September evening and the patio was dotted with lanterns and potted plants. Gill looked out of the kitchen window, knowing she should get back to mingling.

Instead she headed out of the front door of the house and trotted through the fading light towards the barn. Kelly was in Tom's stable, skipping out.

'Kelly, you should be down there!'

'So should you!'

Gill laughed. Despite the difference in years, she and Kelly were very alike, a neat stable and a comfortable horse would always be more important than a new hairdo or nice clothes.

'Thought I had better come up and feed them. It's past their dinner time,' Kelly said, as she finished removing droppings and let herself out through the half-door.

'Thanks, Kelly. And thanks for your hard work today.' Gill caught Kelly's arm, after she had put the muck bucket down, and hugged her employee.

'Well, I think Charlie was the star of the show today! They like being dazzled, these rich horsey types!'

'Yes, but you showed them round the barn and kept the stables perfect. You did a great job. How their horses will be cared for is what should matter after all! Mind you I think some of them are only here for the free champagne.'

'Has anyone agreed to bring their horses here?'

'Not yet, although most of them have expressed an interest, one way or another.'

'You'd better get back to them.'

'Hmm. Stop by the house before you go won't you Kelly, stock up on the nosh – there will be lots left over!'

'Okay, boss!' In new white jodhpurs and a maroon Newman's Arabians jacket, she had somehow managed to keep clean; she looked a picture perfect groom. In many ways she was. Her dedication to the horses and to what Gill was trying to achieve, was priceless. Gill mused, as she strode back down to the house, how much she would have liked Charlie to have felt that way too.

'Ahh, Gillian, there you are!' Mr Abanthy launched into a discussion of tendon injuries in racehorses. Gill realised she was back in the spotlight. As she talked passionately about the importance of bandaging and heat treatments, she tried not to notice Charlie through the kitchen window, slugging from a half-empty bottle of champagne and thinking no one was watching.

By midnight everyone had left. Kelly had fallen asleep on the couch shortly after Charlie had persuaded her to have a glass of champagne. Gill made a courtesy call to Kelly's mother and pulled a blanket over the girl. She blew out the last of the candles that remained on the patio and decided to leave the rest of the clearing up until morning. As she headed back into the kitchen and bolted the door for the night, she heard a bottle slide across the kitchen counter.

Gill turned to see her daughter, heavy eye make-up smeared and hair witchy, taking a pull at a left over bottle. Charlie drank for longer than a seventeen-year-old should have been able to, before lazily bringing the bottle back to the counter with a bang and wiping her mouth with the back of her hand. The girl made cold, hard-eye contact with her mother, challenging Gill to reprimand her behaviour.

'Charlie, I don't mind you having the odd drink, you are eighteen next year, but do you really need to get yourself this drunk?'

'Why not, Mum? Why should you care? I'm not a fucking horse, so you wouldn't give a shit if I dropped dead!' Charlie showed straight white teeth in a wide sarcastic grin.

'Getting drunk and swearing at me is really holding my attention, Charlie, well done.'

'I don't want your attention.' Charlie swigged at the wine again.

'No, darling, of course you don't.'

They stood eyeing each other across the island in the kitchen, which was littered with half eaten platefuls and dirty glasses.

'I'm not clearing up this crap.' Charlie smirked and turned to head into the hall.

'I wasn't going to ask you to,' Gill called after Charlie. If Charlie noticed the catch in her voice, she ignored it. Gill sat on a stool and rested her head on the counter, letting out a wavering sigh instead of tears.

Charlie was studying Law and English at Exeter College and Gill tried to be tolerant of the things students get up to. Unfortunately, Gill's leniency appeared to be creating a foul-mouthed little cow who drank and mistook Gill's good intentions for simply not caring. Did she spend too much time with the horses? Well of course she did, but it was her business – it was what paid Charlie's allowance.

Gill forced her legs to carry her up the stairs to Charlie's room. She stood outside the door and took a deep breath. Since when did you need courage to speak to your own child? Gill had been planning to tell Charlie that she loved her, that it was hard bringing her up and running the business. Gill wanted to offer to spend more time with her. Unfortunately the deep breath took Gill back to her own youth. The smell coming from Charlie's room was unmistakeably marijuana.

'Mum, is that you?' Gill heard Charlie clattering around, obviously trying to open a window.

Gill opened the door and met the red-eyes of her daughter.

'Too late, Charlie, I'm not stupid.'

'I don't know what you're talking about,' Charlie's high pitched protest led to loud giggles at the sound of her own voice.

'We'll talk about this in the morning, when you're not high as a fucking kite.'

Gill went back downstairs. If Charlie had been shocked at Gill's use of the F word, she couldn't have been as shocked as Gill herself, who usually kept that level of profanity under her breath. Gill poured herself a coffee and sat back on the stool in the kitchen. What the hell was she going to do?

'Gill …'

A soft voice brought Gill back to reality from a hazy dream, as she struggled to focus, she saw the empty couch opposite the one she had apparently slept on and wondered where Kelly was.

As if reading her mind, Rosie handed Gill a coffee and told her Kelly had done the morning feeds and gone home.

'So much for her day off.'

Gill realised if Rosie had arrived to help her ride the horses out, it couldn't be very early. She groaned as her friend sat beside her and she caught sight of her watch. 10am. She couldn't remember the last time she had slept until 10am.

'Gill, I just saw Charlie walking down the drive. She was carrying a rucksack and this was on the kitchen counter.' Rosie handed Gill a note:

Gone to see Dad.
Back tomorrow.
C

'My daughter, ever the conversationalist,' Gill sighed.

Half an hour later, the two women were riding along the country lane which surrounded the Shillerton Estate. At the entrance to the estate, Gill swung her leg over Rocky's back and dropped to the ground. She paid a yearly fee which allowed her to ride across the parkland. Gill opened the gate for Rosie and Amber and secured it after them. As they rode along a tree lined path at a leisurely walk, the women had time to notice that a flush of autumn was making the beech leaves blush gently. It was an overcast, late September morning, but as any rider will tell you, if it's not raining, it's good weather.

'So, have you phoned Jules yet?' Rosie said, as she smoothed Amber's proud chestnut crest. Gill was contending with Rocky's eager jigging as the big stallion felt the sheep shorn grass under his bare hooves. She sat easy on the horse, slowly calming him with her secure seat and kind but assertive hands.

'No.'

'Bloody hell, Gill, you don't actually want to fall out properly over this do you?'

'I know. I just don't know what to say? She will still think she is right and he's a great boyfriend and I'm not suddenly going to say, 'Yes he is a great guy, why don't you marry him,' am I?'

'That's a very negative way of looking at it and you know she doesn't really think he's the perfect boyfriend. You need to make up, this is daft. She needs us to support her, not reprimand her for being in love. You know better than anyone you can't help who you love!'

'I know, you're right ... it's just going to be awkward now whatever I do.'

'Why don't I have you both round for a girl's night and dinner next weekend?'

Gill looked down at her gloved hands, which played gently on Rocky's leather reins.

'Gillian Newman, you're not twelve.'

'Okay, yes, that would be good, thank you.'

The horses cleared the tree canopy and they found themselves at the foot of a gentle incline, parkland stretching before them.

'Little canter?' Gill grinned at Rosie.

'Will it just be a canter, or will we end up going flat out?'

'Oh come on, Amber will look after you!'

With that Gill eased her hold on Rocky and he bounded forward in giant leaps. Amber unsettled Rosie by breaking into a dancing canter without being asked. Rosie clamped her hands towards her body and tensed up without thinking. Amber was used to soft hands and a relaxed jockey. Where she would normally have come sweetly under control and found a rhythm, Rosie's sudden tension unsettled her. She stretched her nose upwards, running away from the unnatural pressure Rosie was inflicting on her. The harder Rosie hauled on the reins to ask the mare to slow down, the more Amber fought, her strides interspersed with half rears. Rosie knew not to pull, knew fighting the mare would only serve to increase her flight instinct, but fear swallowed up her rationale.

Had Gill thought to look back at the pair, she would have seen an ungainly wrestling match ensuing between her frightened friend and her sensitive horse. As they reached the brow of the hill, Gill started to bring Rocky back down to a walk. Rosie quickly steered Amber directly behind Rocky so that she slowed down as he did.

'There, see that was very dignified wasn't it?' Gill was beaming and slapped Rocky's neck in praise for not having shot sideways or exploded into a bucking fit, as he was apt.

Gill turned to see Rosie unusually tight-lipped and Amber looking tense. She decided not to comment.

The rest of the ride was uneventful and by the time they returned to Newmans Rosie had, more or less, relaxed again. Even so, she was hugely relieved to dismount and allow her knees to unlock. Amber looked equally relieved that the ride was over and Rosie quietly apologised to the little mare as she gently slid the saddle from her back.

Rosie hugged Gill goodbye and headed back home to do some training with Red.

Gill headed for the house.

A competent horsewoman, blessed with healing hands and a keen eye, Gill had no patience for accounts. She sat in her little office, gazing out of the open window to the paddock. Amber was making snotty faces at the visiting brood mares, reminding them she was in charge.

She smiled at her horse and allowed her mind to wander to thoughts of putting her in foal. She hoped it would be a colt, the beginnings of her own stud. What sort of mum would Amber be?

All too soon she realised from the empty coffee cup in front of her, she had achieved nothing while she had been sat there.

Charlie was on her mind. She slid the cordless phone out from under a disorganised heap of feed merchant's invoices and dialled her ex-husband's number.

'Alex?'

'Gilly, my darling! Have you called to speak to Char, or do you want take a risk and converse with me?' The once great love of Gill's life spewed a confident flow of words which were less conversation and more monologue. His syrupy voice slid from the receiver and clogged her ears.

'She just turned up. I thought you might phone. Had a little girly tiff have we? She really is stunning isn't she, like you, but with a little bit of me thrown in! I think we bred a nice filly, gorgeous glossy mane! Not happy about her chest development though, too much attention from the wrong kind of man. How are those gee gees then, Gilly, made you rich yet?'

'Charlotte,' Gill finally managed to cut him short, 'is getting drunk, and smoking weed.'

'Gilly darling, relax those shoulders, you were young once! Who didn't have a little smokey-jo with their buddies at that age?'

'Smoking, alone, in her room?' Gill appreciated the silence while the big man pondered.

'Ah. Not so good. Still let's not get the firing squad lined up just yet. Do you want me to have a little word? What a naughty filly she is!'

'Could you please take this seriously? She has her final exams coming up in the summer and if she's hung over and stoned she's not going to pass.'

'She's a bright girl, she won't let her studies suffer, and she's determined to be a Barrister! She won't let anything come in between her and the bright lights of the Bar or the sideboard or whatever it is!'

'Alex, she is not the eleven-year-old who watched court room dramas anymore. I'm ashamed to say, she's mouthy and arrogant and drinks like a fish.'

'Surely not?'

'You haven't been around enough to see it. The occasional weekend she spends with you, she puts on a good girl image for Daddy. She might have passed her first lot of exams, but not with glowing colours, she barely scraped through. I'm trying not to be too hard on her.' Gill's voice caught and she realised she was too close to tears to stop them falling. She felt like this was all her fault, when did her smart independent little girl change – had she been too pre-occupied with the business to see it?

She could blame Alex for being a part-time Dad who had often let his daughter down when they had arrangements, but she was her mother!

'Gilly, I still think you are being just a tad uptight. She said she has a free day tomorrow, so I'll bring her back in the evening and we can all sit down and have a proper chat. How does that sound?'

'It sounds great, but by free day, she means she has an English lecture in the morning.'

'Ah …'

'I don't overreact, Alex. I wouldn't have called you if it wasn't getting serious.'

'Right. I'll bring her back tonight. Must dash, Gilly, we're popping over to see Megan. Be there about six. TTFN!' Click.

'Bloody Hell!' Gill grabbed a tissue from the box on the desk and tried to get back to totting up her expenses. Instead she felt a stab of pain at the mention of Alex's live-out lover's name. Megan's voluptuous hips and come-to-bed eyes swam into Gill's head. Megan was the reason for her divorce.

Seven years ago Alex's business had gone into overdrive. He had seen a niche and employed a sales team to help him net the buoyant organic food market. The young, dynamic Megan had quickly turned Alex's little Devon pie business into a nationwide public success story.

At the time Gill had been ecstatic. The success of the company had allowed her to buy Amber and they moved to a brand new house in the affluent West Hill area of Devon. She had it all, rich husband, beautiful child and an Arabian mare. She gave up her job and lived the dream. She lunched with the other ladies of leisure and took her daughter to exclusive dance classes.

But the happiness started to fade for Gill, as the distance between her and Alex grew. She missed the special way he had always spoken to her and the private moments he didn't have time for any more.

One day, Charlie came home from school and asked if her father was having an affair. Gill still didn't really understand what prompted Charlie to say it, but the eleven-year-old girl had clearly discovered more about her parent's relationship than Gill herself had even thought to look for.

Gill thought back to that day when it had all come out. It was also the day she met Rosie and Jules. She had gone to a natural horsemanship demonstration with the woman who had sold Amber to her, an Arabian breeder. Rosie and Jules had been taking a bathroom break, together, as women do, and heard someone crying. The reserved Jules would normally have let the woman bear her pain in private, finding the whole thing embarrassing, but Rosie's empathy saw her knocking on the cubical door.

'You okay, love?'

'No.'

'What's wrong?'

'Listen.' Gill opened the door from where she sat on the lid of the toilet and put her mobile on loud speaker. Alex's voice rang out into the bathroom.

'Megan my beauty! Thought I might join you for that

marketing shindig next week. Cancel your hotel reservation; we'll be staying at a five-star! I'll miss you this weekend you evil temptress. TTFN!'

'Well that's okay, isn't it? He's going with you to your market … thing?' Jules smiled awkwardly, unable to see why Gill was crying.

'He's my husband. And my name's not Megan.' Gill watched as her horror was taken in by strangers who just might understand.

'Oh, bugger.' Rosie understood and had moved into the cubicle to embrace the older woman. 'You poor thing, I'm so sorry.'

It had taken Jules a bit longer.

'If you aren't Megan, why have you got that answer phone message?

'Because people who cheat will always drop themselves in it somehow, he must have phoned the wrong woman.' Rosie answered for Gill.

Rosie had insisted on taking Gill's number that night.

Alex didn't make excuses, or deny anything. He did his best to try and convince Gill that he still loved her and even offered to sack Megan, but the betrayal was such that Gill just wanted out. He moved out the next day. He didn't protest when she divorced him for adultery, neither did he argue with any of her financial demands and the settlement was quick.

She spent a year at the house in West Hill, desolate and lost, desperately trying to look after Charlie, even though she couldn't look after herself. Charlie tried to look after her destroyed mother, but missed her father. What had made it so hard for Gill was that she had allowed him to be her world and in doing so, she had lost the ability to figure out what she wanted. She didn't know who she was any more.

As a divorcee and single parent, Gill no longer fitted in with the ladies what lunched and it was her brother, Mike who had been there for her, popping in and helping Charlie with her school work. Never once saying, 'I told you so' even though he had never approved of his brash and arrogant brother-in-law.

The other saviour through that black time had been Rosie, who had called her the following week, as she had promised. At the time Gill had thought it was a kind offer, but she never expected the sweet brunette to actually phone.

They chatted about the natural horsemanship demo, they told each other about their own horses and when Gill was ready, they talked about Alex. Rosie had insisted on coming to meet Amber and encouraged Gill to ride the mare, while she accompanied them on foot.

Gill was in too much of a state at the time to really comprehend what the comparative stranger was doing for her. Looking back now, with seven years of friendship under her belt, she realised you could expect nothing less from Rosie.

She re-coiled inside for not confiding in Rosie about Charlie that morning, but she was ashamed.

Gill was wondering how the hell she was going to make herself concentrate on the accounts, when Mike phoned. She told him about Charlie and felt altogether better when offered to come over in the evening. She wasn't worried about seeing Alex, anything she felt for him had long since passed. But Charlie? She was, much as it pained her to admit it, very worried about seeing Charlie.

Chapter four

Rosie had been working with Red for a month. He now happily wore his saddle and bridle and moved around her on the ground as desired, subtle and precise, at the slightest of hand gestures. She had also stood on the mounting block and laid over his back a few times, letting him get used to her weight, before she would take the plunge and sit astride him.

But now, with her beautiful, calm Quarter Horse dressed in his Western saddle and bit-less bridle, walking him calmly around the fenced off school – instead of a soft happiness, her heart started to pound. She led him over to the mounting block and asked him to stand; she drew in gulps of air and leant forwards finding it difficult to breathe.

She climbed up the metal steps and stood at the top, her hard hat uncomfortably tight. What the hell was wrong with her? She was unbalanced on the mounting block, like it was too high. She teetered over Red's back with a knot rapidly developing in her stomach. Every time she thought about swinging her leg over the animal for the first time, she had a flashback to her battle with Amber that morning.

She could not control the tension in her arms and legs; it was there now, like an invisible barricade between her and Red. She couldn't do it. He was a young horse who needed security and a comforting rider.

Rosie looked over at Harry. He was grazing just the other side of the fence. If he sensed his master's turmoil, he was choosing to ignore it.

Red had been standing very patiently, but his patience was starting to wear out. He fidgeted and swished his dark chestnut tail. She stepped down from the mounting block and decided to try again later. She tried to do some groundwork, but the tension was still there and he picked up on it. He danced around her and refused to yield to her hand gestures, his giant hindquarters swinging in the opposite direction to her signals.

'Oh, shit!' Rosie fought back tears. She took Red's saddle and bridle off and decided to give it up, before she did the horse any real damage with her own nerves.

Walking back to the house, she tried not to think of the reason she had handled Amber so badly this morning and why she was now unable to work Red properly.

She'd had a bad fall when she was younger. A friend's horse had bolted with her along a main road. The mile and a half of being carted along at a flat out gallop, totally out of control, haunted Rosie so badly she barely allowed herself to think about it. When she did, her heart quickened.

Harry had never scared her at all, but the familiar fear was always there, just under the surface, when she couldn't communicate with a horse properly. She had started riding with Gill to build her confidence and get some more experience to help her to back Red, but unfortunately, it seemed to be having the opposite effect.

While Gill struggled with her family trouble and Rosie struggled with her own ability, Jules was struggling to reduce the swelling on her cheek. She held a cold wet flannel to her developing black eye and glared at herself in the mirror.

'Darling, come here.' Jules sat on the tiled floor beside the toilet and held her free hand out to the puppy, he was rapidly turning into a handsome black dog. If today had been bad for her, it had been terrible for Ziggy, with his sensitive ears. He flopped across her outstretched legs and let out a fitting sigh.

'I couldn't have said it better myself, Zig.'

What a day. It had started okay. Jules had risen early and walked Ziggy over to the farm to see Romeo. She had returned to pair the socks that were in the drier and tackle the mountain of ironing. She emptied the ashtray and tidied the living room.

Since Tristan admitted he had an addiction problem, she tried to get used to it and accept it as part of their lives. She tried not to demand attention, even last night when he had arrived home too late for any kind of evening together. She had sweetly kissed him goodnight and left him to smoke himself into a coma, gently helping him to bed at 4am, when she woke to use the bathroom.

Jules had really tried. She really had.

At midday he had staggered down the stairs in his boxer shorts. She was washing up. He came into the kitchen and drew up behind her. He put his arms around her waist and tenderly kissed her neck. Inside, she melted at his touch and her heart could have cried for joy at the attention.

Unfortunately, or fortunately, depending on how the future now panned out, something in Jules couldn't quite do it. Couldn't just give in and lead a life she hadn't wanted, couldn't let him treat her in a way which devalued her.

When she'd finished washing the dishes, she followed him into the living room. With a voice which came from a part of Jules that she couldn't quite control with her love for Tristan alone, she heard herself say,

'Aren't you going to thank me for doing the housework?'

'For fuck's sake, babe.'

'For fucks' sake what? For fucks sake be a doormat?'

'I'm not in the mood, if you're going to have one of your little episodes, please do it elsewhere.'

She went into the kitchen and tried to hand him the bacon sandwich she had made. He refused to take it. She put it on the coffee table in front of him and sat down to eat her own food.

Tristan ignored the sandwich and called Ziggy. Tristan held the animal's face with his strong hands and spoke to him softly, telling him how good he was.

'Aren't you going to have your breakfast?' she spoke quietly, hoping she sounded friendly.

Tristan ignored her and invited Ziggy up onto the armchair with him.

'Oh, Tris you know he is not allowed on the furniture – his claws!'

Tristan had smiled at her like a naughty schoolboy from behind Ziggy's excited licks.

'Tris, please eat your lunch.' Jules tried to look appealing but the pause that followed was loaded.

'FUCK OFF, WOMAN!' Tristan bellowed. His smile had gone and cold, hard anger greyed his eyes. Ziggy had almost fallen over himself to get off Tristan's lap and away from the sudden outburst.

Tristan had stood up and slowly clenched his fists, breathing deeply, as though trying to control his anger.

'You stupid bitch,' his voice was slow, deliberate. 'You made me frighten the dog.'

Before Jules had time to become outraged by the absurdity of his suggestion that frightening Ziggy had been her fault, he was beside her. He bent over and put his face close to the side of her head, almost touching her. Terrified, she stared down at the plate on her lap and watched tears drip onto her uneaten sandwich.

'HOW DO YOU LIKE IT WHEN I SHOUT IN YOUR EAR?'

Jules let out a scream of shock.

He drew away from her and a sudden defence mechanism of rage kicked in from his assault and she swung a hand up to his face to slap him. She knew what was coming before her fingertips met his cheek. His returning blow was a fist propelled by a fullback's arm. The blow knocked her back into the softness of the sofa cushions and the emotional pain hit her instantly. The physical pain took a bit longer. By the time the throbbing set in, the front door had slammed behind her attacker.

Now it was 6pm. A few hours ago she had phoned Maurice and asked him to feed Romeo for her, saying she had a bad headache. It had since got dark outside and chilly in the bathroom.

The sterile white tiles matched the clinical feeling in Jules' heart. She could not find love. She did not speak the language any more to reason that it was her fault and that he loved her.

She started to realise she was leaving him when she began to plan ahead, not that evening, not tomorrow at work and hiding her bruise, but the future. Coping without someone she had thought she would spend the rest of her life with. She started to mourn her relationship and now instead of crying for him to come home, she cried for herself, for her broken heart and the coming loneliness.

It hurt in a way Jules knew with bleak certainty would not stop for a long time. Realising she was exhausted she allowed Ziggy to follow her into the spare bedroom, where they lay on the single bed. Ziggy snuggled into her back and she found comfort in his warmth between her sobs.

Jules awoke, muggy and in pain, to see Tristan standing at the door. Semi-conscious, her brain tried to piece together the throbbing ache in her face and the fact that she was not in her own bed. She struggled to sit up.

Tristan continued to stand in the doorway, as though a dividing line prevented him from getting any closer.

'I'll sleep here tonight; tomorrow we need to work out what we are going to do,' Jules spoke, with as much self-assurance that she could muster.

He nodded and took a few steps into the hall but came back. He stood in the doorway again and Jules' heart froze. She waited for him to speak, barely daring herself to believe he might tell her that he loved her.

'Do you want me to put Ziggy in the kitchen?'

Jules turned away so he wouldn't see her cry.

'Gilly, my darling!' Alex's bulk filled the doorway and he inflicted a long and inappropriate embrace on his ex-wife.

Gill caught sight of Charlie, who stood behind her father looking sheepish.

'Ah, Michael, good evening,' Alex's confidence was reduced by a peg or two when he saw Mike standing in the kitchen.

Gill gently took her daughter's arm and kissed her soft, peach like cheek as she passed. Charlie smiled quickly before walking to the living room to sit down.

Alex went to put an arm round Gill, who was setting mugs down on a tea tray.

'So, Alex, how is Megan?' Mike eye-balled the man who had crushed his little sister's heart and prevented Alex from carrying out the inappropriate flirtation he was attempting.

'Fine, fine, you know.'

Having satisfactorily thrown Alex off his stride, Mike went

into the living room to join Charlie.

Gill picked up the tea tray to follow, but Alex intercepted.

'Listen, Gilly.' He looked unusually serious. Something about his tone made her put the tray down.

'Little bit awkward and you must really not take offence, but Charlie has asked if she can come and live with me for a little bit.' Alex looked at his feet.

'Right.'

Gill was glad the tea tray was safely on the counter.

'I know, I know, I know exactly what you're thinking, but you should hear what she has to say. I'm somewhat apprehensive about it myself, but maybe I can do this for her, for you, Gilly? Maybe I can help her through this phase where you have helped her through others?'

Gill eyed him with disgust.

'So you want to play Dad now?'

'Gilly, darling.'

'Don't darling me, Gill spat and snatched up the tray, causing the milk jug to slop most of its contents. She stalked into the living room.

Gill tried to compose herself, but ended up dumping the tray on the table in front of her daughter and turning on Charlie.

'So you want to go and live with your Dad, do you? You thought that was clever, did you? Could it be because he's never there and you think no one will nag you?'

'Hang on, Gill—' Mike began.

'No, no I'm sorry. I thought I was going easy on you. I thought giving you a free rein and letting you develop was sensible parenting, but actually, Charlotte, you're just taking advantage now. You think it will be a bed of roses at Daddy's do you? Well just you go then. You go and see how long you last.'

Her fury expelled, Gill sat abruptly down on the sofa, folded her arms, and waited for Charlie to speak.

Charlie simply looked blank. Alex jumped in.

'Gill, I think you are just a bit out of order here.' He looked at Mike's set jaw and added quickly, 'Just a bit, a bit out of order. Charlie will not be getting a free rein at my house; on the contrary, I intend to keep a very good eye on her, at the same time as, hopefully, getting to know my daughter.' He turned to Charlie and put a hand on her knee. She smiled sweetly at him.

Gill could have vomited.

Hurt, but at the same time strangely smug, she decided it was probably best to simply let them loose on each other and wait for the fireworks.

'Okay.' Gill leant forward and opened her palms towards her ex-lover and, what was starting to feel like her ex-child. 'Okay, Charlie, if you think that living with your Dad is what is best for you right now, you should go.' Gill could have laughed at Charlie's stunned expression. 'No, really. If you think being that far away from college, stuck out there in that house on your own will suit you, you go. If you can't have your friends over so much you might actually study more, so maybe this will work out rather well. Not so many drug dealers in West Hill as there are in Exeter, so maybe you'll have to give that up too!'

Gill and Mike both spotted the flash of uncertainty in Charlie's eyes, as she realised that the only benefit of living with her father was to punish her mother and that in fact, it might not be quite the sweet deal she thought she was clinching.

'I agree with Gill, Charlie, if you feel you want to do this, you should give it a whirl.' Mike had cottoned on to Gill's train of thought.

Gill instantly regretted feeling smug, as Charlie clocked her self-righteous smile and went back to plan A.

'Yes, it is what I want to do.'

Later that night, Gill walked up to the horse barn. She needed Amber. When she let herself into the mare's stable, the tears started to fall. She sat down in the straw and sobbed. Sensing her owner's distress, the chestnut lowered her head to Gill's lap and gave her something only a horse knows how to give, her presence, her silence, her time.

Amber touched her forehead to Gills and blew sweet hay-breath into her open palms.

Her daughter had gone, gone to live with the man who had broken both of their hearts. She had gleefully ducked her head into Alex's Mercedes after a businesslike kiss on her bewildered mother's cheek. Mike had offered to stay, but she told him she would be fine, preferring to be alone.

Gill thought about going back to the house, which would be empty and almost started to cry again, but the security light came on in the yard and stopped her. She didn't have time to pray it might be Charlie, because she heard a small, but familiar, voice and the padding of a dog's footsteps as she stood up.

'Gill?'

'Jules!' Gill let herself out of Amber's stable and ran across the barn. 'Oh Jules.'

Gill melted as she saw the red-eyes, one turning purple, above hollow colourless cheeks and an expression which would have haunted the hardest of women.

'I left,' Jules cried from the depths of Gill's embrace. 'I was going to stay the night and leave in the morning. But I left.'

'Honey, you're shaking, let's get you inside.' Gill attempted to start steering her friend back out of the barn, but Jules stood still and looked into Gill's eyes.

'I had to go, he was killing me.'

'You've done the right thing. You can stay here as long as you need to.'

'Thanks, Gill. It hurts, it really hurts.'

Gill rocked her friend, as she convulsed with sobs.

'I know, darling, believe me, I know.'

Rosie crawled along the M4, the Vectra smelt clutchy from all the stop starts. Bloody roadworks.

She had phoned Gill first thing and learned of Jules' arrival. Jules was going to call in sick, she wouldn't have been any use at work anyway and Gill was taking her to collect Romeo from the farm. Rosie promised she would come over that night.

She hadn't exactly lied about where she was going today, Gill had assumed she meant after work and Rosie hadn't corrected her. Even Matt, who had left before she had seen to the horses today, didn't know she had booked a day off.

She needed to do this. She didn't want any advice, she didn't want to confide in her friends or have her husband's support, she just wanted to get it over and done with, so she could move on.

Now it was 11am and she had only travelled five miles in the last hour. She wondered if she would even reach Kent before it was time to come back.

She didn't need to phone her mother in advance, she knew she would be in.

There was a call she did need to make though. She flipped on the hands free and voice dialled Nicola. Nic lived across the valley from Rosie at Mudford. She had a horse of her own and they often rode out together; Rosie half-riding, half-walking and leading the older Harry. Recently she had led Red out to get him used to traffic and Pharoh, Nic's wistful grey pony, had helped the younger horse realise that lorries wouldn't eat him.

'Howdy, Cowgirl!'

'Ha, ha, morning, Nic!' Nicola was twenty-one, a vivacious and energetic naturally blonde artist who lived in a converted barn on her parent's estate. She had been calling Rosie, 'Cowgirl' ever since Red had arrived.

'You busy today, Nic? I'm on a bit of a mission and have to go and see Jules later. She left Tristan last night.'

'Bloody hell. Thought she was going to marry him, not leave him. He is a bit creepy though.'

'Yeah, he is. Safe to say she'll be much better off without him.'

'Are their feeds in the tack room?'

'Yes, thanks honey.' Rosie smiled at Nic's instant recognition of the request that Rosie was getting round to making. She often saw to Pharoh when Nic was away at exhibitions and Rosie would sometimes phone her to return the favour, if she had to work late and knew Matt wouldn't get home until late either. 'I've already pooh picked and the haynets are in the hay barn ready.'

'No worries, will probably do them about six. I've got a customer coming to collect a commission piece at four, so that will work out fine.'

'Oooh is that the Friesian?' Rosie had seen the latest piece the artist was working on in the sitting-room-come-studio of the big open plan living space she had designed for herself.

'Oh no, that needs work. This is a hunter I finished a while ago, but the owner lives in Cornwall and hasn't been able to make it up until now. So what's this mission?'

'Tell you another time, Nic, thanks again, speak soon.' Rosie quickly ended the call as she passed the road works and the traffic sped up again.

Jules stared blankly down at her mobile. Gill drove quietly through the lanes back to Newmans, Romeo on board. Gill had waited while Jules explained what had happened to Maurice. The farmer had given her a brief but heartfelt tweed hug, before shuffling back into the house. She had told him Romeo would be coming with her to Gill's until she figured out what to do, but had insisted she keep paying for her stable. She would want to come back eventually.

'I know he won't want to move out, but it is my house. It's my deposit and my mortgage and I do want to go home.' Jules made Gill jump; it was the first time she'd spoken since they loaded Romeo. He had walked into the box sweetly, joining his spotless tack and multitude of expensive rugs which were already on board.

'Its only day one, Jules. One step at a time?'

Jules threw the mobile down into her open handbag beside her feet. She knew he wouldn't call and she probably wouldn't answer it if he did, but why hadn't he called? She picked the mobile back up and wrote a text message. She read it to Gill:

> I will pay off your car loan and you can have any of the furniture and appliances you want, if you relinquish any common law claim to the house and you move out Juliette.

'But I thought it was your house?'

'It is, but he's lived there with me for the last two years, and he'll try and lay claim to it as a common-law spouse if I don't give him something in return for agreeing not to. I can afford to pay off his car loan and I don't care about the telly or the dishwasher.'

'Send it.' Gill was filled with admiration for Jules. As heartbroken as she was, she was moving on, planning, taking control. It was her coping mechanism and Gill was humbled by it. She thought back to the months she had spent moping around and not dressing at the West Hill house after Alex had gone.

'He won't reply.' Jules sent the text and fell silent again. As

Gill drew closer to Newman's, she had to concentrate on driving through the winding lanes. She didn't notice Jules, face towards the window, silently crying.

Rosie seldom used the key to her mother's house, but she knew if she waited for the door to be answered she might not stick around long enough to do what she had driven for five hours to do.

'Hello, Mum.'

'Rosie.' Selina was matter of fact and didn't appear at all surprised to see her child, which fazed Rosie a little bit. She had, at least, expected some half-hearted attempt at a hug – this was the woman who had been trying to contact her for the last two months.

Selina sat in her usual worn and indented easy chair. The rest of the suite looked un-lived in and fresh, but cigarette burns and years of constant use made the chair look out of place. Rosie was surprised to see her mother nursing a coffee, but as she bent over to lay an unaffectionate kiss on her cheek, she caught a whiff of the whiskey and realised it was Irish.

'I'm not stupid enough to think you have come to see me. You want to hear about your father?'

'Yes.' Rosie perched on the edge of the sofa, clutching her handbag to her stomach.

'Right then. There isn't much to tell,' Selina shook her head at Rosie's obvious discomfort. 'You hate this house don't you?'

'Yes.' Rosie made brief narrowed eye contact with her mother, but looked away before she pissed her off enough to refuse to tell the story. She was unable to be affectionate or make small talk. And she certainly wasn't going to start lying.

Selina eased a cigarette out of a full box and put the end into her small and shapely mouth, the only feature she shared with

Rosie. She reached underneath her bony backside into the folds of the chair and fished out a lighter. She took a long drag, squeezing the cigarette between her slender fingers, before she began to speak.

'You still not smoking?'

'No.'

'Liked you better when you smoked.'

Rosie would have liked to say that she liked her mother better before she started drinking but, as always, she held back. Matt often said that one day Rosie would just let it all go and tell her mother that she hated her for her shitty childhood and Rosie knew Matt was probably right; she probably would feel better. In truth though, Rosie would still have melted if her mother showed her just an ounce of love, or was even momentarily proud.

'When you said you'd given up I assumed you had a bun in the oven but I see from your stomach that can't have been the case.'

Rosie opened her mouth to remind her mother that she had already told her she wasn't pregnant, when she had last seen her in the summer and her mother had rather rudely suggested that could be the only possible reason for giving up smoking.

'Not really the maternal type, are you?' Selina blew out a smoke ring, taunting her daughter with the delicious curls of white smoke. 'I can't imagine you looking after anything that didn't have four legs.'

'And what's wrong with that?'

'Nothing, if you're a bit weird and you are.'

'Can you just get on with telling me.?' Rosie's elbows rested on her knees and she turned her palms upwards, as though praying. She closed her eyes, inwardly hurt but outwardly impatient.

'It might surprise you to know that, once upon a time, I had riding lessons. When Jimmy and I started seeing each other I was having a weekly lesson with my friend. I'd gone along with Claire the first time to keep her company and I didn't really take to it, I'm not really an animal person.

'But I kept going, because your father was one of the grooms at the stable and from the moment I laid eyes on him, I was besotted. I used to pretend to call in there to see the horse I was riding, just to catch a glimpse of him. Can't even remember what the horse was called now and I spent hours pretending to talk to it.'

Rosie wanted the details, not the fairytale.

'What was his name?'

'If you want to hear this, don't interrupt.'

Rosie decided too much information was better than none and finally sat back into the sofa, resigned to hearing the sordid details.

'Jimmy was so supportive of my riding, little did he know.' Selina smiled to herself and Rosie's skin crawled. 'I never thought your real father would notice me, he was such a beautiful man, so strong and masterful. One day I called in on my lunch break and I was by the stable and he just came over, leaned his brown muscled arms on the door and started chatting to me. I was gob smacked – couldn't think of a thing to say. He was telling me about some old injury this horse had and was pointing to his back leg. I couldn't really see what he was talking about and he opened the door and invited me in for a closer look.

As I leant over to look at this horse's leg, I could feel his breath on my face and the warmth of his skin. He kissed me and it felt exactly like a dream. Then he left me stood there and walked off to get on with his work. The next week, while Claire and I were having our lesson, he walked past us and winked at me and pointed to this barn which was round the back of the riding arena. I said goodbye Claire and snuck round there. He was sprawled on a hay bale, out of sight of the rest of the stables, with a farm cat curled up on his flung off boots.'

Rosie decided that, if her mother was going to poison her anyway, she might as well have a cigarette herself. She placed her handbag on the sofa and walked over to her mother, taking a cigarette from the packet on the tattered arm of the chair and lit up.

'There's another ashtray on the mantelpiece,' said Selina. She gave a smug smile as Rosie walked over to stand at the fireplace. 'Didn't think you had really given up.'

Rosie refused to rise to the bait and struggled to stand as her head rushed. Her body swooned and her knees became weak as the nicotine flooded back into her system. She struggled not to cough and was amazed at how easy it was and how good it felt.

'So then you screwed and here I am?'

'Not quite, could have been any of the four times we slept together before he left.'

'And why couldn't I have been Jimmy's? If you had already started seeing him? If you were sleeping with them both, I could still be his?'

'Because – bloody child, you are impatient – when we wanted a second baby, I went and got myself checked out. I couldn't understand it, we'd been trying for over a year and my periods kept right on coming. I was perfectly fine. It was old Jimmy that was firing blanks.'

'But that was years before he went AWOL.'

'Yes, I kept it quiet. Until the day I didn't keep it quiet. Of course he immediately got himself checked out and sure enough, all blanks. Plus you look like your real father, all that brown hair and those eyes. You're short and stubby; Jimmy and I would have had a tall elegant child like us.'

'I still can't believe he came back and forgave you.'

'How naive. He never forgave me.' Selina laughed and added two fingers of whiskey to what could barely be called coffee any more.

'He was so sweet, he earned good money, was about to buy his own business. I knew he was going to be a good father. I missed your real Dad though, desperately, for years. When you started to walk and talk it seemed okay for a while, but I wanted to give Jimmy a child that really was his as well, and the fact that we couldn't have any more was like punishment for my deceit. So bottoms up,' she gestured with the mug and sloshed the lukewarm liquid over her sweat pants.

'The day I found out I was pregnant, I went to the stables but when I got there they said Eddie had gone. He'd taken a job at some posh training yard in the West Country. I came home devastated and Jimmy thought I was scared about the baby. He asked me to marry him that night and bought this house the following day.

He looked after me, he is a good man. He looked after you too. Your real father used me. He told me I was the most beautiful woman in the world; he knew how much I loved him. He had what he wanted from me and didn't even say goodbye. You look just like him, just like Eddie.'

'Is that why you have never told me you loved me, because I remind you of him?'

'You use the word like you know what it means.'

'I do.'

'Ha.' Selina curled her top lip in disgust and Rosie stood up to leave, sensing Selina was about to get nasty and not in the mood to stay for any more of her mother's quips.

'What was his name?'

'Eddie. '

'Eddie what?' Rosie spat.

'Eddie how the fuck should I know!' Selina let out an amused cry as she reached for the whiskey bottle, giving up on the coffee altogether.

'You're disgusting.'

'And you're a smoker! Ha!'

'Bye.' Rosie strode towards the hall.

'Just like your father, leave rather than have a conversation you don't like the sound of.'

'Just like my father?' Rosie turned back to eyeball her mother. 'Which one would that be?'

Rosie took a deep breath after she had shut the front door behind her. She tried to relax her muscles as she walked to her car. She was determined to leave the knot her mother had created in her stomach behind. Now she knew. Now she was going to let it go.

Rosie looked at the clock on the dash as she started the engine; she had been at the house for twenty minutes. 176 miles for twenty minutes. She would need to do some serious recycling to make up for that.

Jules drove towards home. Or what was home. She'd had no reply to her text and she wanted to deliver a letter putting her offer in writing to Tristan, before she could change her mind and get soft. The letter gave him four months to find somewhere else to live; the money would be transferred to his account upon vacation of the property.

When Gill had been begging her not to go and Romeo and Ziggy, bemused by their new surroundings, had needed her with them, she had been strong and resolved. Now alone in the car she felt weak and pathetic, the usual feeling she had when she was around Tristan and his power over her was at its strongest.

She switched the radio on.

A song she had previously thought trite struck her. Lost love and broken dreams spelled out in mournful minor chords was too much; she pulled over, turned the volume up and rested her head back against the seat. She closed her eyes and indulged her heart, wondering where it all went wrong.

Rosie arrived at Newmans that evening, to find Gill getting annoyed with Amber.

'Stand still, you silly mare.'

Gill was trying to rub lotion into Amber's back. Rain scald had burnt hairless patches of sore skin onto Ambers crest and backbone from the recent autumn downpour. The Arabian's thin and sensitive skin made the uncomfortable condition hard to prevent and it wasn't helped by the fact that Amber hated having the treatment, which stung when it was applied. Amber strained at her rope, where she was tied outside the barn.

'Bloody Jules left an hour ago, supposedly just to drop off a letter telling him to get out of her house. She isn't back yet.' Amber stood on Gill's foot as she backed away from her master's unusually vigorous rubbing.

'For heaven's sake, Amber!' Gill bellowed as pain seared through her toes.

Amber raised her head right up in the air and eyed Gill like she had just turned into a predator.

'Oh dear.' Gill gently took hold of Ambers head collar and rubbed the mare's forehead. 'I'm sorry darling. Aunty Jules stressing me out!'

Rosie stepped forward and soothed Amber while Gill finished applying the lotion.

'I need to tell you something.'

'Come on, I can't hang about waiting for her to get back and I need to tell you something as well.' Gill put Amber back into the home paddock and snapped the padlock on the gate shut; a new precaution following the intrusion. She strode into the barn and swung Monty's saddle over his half-door.

'You want me to ride Monday's Eclipse?'

'Well, it's him or Milly, they both need to get out desperately.'

Rosie eyed the huge black horse; he eagerly pushed his muzzle into the crook of her arm. Gill noticed the same tension she had seen in Rosie when she had been on Amber the previous week.

'I know he's a stallion and a racehorse, but he is *the* most sensible responsive ride. Promise. Come on, were losing light.'

Soon the women were riding side by side towards Stoke Rewe Church. Rosie kept her hands light and her seat relaxed. To her surprise the stallion felt calm and solid beneath her, Monty was not unlike Harry to ride.

'Right, you first.' Gill laid a hand on the wither of Marilliams Immortal Mist to sooth the younger greener horse as they passed the Barton Mill Restaurant and a gust of laughter expelled from the open kitchen door. One of the chefs popped his head out.

'Evening, Miss Newman.'

'Hi, George!'

The young man blushed.

As soon as they were out of sight, Rosie giggled, 'Gill, he so fancies you!'

'Don't be daft!' Gill smiled, in spite of herself, she knew it couldn't be coincidence. George was always there when she rode passed. He must hear the approaching hooves and purposely come out to pass the time of day with her, but she couldn't think about someone who couldn't have been older than thirty from the village. Not for too long anyway.

'Come on, Rosie, what did you need to tell me?'

'Right, long story, I'll spare you every little detail, but basically my Dad isn't my biological Dad and I found out in July and I went to see my mother today and Jimmy has known for years but still loves me and I am fairly okay with it, actually, when I think about it.' Rosie felt a bubble of strength rise in her stomach. She really was okay with it, what did it matter, really, what had she lost? She smiled.

'Okay. That was way too fast. You're going to have to start from the beginning, not sparing any details.' Gill was bewildered.

'I thought you might say that. But first, shall we?!' Rosie motioned towards the bridle path on their left, which cut across the valley towards the neighbouring village of Hexham.

Gill smiled and sensed Rosie's bravery was there right now and had to be utilised to conquer the tension.

'Take Monty in front, show him the rhythm with your seat, he won't fight you.'

'Got it.' Rosie urged Monty into a canter; she took hold of his forward impulsion with her seat and rocked him into a balanced and relaxed rhythm. She urged him to work his quarters and felt the sublime oneness as he arched his neck, supple as a rubber ball. Milly and Gill were far less graceful. As the young mare ran ragged along the peat floor of the bridle path, Gill played on the reins gently and encouraged the little horse to find her feet and get comfortable. At the same time though, Gill was exhilarated by the feeling that, for the first time, the mare wanted to overtake the horse in front – maybe the desire to win races was growing at last.

As Monty reached the end of the bridle path, Rosie sat deep and heavy, causing him to slow and break his gait back into a trot. She closed her eyes and smiled from the bottom of her heart. She was a rider, she could teach Red to be ridden.

'You ride him so well!' Gill complimented her friend and

allowed Rosie a few moments to enjoy her precious achievement, when she didn't look tense and neither did Monty. 'But now you have to tell me what this thing with your father is all about.'

'All right, here goes.'

Chapter five

By the time the women rode up the drive to take their mounts back to their stables, Rosie had told the story of her father and Gill had spilled the beans about Charlie's departure. The sun had set and the light was fading fast.

'Just in time,' Rosie said with a shiver, and rubbed Monty's neck for warmth.

'Yep, just in time.' Gill nodded up towards the illuminated barn where Jules was carrying Romeo's water bucket towards the temporary home that Gill had relinquished for him by turning Amber out. Because she was not in training anymore, she could roll and eat grass with the other brood mares. She would be one soon after all. Gill made a mental note to dig out a light rug to slip onto her sore back if it rained.

Rosie dropped to the ground and walked Monty into his stable. She quickly secured the door before approaching Jules, ready to embrace her woe-struck friend.

'It's okay, Rosie, you can un-tack Monty,' Jules tried her very hardest to smile brightly and look busy.

'Of course it's not okay.' Rosie waited for Jules to make eye contact.

'No it's bloody not!' Jules allowed herself to be hugged, as the tears fell yet again, 'I just can't cry anymore, Rosie. I can't.'

'Of course you can, you cry until you are number and less

emotional, and that's what gets you out the other side.'

'No, I mean physically!' Jules drew back and looked at Gill and Rosie, 'My face hurts!' Gill was the first to break a smile. The three stood amongst the animals around which their lives revolved and laughed in spite of their troubles.

Later Jules sat on her new bed in her new bedroom. The loneliness and desolation she felt was never far from her, but the evening she had spent with Rosie and Gill had lightened her mood. She had listened to Gill talk about Charlie leaving and with Rosie had tried to make the older woman feel better, believing her daughter would return home soon enough.

Then she had heard Rosie's painful story about her mother, Jimmy and Eddie. She had immense admiration for these women she was lucky enough to call her friends. How they coped, how they looked after her and each other, made her feel better about her own collapsing life.

Gill was angry with her for going to see Tristan that evening and she understood why. But he wasn't in when she got there and instead of disappointment, she had felt relief. She had been shocked but not surprised at the state of the cottage which without her daily tidy up looked like a bomb had hit it. Beer cans, full ashtrays and an empty microwave dinner container littered the living room and the duvet looked grubby and tired where it lay on the floor by the couch. She was annoyed by the mess, but there was a part of her which warmed to his obvious inability to cope very well without her.

She couldn't help but wonder where he was and although she probably knew he was at his dealer's stocking up on smoke, she found it hard to silence the nagging feeling that he might already have found someone else and be out there right now, being the charming sexy Tristan she had fallen for. Instead of the violent twisted one she had come to rely on for the smallest ounce of praise to keep her going.

As Jules wrapped herself in the strange duvet and tried to get comfortable on the single bed, she tried not to picture Tristan's naked body glistening with sweat as he worked himself into some flawless, faceless, woman. She rolled over and shut her eyes tight to kill the acutely painful image and was glad of Ziggy's soft breathing, as he lay on the floor next to her. Concentrating on his snores she finally drifted off.

Rosie fumbled in yesterday's trouser pocket to find the hotel room cardkey. She knew breakfast was a good idea. She had hardly eaten yesterday and it was included in the price of her stay. She steadied her breath as she left the cocoon of the room she had spent the night in and walked down the corridor.

She didn't like being alone in public and a busy breakfast buffet was one of the last places she wanted to be, sleep shrivelled and vulnerable. But she was here, alone in a strange city to find her real father and if she could do that, she could eat breakfast surrounded by strangers.

Rosie was shown to a seat and accepted offerings of coffee and orange juice. She sat feeling foolish, knowing she now had to get up again to fetch whatever she thought she might be able to stomach, from the array of continental offerings. She wandered self-consciously among the cold meats, cheeses and croissants. She found some cereal she liked and began to help herself. She took it back to her table. The nice waiter had sat her in a corner away from the families and couples, with the businessmen and women who were also alone and she was grateful.

She heard another guest chasing up his coffee order, she hadn't had to chase for anything, the waiter had been as attentive as was possible at a self service meal and, again, she was grateful.

He came over to her table to remove the half eaten cereal she had abandoned after ten minutes of nursing it. He offered her an egg in good English with just a tinge of an Indian accent, she smiled as she declined.

The hotel restaurant overlooked the Avon Canal which ran through the centre of Bath. Apartments which looked like they would have been pretty swanky when built, rose up from the other side of the stone riverbank. Algae from the river's highs and lows had stained the bottom rows of creamy yellow stones and rusted the once white iron balconies. Beyond this was a Mecca of more of the same coloured buildings in varying sizes and it wasn't until Rosie's gaze travelled upwards that she saw the fields in the distance, rising proud over the city.

The bustle and cosmopolitan flavour of the attractive city didn't seem like the place to find her horse-riding father, but those rolling hills did.

The plan was to take the list of livery yards, riding schools and trainers she had compiled and head to those hills. She sat with her second cup of too-strong coffee, gazing at the sprawl of countryside that capped the horizon.

Clear in her mind's-eye, she could see the small shapes of Harry and Red as they danced across the field in the distance, bucking and tossing their heads in a silhouette of freedom. She smiled as she imagined them there, conscious of a glance from a neighbouring table at her sudden brightness.

She thought of home, of Matt carefully following her instructions for the horse's feeding and care while she was away. She thought of her own breakfast table, of the solid wood under her fingertips instead of this bright and shiny Formica. She imagined Matt laughing at the faces Red pulled as he ate. She thought how lucky she was for all she had, all she had left behind to come on this quest to find a man she didn't need.

Tears pricked her eyes, not self-pity, but happiness. She had a father who loved her. Jimmy was more of a 'real' dad than Eddie could ever be, and she decided to refer to Eddie as her birth father from now on. She had her animals, her friends; although her job could be frustrating she could get her teeth into it and believed in what she was doing.

Rosie felt a swift pang of regret that she hadn't allowed Jules to accompany her as she left the hotel breakfast room and passed two women giggling together. A week on from her spilt with Tristan, she knew Jules could have done with getting away for a few days, but when Rosie imagined doing this with someone else bearing witness, it left her self-conscious and uneasy.

Rosie had always preferred to deal with emotional situations alone. During her childhood, sharing problems with anyone but Jimmy had usually resulted in the parents of school friends calling social services or worse, not allowing their child to associate with the daughter of an alcoholic. So she had learned to shut up. She only confided in Gill and Jules when she did because of the bond the three of them had formed and their willingness to share their own troubles.

Rosie left her belongings neatly in the corner of the hotel room and set off for the first of the livery yards she had mapped out as being similar to the one her mother had described. It was going to be a long day.

Meanwhile back in Devon, Gill was thankful for the blessing that October had turned out to be after a drizzly and sometimes unbearably bad summer. Although hard ground was a bad thing for racing horses under usual circumstances due to the concussion to their limbs from running on concrete-like tracks, her light-footed and shoeless Arabians had a distinct advantage when the going was solid. She scowled as she listened to Romeo clopping along behind her and Milly, his iron shod feet smacking down on the tarmac. She could barely hear her own mount's soft footsteps with pebble hard hooves, which could easily cope with any terrain.

It was a requirement when people trained with Gill that their horses had their shoes removed on arrival. She had an excellent farrier, who had immediately paid attention when shoeless horses started popping up in competitions, their owners swearing by their soundness. He had suggested to Gill that they remove Amber's shoes and it had worked better than Gill would have believed, had she not seen it with her own eyes.

Amber's hooves had come back to life. After a transitional period of being slightly footsore, the mare had actually completely changed the way she moved and got faster. Within six months she had gone from a mediocre chance, to the odds on favourite every time. The rest had followed.

She smiled as she remembered Norah's raised eyebrows when Gill had insisted Monday's Eclipse have his shoes off, during negotiation of her contract to train him. Norah had kind of glossed over it at the time, probably thinking Gill was slightly mad, but she had allowed Gill to continue, thankfully.

'He is all right, isn't he, Gill?'

Gill was brought back from the concoction of a plan in her head, to finally persuade Jules to remove Romeo's shoes and have him barefoot trimmed, by yet another panicky enquiry about Ziggy's welfare. Jules had wanted to drive the dog to Dunsford and leave him with Maurice, before she accompanied Gill on a hack. Gill had told her friend in no uncertain terms, that he would be absolutely fine left in one of the stables for an hour. The collie had howled as they were leaving the yard and Gill, who didn't really have much patience for animals who were not horses, had insisted Jules ignore the whining dog and get a move on.

'Jules, he's a dog. I know he is your dog and you love him, but he is still a dog, and being left alone for an hour won't kill him!'

Jules opened her mouth to explain exactly why he was not just a dog, but decided her tone was going to come over hostile and changed the subject.

'So you're taking Milly for the endurance ride next weekend?'

'Yes, her owner wants to breed from her in a few years and the more accolades she has the more her foals will be worth. I agree it's a good strategy. She seems pretty fast but if she's only an average racer, an average racer who is also an awarded endurance horse will be worth more. It is a bit of a stretch from race training, but to be honest, with the way things are at the moment, I'll do whatever the owners want for some extra income. The ride next weekend is just a local event, 10 miles to raise money for the Mare and Foal Charity up on Haldon Forest, but after that I want to take her to a Golden Horseshoe event in Somerset and hopefully get her bronze accredited.'

'Do you think Romeo could do it?

'Well he is pretty fit, you probably do 6 or 7 mile rides on him anyway?'

'I'd like to take him; could we come with you?'

Gill slowed Milly to allow Jules to bring Romeo up beside her and they planned their riding schedule for the week to come. Gill thinking how nice it would be to have a companion on the 10 mile ride and Jules thinking it was just what she needed; something to look forward to. She didn't even need to start getting nervous, it was after all, basically just a long hack with other people around – hardly like competitive jumping!

By the time they rode back into the yard, Gill had convinced her to ride again during her lunch break and take advantage of her work from home day by getting Romeo out for a second time. For the rest of the week Jules would ride out before work every day with Gill and Milly. On Thursday, when she had to go to Bristol for a meeting, Kelly would take Romeo for a four hour ride. Friday, Jules was working from home anyway so they could do another two rides.

On the Saturday, Gill was taking Rocky and Monty racing and they agreed Jules would take Romeo out, leading Milly alongside, for a short brisk hack – but not overdo it, ready for the ride on Sunday.

As the women dismounted in the yard, Kelly came out of the barn looking flustered. Kelly wasn't proxy to the full information about Jules and Tristan, but she had picked up enough to know that Jules wouldn't be very happy about what she had to tell her.

'Jules, um, Tristan was just here.'

Jules looked up sharply from Romeo's saddle flap, where she was loosening his girth.

'What did he want?' Jules' tone was harsh and she snapped the words out, making Kelly blush and shoot a look at Gill for guidance.

'It's all right Kel, let us bring the horses in, put the kettle on and then you can tell us about it,' Gill said.

Kelly went ahead into the makeshift kitchen area which had been added on to the barn, providing hot water for the horses and a place to get tea and coffee without running up and down to the house.

'Who the fuck does he think he is, coming here? At …' Jules looked at her watch '… before eight in the morning?' Jules pulled on Romeo's black leather reins and the horse rushed to follow her into the barn. She continued to rush Romeo until she got to his stable, where she felt immense relief to see Ziggy looking up at her.

Soon they were sitting on the white plastic chairs which formed a small rest area in the middle of the barn, next to the feed bins and buckets.

Jules sipped her coffee and kept her free hand protectively on Ziggy's shoulder. The dog was resting his head on her knee, his intense amber eyes firmly on hers, which were in turn looking expectantly at Kelly.

'He just walked in here, I was sweeping through and he came right up to me and demanded to know where you were. I guess Charlie hadn't answered at the house?'

'Did he try and take Ziggy?'

'No, he barely even looked at him. He wanted to know when you would be back and where you were, I just said I didn't know. Was that okay?'

Jules nodded.

'He said something about your letter being, 'total bollocks' and you wouldn't get away with it.'

Gill and Jules glanced at each other, each raising a wry smile.

'He said you had better call him. He stank of booze. I mean, he didn't seem drunk but you could smell it. He was a bit … scary.'

Jules' hackles rose, angry he could frighten a teenager, moreover that he had the nerve to turn up at all. The one thing she wasn't worried about though, was his reaction to her letter, she knew she had made a reasonable offer and that if it went to court any Judge would see her offer of settlement as being one he should bite her hand off for. She hoped it wouldn't need to go that far, but she felt a rising confidence that if it did, his uninvited and aggressive visit this morning would only stand in her favour.

'Thank you, Kelly, I am really sorry,' Jules said sincerely.

Kelly grinned at the solicitor and excused herself to do the morning rounds, feeding and checking on the liveries in the paddocks.

'I'll phone him today, Gill, sorry.'

Gill had picked up where Kelly left off, sweeping the barn and was thinking about Monty and Rocky's races that weekend. Jules saw Gill was not listening.

'It's okay, I need to get on with some work anyway.' Jules reluctantly left the sweet smells of horse and made for the cottage to fire up her laptop.

Gill came back from her thoughts of keeping Rocky focused during his race and whether she should start getting him used to blinkers, in time to run after Jules.

'It's not your fault, Jules, don't apologise, you'll be rid of him soon, I promise.'

Gill watched Jules walk down the drive, her arms hugging her formerly curvaceous, now slightly gaunt, frame. She glanced over at Kelly, who stood in the nearside paddock shouting at one of the greedier mares to go back to her own feed bucket and stop hogging everyone else's breakfast.

Gill realised from Kelly's comment about Tristan getting no answer at the house, that she still hadn't told her about Charlie's departure. She resolved to tell her when they rode the stallions out together later. She didn't like to burden Kelly with things, but she knew there was a wise head on those sixteen-year-old shoulders and she shouldn't keep things from her.

Just then Sally arrived to ride the now recovered Pebbles and Gill put a smile on, pushing Charlie out of her mind for the moment.

Rosie strode into the fourth yard that day, she wished for the fourth time that day, that she still smoked. None of the yards she had been to so far, had ever heard of an Eddie Gillant. She was starting to wonder what she would do if they actually had heard of him, or worse he appeared from behind a stack of hay bales. She was fairly sure, from her internet trawling and conversations with his old yard in Kent, that Gillant was his surname. She was now starting to worry that she may be going down a blind path if she had got that wrong.

This yard, Thistledown Stables, was slightly more upmarket than the previous ones and she got a more positive vibe from the smart event horses that were being hosed, brought in, led about and generally cared for with the highest regard. Expensive branded saddles sat over newly varnished steel topped stable doors and immaculate cream jodhpurs were worn with matching pale-pink T-shirts by the numerous staff. A short, but impressive woman in the same cream jodhpurs but with jet black half chaps, boots and a white shirt, eased herself from the concrete mounting block onto the back of a 17 hand grey horse with enormous muscled quarters. The woman smiled at the young female groom, who took it as a sign to let go of the grey's bridle. As the woman rode the horse across the yard, the other grooms nodded at her. She was clearly the yard manager and Rosie looked longingly, as the grey flexed his proud neck and became more precise and light with each stride under the woman's commanding hands and seat.

Rosie felt flustered as she realised she was stood in front of the gateway to the enormous outdoor school and the woman was riding the grey straight towards her.

'Good day to you!' The woman beamed at Rosie.

'Hello … er … I was wondering … um.'

The woman, rather thankfully really, ignored Rosie's fumbled attempt at communication and continued talking.

'What brings you to Thistledown? What can we here do for you dear lady on this lovely day?' The woman had an upper-class accent, filled with plummy Middle English tones.

Rosie found her voice again.

'I wonder if you can help me? I'm trying to find someone, who I believe used to, or maybe still does, work in this area.'

'I'll need a name sweetheart.' The woman, realising Rosie was probably not, after all, a potential client, reverted to speaking ordinary English, though her smile did not waver.

'Eddie Gillant.'

The woman faltered for just a split second and Rosie wondered if she had imagined it.

'No one of that name has ever worked here dear. Would you mind opening the gate for me? Quite like to school this fellow!'

'Yes of course, sorry.' Rosie pulled back the spring lever and let the pair into the Olympic sized sand school. 'It really is a lovely place you have here!'

'Isn't it just! Been here nearly eleven years now. Used to take in all sorts but we made a name for ourselves producing dressage horses and that's allowed us to hone in, focus on what we love! This chap is just rising four and he's doing very well, few local tests so far, nothing major, but he is for the big time, aren't you, Revel?' She slapped the big horse's neck as she eased him into a measured smooth trot and continued to talk. 'Of course, people bring their horses here all the time, wanting a finished article by the time they hit their fourth spring, but Revel here is mine, so we're going a bit slower.'

Rosie raised her eyebrows, as the horse, who she guessed had been pre-warmed for the woman, executed a flawless half pass from the centre line back to the outside of the school, where he immediately struck off into a hoof perfect canter. Rosie hadn't even got astride Red, who still looked and behaved like a goofy teenager, and this horse was the same age. She suddenly felt very behind. She also felt like she should give up this nonsense and get home to work on her young horse, who was sat in her field getting fat.

'Do you ride my dear?'

'Yes, I have a retired horse and a youngster about the same age as yours.'

'Splendid, old fella teaching him the ropes. Good show. What's your poison then?'

Rosie's confused look gave her away and the older woman laughed.

'What are you going to do with him dear – what's your discipline – what is he for this youngster?'

Rosie opened her mouth to say 'to love', but thought better of it.

'Well he's an American breed so I would quite like to do Western riding,' Rosie noticed the woman's expression change and quickly added, 'and show jumping, I'm hoping he'll have a jump in him when he is a bit older.'

The woman's expression didn't lift from furrowed distaste.

'Hmm ... never been one for these faddy riding crazes, it'll be circus tricks next! Still, each to their own. Good luck with him dear!' With that the woman broke away from Rosie, asking the grey to extend his canter and float away to the other end of the arena. Rosie guessed she was dismissed and started to make her way back towards her car.

As Rosie was opening the door of the Vectra, a pink T-shirt clad groom appeared from around the corner of the stable block and ran over.

'So, what do you want with Eddie?' Rosie looked up to see that despite her pony-club-style uniform, the groom was in fact in her forties.

'Um, well ... it's sort of personal.'

'Won't find him round here love,' the groom spoke with a thick Bristol accent and had course, unnaturally blonde hair, 'he scarpered years ago, after a falling out with her ladyship over some horse he was trying to sell.' At the mention of 'her ladyship', the groom gestured her head back towards the school, confirming to Rosie the pause when she mentioned Eddie had not been imagined. 'He used to come here a lot, with a horse to sell or some tack. We all liked Eddie, right laugh he was. We 'ad a bit of a thing going for a while!' The groom's eye twinkled and Rosie felt nauseous.

'But then one day those two had a barney and that was that, no more Eddie like. Last thing I heard on the grapevine he was up country, Lancashire or somewhere, up North anyway, on the show jumping circuit up there. Rides beautiful does Eddie. Anyway, better get back to me work – if you find Eddie tell 'im Emma says 'ello!'

With that, the groom scuttled back in the direction of the yard, leaving Rosie wondering if she could get a refund on her hotel room that night. She certainly wasn't about to set off for Lancashire. She wanted to get home to her horses and her husband as soon as she could.

'I don't care if you do that. You can shout as much as you like. The offer I made you is fair and you should take it. Ask Donald.'

Jules stretched her arm out to get her mobile further away from her ear, as Tristan began his next tirade. He was not taking her offer, he was not going to ask the conveyancing lawyer his firm used for advice and he was not going to let Jules take the piss out of him.

'Tristan, it's not 'taking the piss'. It's a reasonable offer.'

'You bitch.'

'Oh, that's grown up. You clearly miss me very much.' Jules' eyes welled at the insult. She felt her resolve to be businesslike and unemotional during the phone call fly out of the open window beside her, along with her new found strength.

She thought about his arms, times when he had held her, when things had been good and he was all she wanted. He was still all she wanted, but she understood now that having him meant letting go of her own wants, desires and rights.

She was about to tell him she loved him, when Gill's head appeared around the door of the Newmans' office. Seeing Jules red-faced and wet-eyed, Gill scowled.

'That's enough, get off the phone,' Gill hissed, snapping Jules back to the really real world where longing to be back with someone who treated you like shit was a bit ridiculous.

'Tristan, I think from now on we should communicate in writing. Send me your demands for settlement and I will consider them. Please do not come to Newmans again, certainly not unannounced.'

Gill smiled before retreating quietly out of the room.

Jules waited for Tristan's reply, but instead she heard a click as he put the phone down. For a second his power over her had threatened to pull her back in, just for a second. Jules set the answer phone on her work mobile and left the office for her second ride of the day.

Gill eased her sore-seat-bones onto the kitchen stool and picked up the phone. She stared down at the cordless handset and shifted her weight around, trying to get comfortable. After riding Milly out twice with Jules and Romeo, she and Kelly had taken Rocky and Monty up to the nearby point to point yard's gallops to do a couple of miles of fast work.

She often rode twice in one day, but three times had pushed her body too far and she momentarily wondered if she was getting old. She laughed as she imagined herself at ninety and still scrabbling up onto mad Arabian racers, towing a Zimmer frame behind.

Her laughter faded as she looked back down at the phone. Charlie had been gone a week now. The last thing she wanted to do was phone and have to speak to Alex, but she needed to know Charlie was okay, hear her voice. Part of Gill almost wanted to leave her daughter to it. If she didn't want to be at her home with her mother, she had to lie in the bed she made – didn't she?

Gill sighed and began to dial.

Suddenly Gill stopped. She hit the end call button and picked up her mobile instead. She laboriously typed a text to her daughter, which she hoped would be light hearted and not sound too overbearing.

Hello Char, its mum. Hope you are
enjoying it at Dad's? Love mum x x

Gill hit send, then instantly regretted it. What a ridiculous text.

'Oh well.' Gill sighed out loud.

'First sign of madness? Or is it sanity!' Jules appeared from the office, bleary-eyed from a long stint at the laptop, but fairly cheerful.

'Get lots done?'

'Tons; broke the back of a new case file and drafted the first letter to the other side. Bloody knackered now.'

'Me too, I should be sat on a rubber ring!'

'Gill, I wanted to say how much I appreciate—'

'Stop there,' Gill interrupted, 'I miss Charlie. More than I imagined I would, because she is such a pain in the bottom, so I really appreciate *you* being here!'

'Good,' Jules blushed, 'shall I start dinner?'

'Can we really be bothered?' Gill held up her mobile, 'order in?'

'Abso-bloody-lutely!!'

By the time Saturday came around, Charlie had not replied to Gill's text, Rosie had not found her father and Tristan had not accepted Jules' settlement offer.

Jules sat uneasily on the skittering Milly, while Rosie enjoyed the comfort Romeo offered all his riders. Jules was jealous of Rosie aboard her perfect gentleman, while she made do with the finicky mare.

She was very pleased Rosie had agreed to come and help out, but she did not enjoy riding Milly. She tried to make the best of the situation and asked the mare to calm down for the hundredth time. Jules wasn't really scared, she was the sort of rider who could handle any horse outside of competition, as long as she knew what to expect. If Romeo had started to behave like Milly was now, she would have been petrified, but because she knew Milly would fuss and dance, she accepted it.

Rosie on the other hand, who had been planning to spend the weekend travelling northwards in search of the increasingly evasive Eddie Gillant, was incredibly glad to be sat aboard the steady Romeo and not in her Vectra on the M5.

'So what made you change your plans?'

'Not ready. Bristol was enough for me. Need a bit of head-space before the next adventure. Plus, I wanted to spend some more time sitting on Red!' Rosie beamed at the thought. She had spent two glorious ten minute periods sat astride her wonderful baby horse so far. She thought about little else. His training, development and how fabulous it felt to be upon him, calm and accepting of her ultimate request. How fabulous that the desire to be astride him had overtaken the fear of doing it when she had returned from Bath. Granted, she hadn't actually asked him to do anything more than wander a few steps from the mounting block, but he was doing so well and she brimmed over with pride at the thought.

'I'll have to come and see him again!' Jules smiled at Rosie's radiating happiness, thinking she deserved it – genuinely pleased for her friend.

'Oh yes, he changes every week!! Whoever said they stopped growing at four, clearly never spent time with a four-year-old horse!'

The women talked about Sunday's ride and Jules tried to get enthusiastic about the endurance event.

Dullness had been building inside her for a few days. She hadn't heard from Tristan. She was settling in at Gills and getting on with her work. Things were starting to feel normal. The more normal they felt, the more the drama subsided, and the more she felt low and despondent.

This was it now. She was so grateful to Gill, but she missed her house, she missed Maurice (strangely) and she missed the quiet times she had with Romeo at the farm. There was always something going on at Newmans, a livery owner arriving, a vet or the farrier turning up, Kelly and Gill deep into racing and now endurance training. She was surrounded by people but she felt lonelier than she ever had before.

'So how are you going to get back to where the box is parked, after the ride?'

'It's a circuit. Starts and finishes on Haldon Hill.'

'Oh I see,' Rosie laughed and wondered if, next year, she and Red might be able to go along, 'are you excited?'

'Yeah, it'll be something different.'

Rosie didn't pick at Jules' lack of enthusiasm. She knew her friend would need time to recover from the heartbreak before anything became genuinely enjoyable again.

Later, Jules looked up from the work she had on her lap and listened. Satisfied the noise was, at last, the returning lorry, she closed her case file and donned her muck boots to walk up to the barn and greet the returning racers.

Ziggy instantly picked up on the excitement which spilled out of the box and leapt forward barking, to join in with Kelly and Gill's laughter.

'Good day?' Jules couldn't help but feel excited and a little bit proud that the yard had obviously been successful.

'Well?' Gill's eyes shone in the floodlight and Kelly giggled as she started to open the ramp, 'Rocky won!'

Jules hugged Gill, genuinely pleased for her friend and unable to stop the infectious joy seeping in.

'And you know what that means?' Kelly called from the back of the box.

'The little bugger can bugger off!' Gill finished Kelly's sentence and the two fell about in hysterics.

'You two have gone mad.' Jules hadn't quite caught on to the joke.

'Patricia said, if he wins this season, she'll retire him to stud in the spring and he'll be going home!' Gill called, as she alighted the lorry through the jockey door.

'Hooray!' Jules cottoned on.

'No more bitten arms,' Kelly sang, as she untied Monty and led him from the box.

'No more barged hips,' Gill shrieked, as Rocky himself leapt from the ramp, disembarking in one effort and dragging her alongside. Gill recovered and put an arm around the wild-eyed and aptly named, 'Fury', avoiding a peevish hoof as his foreleg darted out in front of him, 'You'll be off for a summer of sex and stud feed you little sod!'

'Oh look at you, he's been a nightmare from the start and

you'll miss him!' Jules laughed when she recognised the warmth in Gill's face, as the stallion dumped his ornate Arabian head on her shoulder in a gung-ho gesture of companionship. Reaching up to pull his ear through her hand and kissing his cheek quickly, Gill nodded and gave Jules a sad look.

'Oh you are so soft Mrs big racing yard hot shot!'

As if to break the mood and remind Gill why his departure would be sweeter than it was bitter, Rocky threw his head up in the air and like lightning swung it around to bite Gill's behind.

'Oh, Sod!' Gill rubbed her bottom and caught Jules trying not to laugh. Soon they were both laughing and with Gill leading Rocky, they joined Kelly in the barn to settle the horses down for the night.

Jules felt warmer and happier than she had done all week, as the three did the jobs together, talked about the ride tomorrow and laughed when Gill slid a cold compress, which strictly speaking was for horse's legs, into the back of her trousers.

Monty had won his race as well and the successful day put them all on a high, which stayed with Jules. It allowed her to go to bed with a significant reduction in the despair she fought to stave off since she had left the man she thought she would marry.

Chapter six

At lunchtime the following day, Rosie and Nicola cut across the country lanes towards Newmans in the artist's 4x4, high on their success that morning. Nic had come over early and after breakfast, they tacked up Harry and Red and had been out for Red's first ever ride. They hadn't gone far and it had drizzled the whole way. But Red had been so good, Rosie was almost overcome with joy, partly at her own success with the young horse, but mostly for the infallible laid back attitude he was developing.

Nic had lightly held a long rope attached to Red's head collar from where she sat astride Harry; Rosie had eased herself onto the Quarter Horse. Being led by Nic allowed him to get used to the idea of being ridden out, without the additional concept of being controlled from on top. That would come in time.

Nic hadn't needed to pick up the slack in the rope once, Red had simply walked alongside Harry. He had gawped and stared with prick eared interest at every gateway and house they had passed, but he hadn't shied or jumped once.

'Thank you so much, Nic, I am really grateful for your help.'

'Come on, Cowgirl, I wouldn't have missed it for the world – his first ride! I'm glad we did it with Harry, not Pharaoh. Red trusts Harry so much, it's really sweet. It was a blessing we didn't meet any cars.'

'Yes, for the first time out, but I will have to go looking for them eventually – need to get him used to traffic while I'm on top, not at his head mothering him!'

'You'll get there.' Nic changed down a gear and slowed for a junction. 'It's left here isn't it?'

'Yes, over the bridge then first right.'

Rosie was glad Nic had come with her to Newmans, Matt was away for the weekend at an IT conference with fellow 'computer nerd' colleagues and it was a good opportunity to spend some time with her neighbour. It was Kelly's day off and with Jules and Gill out on the ride, Rosie had agreed to come to Newmans to check on everything, which was a more enjoyable task with the creative and fascinating young woman accompanying her.

They opened the gates and drove up to the barn. Rosie noticed a note from Gill, wedged into the barn's kitchen door.

'Right, we need to check on the brood mares, skip out the stabled ones, and Jules has written, 'cuddle Ziggy and let him out for a pee.' If it's all the same with her I will let him out for a pee *before* I cuddle him!'

'And then we can go out for some lunch,' Nic finished.

'Definitely. We'll go to the restaurant in the village and I can show you the chef that fancies Gill!'

By the time they had completed a circuit of the paddocks and checked on the brood mares and the summer foals, who were getting woolly for the coming winter, and lastly the liveries, the pair were ravenous. Rosie fished the key to the barn from the pocket of her stretchy riding jeans, as they approached the double doors.

'Let's get this done and get some grub.'

Sliding the heavy steel door across, Rosie was surprised that Ziggy hadn't started barking. Her heart sank as she entered the barn and saw Romeo's open stable door. She ran to the stable, Ziggy's bed water bowl and toys were still there, but there was no sign of the dog.

'Oh, no!' Rosie put her hand to her head and tried to think what to do next.

'What's wrong?' Nic had reached Rosie's side.

'Jules' puppy. He should be in this stable.'

The pair looked toward the rear door of the barn which should have been locked, but was ajar. Twenty minutes later they had scoured Newmans, including the house and the lane outside. No Ziggy.

Rosie looked at her watch; Jules wouldn't finish the ride for another hour.

'Why would the back door have been open?' Nic looked out through the back door of the barn. Rosie sat with her head in her hands, knowing that the dog's disappearance would cripple an already vulnerable Jules.

'Gill often leaves it open to let the air circulate in the barn. They must have forgotten to close it this morning – no Kelly on a Sunday.'

'That sounds possible, Rosie, but how did the dog unbolt the stable door? The top door is still bolted?' Nic gestured to the stable, the bottom of the half-door wide open, but the top still shut.

'Now Gill may have left the back door open, but Jules would never have left Ziggy unsecured.'

'So someone took him?' Nic stood up.

'Who steals a collie?'

'A man scorned. Come on.' Nic shut the back door of the barn. 'Bit late but still ...' She walked towards the front doors and started heaving them together.

'Come on Rosie.'

'Oh, Nic, you don't seriously think Tristan came up here and stole Ziggy?'

'Provide me with a better explanation.' Nic allowed Rosie to slip through the gap and out of the barn, before closing it up completely and snapping the padlock shut.

Nic was starting the engine, while a still bewildered Rosie was scrambling to get in beside her.

'Nic, this isn't a good idea is it?' Rosie glanced over at Nicky who was clearly exhilarated by the prospect of gallantly rescuing the dog. Part of Rosie felt she, as the older one, should be preventing this ill advised adventure.

'Look, Jules is going to be devastated if she comes back and there is no dog. Even if Tristan doesn't have him, we need to do something?'

'You're right … Go left.' Rosie pointed at the turning which would take them towards Kysford and began to steel herself for a run-in with the man who had, quite recently, given her friend a black eye.

Meanwhile, Gill was enjoying Milly's relaxed stroll as they cleared the 9 mile marker and neared the end of the ride. For the first 4 miles Milly had literally pulled Gill's arms out. Excited by all the other horses and confused by Gill's insistence that they wouldn't be galloping, the mare had behaved like she was on a racecourse. Amongst the sturdy cobs, the children on ponies and the assortment of hunters ridden by ruddy-faced men and women with loud voices, the cavorting and dancing of the grey Arab had raised eyebrows.

A combination of exhaustion from so many miles of fighting and cantering on the spot while they waited for Romeo and Jules to catch up and what Gill hoped was a final realisation that being so uptight was not worth the effort, had finally seen the mare calming down.

Jules was happily walking along at Romeo's head, giving him a rest he clearly didn't need from her weight. She chatted to him about how beautiful the day had turned out to be and fed him handfuls of grass from the forestry track's green banks.

A gorgeous blue sky now surrounded the Haldon Hills and the Mare and Foal Sanctuary charity ride's participants gently steamed off the morning's drizzle. The flint grey and white stone track underfoot slid around a sweeping corner and the Marldon Tower in all its splendour rose up ahead of them. Instinctively the women slowed their horses to stand and gaze at the white fairytale castle before them, with its beautiful arched windows and the blue sky creating a perfect backdrop, Jules gulped and bit back tears. She and Tristan had visited the Tower earlier in the summer on a rare day when he agreed to go out with her and they had both commented on what a perfect place it would be to get married.

Gill was oblivious to the effect the tower had on her friend, but conveniently provided a distraction anyway.

'Look,' Gill gestured to the orange markers which pointed up a steep, peaty bank and into a tree lined track which was soft and hoof marked, 'on you get!'

Julis buried her head under the saddle flap and tightened Romeo's girths. By the time she emerged and ran down her stirrups to remount she had pulled herself together.

Gill gently squeezed Milly forward once Jules was onboard and was delighted to feel the mare pick up the pace into a relaxed canter. Jules allowed Romeo to follow, his giant rocking horse stride eating up the soft track, and the foursome gallantly held pace to cross the finish line in style.

The curtains were drawn and no noise came from within the

cottage. Rosie felt like an intruder as she eased herself through the gap between the garden gate and the fence at the rear of Jules' house. She made her way up the small but neat garden towards the back door and was mortified when she kicked over a rain water filled candle holder which sat on the small patio.

'Shit,' she hissed and heard barking. So Nic was right, Ziggy was here.

Nic was still at the front of the row of terraced cottages and Rosie hoped she had heard the barking too and would come round. She glanced towards the path which ran along the back of the cottages hoping to see Nicky's curly blonde hair over the top of the fence.

She turned back towards the house and almost jumped out of her skin. Tristan stood quite still at the back door. He didn't open the door but continued to stand the other side of the glass. His cold eyes gave away nothing and Rosie wondered what he would do. After a few more seconds of eyeballing one another, Rosie's anger grew.

'I've come for Ziggy.'

'You'll have a long wait,' Tristan's muffled voice came through the glass, mocking her. Rosie seethed, knowing her friend's dog was right there but not being able to get him.

Ziggy was whining; Tristan reached down to stroke the dog's head to quieten him.

'It's okay boy, you're back with your Daddy where you belong.' Tristan's smile faded as he drew up to lock eyes with Rosie again, 'Get off my property.'

'YOUR property? That's a bloody joke!' Rosie took breath in preparation for telling Tristan exactly what she thought of him, but the curtain was pulled over the glass pane and she heard Ziggy skitter away back into the kitchen. She banged on the door a few times but was ignored.

Rosie made her way back to the street and shook her head at Nic who had her ear pressed against the front door.

'He's got him all right, but he's not giving him back.'

Jules only had a few minutes to enjoy her successful completion of the 10 mile ride. Holding onto Romeo's reins she reached into the cab of the lorry to get her mobile phone before walking the horse round to cool him off after his gallop to the finish. She was wondering if she and Romeo could do the Golden Horseshoe ride with Gill and Milly in two weeks time, when she flipped open the phone.

Seven missed calls from Rosie brought her back to earth with a bump and as she listened to her voicemail the colour drained from her face.

An hour later the colour had not returned and Jules was barely listening to Gill, Rosie and Nic, who were sat in the horse barn at Newmans discussing how to get the dog back. She automatically looked down at her feet where Ziggy should have been sat. But he was with Tristan.

'He doesn't even care about him! I walked him, fed him, and cleared up after him. He ignored him if he was in a mood. He is my dog, not his dog.' Jules stood up and paced up and down the barn ignoring Rocky who was snaking his chestnut head over the half-door, trying to catch her shoulder with his teeth.

'Rocky, behave,' Gill called from behind her mug of coffee. She was trying to stay focused on Jules' turmoil. She thought though, that Charlie residing with Alex wasn't very different to Ziggy residing with Tristan. Although the dog hadn't chosen to go with him, Tristan probably had as much right to the dog as Jules did.

Rosie on the other hand felt no such pragmatic apathy. She

was fuming at the sheer nerve of the great big bastard and was determined to help secure Ziggy's return.

'Who paid for Ziggy?' Nic asked, hunched in her pale blue T-shirt against the diminishing warmth of early evening.

'He did. He did and he knows it.' Jules threw her hands up in the air making Rocky take a step backwards.

'But he was a gift for you?' Rosie shook her head at Jules.

'Legally, the police would consider this a domestic and stay well out of it. In terms of a court, they would determine who had title to the asset and find that person the owner.' Jules shoulders dropped and she started to lose hope hearing her own logic based words.

'Then sod legally!' Nic stood up. 'If you can't get him back the right way, you get him back the wrong way.'

'What do you mean, Nic?' Rosie eyed the artist warily.

'I mean Jules goes round there with Rob on one side and Matt on the other and then asks nicely for her dog back.'

'Oh, now hang on a minute. That's just asking for trouble – and someone like Tristan – straight on to the police!' Gill needed to remind the younger woman that this was not an episode of a TV soap.

'No, no!' Nic put her hand up, 'I'm not suggesting that Matt or Rob actually do anything. I'm just assuming from what you have said and Jules' black eye, this guy is a bit of a coward. So maybe just the sight of some potential muscle is going to at least make him think twice?'

'Will Rob do it?' Rosie looked up at Nic, knowing Matt would do as he was told even though he would probably only just have returned from his conference, but unsure about Nic's relatively new boyfriend.

'I'll call him now,' Nic got her phone out of her pocket and started walking outside.

Jules bit her lip, knowing this rather unorthodox plan was likely to land her in trouble. She wanted Ziggy back and could see no further than that.

A few hours later Jules, Nic and Rosie left for the great dog rescue and Gill was finally alone in the barn. She rugged Milly and Romeo up and turned them out. Now that their big ride was over, they could start their well deserved rest day immediately. She went and got Amber to give her a night in the stable, it was forecast for heavy rain and she didn't want the horse to get wet.

'Proper prissy horse, eh?' She ran her hand down over the mare's fine taut crest, making her arch her neck and lean in for a scratch. 'Can't bear a bit of drizzle!'

Gill let herself out of the stable and leaned against the half-door. She appreciated the quiet. The horses munched their hay and occasionally emitted dull thuds as their unshod hooves walked over the rubber matting in their stalls, but these were sounds Gill found comforting; a more perfect kind of silence. She reached into her pocket and pulled out her mobile phone, it had beeped in the lorry on the way back from the ride. She had thought at the time that the text might be from Charlie and put it to the back of her mind, saving the relief or disappointment, until now.

2 New Messages

Gill opened the first, which was to her delight from Charlie.

Hi Mum, its cool thnx. Might pop over
l8r, 4got one of my law txt bks - C x x

Gill saw the first text had come at 10am that morning and quickly opened the second.

Hi, you wernt there, catch you soon

Gill had missed her. The one day in two weeks Charlie had decided to come home, albeit to collect a book, and as usual her mother had been too busy with a horse. Gill said goodnight to the horses and locked up the barn. She walked back down to the dark house and wished her daughter would come home.

Five miles south in Kysford, the confrontation with Tristan was in full swing.

Jules stood at the front door, feeling acutely the strangeness of being on the outside of her own house. Matt and Rob stood a little way off, chatting to each other with relaxed postures. They weren't being threatening or hostile in any way, they were just a silent threat. Tristan had clearly clocked them because his eyes kept darting over Jules' shoulder at Matt who he recognised and Rob who he didn't.

'I paid for the dog; I keep the dog when you leave.'

'Tristan, do we have to do this on the street?'

'I don't want you to come in.'

'I have more right to be in the house I paid for than you do!'

'You left! You left … so my house.'

'Ha!' Jules' anger was bubbling and she decided this argument was about getting her dog back; the time to fight for her property would come later. 'Please could you let me see him at least, he can hear my voice.' Jules gestured towards the inner door of the cottage which Tristan had shut. The dog was scratching almost rhythmically at the wood and whining at a pitch that was uncomfortable to listen to.

Tristan allowed the dog to come to the front door but as soon as Ziggy saw a big enough gap he hurled himself at Jules and evaded Tristan's hand.

Seeing her chance she picked the animal up and began carrying him resolutely towards her car. Tristan tried to run after her but quite calmly Matt and Rob moved to stand in his path.

'This is not your fight, just let me pass?' Tristan held his hands up and faked a smile at the two men.

The two men said nothing, simply continuing to stand. Tristan thought about trying to go around them but something about the way Rob shook his head and folded his arms stopped him.

Tristan turned to walk back to the house. Once in the safety of the doorway he shouted to Jules, 'I'll just get him again! You won't keep him, he is my dog!'

The bright arrogance of having accomplished their mission saw Matt, Rob and Jules laughing and recounting the rescue all the way back to Orchard cottage.

'Ah, Rob, when you shook your head at him, like, 'don't even try' – that was priceless!' Matt slapped his new friend on the back as they sat in the rear of Jules' car. Ziggy was on the passenger seat, allowed his favourite spot as a treat.

'Yeah, lucky for us he didn't know we were shitting ourselves!' Rob leant forward and patted Ziggy on the head.

'Thanks, guys, you don't know how much I appreciate this.' Jules could have cried to have Ziggy beside her again. Not even Tristan's parting threat could touch her strong resolve. With her friends around her she could accomplish anything. Life could begin without him.

Rosie bounced uncomfortably in the hard man-sized saddle. Used to Red's smaller softer Western saddle, this giant tan settee was making her seat bones ache.

As if reading her mind the instructress, Mel, asked her to

concentrate on relaxing her thighs.

'It's the point between gripping, like you would do for English, and being so loose you fall off! Allow Chip to carry you. You have set him at a pace, jog, now let him do the work. Sit tall and proud, think elegant but effortless. As an English rider you are taught to constantly drive the horse and then harness that energy with your hands. Cowboys rode for hours and hours, days even and riding had take up as little energy as possible. Once you set your horse at a pace, it maintained that pace with no interference until you gave it a different instruction. It meant the horses lasted longer, without getting tired from constant demands and the cowboy could concentrate on the cattle he was driving.'

Rosie nodded and felt just a little bit like crying. She had watched Western riders on you-tube, she had been to some local club shows, and she had been neck reining Harry for years. She thought there was very little to it and the saddle was the main difference. Here at the Henchmore stud with its prize Quarter Horses, expensive tack and supreme knowledge of all things Western, she felt stupid. Moreover she realised that her decision to back Red to Western and compete him with no outside help had been rather naive. This was her third proper Western riding lesson and she was quickly realising she didn't have a clue.

As she bounced around the large indoor arena with Mel's critical but kind eye on her, she racked her brains trying to think if anything she had done with Red contradicted what she was learning today. She had given him single aids and not gripped or squeezed with her legs and she had been very careful not to give him any mouth pressure in addition to what he needed to be aware of her guidance, but those were coincidence and based on her own philosophy anyway.

She was just starting to feel better that maybe she hadn't ruined her horse after all when Chip saw a pole on the floor of the arena and sped up to jog over it. She instinctively drew her knees up from their long Western position and squeezed his reins until he slowed.

'Ha-ha-ha! Reverted to form there a bit didn't you!' Mel laughed 'Chip is very forgiving; some of my horses would have been very confused by that particular English aid.'

'Sorry', Rosie called and smoothed the dun's soft wither in thanks, 'and sorry Chip. He's putting up with me like a gentleman!'

'Nah, don't be daft, he is a horse. You probably aren't in control the way he's used to his rider being, but he is a seasoned chappy and he won't take advantage.'

Rosie continued to caress the base of Chip's mane with the free hand she wasn't quite sure what to do with.

'You'll have to bring Red up for a lesson with me next time. I would prefer to teach you on your own horse. From what you have said it sounds like you're making good progress.'

'Yes, he's such a little star.' Rosie beamed in spite of feeling like a ninny in her cowgirl boots and hard riding Stetson hat.

She thought over the last month. Late October was descending into winter and despite only being able to ride at weekends, she and Red had progressed to the point where she could hack him out alone. They only walked and trotted, or jogged as was a Western horse's gait, but it was major progress for them both.

He was calm and happy out with just Rosie. When there was no Pharoh and no Harry there to give him comfort, Rosie had expected him to spook and be scared, or worse not want to leave home. He had though, as he had done in so many other ways, surpassed her expectations and been bold and brave. Marching high-headed towards scary vehicles and lawnmower brandishing neighbours, he never once turned to run. Rosie was so grateful for his tendency towards meeting his fears head on, rather than bolting headlong towards the horizon. She knew that was something you just couldn't train a horse. They all had individual personalities and predictability; in over half-a-ton of powerful creature it was nothing short of a godsend.

In their short time together she knew Red, she knew his likes and dislikes, how he would react in most situations, she knew the difference between genuine fear and youthful boundary pushing.

What she hadn't expected, she mused as she jogged around the school on Chip, was how much she loved him. She and Red had such a powerful connection. It wasn't planned or something Rosie had worked on, it was something that had just happened.

When his shrill greeting hit her ears in the morning, when she gleefully brought his tack out and he waited calmly to be tacked up, when she said goodnight to him and he stood for a cuddle – there wasn't a second that passed when she didn't appreciate him and the horse he was becoming.

Harry was her life horse, the one who had listened to her childish ramblings, supported her teenage angst, the one she now returned the favour to by caring for in old age. She never thought she would feel anything of the same magnitude for another horse, but she could see the future, bright and brilliant, in Red's huge soft brown eyes.

'Lovely – that's it!' Mel's excited voice brought Rosie back to her lesson. 'You have really relaxed into him – you look so regal up there, real proud rider you are going to be!'

Rosie realised that the minute she had allowed herself to drift off and stopped concentrating on her riding, she had stopped bouncing and at last she and Chip were moving as one.

At the end of the lesson Rosie thanked Mel and said she would be in touch as soon as she had arranged transport to bring Red up for the next lesson. As she hopped out of the car to hit the button on Henchmore's automatic gate and drove away from the perfect arenas and multitude of Paint stallions and imported Quarter Horses, she thought how lucky Mel was.

But would she want that life? A life where staff were employed to care for over 30 mares, foals, stallions and competition horses, where the opportunity to ride in a covered arena was an everyday occurrence? As much as a lottery win and mountains of disposable cash appealed to Rosie, the love she had for her two quite ordinary horses was priceless. She adored Orchard Cottage, a place that she and Matt had worked so very hard for.

Would she feel that same love and gratitude for all she had if it was handed to her on plate? If the best horses the world had to offer were at her fingertips would she still look at her retired Welsh Cob and her ordinary young Quarter Horse in the same way? She doubted it.

'Juliette, darling, would you ring the woman? Now.'

Jules' mother sat on the stool next to the kitchen counter at Newmans. She watched her daughter pace between the dishwasher and the fridge freezer and started to lose her patience. She adored her successful, beautiful child and she had been nothing short of ecstatic when she received the call from Jules and heard that she had left Tristan.

'Your father will be here to collect me at six. I want to be here when you ring.'

Jules bit her lip and eyed her loving, protective and often, overbearing mother. It had taken her a month after leaving Tristan to finally call her parents and tell them what she knew would be good news. Her mother had immediately roused her long suffering husband to drive from Jules' home town in Gloucestershire down to be with Juliette, saying quite rightly a girl needed her parents at a time like this.

Upon arrival at Newmans Jules had been made to recount the sordid story of the break-up. The black eye had long since faded to nothing and Jules saw no point in further fuelling her mother's fiery hatred of her ex-lover so she had left that part out.

She had listened to her mother's loud damning of Tristan, the predictable indignation of never having liked him. Over the last two years Jules had slowly but surely lost almost all contact with her parents, unable to deal with her mother's open and persistent dislike of Tristan.

She had absorbed and felt gratitude for her father's silent sympathetic smile. His eyes reached into her soul and warmed the empty spaces Tristan had left behind. Her mother's exuberance and dominance meant their relationship had always been a quiet one, but his love meant a lot to Jules and without saying a word, she knew she had it.

After lunch, her mother, Marianne had sent her husband into Exeter for some groceries from a deli she liked in order that some serious girl talk could begin. Jules had reluctantly confided in her mother about Tristan's dog napping of Ziggy and refusal to vacate the house.

Since Jules had recovered Ziggy he hadn't left her side. She had started getting into work early so she could sneak him into her office in the mornings. Her concealment of the dog had only been successful for two days. David the partner had come into her office to discuss the court strategy for a case and Ziggy had growled from under the desk.

After briefly attempting to convince him it was her stomach she had to come clean and told the whole story. David had been remarkably understanding and had agreed to the dog accompanying her to work, on the basis that it had to be a temporary arrangement.

Now, Marianne was determined to orchestrate the removal of Tristan from her daughter's hard earned property. Jules wished Gill would come home. She had left first thing this morning to travel to Coventry for the Arab Horse Society's AGM in her cream suit and carefully applied pink lipstick. She knew Gill had to attend the event which Norah Ranger had invited her to, and it was being left alone at Newmans when Jules had decided to call her mother.

Now her mother was here and bullying her to make a call she didn't want to make. Jules began to wonder if involving her parents at last hadn't been a huge mistake.

'Darling, trust me.' Marianne reached forward for her daughter's hand and squeezed her wrist.

'I don't know that she will care and what if she agrees with him that he doesn't have to leave?'

Jules had to admit she had been contemplating calling Tristan's mother ever since the split. She had only spent one long holiday and the odd long weekend in the glamorous matriarch's company when she had accompanied Tristan to Amsterdam. But they had struck up a close friendship – to the point where she would call Jules to catch up every Sunday evening instead of Tristan himself. She had always given Jules the impression she knew how difficult her son could be and despite the great distance between them, she had always taken Jules' side in the few rows she had been proxy to.

'You won't know until you call. It's not like you will ever see her again, if she's hostile you simply end the call and go back to the drawing board. It is your house Juliette you have to try!' Marianne picked the cordless phone back up from the counter and held it out to Jules.

Jules opened her black address book, took the phone and began to dial.

'Speaker phone!' Marianne patted the counter.

Jules set the phone to loud speaker and placed it on the counter. She sat next to her mother who took her hand as they waited for an answer.

'Hallo!' the rich Dutch accent sounded hard consonants out into the kitchen.

'Hi, Ella, its Jules.'

'Well bloody hell, Juliette, where have you been?'

'You haven't spoken to Tristan?' Jules was horrified.

'I've been trying every bloody Sunday for, oh, must be a month and no answer – I thought you had your phone cut off I was going to ask Tris' Dad to wire you some money.'

Jules was shocked Tristan hadn't told his mother about the split.

'Juliette?'

'Sorry Ella, I can't believe he hasn't called you. I left him a month ago … we split up.'

'Oh, I will wring the boy's bloody neck for him. Juliette is it just a little tiff?'

'No Ella, I am sorry. It hasn't been right for a while and we couldn't go on.' Jules was careful not to apportion any blame onto what was, after all, the woman's flesh and blood.

'What did he do?'

'Nothing and everything. We fought all the time and we just weren't happy anymore.'

'Did he clout you? I swear I will be on the first plane to the UK to clout him back!' Jules tried desperately not to give away the emotion which was sloshing about right under her surface. She didn't want her own mother to know and it just wasn't her place to tell his mother that actually, yes he had clouted her and that was the real reason for the split.

'It's more about us as people, Ella, we just want different

things.' Jules tactfully avoided the question.

'What you mean is he wants to smoke bloody pot and you want a life?'

'Sorry, Ella.'

'Oh, Juliette, I'm not a bit surprised. The boy encourages unhappiness. As soon as he's on to a good thing he doesn't stop until he has ruined it completely. Listen, I had better call him and see how he is. Is he still at the little cottage?'

'Yes, but … I'm really sorry to involve you but that is part of the reason I called you. It's my cottage and although he's been contributing to the mortgage payments, obviously, it's all in my name and I would really like to move home.' Jules glowered inwardly when she thought of the pittance Tristan had actually paid towards the mortgage but thought better of bringing it up.

'How much do you need to buy him out?'

'What do you mean?'

'Well, what proportion of the place belongs to him?' Ella became somewhat short.

'None, Ella, I came up with all the deposit and the mortgage is in my name with him as a tenant.'

'What happened to the money we wired?'

'Ella, you've lost me.'

'Juliette, Tris phoned me about the cottage when you had been to look at it, we wired him 20k so he could match what you were putting in and it would be your house together.'

To Jules the room became slightly darker. Marianne gasped. Jules recalled how Tristan had come home with what she now guessed was twenty thousand pounds worth of car and told her he had got a loan, but had been unable to contribute towards the house they wanted to buy.

'I am sorry, Ella, he bought a car.'

Ella didn't speak for a while but Jules could hear the amplified anger in her breathing, swallowing up the air in the room as it emanated from the phone.

'Leave it with me, Juliette. Bye darling.' The dial tone sang out and Jules quickly pressed the end call button to silence the drone.

'Well. I'm not surprised.' Marianne folded her arms and shook her head in disgust.

'Don't, Mum, just don't'.

Chapter seven

Gill woke the morning after the Arab Horse Society AGM to the bedside phone blearing in her ear. She had arrived home well after midnight and realising Jules was already tucked up in bed, had headed straight for her room, exhausted from the day's driving and hobnobbing.

Now it was 8am, the phone was ringing and being a Sunday, all the horses had to be done by her alone.

'WHAT!' Gill shouted and swung her arm out from under the duvet to snatch the phone from its receiver.

'Good morning, Newman's Arabians this had better be good!'

'Ha ha ha ha, late night was it?!'

Gill softened when she heard Rosie's laughter.

'Actually it was well worth going, may have got some more business out of it! Girl with an Arab going off to university – might want to try him at racing while she can't ride him anyway.'

'That's brilliant. Actually I'm just about to ride Red out but I wanted to ask you when you could take him and me up to Henchmore for a lesson? I had a lesson on one of their horses yesterday, but Mel, the instructress, suggested I bring the boy up next time!'

'Um, I've got another endurance ride next weekend, the weekend after I am having a new horse arrive.'

'Brilliant – who from?'

'One of Norah's young stock. She wants somewhere to winter him before he starts training next spring when he turns four. Fingers crossed when he starts training he'll stay here to have it!'

'And in the meantime its livery dues, for you?'

'Yes, which is another £30 a week I could do with! Listen thinking about it, is today too short notice?'

'Why are you free?'

'Mucking out and feeding but that's it.'

'Let me ring Mel and I'll ring you back!'

'I'm mobile – I have got to get started on these poor horses!'

Two hours later, Red happily ambled onto the low ramp of Gill's two-horse transit van followed by a nickering Harry who didn't want to be left behind. Red had apparently forgotten all about his ordeal in the breeder's box the day he had arrived at Orchard Cottage.

In future Rosie knew the horses would have to get used to being separated for longer, but today Mel agreed Harry could have a stable while she had her lesson and it seemed mean to leave him behind to fret about his lost companion when he could just as easily come along.

Soon they were heading towards the M5 to make the fifty minute journey north to Weston-super-Mare. The horses travelled easily in the rear facing van and looking at Red who was gazing out of the small window, Rosie was delighted at how calm he appeared.

'I haven't seen you since the Golden Horseshoe Ride, how was it?' Rosie was determined to make enough small talk not to focus on how nervous she was about her lesson. Red had never even been in an arena. She tried not to think about how exciting he might find the new smells and strange horses.

'Great! Fabulous riding over Exmoor, don't think their feet

saw tarmac once! I think Milly is going to be good at this, possibly better than at racing. Her heart rate at the midway checkpoint was so good the vet asked if we were only just joining the ride when in fact we had already done 15 miles! She is bronze accredited, so is Romeo, although he was quite tired at the end, only just passed the vet.'

'Is Jules going to take him to the one next weekend? '

'No, that's a 50 miler and she's been working so hard she just hasn't been able to get him fit enough. I saw her just before I left, she told her parents; they spent the day with her yesterday'. Gill carefully negotiated the motorway slip-road and slid the four-year-old vehicle into fifth gear.

She loved the two-horse van and although she had to admit it was struggling slightly with Harry and Red's bulk in the back, it was so much easier to drive than the big box. She bought it six months ago and with the fuel she had saved using it whenever she could, it was already making its money back for her.

'How has she been?'

'Up and down, and between you and me – completely neurotic over Ziggy.'

'Understandable though.'

'Yes. She's thrown herself into work, which is probably good for her. She misses Tristan like mad and some nights you can she struggles to stop herself getting in the car and just running to him. But she's a strong girl, she won't.'

'Speaking of strong girls, how is Charlie?'

Gill took her eyes off the road to give Rosie a withered look.

'I've spoken to Alex a few times but she doesn't seem to want to speak to me herself.'

'Sorry, I'm sure she'll be back soon.'

'I hope so. But she's a young woman now, if she feels this is the best thing for her and she needs to get to know her Dad, who am I to stand in her way?'

'That's very unselfish of you.' Rosie looked at Gill who was scowling in her wing mirror at a juggernaut driver who was getting too close for comfort.

'Motherhood, eh? Stick to your boys Rosie!'

Jules sat in the office at Newmans, pleased after the phone call she had received from Tristan's mother. She dialled her mother's number to give her the good news.

Jules laughed at her mum's delight when she told her Ella had been adamant he would be out by Christmas. She left out the distinct impression she got from Ella that Tristan was not in his parents' good books, having spent their money on an overpriced hatchback instead of a step on the property ladder.

'He really should be getting out right now not by Christmas, but he is going, that's the main thing. And it's probably very good that you'll stay with Gillian for a few more months, it is nice for you not to be alone darling.' Jules listened to her mother twitter on for a few more minutes, before promising to come and stay soon and ending the call.

Jules thought about calling Tristan for physical confirmation of his mother's promise, but she decided to leave well alone. Ella had a distinct power over Tristan and gripped his admiration in a way Jules scorned herself for never being able achieve. She held many of the same qualities he had often praised Ella for; the ability to work full-time and run a household, her strength of character and professional ability. But somehow, Tristan had never recognised those qualities in Jules.

'Right then, Ziglet, let's go for a little ride.' The dog immediately got to his feet and stood at the office door, tail wagging, open mouth smiling.

Jules had been working in the office for most of Sunday

morning and deciding she and Ziggy needed some fresh air she donned her boots and made for the barn. Ziggy walked to heel with no lead or voice commands now, and Jules wanted to see if he would be able to accompany her and Romeo out on hacks.

After running a body-brush over Romeo's already gleaming coat and routinely checking the fit of his perfectly balanced saddle and precisely adjusted bridle, Jules led him out into the yard towards the mounting block. Once she was on board and had tightened Romeo's girth, she laughed to see Ziggy, who stood hesitantly at the door of the horse barn.

'Come on then!' Jules called as she turned Romeo to walk down the drive. Ziggy trotted over and fell in step beside Romeo. They had got used to each other around the barn and in the field and Ziggy quickly applied heel to mean Romeo's legs.

'Good boy.'

Ziggy wagged his tail and looked up at Jules; it was as if he had been doing it all his life. The trio walked out onto the lane and when Jules asked Romeo to trot Ziggy kept pace. Jules smiled a wide genuine smile and for once, didn't feel lonely at all.

'He is a nice little horse this one.' Mel ran her hand down Red's slightly sticky neck and patted his broad withers. Here among Henchmore's many Quarter Horses bred for various disciplines, it wasn't difficult to confirm Red was of cattle horse stock. His thick chunky hindquarters, close coupled short back and powerful neck gave away his bloodline's intention – to round and rope cows. He was quite different from the taller, lighter 'trail' or hacking bred Chip, who Rosie had ridden the day before.

'I'm so proud of you!' Rosie threw her arms around Red's neck unable to maintain professional horsey decorum any longer. The lesson had gone brilliantly. Mel had confirmed Red's natural ability for Reining Competition, which was a Western discipline requiring the horse to spin and turn on a sixpence, going from a gallop to a standstill in one quick sliding stop. Of course they hadn't actually performed any manoeuvres during the lesson, they had only walked and circled, but Mel had shown Rosie how to perform the basics for these movements on the ground with Red and given the pair lots to work on before their next lesson.

Gill and Mel laughed at Rosie's delight.

When they had arrived Mel had suggested they turn Red out in the arena and leave him loose to get used to the area he would be working in. Harry was given a small stall overlooking the large sand school and they had gone into the enormous barn's integral office for a coffee while Red exhausted his enthusiasm for his new surroundings.

By the time Rosie had walked into the school carrying his saddle and bridle, conscious of Mel and Gill watching her, Red was ready.

She called him softly as she swung the heavy saddle over the post and rail fencing which bordered the arena. To her delight he walked, ears pricked, straight to her and stood in close to her familiar body. Talking to him, Rosie gently slid the soft leather bridle onto Red's poll. The familiar motion gave comfort to them both and Rosie hauled the saddle onto his back as he stood perfectly still. By the time she led her brave young horse over the mounting block in the corner of the school she was fairly confident the lesson would be a good one.

'Nice to meet you, Mel, give me a call if you want to talk more about breeding!' Gill called as she sprang into the van.

'Byeeee!' shouted Rosie as they left the stud. 'Thank you, Gill, for bringing us, I'll settle up with you if you let me know the mileage.'

'My pleasure, Rosie, although something towards the diesel

would help! I'm so impressed with what you have done with him, considering he was unbacked six weeks ago you must have really worked your little bottom off!'

'It's a great feeling, Gill – well you must know that with the Arabs, real progress from hard work. Unlike searching for your long lost father, which is just plain soul destroying.'

'How is the hunt going?'

'I just don't care anymore! I've got a Dad, I don't need another. The trail went cold after Bristol and I'm certainly not buggering off to Lancashire on the say so of one slightly slutty groom. I've got everything I need right here.' Rosie smiled at the CCTV image of her horses swaying gently in the van behind her. Gill wished she could be as self-assured as her friend.

Rosie sat in the bath that evening, wishing she owned a shower. It wasn't that she minded particularly, she quite liked a bath if it involved a glass of wine, maybe a book or a chat with a friend on the phone. When she had lots to do though, she missed the convenience of a shower, hopping in and out, nice ten minute affair. In the bath it took her ten minutes just to wash her hair.

Her hair had a natural wave and became frizzy easily. As she used a jug to rinse the thick masque of conditioner she had applied five minutes before, she wondered if she was too old for unruly locks which fell almost to her bottom. Maybe she should go for a neater trendier style. Jules had sleek, almost black, shoulder length hair which was always beautifully straightened and chic with a sweeping fringe.

Gill's blonde bob was cut into easy to manage layers which fell into place naturally and fitted in with her hectic schedule. Even Nicola the artist who had a fey quality and hippy style anyway, always seemed to have her blonde ringlets under control. It's only me, she thought as she rang the last droplets from the dripping mass, who always looks slightly scruffy.

'I don't care! It's my hair,' Rosie muttered indignantly as she stood up abruptly causing the bath water to slosh to the end of the narrow bathtub.

'Yes, it is your hair, who said it wasn't?' Matt laughed as he walked into the hideous green and brown bathroom they would eventually get around to gutting and replacing. Rosie smiled at her husband, still wearing khaki shorts and a fawn T-shirt around the house even though it was November.

Matt reached into the airing cupboard and pulled out a large white bath towel. Rosie stepped from the bath and he wrapped her up, strong arms pressing her into the warmth of the soft fabric. He kissed her wet head and allowed her to move away to wrap her hair in a second towel before embracing her again.

She had told him all about the lesson when she'd arrived home and as they stood in silence she smiled as a lingering aroma of spices and slow cooking wafted in from the oven.

'What would I do without you?' Rosie sighed.

'Be very unhappy!'

Rosie laughed as she nodded, she really couldn't have been happier. She was doing well with Red, who was in the field with Harry, just outside. Jules was on the mend and work was ticking along nicely.

Rosie twinkled her eyes at Matt before pressing her small but full lips against his. He kissed her back, tenderly but with just enough pressure to make her feel safe and feminine. Matt gently took her bottom lip between his teeth, causing a delicious wave of arousal to course through her. Rosie wriggled her hips, allowing the damp towel to drop to the floor. Matt didn't need any more encouragement and grabbed her hand. She followed him buck naked and giggling uncontrollably to the bedroom where they energetically dispelled the myth that married couples don't have great sex.

'Gillian!'

'Yes, Norah, sorry.' Gill was trying to concentrate on Norah Ranger's words but she couldn't stop her attention being pulled away from the office and the telephone call she was having. Through the open window she could see Kelly working with one of the youngsters. The six-month-old Monday's Eclipse colt was playfully nipping at Kelly's calf as she prised his dainty little hoof up from the ground to inspect the sole.

He had previously been quite a flighty little creature but Kelly had clearly put in some time with him now that the last Arabian Racing fixture for the season had been and gone. It was good for Kelly's college portfolio to work with the youngster and hopefully this foundation training would impress the owner and encourage her to continue to keep the foal at Newmans over the winter. 'Total Eclipse' was out of a mediocre Arabian mare, but there was something special about the cocky colt whose chestnut coat was wintering out to a darker shade. The more he lost of his downy baby fur the more it seemed certain he would be as black as his father, and hopefully as well put together.

'Gillian, my youngster. He is quiet as a lamb and very well mannered, bit dopey actually. I hope to goodness he gets some go in him by spring as I want to him to have his first few races at the end of next season.'

Gill was brought back to the conversation by the mention of racing the three-year-old. She didn't want to ask Norah outright if that meant he would be staying with Gill for his training but from what Norah was saying the chances sounded good.

'The calmer ones always do well. The less energy he uses up before the race the more he can put into running. I have a mare here, who could really have potential but she gets herself so stressed out before the race, fretting and pacing, she is burnt up by the time she gets to the start. I'm sure your—'

'Gillian I must go, I'll bring him over on Friday, 10ish?'

'Right yes, sorry, Norah, bye.'

Gill hung up and wondered whether she would ever have the measure of the woman. She must have trusted Gill or Monday's Eclipse wouldn't have been placed at Newmans, and now a second horse would be arriving at the end of the week.

Why then did Norah never have time to listen to anything Gill had to say? Gill decided while the going was good she wasn't going to dwell on it and leafed through the pages of the diary to make a note of the new arrival.

She opened the window and called to Kelly who was laughing at Total Eclipse. He tried desperately to bite at the small length of webbing which hung from the foal slip she had gently slipped onto his pint-pot-head.

'Wait there, Kell, I'll get the baby rug!' Gill shut the window and ran up to the barn to get the tiny gortex rug the little horse would soon need to start wearing.

Gill stroked the young horse's nose and talked to him while Kelly gently placed the rug onto his back. She heard a car pull into the yard and glanced at her watch. She thought it was rather early for Jules to be home from work, even on a Monday and she stood up from where she had been crouching with the foal to see who it was. The foal jumped, surprised by Gill's sudden doubling in height and almost tripped over Kelly who was crouched and reaching under his belly to fasten the cross straps which secured the rug in place.

'Sorry Kelly.' Gill reached her hand to the groom who had fallen backwards onto her bottom. 'I think I had better go and see who that is, I don't recognise the car.'

'Shall I leave the rug on him for a minute, let him get used to it?'

Gill nodded and headed for the gate. Kelly walked over to the foal's mother who had been watching and patted her neck for allowing them to interfere with her baby.

By the time Gill reached the yard, the two occupants of the white Ford Fiesta were getting out of the car.

The man had a broad Irish accent and looked rather un-horsey in tight black jeans and a leather jacket.

'Hello there. Looking for some livery for my lady's horse!' Gill shook the slight hand of the dark haired man and turned to the nervous looking woman who was wearing remarkably clean, cream jodhpurs and new black riding boots.

'Right. I'm Gill, this is Newmans.' Gill reached forward and shook the woman's hand, who mumbled that she was Cathy.

'Cathy here has just got her first hoss! Been having lessons for a while but we took the plunge got her a nice horse, hunter isn't he Cath?'

'Yes.'

Gill thought Cathy didn't look very enthusiastic about her hunter.

'Where do you live?' Gill asked the rather odd couple.

'I work up in Bristol so Cath is in Exeter on her own most of the time.'

Gill recoiled inwardly thinking if the woman was lonely she would probably hang around the yard a lot and then chided herself, for any income was income, even if it meant putting up with the shy woman. Gill was lucky in that most of her current livery owners were very much weekend riders and the race horse owners barely visited the yard, but she had always known the grace of a quiet stables wouldn't last.

'Well, let's give you the tour and then we can talk about

prices.'

Ten minutes later they were stood in the barn. Gill still hadn't learned much more about the pair and was losing a little patience with how nervous the woman appeared.

'Blimey, he's a beauty for sure!' The man ran his hand down Monty's sleek neck as the stallion stood politely with his head over the half-door.

'Yes, he's a racing Arab, stallion too,' Gill looked at Cathy who was looking at her feet. 'I assume the horse you have bought is a gelding?'

'Yes.'

'Right, here is my fee plan.' Gill handed the man one of the flyers she had had made up which detailed her race training, brood mare and full and part livery fees.

The man raised his eyebrows at Gill's prices and the couple quickly left saying they would phone.

'Well that was a waste of time,' Gill said to Kelly, who was approaching with the foal rug as the fiesta made its way down the drive.

'You win some, you lose some?' Kelly smiled and placed the little rug onto the large shelving wrack which lined the far wall of the barn.

'Better lost in their case, odd pair,' Gill shook her head.

'Best get Milly out before it rains?' Kelly reminded Gill.

'Okay, would you like to ride Monty? He's bored!'

Gill enjoyed Kelly's company and the girl didn't have to be asked twice to ride the stallion and quickly fetched his tack. The racing season was finished but the horse needed to be kept ticking over for the winter. Milly had her big endurance race in two weeks time and Gill would have to ride her for at least three hours a day, with some all day rides thrown in before then. As much as she was pleased at Milly's progress, she was beginning to find the time endurance training took up a bit wearing.

'Over to the estate or up to Silverton?' Gill smoothed Milly's silky white forelock so that it sat under the headstall of her bridle and decided she was quite fond of the mare, especially now that she was becoming a more relaxed ride, at least endurance was good for something.

'Let's go to the estate,' said Gill, and she laughed as she saw Kelly melt at the thought of Monty's luxuriously smooth canter over the parkland.

'I love riding Monty, thanks Gill. I will pooh pick the paddocks when we get back!'

There was certainly something about Monty and she knew it would be a sad day when he retired from racing and went back to Norah's small stud farm, or worse, if Norah ever moved him to a different trainer.

Jules stretched her arms upwards and arched her back, feeling the confinement of her office chair after a long day. It was 5pm and she'd had enough. She decided to pop across to the Princesshay shopping centre round the corner from her firm's building and do a little shopping before the stores closed.

She had worked most of the weekend and didn't feel in the slightest bit guilty about leaving early. Jules left Ziggy on his blanket in the back of her car with the window slightly open to let in the cool evening air and she promised not to be long.

Jules couldn't help smiling openly as she walked along the bright arcade. She hadn't really been shopping since she had left Tristan and was delighted to feel the familiar desire for some new shoes or cute little top. She must have dropped at least a dress size since the split and decided if there was one upside to tremendous heartache; it was that if you were miserable enough, you lost your appetite. Jules loved clothes.

She wasn't too obsessive about fashion but she always felt a surge of excitement when a new season's colours and styles hit the shops. The winter style was well in, and leggings worn over knee-high boots topped with an oversized jumper or figure hugging dress were certainly looks she could pull off, especially now she would be a trim 12 instead of an occasionally wobbly 14.

Jules bit her lip as she passed the window of her favourite designer store and saw a vibrant green jacket. Double breasted with oversized lapels she imagined it hugging her ample bust before falling away over her new smaller hips and decided she had to go inside and try it on.

'Hey, Jules.'

She knew the voice before she saw Tristan's face.

'Hi.' She was nervous, embarrassed even, especially having involved his mother over the cottage. He was also the last person she expected to see, knowing he usually sped straight home as soon as he left the office to make himself a joint.

'Just off to pick up my dry cleaning,' Tristan's voice was light-hearted and quite friendly. He looked relaxed, completely unemotional. Jules had to thrust her hands into her trouser pockets to stop them shaking. She didn't know what to say.

'Oh …'

'Well, good to see you, take care.'

Jules froze as Tristan leaned in to kiss her cheek, before making his way along the pedestrian-only street. Tears welled in her eyes as she watched him walk away from her. She knew he was emotionally stilted and never behaved in a predictable way, but she hadn't expected that the first time she saw him out of context he would act as though their relationship had never happened. She could have been any random acquaintance.

The new jacket forgotten she hurried back to the safety of her car and Ziggy, and headed for the Newmans wet-eyed. She didn't know what she had expected, but it certainly wasn't that.

'Bloody weirdo!' Jules shouted as she drove out of the city and towards Stoke Rewe. Ziggy, surprised at her sudden and unusually loud utterance, barked in agreement.

Jules was pleased to see Rosie's car parked in the yard as she drew into the driveway of Newmans, which was starting to feel like home.

She went straight into the barn to greet Romeo and found Gill and Rosie drinking coffee, Rosie still in her work clothes having come straight from Exeter's Civic Centre where the City Council housing officers were based.

'Hey, honey!' Rosie patted her lap. Jules sat across her friend's legs and put an arm around her shoulders. Ever since she and Rosie had met over a mutual client, who had found himself both homeless and in need of a solicitor, they had found an ease in each other's company. Realising they both had an interest in horses they had arranged to have lunch. Their line of communication was like a tangible strand between them and even early on they had found themselves plunging straight into deep and meaningful conversations. Jules had admired Rosie's down to earth nature, willingness to speak her mind and obvious ability to consistently do the right thing in all situations. Rosie in turn enjoyed the neat stylish solicitor's intelligent company and sense of humour and although they were quite different and had had polar opposite childhoods, their mutual respect quickly turned into a genuine love for one another.

'Saw twat face today,' Jules sighed, 'he was friendly and normal and even kissed my cheek before he walked away. If his intention was to totally freak me out he succeeded.'

'Are you all right?' Gill looked concerned.

'Yeah, I'm fine, really.'

'Twat face?' Rosie exclaimed. Jules started to giggle and Gill and Rosie followed suit until the three neared hysterics.

'So what brings you here Rosie?' Jules hopped off Rosie's lap and pulled up her own chair.

'I was just getting round to seeing if Gill might be free to take Red and I to a Western riding show on Saturday?'

'His first show, how exciting!' Jules leaned forward and mentally cleared her diary. 'I'll be your groom – oh, I'll have to get myself a cowboy hat!'

Gill had been about to say she was too busy with the endurance ride the following weekend to spare the time, but seeing the delight radiating from Jules and the undisguised pleading in Rosie's eyes, decided she would manage.

'I reckon I could do that.'

'It's just the morning Gill, starts at 8am, and finishes at 1pm. It's the Devon Western Riding club's young stock show. I'll just be doing an in hand – or Halter as they call them – Quarter Horse class and a ridden walk and jog – which is a trot by the way!'

'Even better, I can ride Milly in the afternoon and Kelly will be here in the morning.' Gill smiled, now that Norah's new youngster was arriving on Friday and she could enjoy a morning with her friends she saw no reason not to.

'Mel from the Henchmore Stud phoned to tell me about it today, she emailed a schedule and suggested my classes. She also said if she saw you there she could talk to you more about Quarabs – what the bloody hell is a Quarab?'

'While you were getting Red ready at the stud I spoke to her about the newest hottest breed – Quarter Horse cross Arab! I get free covers from Starfighter while he is here so I wondered if I could arrange to have one of her mares on a breeding loan.

Trouble is some of the ones I've seen have got tiny heads and giant quarters, so it would have to be the right mare or we could end up with a bit of a dog.'

'And they're called Quarabs?' Jules smirked.

'Sounds like something you'd get from a one night stand!' said Rosie.

Jules threw her head back unable to contain her laughter.

'You won't be laughing when it makes me rich!' Gill said mockingly.

'Rich or ITCH?!' Jules howled and Gill shook her head as the two younger women collapsed into helpless fits of belly laughing.

Later when Jules had gone back to the house and Rosie had headed home to see to her own horses, Gill removed the last droppings from the stables of the boxed horses.

Rocky had gone back home to his owner now that he had won the last race of the season. Although the lost training fee was something Gill could scarcely afford, she was pleased to have a stable for Amber again. Although generally speaking when a horse wasn't in training Gill preferred them to live out in one of the paddocks, Amber liked her creature comforts. Sharing one of the field shelters with other mares when the weather was bad made the mare cranky and on a windy night like this one, Amber was in her element nestled in a cosy straw bed with a full haynet and Monty's appreciative company in the stable next door.

Amber immediately left her haynet when Gill walked over to stand at her stable door and joined Gill in her soft companionable way.

'Oh, Amber,' Gill sighed, 'when will Charlie come home?'

Amber softly brushed her cheek with her muzzle, chestnut whiskers tickling Gill's neck, but the mare had no answer to her master's question.

Rosie rolled over and nearly fell out of the single bed. She was too nervous to sleep. Moonlight flooded in through the window of Charlie's bedroom and illuminated the teenagers abandoned possessions.

Gill had collected Harry and Red earlier on in the evening so they could set off southbound for the Grove in Okehampton first thing in the morning. The week had flown by and Rosie started to wonder if she wasn't making a huge mistake taking her recently broken youngster to a show so soon.

Harry would stay at Gill's in the barn while they took Red on to the show and both horses were currently in the paddock outside, fed, watered and grazing happily despite being in a strange field.

Rosie resisted the temptation to go to the window and look down at the ghostly outlines of her horses, as she had done countless times already. She looked at the bright blue numbers of Charlie's digital alarm clock. It was 2.20am. Three hours since she had said goodnight to Gill and Jules and come to bed. She had to be up at 5am to prepare Red. They needed to be loaded and on their way by 6:30 in order to reach the show in good time for the 8am first class. Rosie's class was the third of the morning, but being her first Western show she had no idea how long the classes would take and therefore what time she and Red would be called.

She glanced over at the new show halter which hung on the back of the door. She had ordered it on Tuesday from an online Western tack shop and had waited with baited breath. Luckily it had come this morning in the nick of time.

The tan coloured leather halter was decorated with intricate patterns in silver thread and the long leather lead rope matched in colour perfectly. It was the only thing she needed for the show that she didn't already have. The first thing she had bought after she had paid the deposit and agreed to purchase Red was a

Stetson and she smiled to herself in the darkness as she recalled the way Matt ribbed her and said she only wanted to take up Western riding so she could get a cowboy hat and boots.

Her black wrangler jeans and grey long sleeved shirt hung in front of Charlie's wardrobe. Rosie was worried about her outfit, but Mel had assured her there was no need to buy a fancy rhinestone jacket for a small club show.

She turned over again and shut her eyes, determined to get at least a few hours sleep. She finally drifted off by imagining she was at home in her own bed with Matt beside her.

'It's a good job we brought him straight in – the first class is over!' Jules ran over to where Rosie was trying to make Red stand still, holding the cowboy hat she had managed to find in a charity shop onto her head to stop it flying off.

'What do you mean?' Rosie couldn't believe it. They had arrived at ten to eight, after Red had decided he wasn't too keen on getting into the horse van after all, despite having travelled to Gill's beautifully in it the day before.

The Grove Equestrian Centre was well equipped with a huge indoor arena, viewing gallery and adjoining collecting area. Red was somewhat overwhelmed by his surroundings.

Rosie tried to control her own terror when she thought about having to get on his back later for the ridden classes. He bounced around her, the whites of his eyes showing as he jumped and fretted at the loudspeakers and passing horses who all looked incredibly calm in comparison.

Her heart warmed when an older lady leading a large bay Quarter Horse smiled a sympathetic smile as she passed. It was Red's first show after all and Rosie reminded herself that the most important thing was that he had a good day and a positive experience.

When the three women had arrived, Rosie had dashed to the makeshift steward's office to quickly join the Devon Western Riding Club in order that she could make her last minute entries to the two classes.

She had returned to see Jules trying to lead Red around the lorry parking area. Her precise British Horse Society approach to handling a horse did not sit well with Red who was used to Rosie's slack roped approach.

'You trot into the arena one at a time past the judge, then line up at the far end. She comes over and inspects your horse. Then she considers everyone for a minute and you are called to line up in your placing. And that's it! Not a bit like English showing when you have endless walking and running round and round the judge.' Jules noticed Rosie was struggling with Red who was reacting to the announcement of the winner of the first class as though firecrackers were being set off behind him. 'We had better get him up to the side of the ring; he might settle when he sees inside?'

Rosie nodded not trusting her voice, and Red cavorted beside her.

'Ah, here she is!' Mel called from the entrance to the arena where she was stood talking to two other women, 'Jane, Wendy, this is Rosie with the youngster I was telling you about.'

Rosie managed to slow Red enough to stop and say hello.

'Bit nervous is he?' Wendy smiled. 'Bound to be at his first show, don't worry dear we're very relaxed here, happy to support newbie's making the effort to turn out!'

'Thank you,' Rosie replied. It was just a little trip out for her and Red, an opportunity for him to get used to competition in a friendly setting. There was really nothing to worry about.

Almost immediately Rosie relaxed, Red relaxed too. She walked him around the covered collecting area and watched the three-year-old class leaving the arena. One of the horses, an attractive black colt, pranced at his handler's side. At least Red wasn't the only horse who was excited. Rosie concentrated on working Red, asking him to turn when she turned, stand when she stood. The horse found comfort in the familiar ground work Rosie had done with him so often and eventually she was able to rub his shining neck until his head dropped in acceptance.

'Your class will be called now. Wait until they call your number and trot him in. I'm going to join Gill in the viewing gallery – good luck! Oh, hang on your number is squiffy.' Rosie breathed deeply as Jules straightened number pinned to her back.

'153,' the steward called. Rosie led her young horse towards the entrance of the arena.

'Trot on, baby boy,' Rosie murmured as she passed the steward and smiled. To her delight Red immediately lifted into his long striding jog and the lights of the arena shone on his white flecked chestnut coat as his gleaming legs carried him forth.

Chapter eight

'Pity about the first class, but you did us proud in the second!' Gill grinned from the van's driving seat at Rosie, who was still in shock.

'Don't worry about the first class, it was a learning experience and you'll know next time, standing still is something to work on,' Jules added, from her position squashed between Gill and Rosie. Red's head was down and the tired horse dozed as he travelled in the back. Rosie wasn't surprised he was tired, today had been quite an ordeal for the adolescent. However tired he was though, Rosie was sure he'd had a good day. He had enjoyed the praise and clearly relished the sights and smells of the show.

Although his first halter class had been a disaster, from Rosie's point of view, Red had been none the wiser and thoroughly enjoyed his first spell in the arena. Red had trotted (or 'jogged' as Western trained horses should) beside Rosie beautifully, but was rather put out at then having to stand still in line, while the judge inspected the entrant's for their confirmation and closeness to the desired Quarter Horse breed type. The judge had a fair crack at trying to assess Red, but the excited horse, fired up from his jog into the arena, had failed to stand still, even momentarily, while she had walked around him.

Embarrassed, Rosie had struggled in vain to keep Red from bashing into his statuesque, doe-eyed competitors, as he flailed from side to side. He had come 5th in a class of five. Rosie looked down at the green rosette in her hand. During the class she had been devastated, thinking that coming in last place had meant the judge did not think Red was very well put together, or was a bad example of the breed. She had been gushing and grateful when the judge's steward had followed her out of the arena after the class.

The steward explained that, while the judge had liked Red very much, she was unable to place him where she would have liked, due to his failure to stand up for her. The steward had added kindly that they ought to have been eliminated for this breach of Western showing rules, but that as it was Red's first show they had allowed the pair to stay in the ring and awarded the last place rosette out of kindness.

By the second class Red had got used to the arena and was less excited by the close proximity of strange horses. He had walked beautifully round the arena and when the command came over the Tannoy for competitors in the novice, 'Walk Jog' class to jog, he had transitioned beautifully. His jog had not remained beautiful and there were moments when Rosie had struggled to stop him napping towards the middle of the arena, his head and shoulders crabbing awkwardly.

Overall though, he had performed well enough to earn himself 4th out of the seven entrants and Rosie was delighted with her placing. When she had first mounted Red before the class and felt him unusually charged beneath her, she had almost wanted to get off. But fuelled by a determination to go through with the class, she was so pleased she had stayed on.

'I'm so proud of him,' Rosie said, for what was probably the twentieth time during the journey back to Newmans.

'We know!' Jules and Gill cried in unison.

'Right,' Gill said, as she gently swung the van off the lane and up the drive, 'Rosie, go and grab Harry and we'll load him straight away, no point getting Red out, I'll take you straight on home.'

Rosie started to undo her seatbelt as the van drew to a stop in the yard. Something about the sudden tension in Jules next to her, made her look up. The three women sat rigid for a second. Wide-open stable doors could be seen through the open front of the horse barn.

Gill was first from the box and as she opened the driver's door, the shrill sound of desperate whinnying from Harry met her ears. As she ran, numb, towards the barn her legs felt as though they were not her own. A heavy sense of killing dread crashed down upon her because, even before she reached the entrance, she knew something was very wrong.

Gill barely heard Jules and Rosie come up behind her as she stood in the doorway, frightened to enter the barn because she could already see that a frantic Harry was the only horse left. Rosie ran ahead of Gill to get to Harry, but as she passed Monty's open stable door, she caught sight of the prostrate form of Kelly through the bars. The girl was slumped in a corner quietly sobbing. The top and bottom doors of the stable were bolted shut and Rosie struggled to get them open in her haste to get to Kelly.

Rosie knelt at Kelly's side and the bleary-eyed groom clutched at Rosie's hand. Kelly's eyes met Gill's as she too came into the stable.

'Gill, I'm so sorry, I tried to stop them …' Kelly's wail and streaming tears barely reached Gill. She froze to the spot, her dread confirmed. Amber, Monty and Romeo were gone.

An hour later, two police officers stood in the barn. Gill had to hear Kelly's sob-ridden story for a second time as the officers took details in their leather bound notebooks.

'I heard a horsebox pull up. I wasn't expecting one,' Kelly's wavering breaths came rapid and slowed her speech. 'Three men came into the barn. They had head collars in their hands and one of them had a crow bar and I asked them what they wanted, but they ignored me. The one with the crowbar … went straight over to Monty and started to put the head collar on him. I ran over, but he shoved me out of the way. I tried to stop him opening the door to the stable, but he kicked me. I tried to grab the lead rope from his hand, but he pushed me into the foaling stable and tried to lock me in. I ran at the door but he swung the top door and it hit me on the head. As I fell, I could see Romeo being led out of his stable. I must have passed out for a few minutes I think. When I came to I was locked in the stable and they had gone. My mobile is in my coat pocket on the peg in the kitchen …'

Kelly turned to her, pale-faced, white-lipped employer.

'Oh, Gill I tried to stop them. Jules I'm so sorry.' Kelly looked through tear-streaked eyes at Jules, who was crouched down holding Ziggy tightly in her arms. Jules returned from the horror of her own imagination at the sound of her name, but didn't speak.

'It's all right. It wasn't your fault, you tried.' Gill leant over the devastated girl and held her. Gill left Kelly alone at the yard all time without thinking anything of it. A wave of guilt swept over her as she noticed the egg-sized swelling and rapid colour change to blue of the skin over Kelly's temple.

After Kelly had finished describing the three men and the horsebox as best she could, her mother, who they had called straight after calling the emergency services, whisked her away with a paramedic into an ambulance.

Gill hugged the groom and whispered to her again that it was not her fault before they drove away.

The afternoon passed in a blur for Jules. She was numb and isolated from the twenty or so people in various states of shock and activity, who were filling the ground floor of Newmans cottage. The police officers were still there and a community support officer, who had only just arrived, was taking photocopies of the three horse's passports as proof of ownership. Gill's brother Mike was making tea for Norah Ranger. The large woman was trying to discuss a plan of action with Gill, who was clearly unable to think straight.

Rosie's husband, Matt, Nic and her boyfriend Rob were trying to offer whatever support they could, but were also clearly shell-shocked. Various people from the village and those who lived along the lanes in either direction from Newmans were recounting anything they had seen.

Two of Gill's immediate neighbours had seen a large blue horsebox, but used to comings and goings from the yard, could not possibly have known to note the vehicle's registration.

She noticed that two of the Chefs from the Barton Mill restaurant in the village had arrived with trays of sandwiches. The taller of the two chefs couldn't take his sympathetic green eyes away from Gill.

Under any other circumstances, Gill would have been warmed and humbled by the support of her community, but instead, it was as if she was part of a living nightmare. Every time she closed her eyes, all she could see was Amber's face. The only sound she could hear despite the chatter and activity in the room was the soft nickering of her beloved horse, ringing out over and over in her memory, as though it was frightened of being forgotten.

Later that evening, Rosie walked into the dark paddock to check on Red and Harry. She knew she was needed by her friends and while the police were questioning Kelly, she had turned her horses out into the paddock next to the house. Gill would not have been in a fit state to drive them back anyway.

Rosie reached Harry and put her arms around his neck. She held on too tightly and the old horse took a step back in protest, eyeing his owner with a cocked head and questioning expression.

She vaulted onto his broad, rug covered back. Sitting astride him she leant forward and rested her cheek on his mane, her arms around his withers. She exhaled in utter relief to feel the strong warm bulk of her horse beneath her.

For the first time, Rosie was thankful for Harry's dipped back and age-sagged eyes. She was sure they hadn't taken him because he was so clearly an old horse, who really wasn't worth anything. He was worth the earth to Rosie.

Eventually Rosie gently slid from her horse and walked stiff legged, to securely padlock the front gates of Newmans. As hard as she tried, she couldn't ignore the creeping guilt which lay its icy fingers along her spine.

The horses may not have been taken if Gill and Jules hadn't been at the show.

Gill woke as the sun began to rise. An unwelcome shard of light slid across her bed and made her feel exposed. She had probably only had an hour's sleep all night.

When had everyone finally left, and Rosie had retired to Charlie's room, she sat with Jules in the living room. They hadn't really spoken to one another as the hours dragged past. Consumed with fear, they needed the silent comfort that each understood what the other was enduring.

Heavy-footed, she had eventually gone up to her room where

she had laid on top of the bedclothes, feeling a cold desolation she hadn't thought possible. Even when her marriage had broken down the sadness and loneliness had not come close to this, because at least then, she had had some control over the situation.

Gill hadn't even begun to contemplate what Monday's Eclipse having been stolen meant or how Norah must be feeling about a horse entrusted to Gill's care being taken.

All she could think about was Amber, twelve-year-old Amber with her rain scald and her occasionally fiery temperament. Monty and Romeo were valuable assets, a stallion capable of producing offspring and a seasoned competition horse. The possible consequences didn't bear thinking about.

Gill still felt like it was happening to someone else. Shock prevented tears; she was isolated from her own self.

Still dressed from the day before, she pulled herself from the bed and wandered towards the staircase, not really sure what she would do when she got downstairs.

Jules hugged her knees to her chest. She barely looked up when Ziggy, hearing Gill's footsteps in the corridor, padded out of the bedroom. Her red eyes stared straight ahead.

Where was he? Where was her chestnut horse? With his gentle eyes and his proud roman nose. What was he doing right now? Was he in some grubby lorry with tired, travel weary legs? Was he hungry? Did he wonder where she was? Was he being the perfect gentleman as always? In rough hands, that wouldn't recognise his manners? Who wouldn't see the amazing horse he was?

The horse he was to her. Was he being ridden by some heavy handed woman? Did she ask him to jump in a badly fitting saddle, a rusty bit and tough bone-like leather headstall?

The images flashed through Jules' mind. She was helpless to stop the steady stream of her own cruel imagination. When had Romeo last had a drink?

He loved his water bucket, ducking deep into the cool clean water and sloshing his muzzle back and forth as he drank. Jules thought of all the times she had cursed him for making a mess on the floor of his stable, for wetting the straw with his exuberant thirst quenching. Her fingers raked up through her hair until she was holding her scalp so tightly, her nails dug into flesh. It wasn't until she felt the sticky wetness at her fingertips, that she realised she had drawn blood.

'WHY didn't you call me?' Carol's face was flushed with anger as she crashed through the back door. Gill was stood in the kitchen. Taken by surprise, she really didn't understand what the livery owner was saying. She had been at the kitchen counter for about ten minutes, shrouded in grief, closed off from the world around her.

Gill opened her mouth to respond, but no sound emitted. She truly didn't know what to say.

'Jasper and Ryan are fine, I checked them myself many times, Carol,' said Rosie, dashing into the kitchen to Gill's rescue. 'Come into the lounge and I'll tell you the whole story.'

Rosie led the furious Carol away. Gill didn't realise her friend was saving her from an earful. She didn't even register that Carol ought to have been called last night. Nothing was real any more.

Gill looked blindly around her before she realised the other person in the kitchen was Mike. He made her sit on a stool before making her a coffee.

'Rosie and I have seen to the horses,' he spoke softly in his usual gentle voice.

‘Right.’ Gill felt alien in the kitchen. It was as though she didn’t belong there anymore.

‘I called Alex, Charlie will be here later. Norah called this morning, she’ll be here in a minute.’ Mike gently squeezed his sister's hand as he passed her to fetch mugs and the physical contact made her swoon. She clutched at her brother’s arm.

‘Can’t bear it, Mike. Where are they?’ her voice was small, bordering on hysteria.

Mike took her by the shoulders and stood in front of her.

‘Don’t. You will find her. You will find all of them. I promise.’ Gill met eyes with her sibling, clutching to his positive words. ‘You have to be strong now, for Amber?’

Gill nodded feebly. She glanced over his shoulder and out of the window.

The brood mares grazed in the paddock as though nothing had happened. Tom drank from his water trough in the high fenced stallion enclosure. The horses looked relaxed, like it was any other day.

Jules walked into the kitchen. Weighed down by lack of sleep and barely coping with the adrenaline which was still pumping through her. Adrenaline her body produced to help her find her beloved animal, who was surely in danger, but that she was powerless to use effectively. Shock bound her into futility.

‘Morning, Jules,’ Mike smiled warmly. ‘Would you like me to call your Mum?’

Jules nodded, the corners of her mouth lifted at the kind offer but her eyes stayed dark. She wandered into the living room and sat on the sofa, drawing her knees up to her chest, in what had become a familiar unconscious action.

Rosie finished calming Carol down and the woman became

sympathetic to the plight of Jules, Gill and Norah almost immediately, as soon as she realised her horses had remained padlocked in their paddock, as had all but three of the yard's equine inhabitants, she was ashamed of her treatment of the obviously traumatised Gill.

'Really it's all right, Carol, I'm sure she didn't take it in, anyway.' Rosie promised Carol she would call her if there was anything at all she could do.

After she had shown Carol out, she sat in Gill's office. She leaned forward to switch the computer on. She didn't know where to start. She was full of compulsion to do whatever she could to help her two friends, but where the hell was she supposed to direct it?

The police yesterday had said to start checking sale catalogues. She clicked on Google and typed in, 'horse sale'. She stared blankly at results 1 – 10 of 1,210,000.

What types of sale might two Arabs and an Eventer be taken to? Where should she look?

She decided instead, to start posting details on the many horse chat forums the UK equine lover had to choose from. The desperation she felt for anyone who had had a horse stolen, never mind two of her closest friends, must surely be a feeling shared by the hundreds of other horse owners out there?

The three horses' passports were still on the office desk and using the details she described the animals in a post she titled, 'Horses stolen yesterday from Exeter, Devon – please help'. Using New Rider, Horse and Rider Magazine's online forum and Adhorse as well as a multitude of others, Rosie sent information out into the ether.

Rosie realised as she sent the last post, she may have just made things worse for Gill. As much as she wanted to get the horse's details to as many people as possible, she knew Sally and some of the brood mare and racing owners probably still hadn't been called. Rosie couldn't run the risk of them finding out about the thefts via some chat-room that they might happen to stumble across.

Rosie noticed a typed list on the office's pin board. Each owner, along with their telephone number and the names of their horses, were listed neatly. Rosie unpinned the sheet and set it beside the phone. Acting as ambassador for the yard, she began making calls to the owners. Their reactions ranging from shocked disbelief to outright anger. All, though, couldn't hide their relief that their own horses were safe. Rosie was glad to have spared Gill the agony of their joy penetrating her own despair.

An hour later, Mike showed Norah in and for once, the woman had lost her brash assertiveness. A night to sleep on the appropriation of her best stallion seemed to have weakened her.

Gill recognised for the first time in the eyes of the woman she had previously thought was all business, sadness at the theft of her prize stallion, which clearly went deeper than the asset he was.

Gill reached across the kitchen counter and put her hand on Norah's. As their eyes met, Norah smiled sincerely at Gill. It was probably the first eye contact she had ever shared with her powerful client and she was momentarily warmed that the woman was so worried about Monty.

Gill quickly retracted her hand and stood up to greet a woman who was opening the kitchen door and introducing herself as Detective Inspector, Lila Gregory.

Jules barely noticed her parents arrive. She could hear and see her mother, being loud and demanding with the Devon and Cornwall Constabulary officer, who was trying to explain what would happen next. But it seemed like there was a distance between her and what was happening around her. Much like Gill, she was trapped inside her own private hell, powerless to do anything.

Rosie was listening attentively to the female DI, who seemed fairly passionate about recovering the stolen property. Jules could see Rosie making notes and asking questions. Jules understood from the periphery of her senses, they would be notifying Trading Standards, the Department for Farming and Rural affairs, the larger horse societies and pretty much anyone else who attended horse sales on a regular basis.

Jules pictured Romeo at a horse sale, his tall powerful frame reduced like a caged bird, within the confines of a small bidding ring.

Jules was so fed up with the images in her head, but she could find no mechanism to switch them off. They just kept coming.

Just then something that Lila, the DI, was saying brought Jules back into the room and the present with such force, she almost expected someone to greet her.

'... unfortunately the eyewitness account that the men were wearing gloves, coupled with the lack of finger prints, means we are likely to be dealing with career thieves. They walked in here bold as brass and were prepared to commit assault to get what they came for. That usually means they are also better at covering their tracks further down the road, in terms of hiding the horses and selling them on under the radar.'

'What about Romeo's Microchip? No one asked me?' Jules looked up at the DI. It was the first time she had spoken and she was conscious of all eyes in the room turning on her.

'Well, unfortunately, the microchip only helps if someone is suspicious enough to ask a vet to scan it and of course, if you find the horse to prove ownership. This afternoon I'll enter the details of all three horses on the Stolen Horse Register, that way, anyone who is suspicious about a new horse turning up at a yard or at a sale with no passport, can see if it is a registered missing horse.' The DI smiled warmly at Jules, delivering the news gently.

'What will you actually be *doing* to investigate this? Other than notifying few enforcement agencies?' The words were out of Jules mouth before she had time think she might sound hostile. If Lila noted the hostility, she chose to ignore it. She sat on the arm of the chair and opened her palms to the expectant room.

'The truth is Juliette, other than the descriptions of the horses, we haven't got a lot to go on. Looking over yesterday's statements, we have some weak descriptions of the three men who sound fairly generic, we have no registration number for the horse box and the description of that is pretty loose too. But, people do get their horses back, sometimes in cases where we don't even have descriptions of the suspected thieves to go on. Often it's the determination of the owners that get these horses back.'

'I've posted descriptions of Amber, Romeo and Monty on all the horse forums,' said Rosie. She felt she had done the right thing, when Lila smiled enthusiastically and nodded.

'Horse insurance companies will sometimes offer a one off sum to assist the owners in searching for their horses, having posters printed and such like, you should check your policies.' Lila stood up.

Gill and Jules locked eyes. They barely noticed the DI leave.

The two friends recognised in each other's expressions, a dawning of realisation. If anyone could get the horses back, they could. With love, determination and the sinking knowledge that life like this was too black to ever be satisfactory, they knew they had to try.

After the DI had left, it was as though a new life force had taken over at Newmans. Instead of a drab misery clouding the atmosphere, Jules and Gill finally began to spring into action. The bleak helplessness had not left them by any means, but their sadness had a channel, their grief a direction, as they made arrangements to leave.

Are you sure you don't mind, Rosie?' Gill asked her friend one last time, as she loaded the last of her bags into the horse box.

'Absolutely, as long as it's just looking after them all and not training, Matt and I will stay here as long as we need to.' Rosie had already phoned Matt. His initial grumbles at having to move in to Newmans were instantly revoked when Rosie reminded him it could have been Red and Harry stolen and she who needed help.

Gill was grateful to Rosie for phoning the owners of the remaining horses that morning. The owner of Marilliam's Immortal Mist had thankfully agreed that Milly's endurance career would be suspended, while Gill left to search for Amber and Monty.

Gill knew, if the search continued for too long, the owner would probably move the mare to a better resourced yard, but for the moment at least, she was grateful for the loyalty. She was also grateful for the support Norah had given before she had left. She had promised to contribute to the costs involved in spending days on end in the lorry, travelling from sale to yard to event. Gill knew she would have to charge a reduced fee for Milly, while she was not being ridden and that she would also now lose Monty's training fee from her income.

A harder woman might have decided she needed to concentrate on running her business, might have left the search to Jules. But as Gill headed into the barn and picked up Monty's soft brown leather head collar and Amber's delicate black halter and held them in her hands, she knew she had to go. She knew she couldn't stay here and pretend things were normal, get on with her job.

Jules joined her in the empty barn and reached for Romeo's spotless, padded head collar. The pair stood looking at the garments of their horses. They would have given all they had in the world to slip them onto willing heads.

But the barn was empty, the silence deafening. No rhythmic munching on hay, no footsteps on the straw.

'Come on, I have a few more calls to make, then we can go.' Jules squeezed Gill's shoulder, as Gill bit back tears. She allowed Jules to steer her out of the barn and fell in step with her friend's purposeful stride back to the house. Gill looked at the set determination in Jules' jaw, whitening the taut skin over her cheekbones. She knew that determination and knew she had to use it herself to replace the helplessness, which was threatening to crowd her again.

'David Barker for you, Jules.' Mike held the cordless phone towards her, as they reached the door. Jules would never dream of calling her boss at home under normal circumstances and the message she had left with his wife earlier must have raised alarm bells, because the senior solicitor's tone was urgent.

'Juliette, are you all right?'

'Yes.'

She tried to sound convincing, as she started to explain what had happened. She made her way towards the office and shut the door. She told the story in what started as a level voice, but by the time she had got to her closing statement, her words sounded weak and tears slid down her face.

'... So I have to find him. Have to, David. I am sorry.'

David tried to convince Jules it was for the police to find the horses and that the search could be dangerous, especially if these men did not bat an eyelid at knocking out a teenager. But she didn't care. She articulated her feelings slightly better than, 'I don't care', but the point was made.

David eventually agreed to a sabbatical period, effective immediately. Jules would not be paid, but he would do his best to keep her position open for her. It would be for a month, initially. David made it clear that, because he would have to employ a temp to cover Jules' work even if she found her horse in the first week, she would still have to take the month off, unpaid.

'That's very reasonable, thank you, David.' Jules felt relief at his agreement, but she had been quite prepared to be fired if David had refused. Her victory was comforting, but not essential.

The loneliness Jules felt as she continued to sit on the leather chair extended beyond the absence of Romeo. Because this loss, this agonising loss, was not something which much of the population would understand. It was not a mainstream tragedy. The grief of losing an animal she had learnt with such clarity when her dog had been taken from her, was something many would view as nothing more than a shame. Only those with a strong connection to animals, a horse of their own, could begin to imagine this feeling.

She wished it could be on the news, with offers of help flooding in. The rallying round of family, friends and some of the villagers yesterday had been nice, but it was on nothing like the scale Jules found fitting for her grief.

Jules couldn't have children. The ability to carry a child had been removed when she had survived ovarian cancer. A year after the operation, she had bought Romeo. It wasn't that she had been broody and needed a replacement, she had been quite philosophical and wanted to adopt when she was ready, when she had found the right partner. But she had felt a need to direct her love, a desire to turn lessons and rides on Harry into her very own rewarding dependant, when the chance of falling pregnant became zero.

She knew the only way to get Romeo back was to find him herself.

'Mum?'

Gill had been taking Rosie over the feeding arrangements and amounts for the horses, when she heard Charlie's voice.

Before Gill had a chance to greet her daughter, Alex was up close and personal. Holding on too tightly for too long he clamped her into his flaccid embrace.

'Gilly, my darling, my poor, poor darling how truly awfully terrible for you.' Gill suffered the invasion to her personal space until he finally let go. As she made her way past him to get to Charlie, she could hear his words spilling out in torrents, could he help with the insurance claim, could he provide money from his own pocket to bail her out? But Gill disregarded his arrogant offerings.

'Thanks for coming.' Gill held her hand out to her daughter, who shyly took it. They looked at each other for a moment before Charlie pulled her mother in and put her arms around her.

'Sorry, Mum,' Charlie's voice was almost a whisper, but even over Alex's incessant chatter, Gill could hear the sincerity which reached into her heart like a lifeline.

For a moment, Gill felt compelled to keep Charlie beside her. The comfort she felt just from having her child near was immeasurable. Gill could hear the words forming in her mind and she had to stop herself from asking Charlie to come with her and Jules. Gill knew she could not take her daughter away from college, away from her future, as strong as her own desires were.

'Will you SHUT UP.' Gill turned on Alex, who was still talking away, his words only really of benefit to himself. Had Gill's eyes not been burning into Alex's ham-like face she might have noticed Charlie's concealed amusement.

'Well, Gilly, I can see you are still very very understandably upset and not quite ready for sensible discussions about this.' Alex had a way of keeping the upper hand, no matter how hard Gill shot him down, but she continued to glare at him as he put an arm around her shoulder, 'Good Luck, Gilly, I do sincerely hope you find your Arab. If you don't manage to recover her I promise to buy you any horse your heart desires.'

Before Gill had time to explain exactly why that was one of the most hurtful things he had ever said to her, Charlie gasped.

'Oh Kelly!' Charlie didn't try to hide her reaction. As Kelly entered the barn, even Alex was momentarily speechless at the sight of the formerly rather attractive sixteen-year-old. Hot, tight, angry swelling had all but completely swallowed one blue eye and an unholy purple and green bruise spread from her hairline down her face, reaching almost to her jaw. Kelly's mother stood behind her and Gill noticed the worry in the woman's eyes.

'Kelly, you should be in bed.' Rosie stepped forward and put a hand on Kelly's arm.

'Thank you,' Kelly's mother sighed. 'I've been telling her that, but she won't have it, said she had to come here – said you would need her.' The woman eyed Gill with just a hint of accusation, torn between the admiration and infuriation she felt for her dedicated, guilt-ridden child.

Gill took Kelly's hand and together they left the barn. Conscious of the audience, Gill needed to be alone with her young employee.

'I'm leaving soon, with Jules; we're going to look for the horses.' Gill recognised what Kelly was about to say and stopped her, 'No, no you can't come.' Kelly went to protest, but Gill continued, 'No. You're not well enough and Kelly listen – Rosie needs you here. She and Matt are going to move in to keep an eye on things but you are the one, I know, who will keep things running. I trust you Kelly, hand on heart and I wouldn't be happy going unless I knew you were here. But, and this is important, not until you're better. You need to go home and you need to rest. Then you need to come back here and you need to run my yard for me. You know what these horses need and without me, they are going to need you so much, Kelly. You know that Tom will only let you catch him if you ignore him first; you know that Bramble needs to have her feed separate from the other mares; you know Milly has to have her sweet itch lotion twice a day. You know these horses.' Gill noticed Kelly's mother stood listening and the woman smiled in thanks.

'You mean I'm not sacked?' Kelly burst into tears.

'You're not sacked, you are my hero – you tried to save them and look at your poor face.' Gill tenderly brushed the back of her hand against Kelly's good side. She felt a rising confidence as Kelly smiled in gratitude 'and when I have found them we'll go back to normal, just us and the horses.'

Gill's smile faded as she saw Charlie beside Kelly's mother.

'We're off now,' Charlie's voice was cold, the sympathy and desire to give heartfelt comfort to her mother had melted away.

'Oh Charlie, don't go?' Gill moved over to her daughter and hugged her. Charlie hugged her mother back, but did not change her mind about leaving.

Once Charlie, Alex, Kelly and her mother were gone, Gill had to concentrate on her preparations for leaving.

Mike and Rosie stood in the yard waiting to bid farewell to Gill and Jules, as they stowed the last of the provisions into the living quarters of the three-horse box.

'Good luck.' Rosie smiled up at Jules in the passenger side of the lorry's cab. She wanted to say so much more. Be careful, look after yourselves, and eat properly. But she was perceptive; she could almost see the words she and Mike had offered, bouncing off the hard exteriors of Jules and Gill. A thick coating of resolution had been applied, single track minds set on recovering their animals.

As the lorry swung around the yard and made its way down the drive, Mike briefly squeezed Rosie's hand, before heading into the barn. Rosie watched Mike, as he walked through the open double doors, his jaunty stride carrying his large but lean frame. An only child, she had missed out on having a sibling. She thought how lucky Gill was to have a brother like Mike.

Chapter nine

Later that evening, Rosie sat in Newmans office nursing a headache. It had been an emotional and stressful afternoon and she could have done without the task ahead of her.

But, Gill and Jules would be awaiting a list of sales and events scheduled for the coming week and she needed to get her brain into gear. They had already decided to attend a horse sale at a Livestock Auction in Shropshire the following morning. Norah had given Gill the details of an Arab breeder she knew who had indicated the sale was large and drew in the crowds. The breeder had offered to attend the sale to help them look, so it seemed as good a place to start as any. Rosie glanced at her watch and knew they would have arrived by now, to park up nearby and wait for the gates to open first thing.

Rosie couldn't believe how hard she had found it to look after all the Newmans' horses, plus her own rather disorientated equines. She knew coupling her new duties with a full seven hours at work tomorrow was going to leave her too drained to try and complete her research task come the evening, so she had to do it now.

After Jules, Gill and Ziggy had left; she had driven home to Orchard Cottage to help Matt to pack for what was an unknown stay at Newmans. Together, they had lugged sacks of Harry's feed into their cars, along with their clothes and other necessary items.

When they returned to Newmans, Rosie had been grateful to see Mike picking up dung from the paddocks. It meant one less job on the long list.

Having two horses, although not unpleasant, could be hard work at times. Now, looking after 25 equines, she realised what a walk in the park her normal life was.

She had no idea how long it would take her friends to recover the missing horses, or give up the search and come home empty-handed. She tried not to think about the latter, which would have dire consequences for the long term happiness of both women. Rosie was determined to do her very best to help and support both of them. It was going to be tough going.

Earlier when she and Matt had mucked out, fed and tended all of the horses outside and inside the barn, they had both felt drained afterwards.

Then, as though in punishment for thinking they had finished, the afternoon's lazy showers had turned into insistent downpours, meaning the brood mares with smaller foals had to be brought in for the night and stables prepared. Already emotionally exhausted, the physical fatigue took its toll.

Rosie gritted her teeth. She trawled through livestock auction websites, searching for the day of the week when their respective horse sales would be held and tried to work out a timetable which made geographical sense. She followed the Detective Inspector's advice and chose sales which were low profile enough for thieves to think horses could be sold undetected, but large enough to ensure the precious goods fetched a decent price. For every sale on every day, Rosie knew there was another sale going on somewhere else, where the horses might be. It was like playing Russian roulette and the prize would be picking the right sale on the right day. Pot luck. But there was no alternative.

Rosie imagined Gill and Jules in the lorry. Heating the soup they had taken with them on the small stove in the living quarters and laying out warm duvets in the bunk above the cab. She hoped her friends would sleep; they would need their wits about them in the morning.

'Rosie,' Matt gently nudged Rosie's arm where it cradled her head. 'Bed.'

She realised she had fallen asleep at the desk and stood up, woolly but resolute. They had to be up at 5am to see to all the horses and it was already 11pm. Matt put an arm around his wife and they headed to Gill's bedroom, where they would be sleeping until further notice.

'I do hope Kelly's better soon.'

'Good morning. I have the details here of some stolen horses we're trying to find and I was—.' The auctioneer's clerk stopped Jules mid-sentence.

'Arabian Mare, Arabian Stallion, Irish hunter.' The man read from a piece of paper he recovered from the mountains of sale entry ledgers he had on his desk.

'Yes, that's them.' Jules nodded. She handed the colour photographs of each of the horses to the man, who promised to get them to the auction room staff before bidding began.

Jules headed back out of the market office towards the holding area, where Gill would already be scouring each pen for a familiar hock or head. Bless her mother and Rosie. Since Rosie had produced a sale timetable for Jules and Gill to work from, Jules' mother had set about faxing details of the stolen horses to the markets, so that they had them in advance of horse sale days. Her mother had also faxed details of the horses to every corresponding police station and Jules was grateful for her mother's help. She would see her mother that night, as they were attending a sale in Cheltenham the following day and the temptation of a proper bed to sleep in for a night, a shower and a good home cooked meal a few miles down the M5 in Gloucester, had been too strong to resist.

It was Thursday morning and after four nights in the lorry both women were starting to get cabin fever.

The three sales they had already visited during the week had proved fruitless. On Monday at the first sale in Shropshire, Norah's friend had helped them watch the bidding ring and check the pens and boxes for the horses. Anxious to help in any way she could, she had made up posters for them to put up around the sale. They handed the posters to any sale goers who would stop long enough to listen as well, encouraging them to put them up at their local yards and tack shops. Each poster bore a description of the three horses next to a colour photograph and contact details. They had been making copies of the photographs of the horses and the posters at every opportunity, stopping at local stores boasting a colour photocopier in the window. Jules' mother had been to a printer's and tonight they would collect a thousand copies, which should save them time and hassle the following week.

If no leads came from the posters and they didn't find the horses before Saturday, they would be heading back to Newmans for the weekend. Jules prayed something would happen to prevent the return journey.

While they were attending sales there was hope. Each new day was a day when they might find the animals they so craved and Jules couldn't bear the thought of being back at home in Devon. Sitting at Newmans where there was no chance of making a discovery, waiting for Sunday evening so they could set off again.

Both women were tired from driving long distances, nights on the hard bunk above the cab and unrelenting shifts between watching the sale ring and scouring the holding pens. The defeat of heading home to Newmans ought to have had the upside of an opportunity to rest, but the inevitable loss of adrenaline and a lull in the urgency to keep moving, would give the exhaustion a window to get the better of them.

Jules smiled down at Ziggy, who padded beside her, resenting having to be on a lead. He had been such a good boy, guard dog at night in the lorry, her constant companion. It was good to have someone to hug. She had always been a tactile person and she missed the intimacy that being in a relationship offered.

'It's the rules, Zig,' Jules ruffled the dog's head as they moved through the sale crowd, 'all dogs on leads at market.'

Ziggy cocked his head and looked up at her with a mournful brown eye. She knew he didn't need a lead to stay by her side and under control, but the auctioneers probably didn't care very much about the level of obedience the dog would have displayed if given the chance, and she needed to keep the officials on side. The more of a good impression she and Gill made, the more, in theory, people would try to help.

'Anything?' Jules mouthed as she approached Gill, who was handing a poster to a small group of women huddled around the pen of a young gypsy cob. Gill retreated from the sympathetic smiles of the women to move over to Jules.

'Diddly-squat,' Gill shook her head and leant against the bars of an empty pen. It was going to be the fourth long day in a row.

'Oh what NOW?' Rosie had finally settled down for the evening and the doorbell was the very last sound she wanted to hear.

Fridays were usually relaxing for Rosie. At Orchard cottage she would have had the house to herself, time to play with the horses, catch up on housework and maybe see a friend for lunch or coffee.

A Friday, running Newmans, was rather different. Rosie genuinely knew she'd had a harder day than if she had been at work. When she'd finally settled down with a takeaway in front of the telly, she had been hoping not to move from the sofa again until bedtime.

The day had started with the usual gruelling rounds, seeing to all of the horses. Then the vet had arrived for an appointment to swab Amber. It was a pre-conception health check required by most stallion owners. It had obviously been arranged before the mare had been taken, when Gill had been planning to put her in foal. The vet was very understanding and agreed not to charge for the wasted visit, something Rosie was grateful for and which confirmed her decision not to mention the forgotten appointment to Gill.

The farrier turned up an hour late and completely threw Rosie by asking which horses he would be doing. Rosie had absolutely no idea which were due and which weren't and as much as she hadn't wanted to bother Gill, she had to phone her to ask who needed a trim. Rosie then had to bring in each of the horses who needed a pedicure from the mud-sea fields, which were waterlogged after the week's incessant rain. She washed and towel dried their feet individually, working as quickly as possible to have the next horse ready when the farrier had finished with the last.

By the time he left, Rosie realised it was time for the evening routine to begin and she started feeding and bedding down.

She hadn't had time for lunch or to spend any proper time with Red and Harry. She had been leaving them until last, saving her own familiar animals until all the other jobs were done.

But, inevitably, by the time she got to them, the 5pm darkness of mid-November had descended and the daily rain had set into a steady rhythm, so all she could do was feed them and check their rugs, before plodding wearily back to the cottage.

She was cross and gritty when she answered the door, leaving Matt on the sofa with the remains of her pizza.

'Hi, I just came to see if there was anything I could do to help, is Miss Newman here?' The tall man looked past Rosie and into the hall behind her.

The white chef's coat he wore was rain-darkened and clinging to a red T-shirt underneath. His blonde hair was slickened by the downpour and tendrils hung over his forehead, spilling rivers down his handsome face and wide angular jaw.

'It's George, isn't it?' Rosie recognised him as the chef from the Barton Mill, who she had seen whilst riding with Gill, and who had brought food the day of the theft. Despite her fatigue, Rosie felt quietly excited that she had been right – he must fancy Gill or he wouldn't be here.

'Yes, that's right.' He gave a winning smile and his white teeth gleamed. Rosie felt a butterfly in her stomach that would have made Matt jealous.

'Come in, come in – you look drowned!' Rosie gestured and he followed her to the kitchen.

'I left my car at the gates. I climbed over and walked up,' George explained his appearance. 'Can't blame Gill for keeping them locked after what happened.'

Rosie went into the utility room next to the kitchen to fetch George a towel, before putting the kettle on to boil.

'Gill is away with our friend, Jules, her horse was also taken. They're travelling round the sales looking for the horses. Matt, that's my husband, and I, are looking after the place while they're gone.'

'Oh.'

George didn't hide his disappointment very well.

'Stay and have a hot drink?' Rosie offered.

George shivered and nodded.

'They were due to be back for the weekend tonight, but they had a tip off about a hunter trial at a Riding Club near Cheltenham tomorrow, so they'll be staying away after all.'

George wrapped the towel around his shoulders.

'What's a Hunter Trial?'

'Not a lot to do with hunting actually, these days. It's a jumping event; the jumps are spread out in a big course across country. It's often called Cross Country. Romeo, that's Jules' horse, is an eventer and his forte is Cross Country. Someone at the horse sale they went to today said it was a big event and horses for sale were often taken there to show off their ability.'

'What about Gill's horse?'

'Well, it's probably an unlikely place to find an Arab Racing mare, but to be honest I don't think either of them wanted to come back here. Not without the horses.'

George nodded, he understood immediately and Rosie warmed to him even more.

'And I guess if they find one of the horses, it could lead them to the others?'

'Yes, exactly.' Rosie smiled at the man. He was quite obviously genuinely upset for Gill and although he couldn't have known her very well, Rosie sensed an affection which seemed to go beyond neighbourly concern.

George noticed the colour posters detailing the three horses on the kitchen counter. He offered to take some to put up around the village and in the restaurant, which attracted visitors to the area as well as locals. Rosie gratefully gave him a handful. They continued to talk about the horses for a while and George promised to do all he could, saying he had a cousin with horses in Sussex and he would email the poster to her.

'George, this is Matt.'

Rosie jumped up to help Matt who was about to drop the precarious stack of plates, pizza boxes and empty glasses he was carrying.

'You wouldn't last long working for me!' George laughed.

'You work at the Barton don't you? Was very nice of you to bring those sarnies at the weekend,' Matt smiled at George, but put his arm around Rosie. She raised a questioning eyebrow at her husband's protective gesture. Matt had nothing to worry about, Rosie was completely devoted to him, but he clearly felt threatened in the presence of what Rosie had decided was a truly beautiful man.

George sensed he was intruding and drained his coffee before standing up to leave.

'Well, the rain has eased off a bit. Please tell Gill I stopped by.'

'Oh I certainly will!' Rosie smiled with just a hint of devilment.

'That's great news, Kelly, thanks for letting me know.' Gill hung up her mobile and continued to walk along the rows of horse boxes.

Kelly had called to say she would be back at work on Monday and Gill made a mental note to give Rosie the good news when she called this evening, for the nightly update on the yard. She knew Rosie must have had one hell of a week looking after all the horses and her own, as well as working four out of the six days since Gill had left.

Gill continued to walk between lorries and trailers of various sizes. Ziggy walked beside her, a quiet companion, but a welcome one.

She didn't feel like she would find Amber here, surrounded by giant, muscled horses being prepared for their turn to brave the cross country course. Solid quarters gleamed under attentive brushes and protective boots were securely fastened to precious knees and cannon bones.

Amber and Monty were horses of air and fire, who floated over the surface of the earth, graceful as dancers, their tails pointing towards a sky as free as they were. Here, 17 hand high chargers pounded the ground with enormous hooves and devoured jumps with powerful leaps.

Gill looked down at the poster in her hand. Her eyes locked on the picture of Amber, as they had so many times over the last week. It had been taken in the summer. The mare's bright copper coat gleamed in the sunlight, her dished white face luminous. The picture took Gill back and for a moment she could almost feel the warmth of that clear July day and Amber's silky mane, as she ran her fingers down over the proud arch of the mare's neck. The memory touched each of Gill's senses, giving her just the briefest respite from missing her horse.

All too quickly, Gill was back under a heavy grey November sky and Amber was confined to a photograph.

Gill spotted Jules talking to an event official and made her way towards her. Jules was thanking the official, who was making the promises both women were now used to hearing. Ziggy leaned towards Jules and strained on his lead to reach her.

'Yes of course, I'll get these posters put up at the Stewards Office today and I'll take some back to my yard. I really hope you find them.'

Hope. If only it could be quantified and traded for a reality. All the hope which had been offered by the countless people they had met since their search began didn't seem to get them anywhere.

As the official walked away, Jules smiled awkwardly at Gill, knowing that a cross country event was only likely to be useful for finding Romeo. He was bred and trained for this type of event and, although Amber was in fact quite a good jumper, she did not have the size or aptitude to be competing here. At the sales Gill had been pro-active, energetic and focused on finding the horses, but today she looked lost. Jules spoke briefly to Ziggy but didn't take his lead from Gill. They were starting to form a bond and Jules wanted to encourage his being less dependent on her alone.

Jules awkwardness extended further than guilt, because she had received some news which Gill was unlikely to take very well. She now felt as though the last week had been a complete waste of time and Gill was low enough already. But she had to tell her.

'Lila, the DI called me,' Jules said, looking down at her gloved hands.

'And?'

'And, she said that whoever stole the horses would be unlikely to try and sell them on for at least a few weeks, maybe even months.'

'What?' Gill had been praying for Monday to come quickly, when they could start the next week of visiting horse sales. At the sales she felt hopeful.

'She said that because it's illegal to travel or sell a horse without a passport, they would be unlikely to move them around or take them to sales, until they get new false ones.'

'But how would they get false ones?'

'It's very easy to get a passport for a horse, apparently, as long as you know the right people and you understand how to work the system. I get the impression organised horse thieves can find their way round most things.'

'So they won't be sold until they have them?'

'Lila didn't seem to think it was likely.'

'So we might as well go back to sodding Devon?' Gill threw her hands in the air, making Ziggy step back. Tears of anger and frustration threatened to fall. 'What are we supposed to do now?'

Jules decided, as Gill was already infuriated, she might as well deliver the second blow the DI had inflicted over the phone.

'And there's worse. She also said that, often, thieves will respond to wanted adverts for a certain type of horse and make direct contact with the would-be-buyer, which means the horse never actually goes to a sale and never gets advertised or listed anywhere.'

Jules waited for Gill to react. Instead of rage, when Gill turned to face her, she simply looked defeated.

'And a stallion like Monty might never be sold. The same applies to Amber. If the people who took them know their pedigrees from their racing form, they are just going to breed from them. Even if foals were conceived now, they wouldn't be ready to sell for at least two years. Wouldn't be ready to race or show for four or five. By then, whoever stole them would have covered their tracks and be long gone.' Gill looked at Jules, challenging her to disagree with the logic Gill had been fighting in her head since the horses were taken.

'But we just don't know. Not really. They could be itching to get rid of them and cut all ties with the offences they committed by stealing them? The truth, is we don't know.' It was Jules' turn to get frustrated and she almost shouted the last of her words, looking wildly around her, feeling that if one of the thieves were to walk past her, she would happily have committed an offence herself.

Jules looked back at Gill. She could see her hope had faded. The women had spent twenty-four hours a day together over the last week. Jules realised that the same shroud of desolation which had rendered them both helpless in the first hours after the horses were taken, had returned.

'I just want them back.'

'We will find them.'

Jules hugged her friend and prayed with all her heart that she would be proved right.

They stayed at the event until both of them had seen every horse there at least twice, before returning to the horse box and parking up at a motorway service station. They ate lukewarm tedious food in a depressing and soulless cafeteria, without speaking. Jules tried to shrug off the effect the day had had on her. She was trying to stay strong while Gill was weak, but she had felt an acute longing for Romeo at the cross country event, which would not release its hold.

The smell of hoof churned soil, sweaty horses and the excitement of the competitors and spectators was so familiar to Jules. Without Romeo, she was on the outside, no longer part of the activity. She vowed if she found her horse, she would never again get nervous about competing. Watching riders getting frustrated with their horses, Jules longed to shake them, to tell them they were so lucky, that it didn't matter whether you won or not, that to be there experiencing the thrill of jumping the course with your partner was the most precious gift in the world.

Gill watched the food on her plate slowly congeal. Cauliflower which defied the logic that it had once been a vegetable, and fatty lumps of tasteless cheese swam in transparent oil, which hardened as it cooled. She put her fork down in disgust, she wasn't really hungry anyway.

'I miss your Mum's cooking,' said Gill, and smiled for the first time since the morning.

'I do too.' Jules tried to swallow almost-stale bread which had successfully resisted her attempts to chew it. They had spent two nights at Jules' parents' house. Marianne's lovingly home prepared meals had been a welcome break from tins heated on the stove in the lorry and overpriced convenience food.

Jules finally finished her mouthful and remembered the other thing the DI had said.

'I forgot to tell you what Lila was actually phoning for. She told me about an organisation called Horsewatch.' Jules took a sip of her orange juice and Gill waited for her to continue, 'Apparently there are local branches all over the UK and they work with local police to help people get their horses back. It's a five-pound registration fee to become a member, it's run by volunteers and there's a branch in Okehampton. Lila suggested we meet with the coordinator down there.'

'It's got to be worth a try,' Gill nodded her agreement.

'She also said that it was worth contacting the local Animal Shelter and giving them the details of the horses, as they can circulate them across their other rescue centres and make inspectors aware.'

'In case the horses are so neglected someone reports them?'

Gill was horrified at the thought Amber might actually be mistreated by the people who had taken her. She had assumed, at the very least, they would be well cared for given their value – or what was the point in taking them?

Jules, on the other hand, had pictured Romeo in a state of malnutrition so many times she was surprised she hadn't contacted animal shelters already.

'Mind you, at least if they were a bit ribby and someone reported them, we might get them back,' Gill reasoned.

Jules nodded. She hadn't cried all day but now she had tears gathering in her eyes. She prided herself on the way she looked after Romeo, he had never wanted for anything. The thought of him hungry, or worse, beaten and soured, broke her heart.

'Let's go home.' Gill stood up, the metal legs of the chair scraping on the tiled floor and making people turn to stare.

Jules continued to sit and a tear spilled over to run down her face and land on her coat.

'Come on,' Gill had her urgency back, 'we'll drive home now and we can see this Horsewatch person and visit the Exeter Animal Shelter tomorrow.'

Jules looked unsure, she so desperately hadn't wanted to return to Newmans, but she didn't really have any better ideas for killing the time until Monday.

'And then leave Sunday night for the sales again Monday? I don't care what Lila said, I want to keep going to the sales.' Jules eye's pleaded with Gill. Gill thumbed away Jules' tears and nodded.

'Me too.' Gill had come to the same conclusion, despite the DI's suggestion that the horses would not be sold on again so quickly, they had to keep looking regardless.

By the time the pair pulled up at Newmans, Saturday night had become Sunday morning. They decided to leave the horsebox locked up in the lay-by overnight to save unchaining the gates and driving the noisy vehicle into the yard. They climbed over the gates as quietly as they could with their holdalls and walked softly towards the cottage. Ziggy slid under the metal bars to follow them.

As Gill unlocked the front door, she almost jumped out of

her skin to see Rosie stood in the hallway brandishing a rolling pin. Rosie slumped against the wall in relief to see Gill and mumbled something incomprehensible about having a heart attack.

'What would you have done if we had been thieves? Made us a pie?!' Gill laughed at the rolling pin, which Rosie then pretended to hide behind her back.

'First thing I laid my hand on!'

The friends hugged in turn and headed for the kitchen. Rosie sat at the counter in her dressing gown stroking Ziggy's shiny black head while Jules put the kettle on.

'How did you know we were coming?' asked Gill.

'Ah well, we have some new technology, but I'll tell you about that in good time – what made you come home? We weren't expecting you until next weekend.'

Jules explained about the DI and the organisations they needed to make contact with. Rosie said she wanted to go with them and Gill agreed enthusiastically, Rosie always had good ideas and was a better listener than Gill, who tended to get lost in her thoughts.

Jules didn't mention the DI's comments about it being too early to visit sales and although they hadn't planned not to tell anyone as such, Gill didn't bring it up either.

'It's weird being back,' said Gill, looking around at her kitchen. The week since they had left to search for the horses could easily have been a year and her home felt like some strange, unfamiliar parallel universe. She wondered if it would ever feel like home again, if Amber didn't come back.

'Yes, but we'll be leaving again tomorrow night.' Jules set mugs down in front of her friends and drew up a stool. This was temporary, she decided, nothing more than a necessary pit stop and that would be how she coped with being back.

'So, how did you know we were coming?' Gill asked again, puzzled.

'Well, Mike and Matt were talking this morning. Mike came and helped out all day today, he has been such a star. We were a bit worried about Kelly, when she comes back she will be here alone during the day.'

Rosie paused to sip her coffee.

'Monday,' said Gill, remembering she needed to give Rosie the good news.

'Hallelujah!' Rosie laughed, trying to sound light-hearted to hide her intense relief.

'Well, after much faffing about and Matt in his element with a new gadget to create – there's now a little infra-red sensor thingy either side of the main gates. If the beam is broken by someone coming in, an alarm sounds in the house. They also rigged it up so a light flashes in the barn. That way you know down here, but also, if Kelly is alone in the barn, she'll know when someone is coming up the drive.'

'Oh that's wonderful. I was so worried about Kelly coming back.' Gill stepped off her stool and moved round the counter to hug Rosie, showing her gratitude in a way more fitting than words.

'I guess Kelly can just lock herself in and use the phone if she's worried?' Jules thought over the new security measures, trying not to allow wishing they had been in place a week ago.

'We've kept the main gates locked all the time. We only open them to get our cars in and out. Some of the owners couldn't find their keys, so I had a load cut, they're in the office.' Rosie didn't mention that Mike had paid for the keys and the PIR sensor for the front gate, and that the rest of the new kit had come from Matt's own supply of electronic equipment.

'I gave them all keys but they never needed them so I'm not

surprised they lost them. We never locked the main gates.' Gill stared blankly ahead, as Jules and Rosie eyed each other awkwardly. 'I mean, after that night when someone let the horses out, we started locking the field gates, and the barn was always locked if no-one was here. I just didn't think about it. You just don't think someone is going to walk onto your property in broad daylight and steal from you.' Gill shook her head, guilt tormenting her.

'At the farm, Romeo wasn't even in a locked barn. His stable is in the middle of the yard and if Maurice was at market or out in one of the fields, anyone could have walked right up to him and just led him out.' Jules knew she could apportion no blame onto Gill; Romeo would have been even easier to take before she had moved him to Gill's.

'Look, my tack room doesn't even have a lock on it,' Rosie leaned forward and took Gill's hand. 'At the Cottage we're so far off the beaten track we don't even lock our front door. Neither of you could have foreseen or prevented this. It's Devon! You just don't expect anything to be taken and let's face it, we all know if someone really wanted to take something from you, even padlocks and sensors wouldn't stop them. The DI more or less said so herself.'

'I've been trawling the internet for sales and adverts and I've done some research on horse theft in general. If someone wants your horse badly enough and they are prepared to pay enough to get it, there are people who will get it for you by any means necessary.' Rosie finished her speech and saw from the bereft faces, she was probably making them feel even more depressed.

'Look, remorse is a wasted emotion. Feeling guilty doesn't accomplish anything. We were all lapse about security and we won't be again. That has to be the beginning and the end of it. Finding your horses is the important bit now.'

'You're right, Rosie.'

'Right, on that note,' Jules decided to break the low spell, 'let's work out what we are going to do tomorrow, then, I don't know about you two, but I could do with my bed.'

The next morning, Rosie awoke to find that Gill had already seen to all the horses. She was furious with Matt, who hadn't woken her when the alarm had gone off. He knew she could sleep through a tornado. She had dressed as fast as her sleep weakened limbs would allow and dashed downstairs, knowing it was already an hour past the usual morning feed time, just as Gill was coming back in from cold, crisp morning air.

'Gill, you shouldn't have done it!'

'Don't be silly I was here and you needed a morning off!'

'Yes but … was it awful?' Rosie screwed her face up in disgust at her own laziness, thinking how horrible seeing to the horses without Amber and Monty there must surely have been for Gill.

'Actually no … Well, I had a bit of a cry when I saw Amber's feed bucket, but to be honest it was nice to see the horses and do something familiar. Every morning I wake up in that lorry I have this horrible empty feeling. It's though my body is expecting me to get outside and get cracking with my morning jobs. As much as it hurt, at least I feel right in myself today.'

Rosie started to grind coffee. Gill's words didn't entirely absolve her from oversleeping, but she was pleased about the apparent therapeutic benefit.

'Where is Jules?' Rosie asked, as she switched on Gill's coffee machine, feeling uncomfortable at how comfortable she had become in the kitchen, now that its rightful owner was back.

'She was up early too, taken Zigs for a walk … there she is, look.' Gill pointed through the kitchen window. Jules was speaking to Harry, while Ziggy sat waiting the other side of the fence to the paddock, wanting to be with Jules, but nervously eyeing Red, as the young horse stretched his eager head out towards the dog. Jules had ridden Harry many times before she had bought Romeo and she softly stroked the horse's white forehead, smiling at his familiar course coat.

'They look pretty settled,' Gill said, still looking out towards Red and Harry. 'I wasn't sure what Harry had for breakfast, so I haven't seen to them.'

'No problem, they're used to me oversleeping! I'll get out there now.' Rosie poured herself a cup full from the large jug on the hotplate and donned her boots at the door.

'I had better get ready to go, leave in half an hour?' Gill made for the staircase, to get out of her mud splattered jeans. 'Forgot how quickly it all became a quagmire here!'

Rosie rolled her eyes in agreement and set off to splosh over the rain-filled hoof marks, which had created a sea of tiny puddles across the paddocks.

Chapter ten

'… And contact the associations direct. Two Arabs – let the Arab Horse Society know and they can get the info on their website. Other one is a hunter, contact Horse and County; they might do an article if you're lucky.'

Gill nodded enthusiastically as Janet, the Horsewatch coordinator for Devon, reeled off lists of people to contact to assist with the search for the horses.

Rosie scribbled frantically, trying to keep up with what the woman was saying.

'Let me just check that back. Local press, local Animal Shelters, well Jules is there now, World Horse Welfare, Arab Horse Society, Horse and County. Is that it?'

Janet thought for a moment. They were sat in her dining room at a large oak table. Her house, on the outskirts of Okehampton, was cosy and homely. The sideboard next to the table was crowded with thank-you cards and photographs from grateful owners, who had found their horses with this vibrant woman's help. The cards warmed Gill and she quickly got lost in her mind's image of an emotional reunion with Amber. It was lucky Rosie was there to make notes.

Meanwhile, to the east of the County, Jules was leaving the

Animal Shelter's Devon headquarters. She opened the back door of the car for Ziggy and waved goodbye to the staff who were watching from the reception building.

The Shelter Manager promised to put details of the horses in the national weekly Inspector's bulletin and to send them to other shelters. While she and the other staff and volunteers had been sympathetic and expressed genuine hope that the horses were recovered, there had been a distinct lack of shock in their faces when Jules had told the story. As Jules negotiated the short winding driveway back onto the road into Exeter, she guessed that, if they saw such unbelievable cruelty on a day to day basis, it was natural they would become somewhat hardened by it. She mused that, if you regularly witnessed the extent of the inhumane behaviour people could inflict on those who would not fight back, you would eventually be numbed.

Jules looked at her watch and hoped Gill and Rosie had had better luck with Horsewatch.

After a week on the road, Jules had no clean clothes left and she wished she had put a load of washing on that morning. She also needed more jumpers and her thick winter coat, which were still at the Cottage in Kysford.

As she headed towards her old home, she decided she really didn't care if she saw Tristan. Considering what she had been through over the last week, seeing her ex was hardly going to be a challenge. Yes, she still missed him, but like so many other things in her life, since Romeo had gone, it hardly mattered. Besides, he had been so carefree and polite with her the last time she had seen him, she doubted there would be any overflow of emotion. She made a mental note to leave Ziggy locked in the car when she arrived.

As soon as they got home, Gill announced she was going for a ride on Milly, with an exuberance which had become a rarity of late, she bounced up the drive towards the barn, needing the freedom of being astride a fresh, excitable horse.

With a few moments hesitation, Rosie declined Gill's invitation to accompany her with Red. She hadn't ridden him for over a week now and would need to take it more gently than Milly was capable of.

Matt was out for the afternoon and she was filled with a new hope, so she made herself a pot of coffee and settled in the office to put into practice the suggestions made by Horsewatch.

She began updating the posts she had made on online forums and drafted emails to the Arab Horse Society and local press. She knew, technically, Gill or Jules should be doing these things, but Gill needed a ride and they both needed to get ready to set off again tonight.

Jules arrived in Kysford and parked in her usual spot in front of the house. Seeing Tristan's car further up the lane didn't faze her, she was simply picking up some clothes. If she applied his apparently cold logic to the situation, he was really no more than a lodger who would reside in her home until Christmas.

On that note, she decided to ring the bell instead of using the key and, waiting with it in her hand for him to answer the door, she expected the nerves to set in, but they didn't.

She gave it a full minute then used her key. She stepped into the house and looked around the relatively tidy, but clearly mucky living room. Glancing at the possessions within it, she didn't care if he took the lot. The things they had chosen together had lost their sparkle and the prospect of choosing new furniture alone with no debate, gave her a tinge of excitement.

She decided he must be out, despite the presence of the car, and headed up the stairs to the bedroom, intending to fish out the suitcase from under the bed and pack whatever would fit in it. She winced as she passed the framed photograph of herself and Romeo clearing a large show jump. The memory of the day distant, like the house, and her heart grew colder.

Jules pushed open the bedroom door and began to stoop down to reach for the suitcase when she realised Tristan was in the bed.

'Oh!' she cried. He was alone, it was something to be thankful for at least.

He gazed up at her and smiled, drowsy but to her surprise, happy to see her.

'Hey, you,' his soft sleep-weakened words sounded so familiar.

'Sorry, Tristan, I came to get some things; I'll wait for you to dress,' Jules flushed, and turned to leave the room.

'Don't be silly,' Tristan sat up revealing his well-defined and hairless chest. He patted the bed beside him. 'Come and sit down, how are you?'

Jules contemplated for a moment. She didn't really want to tell him about Romeo, to become closer to him through sharing what she was enduring.

'Jules, you look thin?' He patted the bed again.

She sighed and sat, but at the end of the bed, not up close to his apparently naked body, where he wanted her to sit.

'Romeo was stolen.'

'Jules, baby.' He slid down the bed towards her and took hold of her hand, sincere, questioning, warm for once.

By the time she had finished telling him the story, she had tears in her eyes and she cursed herself for crying, not wanting to be that weak in front of him. The familiarity, being in their bedroom, the smell of him was overpowering. He was sympathetic, strong, the Tristan of the early days again.

He slid his legs around her hips and held her with all four limbs, gently pushing her head into his chest. She knew she should get the hell out of there before anything which would drag her back to him could happen. She had come too far, been through too much hell to move forward from the heartbreak of their split.

But for a moment, just a divine moment, she allowed herself to be held, to feel small in the safety of his arms.

She untangled herself from him gently, kissing him on the forehead before she stood up.

'I had better go, Gill and I are leaving again soon, to look for the horses.' She quickly stuffed clothes into a carrier bag which she found lying in the bottom of the wardrobe, abandoning the suitcase.

'I hope you find him, if there is anything I can do?'

Jules nodded, trying not to make eye contact with him. She called goodbye as she descended the stairs, shutting the front door behind her and breaking into a run to get back to the car.

She dumped the carrier on the passenger seat and stroked Ziggy, who was trying to lick her face from the seat behind. It had taken such immense strength to leave him when he was so loving, so earnest in his thought for her. She allowed herself the comfort of knowing that with only a small bag of clothes collected, she had an excuse to go back.

Rosie insisted on cooking an early dinner for Gill and Jules before they left.

Gill enthused about the meeting with Horsewatch and Jules listened intently, as they relayed the suggestions made. Rosie had already reeled off some emails and seen that the horse's details had appeared on the Horsewatch website already.

'More chips?!' Rosie offered the large bowl to Jules, who

declined. She didn't mention seeing Tristan. She had convinced herself it was fairly insignificant and not worth discussing, but she didn't seem to be able to stomach very much of the steak Rosie had prepared.

Gill's phone vibrated in her pocket and she scrabbled to retrieve it, hoping the text would be from Charlie. She had been having a slow conversation with her daughter via text messages, during the week since the horses were taken and she unlocked the keypad to see what her daughter would say.

'Oh.'

'Oh what?' Rosie smiled, as she shovelled more chips onto Gill's plate. They both looked so gaunt, she wanted to get some carbs into them.

'It's from George. That chef from the village. Something about his cousin.'

'Oh yes, he came over the other night, took some posters for his cousin in Sussex, has her own livery yard apparently. I have got to tell you Gill,' Rosie's eyes twinkled. 'He is so smitten with you.'

Jules smiled, catching Rosie's eye.

'He is not! He has got to be, what, thirty? What would he want with an old bag like me?'

'He's very concerned about you, he wants to help any way he can, he told me.'

Gill caught the devilment in her friend's face and laughed.

'That's fine, you just tease me then. Thanks a bunch.'

'Seriously, Gill, he was so gutted when you weren't here, it was quite sad, really!' Rosie sniggered.

'Shut up.' Gill stuffed a forkful of steak into her mouth, and then she noticed Jules was laughing as well.

'And you shut up too!'

Matt drove into the yard just as Rosie was closing the gates after the horsebox.

'They're off again already then?' He helped her to secure the chains. 'Did you tell her about the feed merchant?'

Rosie bit her lip.

'Rosie, we can't afford to pay Gill's bills.' Matt looked stern and refused the embrace Rosie tried to soften him with. 'That's four hundred pounds out of our account now.'

'I know, I will tell her, she'll phone tomorrow, I'll tell her then.'

'Promise?'

Rosie nodded. As she headed up to the barn to do the evening feeds, she raised her face skywards to look at the blanket of stars. She knew Gill was already in trouble, how on earth was she going to break it to her that the feed merchant had arrived demanding payment?

'Could Gillian Newman and Juliette Walker please report to the Market office immediately?'

Jules left the man she was talking to over a poster, which she almost threw at him, as she dashed through the sale ground towards the office. As she burst from the bidding ring and up the covered corridor, she and Ziggy almost collided with Gill. They ran together, not speaking. Neither allowing themselves to hope they may have been summoned to be given good news.

It was now a month since the horses had been stolen and a week before Christmas. The women knew they were attending one of the last sales before the Christmas and New Year break and as their feet fell in time pounding the paving slabs which lined the pedestrian walkway, each said a silent prayer.

Jules' month long sabbatical was up just as the Christmas break began and if she didn't find Romeo soon, she would have to call the office and attempt to extend her unpaid leave to go on searching in the New Year.

Jules had barely dared to imagine what Christmas was going to be like. No Tristan, no Romeo. She couldn't even go home, as Tristan wasn't due to move out until the 27th of December. His parents would come to stay for a week's holiday, and then he was moving into a flat his father had rented for him in the centre of Exeter.

Some people never suffered for anything. He had everything handed to him on a plate. Jules' own finances were not in dire straits, but the month without pay and the constant fuel contributions and convenience food were starting to make her balance run low.

He had phoned her a few times, since she had seen him at the house and told him about Romeo. She had slipped into the back section of the horsebox and stood with her arms over the partition while she spoke to him, not wanting to endure Gill's disapproval. She appreciated his calls more than she would ever let on to herself.

'Not the dog.'

A market steward tried to prevent Jules walking into the Market office with Ziggy, but a more senior gentleman standing behind the desk decided to make an exception for the breathless and pitifully hopeful-looking women.

'It's all right, just keep him on the lead.'

The steward reluctantly stood aside and the women were invited to sit down. The senior gentleman smiled warmly and quickly put them out of their misery.

'We don't believe your horses are here today.'

Gill's eyes fell to the floor and she mustered what little strength was still within her, not to throttle the apparently perfectly nice man.

'However, my clerk here did find something which might be of interest to you.' The man gestured to a skinny blonde girl with milk bottle thick spectacles, who almost fell over a chair to move towards her boss.

'Here look.' She thrust forward three entry forms. 'I noticed these hadn't been collected and then Mr Harris said about keeping an eye out for your horses and I wondered if these might be them.' The girl spoke with a Yorkshire accent as broad as some of the farmers in the sale ring and it didn't seem to fit with her slight appearance.

Jules' eye flashed like lightening over the entry forms.

Arab, Mare, Chestnut, 14.3hh age 9
Arab, Stallion, Black, 15.1hh age 6
Hunter, Gelding, Chestnut, 15.2hh age 7

'It's them.' Jules was incredulous.

'But the ages are wrong, they are all too young?' Gill's tone was almost demanding.

'It's fairly common practice to reduce the ages of horses to get a better price,' the man said, 'the fact that the forms weren't collected means they haven't actually been brought here today. If you're fairly sure these entries relate to your horses, I'll call the local police.'

'Positive.' Jules looked up at the man, making direct eye contact to show her certainty.

That evening, Jules stirred the rice, which was bubbling on the hob in the horsebox. Gill lay on the sofa bench and wrapped a blanket around her shoulders. It was bloody cold, even with the gas heater they had purchased as a necessity for living in the box.

Ziggy sprang lightly onto the bench and laid around her feet, as though sensing her need for extra warmth. Gill felt her mobile vibrate in the pocket of her jeans. She unlocked the screen and a little butterfly flapped in her tummy when she saw it was a message from George.

They engaged in texted banter, which bordered on flirtation, and had every evening since they'd left. She looked forward to arguing with the young man, whose twenty-word views on the world were refreshing and brought light relief. He usually texted her during quiet periods in the restaurant and she liked to picture him there in his white hat, spatula in one hand, phone in the other. She dreamed about him sometimes. They never actually had sex in the dreams but they were certainly pleasant and brought a welcome respite from nightmares about Amber.

Jules got plates from the small cupboard beside the hob. If the horses had been due to attend the sale, they could be nearby. She couldn't shake the feeling of proximity to Romeo, as foolish as the rational side of her brain told her that was. If the thieves had been frightened into wasting their entries fees for the sale today, they had probably moved the horses well away from the area by now.

The police had taken the entry forms as evidence but hadn't held out much hope. The entries had been made by telephone and paid for in cash. The envelope had been hand delivered and the chance of recovering the thieves' finger prints had been reduced to zero, when the skinny clerk had reluctantly admitted she had thrown the envelope away. She wasn't to know.

'I think we should spend the day visiting all the yards round here tomorrow and Friday. Anywhere we see a horse, we stop and ask. The sales we were going to go to have the horse's details and there's got to be a chance someone saw them. Saw something …' Jules stood still and waited for Gill's reaction.

'Yes,' Gill nodded. She was concerned that the horses would

be quickly entered elsewhere to get them sold and moved on, but she knew their presence at two out of probably hundreds of sales taking place tomorrow, was unlikely to make much difference.

She had called Janet, the Horsewatch coordinator that afternoon, who had suggested that now they finally had a lead, they should follow it. Gill felt detached from reality, they had come so close, but seemed no further forward. It was difficult to deal with.

'I wish I knew what stopped them bringing the horses there today. How did they know we would be there?' Jules paced in the tiny living area.

'They might not have known anything about us, might have been pure coincidence.' Gill mused, trying not to dwell on the idea that their every move could be being watched. Despite the comfort of the sleeping Ziggy at her feet, she suddenly desired the safety of a public place instead of the dark lay-by they had stopped in. 'Let's eat, and then we'll park up at the services for the night.'

Later, as Gill stirred in her sleep, Jules resented the movement of her constant companion; she was restless, her imagination playing out a reunion with Romeo, as it so often did, to bring her comfort in the small hours. Gill broke the spell by moaning softly. Jules rarely slept a night through. She was still waiting to drift off, when some of the lorry drivers nearby started warming their engines and fetching morning coffees.

They hadn't been back to Newmans for three weeks, apart from two stop over's with her mother, they had been in the box almost solidly. Jules longed for some time to herself, longed to take a shower in the morning for granted.

As Gill's finances got inevitably worse and Jules' own concern for her bank balance grew; the nights in budget hotel chain's and B&B's became rare. Jules loved Gill, but their combined misery and the steady loss of hope, which they both fiercely denied, was starting to make the unity of the early days weaken. Detective Inspector Lila had danced around the subject, before suggesting they start moving on and getting on with their lives. She had been surprised and intrigued when Jules phoned to tell her about today's development. But, she had been quite blunt in her opinion – that the lead was not really a lead, since they hadn't actually gained any evidence.

It was as though everyone but Gill, Jules and Rosie were starting to give up. Rosie's agreement to stay at Newmans must surely have come from loyalty now, rather than genuine belief they would find the horses. With Kelly back to work full-time, Rosie seemed to be finding the yard easier. Even Jules' mother had started to twitter about Jules' career recently. The only person who hadn't even hinted at a reality check was Tristan. He never questioned her continued conviction.

'What time is it?' Gill was groggy.

'Six-ish.'

'Might as well get up, be light in an hour.'

Jules nodded and eased herself from the bunk. She hadn't slept at all, but it was a feeling she was becoming accustomed to.

Rosie linked arms with Val as they walked along the high street. They were heading back to the office after the department's Christmas lunch and they lagged behind the others, so they could talk. With only a week to go until the council shut for Christmas, they both should have been in high spirits. As it was though, only Val was relishing the prospect of time off with her family.

'It's not that I don't want to see them. Having them back means, at least, I'll get a rest from seeing to all the horses. It's just they are such hard company, V. They are, understandably, so down all the time. It's exhausting to make the effort to be bright. Oh dear, I sound like a bitch don't I?'

Val laughed and rubbed Rosie's arm affectionately. They had worked together for nearly ten years and although they rarely saw each other outside of the office, they had become incredibly close, daytime family.

'Rosie, you're not the patron saint of caring for everyone. It's perfectly understandable that you were looking forward to a nice first Christmas with Matt at the cottage and not running around after other people. And all those horses – I hate to say it but you look terrible woman, it's too much work!'

'Matt is right pissed off. Wants to go home. I feel the same, but I can't drop them in it now. As soon as the sales start up again they'll want to carry on looking and I'm not going to stop them going by leaving, am I?'

'It's a tough one. I can't tell you to sit them down and explain you need to go home. I know you would feel too guilty.' Val sighed and gazed at the festive shop windows with their twinkling lights. Panicky looking shoppers queued to buy gifts, completely oblivious to the ridiculousness of it all. 'Couldn't you go home for Christmas? Leave when they come back and then agree a date to move back in again afterwards? At least then you could still have Matt's family over.'

'We've already arranged to go to them. We are going up to Somerset on Boxing Day, seeing them, then spending the night in London with Dad and Crystal, and coming back. At least with Red and Harry at Gill's already, we can have a night away.'

'Sounds like a big rush. Make it two nights, at least – you need it Rosie.'

'Yeah, you're right. I'll speak to Matt later and maybe ask Gill.'

'Phone him now.' Val unlinked her arm from Rosie's, to

allow her to fish in her handbag for her phone.

Rosie did as she was told. Of all the people Rosie knew and loved, Val was the most maternal and Rosie never grew complacent about how much she needed someone else to be that kind of friend to her.

'Well, thanks for your help,' Jules shook hands with the rugged-faced woman, who nodded and strode back towards her small yard to go about her duties. Gill unlocked the horsebox and they climbed into the cab. It was the fifth yard they had been to and it was the same story every time. Each yard owner or groom had been incredibly sympathetic, taken a poster and volunteered to keep an eye out.

'Nothing suspicious about that place either,' said Jules, and she blew air noisily from puffed cheeks in an expressive sigh.

'Nope. Reckon she was genuine too. If only someone had seen something.'

'We've got the rest of today and all day tomorrow. We're bound to come across something or someone?'

Gill nodded and started the engine, trying not to focus on the fact that after tomorrow, they had no more sales to attend and would head home for Newmans to sit in agonising static, until the New Year.

'Right, next place is in Bury.'

Jules punched the postcode into the GPS system and ticked off the yard they had just visited. They had collected a free local equine publication from a tack shop that morning and were working through the listed yards. Jules used a map to organise a logical progression from yard to yard, but they relied on the sat nav to direct them.

'Reckon we can do another five before it gets too late to go knocking on doors. Then the rest tomorrow and then …' Jules trailed off not saying the last bit of her sentence – and then home.

'At least I'll get to see Charlie,' Gill picked up on Jules' train of thought, 'and you'll get to see your Mum.'

'Yes. Are you sure it's okay for my parents to come down?'

'Of course it is, Newmans is your home,' said Gill, inside, she felt that she would rather have spent Christmas day under a duvet, blotting out the rest of the world and its festive cheer. But, she knew Charlie's visit would mean she had to 'do Christmas'. Maybe that wasn't such a bad thing.

'I still feel awful about not buying anyone presents,' Jules said, twisting her hands together, embarrassed at the prospect of having nothing to give to her family and friends.

'Oh, nobody cares; it's not as if we have been doing nothing!'

Gill changed gear forcefully, slightly irritated. She knew she would have to get Charlie something, but not only had she not had time, she knew, without even looking at her bank balance, any present she did manage to find would have to go on credit card, with a bill coming back to haunt her later.

'Could we pull over here so I can let Ziggy have a run?' Jules pointed to a green Public Footpath sign beside a lay-by. She was conscious he had been cooped up in the box most of the morning.

'Good idea, I could do with a wee myself.'

'Oh brilliant!' Rosie dropped carrier bags of shopping on the floor in her haste to retrieve the magazine. Amongst the large collection of post for Gill, the Horse and County Magazine she had been waiting for had arrived. Rosie stood leafing through it, searching for the right page, until Matt shouted at her to close the front door.

'Rosie, I've only just got this fire going, you're letting cold air in!' Matt had organised for their winter log delivery to be brought to Newmans, so they could light the woodburner, instead of running down Gill's domestic oil supply.

'Sorry, love.' Rosie nudged her bags out of the way to shut the door and walked slowly into the living room, without taking her eyes off the Horse and County.

'Here it is!' she exclaimed. Amber, Monty and Romeo's faces stared back at her from the 'missing horses' section of the classifieds.

Matt stood up and had a look at the half-page advert.

'Must have cost a fair bit.'

'Yes,' Rosie bit her lip, 'but it was the best present I could think of for Jules and Gill.'

Matt put his arm around his wife.

'It is very eye-catching.'

'And, I did get a discount!'

Later that evening, Rosie wearily donned her headlamp and braced herself to head into the cold, dark field.

Since Kelly had returned to work, she did all of the morning feeds and as many of the jobs as she could, including schooling Milly in the field (Gill wouldn't allow her to hack the mare out alone any more). Unfortunately, she left too early in the evening to do the night feeds. Her mother collected her as soon as the sun started to go down, which left Rosie to battle through the darkness and see to the outside horses herself.

The ones in the barn were easy. Kelly left the feeds ready and the haynets outside each door. Rosie could feed them, top up their waters and removed any fresh dumps within ten minutes. But the outdoor horses, they were a bind.

Each field containing horses, including the one next to the house where Red and Harry resided, had to have a large wheelbarrow full of haylage dumped into a feeder. Then she went round with the wheelbarrow again, loaded up with feeds, to doll out to each horse. By the time she had got to the last horse, it was time to start collecting in the empty buckets again, ready for the morning feeds.

'Marcy, give OVER,' Rosie yelled at the greedy mare and threw her hands in the air to chase her back to her own bucket. She was heavily pregnant with a foal due in the spring, but that didn't stop the little bay horse from weaving her way around the buckets, snatching mouthfuls from each, before the horse trying to eat from it chased her away.

Rosie waded back through the mud to push the wheelbarrow along to the next field. As she climbed through the post and rail fencing, she left a welly behind and had to hop on one foot, whilst reaching back into the field to retrieve it. As she made a grab for it, she noticed one of the youngsters trotting up and down the row of buckets and realised she had forgotten his feed.

Rosie grabbed at the bucket, spilling the contents over the gravel track alongside the fence, as she tried to climb back in the field.

'FUCK!'

As though on cue, the heavens opened. Huge droplets splashed onto Rosie's head, sliding through her hair before running down her forehead.

After what felt like an eternity, Rosie finished her rounds. Cold wet jeans stuck to puckered white flesh and she began to itch as she pushed the wheelbarrow of emptied buckets back into the barn. Dumping the handles down in disgust, she had an overwhelming urge to peel her jeans off there and then. Her mobile rang and stopped her.

Frantically drying her hands on a rug Rosie, picked up the phone from the table in the barn and held it an inch away from her dripping ear. It was Nic.

'This is Rosie Hall, soaked to the skin, covered in mud, exhausted and in need of a bloody DRINK!'

'Ha ha ha ha ha! Come on cowgirl, can't be that bad!' Nic giggled at Rosie's outburst of an opening line.

'It is, and worse. I just don't know how Gill coped with this!'

'Probably, because she didn't do a full day's work first?'

'Err, you're right maid, I do deserve to be this pissed off.'

'Speaking of work, are you tomorrow?'

'Nope, Friday, so I'll be helping Kelly and dealing with the vet – why?'

'Well, I've finished all my Christmas present commissions, so I thought I would come and give you a hand!'

'Oh you star!' Rosie knew how hard Nic had been working to get all her gift commissions ready for their Christmas destiny and was truly touched that Nic was now turning her attention to helping out at Newmans. 'Are you sure you don't want to just relax now, you must have been going round the clock.'

'Hell no! Been cooped up in the studio for weeks. I need to get outside and do something physical. Pharoh lost a bloomin' shoe yesterday and the farrier can't come until the New Year. If I can't ride him, I might as well come and see you!'

'Just love you, utterly fabulous woman!'

'See you at ten-ish?'

'Can't wait, bring cake!'

'Will do!'

Rosie spirits lifted, not just at the prospect of an extra pair of hands, but by the thought of a day with Nic. Her bubbly personality and wicked sense of humour were just what she and Kelly needed, especially with Gill and Jules due home in the evening.

She walked back down the house, undoing her jeans as she reached the door and kicking her wellies off, she was almost naked by the time she reached the shower room and she got straight in to warm up.

Later, as Rosie sat nestled in her dressing gown waiting for Matt to bring her some soup from the Rayburn, she picked up the Horse and County to look at the advert again. As she read through the wording, making sure the horse's descriptions and telephone numbers were right, an advert on the opposite page caught her eye.

> Schooling and Training Services, all types
> and temperaments considered I travel to you
> so no need to move your horse.

Rosie's eyes widened and her body become light and alien, as she read the name next to telephone number. How many horse trainers called Eddy Gillant could there be?

Christmas Eve, Jules decided, was not turning out to be altogether unpleasant. On the way home in the horsebox the night before, she and Gill had barely spoken. The gloom of spending almost a week not looking for the horses had filled the cab.

But after a good night's sleep in a proper bed and now, as she watched Ziggy stretching out beside the glowing fire, relaxing properly at last, she started to feel a break was needed. It was good to have an enforced rest. She and Gill could have gone on living in the box and searching indefinitely, but as there were no sales until the New Year and they could hardly go knocking on doors and visiting yards at Christmas, she didn't have to feel so guilty about stopping. Just for a week.

Her phone bleeped. She was expecting it to be her mother, texting to say what time they would be arriving that afternoon, but it was from Tristan.

It was a strange arrangement, they didn't discuss their relationship and there were no recriminations. It was a comfortable friendship, companionship with no expectations. Although it was nice and quite a feat to have become better friends after their relationship than they probably had been during it, she still had just a touch of unease. She played it down to Gill and Rosie and she certainly wouldn't be telling her mother.

Tristan's message asked if she could meet him for a drink that evening, since she was back in Exeter. She felt an unwanted thrill at the prospect of seeing him, but quickly tapped out a response declining the invitation, explaining her parents were coming and loosely suggesting they do it another time.

'Fancy a ride?' Gill popped her head around the living room door. 'I need to get Milly out and Kelly has gone home so Badger needs a rider.'

Jules looked at Ziggy, sleeping contentedly by the fire. She got up quietly to follow Gill. She hadn't ridden since Romeo had been taken and she was tired enough to have got down on the floor with Ziggy and slept, but an hour in the saddle was a treat she was decided she shouldn't pass up, even if she would miss Romeo like hell.

She walked with Gill towards the barn.

'Doesn't Rosie want to ride him?' Jules asked, wondering where Rosie was.

'She and Matt have gone last minute shopping. Poor girl is worn out. She did ride Red this morning, first time in a long time and he was a bit full of himself – not sure she would fancy another ride today.'

'Badger is such a horrible name for a horse, poor boy.' Jules slapped the neck of her mount. The short stocky Arab had choppy pony strides and a barrel shaped middle, but was quite safe beneath her and thankfully, felt nothing like Romeo.

'I know it's a bit of a shame isn't it!' Gill laughed, watching Badger from Milly's back, impressed at how calm and collected the mare was. Kelly's schooling in the paddock seemed to be paying off.

'His owner is going away to university. She didn't want to sell him and money doesn't seem to be an object so she decided to put him in training for a few years. See if he had a racer in him somewhere under all that flab. I don't know how I'm going to get him up to scratch for the new season, especially seeing as we won't be here again after the New Year, but Kelly will start schooling him in the paddock and hopefully she can get him to stride out and shed a few pounds.

His owner knows what has happened and she is quite happy to pay a reduced fee, if I can't get him ready in time. She is so funny with him. He's had too many titbits and been allowed to get away with murder, from what I can gather, but it doesn't seem to have harmed his manners too much, he's good in the stable and gets on with the mares. She calls him, 'Bag' and she is always telling him to, 'get a wriggle on!''

'Get a wriggle on, Bag!' Jules laughed, her legs aching from the amount of encouragement the overweight horse needed just to keep up with Milly. Badger was predominantly black, but he had a messy spattering of white hairs across his forehead and over his knees, which made him appear an almost dirty-grey in places.

'The worst of it is, his registered name is, Badger's Hole. Can you imagine it over the Tannoy at Taunton, *'and its Badger's Hole bringing up the rear!'* "

'Oh how embarrassing!' Jules laughed.

'It's all right being back isn't it? Just for a bit,' Gill confirmed she was feeling the same way as Jules.

'Yes – just for a bit.'

Chapter eleven

Rosie clattered pots and crashed baking trays as she dashed around the Newmans' kitchen. Jules' parents had arrived and they were busy catching up on her news in the living room. Gill had gone up to do the evening feeds and Mike would be arriving any minute. Nic and Rob were coming over later on too. Rosie was worried she wouldn't have enough food. It was 7pm already, and as soon as Nic arrived, she was going to need to feed everyone. She just hadn't had time to prepare anything and was wondering how to stretch the party-food she had picked up earlier from a supermarket, to accommodate nine people.

Gill walked back into the kitchen, flushed from the cold.

'It's starting to snow!'

'Oh, a white Christmas,' Rosie said, as she frantically searched the freezer for more bread.

'What's the matter, Rosie?'

'I got everything for Christmas day ages ago, but I'm running out of things for tonight!'

'Don't worry, George will be over soon, the Barton only opened for lunch and he said he'd bring some cold meats and things with him, I should have told you sooner.'

'George is coming over!' Rosie stopped what she was doing, her food problem solved. And Gill had her full attention.

'Don't look so shocked.' She didn't really want any attention.

'Gorgeous George, who fancies the arse off you?'

'It's nothing like that, we've been texting a bit and he offered to come up with some left over's, that's all. It's not a date.' Gill laughed a high pitched laugh, which was intended to sound like scorn, but came out as pure nerves.

'What are you going to wear?' Rosie's eyes sparkled, full of mischief.

'I thought my cream slacks and a black T-shirt?'

'Nooooo!'

'What?'

'Too neat! What about your green tunic – the one you wear in summer as a dress – and some leggings underneath?'

'I don't have any—'

'Come on.' Rosie checked the timer on the oven and ushered her friend upstairs.

Later Gill stood in the kitchen feeling uncomfortable in a pair of Rosie's calf length, black leggings and a shimmering green tunic which hugged her slender frame and neat chest. Rosie insisted that Gill didn't look like she had made an effort, she simply looked festive. Gill tried to convince herself that, just because she wasn't in muddy jeans and a man-sized sweater, it didn't mean she was 'dressed up'.

Gill had, point blank, refused when Rosie had suggested she finish the outfit off with a pair of black high heels. Now her bare feet were cold on the tiles and she wished she could put her tatty old brown slippers on.

'You look nice!' Jules breezed into the kitchen, still laughing from the conversation she had left in the lounge.

'Thanks.'

'So, what time is he getting here?' Jules asked, teasing Gill.

Gill shook her head.

'I'm going to kill Rosie.'

'Come and join us, Mike is just telling us how, when you were ten, you used to have tantrums if you weren't allowed to sleep in Prince's stable!' Jules picked up the bottle of wine she had come in for and headed back into the lounge.

Gill had fond memories of Prince. He had been a part-bred Arab, only 14.1hh but he was more like a Roman War Horse than a crossbred pony. He had long reaching strides and carried himself with an air of elegance she hadn't seen again until the day Monty had arrived at Newmans.

He had been such a gentleman and as a seven-year-old she had begged her parents to buy him for her until they had given in. Theirs was a special partnership, much like she had now with Amber … or did have.

She thought, gloomily, that she would have to visit her mother tomorrow. Gill and Mike had lost their father when Gill was just twenty and Mike twenty-five. Her mother seemed to cope for a while and even had other relationships, but years of high blood pressure got the better of the capillaries in her brain when she turned sixty. It started off as a little short-term memory loss. They had both teased their mother in the early days when she just seemed a bit ditsy.

But before long it became apparent there was a serious problem. The worse her memory became, the more she missed Gill's father. It was as though she was re-living the pain and grief all over again. Last week faded to total amnesia, but thirty years ago crystallised and she truly lived in the past.

She had moved in with Mike and his long term partner, Ginny for awhile. Gill could still remember the helplessness as Mike told her how their mother would wake in the night screaming their father's name.

It was a strange relief when the dementia took over

completely. Now she lived in a constant dream, oblivious to the world. It was not ideal, but she seemed at peace.

She and Mike had taken the decision to sell their childhood home to pay for residential care in Exeter, when Mike had no longer been able to care for their mother. Mike visited all the time, but Gill tended only to go on special occasions. Her mother didn't know who she was and she didn't see the point in going more frequently. She certainly didn't believe in dragging Charlie along.

Just as Gill was wondering whether to pay the obligatory visit before or after the Christmas lunch Rosie would be preparing, the doorbell went. Her heart leapt into her mouth and she wished she hadn't built seeing George up so much in her head. She walked along the hallway, towards the front door feeling like a teenager on a first date.

Texting George had been easy, fun. She had even flirted a little. Walking towards the door to actually see him in person, any confidence she had found electronically, faded. She took a deep breath and tried to adopt a more natural facial expression, as she opened the door.

George stood in the doorway, snow falling gently around him. Laden with bags of food he struggled to hand her a bunch of flowers.

'Hey', Gill said, relaxing at the sight of his warm smile.

'Hey, you.'

Jules gazed around the room from behind a large glass of white wine. Ziggy was nestled adoringly into her father, who was sat on the floor by the fire. The dog wanted to be as close as he possibly could to Martin and the pair sat quietly, as though their own special silence surrounded them.

Jules looked at her mother and couldn't help grinning.

Marianne was being loud and jovial and holding everyone's attention, as she quizzed poor George.

'So, do you get anyone famous in this restaurant of yours?!'

'Well, once we had Dawn French in … The booking was under someone else's name, so when she walked in, the maître d' nearly wet himself.'

George was holding up well under Marianne's scrutiny. She had quizzed and questioned him for a full ten minutes, encouraging him to talk about himself and in her own special, but slightly intimidating, way, was integrating the newcomer.

Nic and Rob were joining in the conversation from their vantage point, snuggled together on the window seat. Rosie sat on Matt's lap, almost asleep.

Jules noticed that Mike looked quietly amused. He was watching Gill and Jules quickly saw why. Gill was transfixed by George, drinking in his every word, but sat a little way back from the circle on a hard chair, thinking no one would notice her.

'I would like to propose a toast!' Marianne stood up, gesturing around the room, her long dress and ankle length cardigan swinging about her. 'To health happiness and finding those horses in 2013.'

George stood up too and raised his glass high.

'To finding the Horses.' He looked at Gill and blushed gently. She in turn was too embarrassed to make eye contact.

They all joined in the toast, but as Jules raised her glass a prick of guilt stabbed at her. Here she was enjoying herself, laughing and drinking, while somewhere out there Romeo could be suffering.

Gill awoke, surprised she didn't have a hangover. She gave a long luxurious stretch, appreciating the warm bed, soft duvet and absence of the sore back the lorry bunk usually bestowed upon her.

She bit her lip as she thought about her dream. It was lucid in places and soft and hazy in others. She was with George. She couldn't remember where they had been or what they had been doing, but she had a strong yearning for him. The feeling of his strong, warm and masculine hand around her own stayed with her. As she recalled the dream, a desire to see him again was overwhelming.

When he had left the previous night, Mike and Ginny, Nic and Rob had decided to go at the same time, so the mass goodbye had been very public.

As they milled in the hallway donning coats, Rosie started talking to Nic about going away on Boxing Day. George saw his opportunity and promptly invited Jules and Gill to the Barton to sample the Christmas taster menu in the evening when the restaurant re-opened. Gill had politely said she would see and let him know, but this morning she felt a strong compulsion to go.

She dressed and prepared to go outside and see to the horses, who didn't know it was Christmas Day and still needed to be fed, she realised for the first time since Amber had been taken, she hadn't woken with a cold dread. Thinking about George provided a welcome respite from nightmares about her horse.

Rosie waved to Gill, when she saw her walking up the track. She was in the field with Red and Harry, giving them the traditional Christmas breakfast Harry had enjoyed for the last 15 years. In addition to his usual morning feed, he enjoyed an extra bucket filled with chopped carrots apples and parsnips, decorated with polo mints and triangles of cold toast.

She had so looked forward to her first Christmas at the cottage and with Red. She smiled at the youngster, who greedily crunched the vegetables and apples, white foam covered his dark grey muzzle from his enthusiastic and squelchy chomping.

Rosie had been up at 5am to wrestle the large turkey into the biggest oven of the Rayburn. It had just about fit. She didn't need to do anything now until noon, when the potatoes and stuffing would need to go in. She had plenty of time to take Red for a ride.

She stood with him and scowled. Things had been going so well, until yesterday. She had taken him out along the lane and he had been walking along nicely, but when they reached the crossroads he backed sharply, without being asked, onto the verge. He had then refused to walk forward. His ears went back when she put more pressure on, asking him to walk on again and he threatened to buck. She eased off quickly, not knowing what to do. In the end she had dismounted and led him home.

She was embarrassed and annoyed with herself. She had dismounted for all the right reasons, she hadn't wanted to have an argument with Red and he was clearly not behaving like his usual self, but she was disappointed and now slightly apprehensive about getting on him again. She knew he was questioning her leadership, but she hadn't been a strong enough leader to overcome it from his back, due to her own underlying fear at the thought of him bucking.

She decided to give them both a day or so off and come back fresh when the fear had subsided.

She collected up the buckets. Looking after Newmans, work and the dark evenings, meant the opportunity to ride was so rare. She knew she should have taken him out, but her gut instinct told her not to, that it wouldn't go well. She recognised the warning and she listened. She was so terrified of ruining Red with her own fears and lack of ability. If she felt like she wouldn't be able to ride him, she probably shouldn't.

She hoped the desire would come back after she and Matt had had their two night break to see Matt's parents and Jimmy.

She decided to use the time to pack instead.

Rosie finished basting the turkey; she heard Alex and Charlotte coming in through the front door.

'Hello, Rosie Posy! And a Merry Christmas to you!' Alex bustled forward to kiss Rosie's cheek as she stood up from closing the oven door. She recoiled but refrained from telling him to bugger off, for Charlie's sake.

'Hi, Char, Happy Christmas!' Rosie hugged her friend's daughter warmly, she knew how pleased Gill would be to see her and was glad the girl had come, albeit with her father.

Gill hurried back from the barn, having seen Alex's car pull up by the cottage. Any recriminations or awkwardness temporarily dissolved, she was simply genuinely pleased to be seeing her daughter.

Alex was unusually gracious and, after he had lavished some unwanted attention on Gill, he left saying he was going for a walk.

Gill sat with Charlie in the living room, they were alone as Jules and her parents had gone to the village pub and Rosie and Matt were upstairs organising the heaps of washing they had fallen behind on whilst looking after Newmans. It was the first time she had seen her daughter since the day the horses were stolen. Apart from the odd text, Charlie had not volunteered a lot of support to her mother in this time of crisis, but her attitude to Gill had clearly changed and Gill decided that was probably worth more in the long run.

Charlie talked about college and how well things were going. She had made some new friends who lived in the West Hill area and also went to Exeter College. From what Gill could gather from the way Charlie spoke about study dates and visits to the

Exeter Crown Court public gallery to watch cases, they were a much better influence on Charlie than the pot-smoking hippies she had previously been hanging around with.

Charlie was genuinely grateful for the gifts Mike and Ginny had thankfully purchased for Gill to give to her. They were only clothes vouchers and funky pair of earrings, but Charlie accepted them with heartfelt thanks and talked about the dress she was hoping to buy.

Gill's heart sank when Charlie mentioned the car Alex had given her as a Christmas present.

'I didn't even know you were having lessons?' Gill tried not to spoil the nice time they were having together with the desolate feeling that she didn't know her child very well anymore.

'Oh I'm not, yet, but I have got this intensive course booked for the New Year. I start on the fourth of January!' Charlie looked excited and Gill was happy for her, regardless of the terms attached to it. 'Dad is paying and I already passed my theory test.'

'Well done, darling! So, tell me all about your car!' Gill encouraged Charlie to describe her car, a four-year-old Peugeot.

Charlie started off playing the car down, conscious of the comparison between her father's enormous gift and the vouchers in her hand from her mother, but soon she was enthusing about the cool purple colour and built in sat nav.

'And once I've passed my test I can come to visit more, if you want me to?'

'Of course I do. This is still your home and it always will be.' Gill reached out and enveloped her daughter in a long cuddle.

They were still cuddling when Alex burst into the living room. Charlie sat up from where she had been resting her head on Gill's shoulder.

They talked briefly about the search for the horses and Gill's plans for continuing the search in the New Year. Alex refused the offer of a coffee and announced they must leave to arrive at Megan's house in time for a 'glorious' pheasant'. It dawned on Gill that if Charlie had to spend some time living with her father, now was probably the best time. She had been living almost entirely on the road and could continue to do so indefinitely. At least with Alex she knew Charlie was safe.

When they left and Gill had one last hug with her daughter, she thought about her promise. If she had to sell Newmans to continue to search for Amber, there would no longer be a home for Charlie to come back to.

Later that afternoon, Jules sat on her bed. Ziggy sat expectantly on the floor beside her, amber eyes searching for any hint of movement from his master that might suggest a walk, or even just a run outside.

Jules sighed and looked down at her dog. The fun and festivity of last night, the large and extravagant Christmas lunch, the wonderful present from Rosie in the Horse and County. It had been just enough to keep her from sinking again.

But now, her parents were heading home before the snow got any worse, Rosie had fallen into a deep sleep and was snoring loudly on the sofa with Matt. Jules didn't want to walk Ziggy or do anything else either.

Gill had the right idea, when lunch was over and Marianne and Martin were safely on the road, she had taken herself off to the horse barn. Jules saw her ride past the window, astride Milly with Badger on a lead rope walking beside her. The concentration required and the adrenaline resultant from controlling a high spirited horse like Milly, whilst keeping a plod like Badger going at an equal pace, would allow Gill no time to think about anything else.

Jules took her mobile from her pocket to read a text from Tristan. It simply said, 'Happy Christmas'.

She replied and asked him what he was up to and sent her love to Ella. His reply came so quickly, Jules had expected it to be from someone else.

> They didn't come, long story. Not much, just watching the Christmas shi te on telly

Jules read the text over and over, her heart swooned in compassion. If his parents hadn't come over for Christmas, he was probably alone and probably had been all day.

Ziggy sensed a change in her emotion and put a paw on the bed, cocking his head and pleading with her.

'Oh come on then dog,' she said affectionately and stood up, Ziggy nearly unbalanced himself with furious tail wagging and excited pirouettes. 'Walkies now, then later we might go and see Daddy.'

'That's it Bag, get a wriggle on!' Gill laughed at the mottled black and grey Arab, as he jigged eagerly, ears pricked, looking forward to being back in his stable. The snow fluttered about them and the lane which led to Newmans was noticeably whiter. Badger had mostly made Gill's arm ache trying to keep him alongside Milly, until he had recognised they were nearly home. He picked up the pace and brightened, as he thought about the feed that would await him. Once his excited spurt drew him level with Milly, he didn't fall behind again. Gill made a mental note for Badger's future.

He had probably been used to being tucked in behind his companions, or allowed to plod at his own pace, but a combination of going towards the yard and being allowed to go level with Milly seemed to have awakened something in him.

Gill figured, if she kept him in short races, a mile or less, he would be going down to the start line then turning around to race back towards the finish post – but more importantly, he would race towards his temporary loose box and companions. If the jockey also kept him up with the pack at all costs, rather than allowing him to tail off and lose heart, he just might not be the hopeless racer she had anticipated. Even if he only came in middle of the field each time, it would be more exciting for his owner, and less embarrassing for Newmans than a last place finish.

'That is if I keep training,' Gill said, and looked down at Milly's withers.

Being back at Newmans for the last few days had made her think about the future. Certainly more than she or Jules had during the days and long nights in the box, when they focused on survival and searching and hadn't had the energy for much else.

If she didn't find Amber soon would she have to send the Arabs in training back to their owners? Tom back to France? Sell the house and give up on her dream? It just didn't seem right to carry on without Amber by her side and she certainly couldn't afford to go on searching if she didn't have the training fees. But where would the liveries go? And Kelly? Where would she keep Amber if she had sold up and then found her? Would Gill have to put her at livery, rent some grotty flat somewhere and get a job?

Gill knew in her heart she couldn't go back to an office job. How could she sit behind a desk and work for someone else, when she'd had all this?

She had to focus on the horses again as they rounded the corner into Newmans and Badger broke into a gleeful trot, making Milly skirt sideways and pin her ears back at the gelding.

'The snow is settling, Jules, where are you going?' Gill rode up the drive just in time to see Jules getting into her car.

'Yes, I was a bit worried, but I wanted to drop Maurice his Christmas card and say hello.' Jules' face was already red from the cold and it hid a flush of embarrassment from the lie. She had already phoned Maurice to wish him a Happy Christmas yesterday and he had said then he was going to his son's for the day.

'Take the Discovery,' said Gill, 'it's behind the barn, the keys are in the kitchen.'

'Thanks, Gill, that would be great!'

'No worries, the gear stick sticks, but at least its four-wheel drive!'

Jules was guilt-ridden as she drove down the drive. The snow was starting to stick, falling in soft white clouds as it became heavier. If Gill had known where she was really going, she probably wouldn't have offered the old vehicle so readily, if at all.

She knew going to see him was silly. But the thought of him there alone on Christmas day? Jules ignored the voice inside her. The one trying to remind her that of all the people she knew, he was the least likely to mind. The one telling her it was her own need for a distraction that saw her making her way to Kysford.

'Hi, sweetie.' Rosie looked up from the computer screen in Newmans office as Gill came in. Gill had a strange smile on her face and Rosie recognised her friend had something to share.

'I saw George.'

'Out on your ride?'

'Mm, I rode past his house in the village. I did know he lived there.'

'And?'

'He was outside in the snow with a little girl, nearly hit Badger with a snowball!'

'His?'

'No. No! He introduced her as his niece. He mentioned Jules and I going to the Barton for dinner tomorrow night again. Insisted it was his treat.'

'Are you going to go?'

Gill nodded shyly.

'Think so.'

'Oh, how exciting! I wonder what his cooking is like? Way to a woman's heart and all that!'

'I don't know. I've never actually eaten there – too expensive for me!'

Rosie recognised the need to be sensible, as she looked at Gill's anxious face. She knew without asking that Gill was wondering whether getting involved with someone when so much was going on, was a good idea.

'Well it will be nice. Have a bit of fun, you don't have to commit yourself and you don't have to do anything you don't want to. With everything you have been through lately you deserve some light relief.'

'Will you help me pick an outfit?'

'Of course, Matt and I don't leave until lunchtime tomorrow, we can have a look later.'

Gill nodded. She was embarrassed and wanted to change the subject.

'So, what you up to?'

Rosie looked at her friend. She had only discussed it with Matt so far and she hesitated, before deciding to tell Gill.

'I think I've found my Dad.'

'Really?' Gill dumped a pile of horse passport forms onto the floor so that she could pull the spare chair over and sit beside Rosie at the desk.

'Look,' Rosie pointed out the advert on the opposite page to the horses, in the Horse and County.

'Oh my … What are the chances?' Gill's mouth dropped open. 'And that's definitely his name?'

'As far as I know.' Rosie wiggled the mouse to dissolve the screen saver on the pc in front of them. 'And look.'

Gill looked up from the magazine; she couldn't believe what she was seeing on the screen.

The website was amateurish, in gaudy turquoise colours with a crude animation of a horse's head alongside the title, 'Eddie Gillant Horse Training and Re-schooling'. There was a short blurb about the training services offered, no mention of a yard, but an offer to travel to any horse within 50 miles of the city of Reading. In the bottom left hand corner of the screen, next to a mobile number, was the reason for Gill's disbelief – a portrait photograph of a man stood next to a tall grey hunter.

Gill looked at Rosie's face, a mixture of excitement and fear, and back at the screen.

'He is your Dad. Absolutely one hundred percent,' Gill said and continued to look at the photograph. The man had such a familiar face; Rosie's eyes stared back at them, his tousled brown hair was an identical shade to Rosie's long wavy locks and it appeared to be almost as unruly.

'It's him isn't it? I have found my Dad.'

Later, sat in the living room with Gill and Matt, Rosie made a decision.

'I'm not going to do anything until we get back,' she said loudly.

‘That’s a good idea, honey,’ Matt smiled warmly, trying to be as supportive as he could. With parents who were still in a secure relationship and a happy wholesome childhood, he struggled to comprehend how this must feel for Rosie.

‘Give yourself time to think, don’t rush into anything,’ Gill added.

‘I might think about going to bed now.’ Rosie stretched and yawned, it had been a long day and the enormous amount of food consumed still sat heavy on her stomach. ‘Do you think Jules is all right?’

‘Oh, you know what Maurice is like with the cider at the best of times, let alone Christmas day, I’m sure she’s fine,’ Gill assured her, and decided to turn in herself.

Jules watched Tristan sleep. His breathing quiet and even, he looked completely serene. From where she sat on the bed, she could see the snow outside getting heavier. Through the open curtains, a light wind blew tiny flakes into a wintery dance. She glanced at the bedside table. It was 2am.

She should go, an uneasiness prevented sleep, but she knew the journey would be dangerous, the roads slippery.

She didn’t want to wake up next to him in the morning, didn’t have the energy or desire for a last goodbye. They had said their goodbyes already.

When she had arrived at the cottage earlier on in the evening, he had been pleased to see her, but there was no acknowledgement given to her making her way through the snow on Christmas day. Spending the day alone had no real impact on Tristan, he didn’t really think anything of it. She hadn't wanted to allow someone she cared about to be on their own during the most family conscious day of the year, but she should have known it wouldn’t have dawned on him; it mattered little to him.

When he told her why his parents had not come to England to stay at the house as planned, she had waited to be upset but it simply hadn't come. They hadn't come because when he vacated the house, her house, the day after Boxing Day, he would be going back to Holland to live.

It made sense, he said, he could sell his car and pay off his debts and also have the lump sum Jules had offered. He could live with his parents in the market town of Harleem, just outside Amsterdam, and get into real estate over there. He would, of course, eventually get his own place once he could afford it. Most importantly, he could smoke as much pot as he wanted without getting arrested, thanks to his Dutch passport.

Jules felt guilty at first, worried that his uprooting and leaving the UK was down to her. She started to feel better as the evening wore on and they chatted. His performance at work was slipping, his firm weren't very happy with him and a partner suspected he was using drugs. It was time to move on. 'Time to get out,' he said.

Jules still had affection for him. It wasn't the same love she felt when they were living together, which was overpowering and destructive. It was a wishing of well-things, a special place in her heart could always be kept for him. But with him out of the country, a clean break would be easy.

Over the last two months a reliance culture had built between them again, even if it was just phone calls and texts. His moving to Holland would be a natural end to the situation, her escape. It stopped her following the path she had been coasting towards.

For the duration of the evening she had enjoyed his company, talked about a separate future with no recriminations. He even suggested a holiday to Holland to visit him in the spring; she nodded, knowing she would never go. Her mum would talk her out of it, even if the desire to see him saw her contemplating the visit.

He hadn't invited her to spend the night, neither had she asked, but two hours ago he had stood up and held his hand towards her.

'Bedtime?'

She looked up at him. Drinking in his dark eyes and the way his sun-kissed hair curled so perfectly over his forehead.

'Yes.' She took his hand and together they walked upstairs to what had been their bedroom.

He had undressed her so tenderly. Not touching her skin or trying to kiss her until he had pulled back the duvet and invited her to slide her naked body in. He kissed her softly where she lay, for what felt like hours, until she was so aroused she wriggled beneath him, signalling she was ready. They made love slowly, holding eye contact by the soft light which flowed in from the landing.

It was a perfect goodbye. Jules knew the act would make her miss him all the more, would make her question the break-up and irrationally connect the physical sensation to meaningful emotions. But, knowing he was leaving allowed her to indulge one last time, because even if she weakened, she couldn't come back.

Now, watching him sleep, Jules knew there was no more to be said and that waking up together would only serve to make it harder to go.

She dressed in silence and left the house.

Gill and Jules waved Rosie and Matt off as they headed down the drive in Gill's Land rover. The snow was thick on the roads the Council hadn't gritted and Gill insisted they make the trip to visit their parents in the 4x4.

Rosie had taken Gill through Red's routine and Harry's feeding schedule in more detail than had passed the other way when Gill left Rosie in charge of the whole of Newmans. Rosie had prepared their feeds already in knotted carrier bags which simply had to be emptied into buckets, so there really wasn't a lot to do, but Gill affectionately afforded Rosie her neurosis.

Rosie showed no outward signs of the turmoil that must be within now that she had found her biological father.

Jules however, seemed very subdued. Gill reminded her about their meal at the Barton that evening.

'Sure, I'll be ready to walk over at eight as planned,' Jules confirmed. She really didn't feel like going out for dinner, but she would go for Gill. It was nice for her to have a bit of male interest. Jules asked to ride Badger, wanting to be alone. Gill agreed. They would be on the road again soon, just the two of them. They could probably do with as much space as they could get in the interim.

Gill headed to the office, deciding to utilise the time to face some paperwork. She couldn't stop thinking about George, about seeing him. She shut off the voice in her head questioning her decision to go along this evening. She silenced the inner reprieves about George's age and her emotional state, with firm assertions that it was going to be more of a party. From what George had said, half the village would be there. She hadn't had so much dialogue with herself since the last time a man had been in her life.

Gill went through the pile of new feed merchant's invoices and farrier's bills. She realised the float of cash she had left Rosie must have run out awhile ago. She reached into the top drawer for her calculator and did some sums. Based on the number of paid invoices and the amount she had left for Rosie, Gill owed her friend in the region of £500.

She decided to go through the rest of her post. Although the credit card bill and utility bills would be even more depressing, there should also be some money in at least a couple of the envelopes from the liveries who paid in cash. By the time she had finished with the stack of direct debit notifications, she realised she must be seriously overdrawn. Luckily the Newmans business account had a pretty large overdraft facility, but even with that extra cushion she must be skating close to the edge.

Gill saved the handwritten envelopes until last. When she had opened them all, she had £168 pounds in front of her.

'Oh fuck!' She banged her fist on the desk.

Mike wouldn't expect to be paid for Charlie's Christmas present just yet, but the horsebox would need to be filled up with diesel as soon as they set off again on New Year's Day. Money came in from the other liveries and the horses in training via standing order, but that would only accumulate until the next direct debit came out. With Monty's fees suspended and Rocky gone, she wouldn't clear zero.

She was going to have to ask Mike to bail her out. It was something she had avoided doing the whole time she had been running Newmans. In the early days she had subsidised the young business with her divorce proceeds, confident in the belief she would soon start to turn a profit.

And she had started to, for about six months over the summer she had actually done more than broken even. She had taken the profit and any winnings percentage she got from generous owners and put it in a separate account, enjoying the security and sense of achievement in having her own real money. She had even been able to give Kelly a few bonuses, which she so deserved.

That had gone now. It turned bad so quickly, it had only

taken losing two paying horses, living off motorway service station meals and using a lot of diesel, to put the business into reverse.

It was hard to connect with her apparent financial ruin. She cared more about finding Amber. She would probably have to sell now anyway.

The crumbling business and failure to prove to herself and Alex that she could be a success were just additions to her incredibly low, low ebb. If she still had Amber and she hadn't lost Monty, she would have fought, advertised, cut costs any way she could. But now it all seemed so pointless. At least Kelly's wages came out automatically the day after the standing orders went in, while there was still money in the account. She couldn't afford to lose Kelly now, not if she wanted to carry on searching.

She sighed heavily and dialled Mike's number. He and Ginny were pretty well-off and he had already offered. It didn't make calling her big brother to bail her out of a hole any less degrading.

Chapter twelve

'Well?'

George made Jules jump when he sat down beside her. It was the first time they had seen him all night. She fought not to laugh at Gill who was trying to be nonchalant, but not succeeding.

'This is absolutely delicious, George,' Jules said, between mouthfuls of the most exquisite crème brûlée she had ever tasted. Sharp raspberries cut through the perfect light crème and sweet hot caramel. The whole meal had been decadent. Beautifully presented on square white plates, a delicate mixture of flavours and colours lit up every course.

'I had no idea this place was so posh – it's like being at a Michael Caines!' Gill had been nervously necking smooth red wine all night. Her glass was re-filled almost immediately each time she drained it. Her voice came out louder than she realised it would.

George laughed; a genuine smile rose up from the bottom of soul to see Gill enjoying herself.

'I'm going to go ahead and take that as a compliment.'

'Here, won't the boss mind you sitting with us?' Gill leaned towards George, alcohol dilated eyes flirting. 'Will you be in trouble?!'

'Oh, I don't think he'll mind, you're the guest of honour.'

Gill looked around the dining room, many diners had now

left, but there were still tables full of people from the village, including the local councillor.

'Me? Oh no, I don't even know the owner! I can't be the guest of honour.'

George smiled at Jules mischievously.

'Oh, but you are. The boss thinks you're very special.'

'A man who I have never met thinks I'm special? Ha – stop winding me up!'

Jules rolled her eyes, Gill was not going to cotton on.

'I think what George is trying to say is that he is the boss!'

'What, you own this place?' She swept her arm out in a semi-circle to encompass the restaurant and caught the handle of the spoon in her empty desert dish, sending it flying onto the floor. 'Oh bugger!' Gill giggled and then clamped her hand over her mouth.

Jules looked at George. He laughed out loud and laid his hand on Gill's after returning the spoon to the dish.

'Part own, but don't say it too loudly, everyone will know!'

Later, Jules sat at the bar. George and Gill were still sat at the same table. He rested his chin on his palm and watched her as she talked, animated, about everything and anything. Gill's inhibitions momentarily forgotten, in the safety of a public place, she poured out her personality in vivid colours. She was usually so reserved, preferring to keep conversation functional. George was clearly captivated.

The rest of the diners had left and only staff and a few of their friends remained. She supposed this was what a lock-in was like. Chart music played over the sound system instead of the ambient classical sounds during dinner service. A couple of the waitresses had started to dance around the tables and the sous-chef burst from the kitchen and sidestepped his way towards the girls to join them. The man behind the bar offered Jules a cocktail.

'Surprise me,' she said, and smiled at the man, who was in his late fifties.

'So you're here with Gill?'

'Yes, George invited us. How do you know Gill?'

'Oh I don't, not personally anyway, but pretty much all of us have heard about Gill. George is rather smitten with her.'

'Yes, you can tell.' Jules befriended the man as he placed a screaming orgasm in front of her.

'I added some chocolate sauce and finished it with coffee ice-cream. I sense you like it creamy and rich.'

'I'm very impressed.' Jules genuinely was, although her appetite had dwindled and her figure dramatically reduced of late, anything creamy would usually have been her weak spot. The man watched as she took a sip and smiled, taking her pleasure as personal gratification.

'Rob Brandswell,' he offered his hand. 'I'm George's business partner.'

'Nice to meet you, Jules.' She took it and smiled as he squeezed her fingers.

'Oh yes, so sorry to hear about your horse.'

'To be honest Gill, after this amount of time, it's not going to make that much difference if you miss one sale. We've got information out to all the markets and police stations, the horses details are on our site and all the main forums.'

Gill remained silent. She knew she couldn't refuse Rosie, but she was anxious about missing the first two sales after the New Year. As much as being back at Newmans and having some semblance of normality had been nice, comforting even, she had a burning desire to get back on the road and continue the search.

'Okay, Janet, if you're sure.'

The Horsewatch coordinator sighed.

'Look, if you are that worried about missing it, I'll ask my colleague in Newmarket to go to the one up there for you. The one in Truro is small, as long as you get details to the Market supervisors, they'll spot an expensive Arab if one turns up, no trouble.'

'Janet, I don't know how to thank you.'

'Don't mention it, Gill, chin up.'

Gill thanked Janet profusely, before hanging up. She felt a bit better. She thought briefly that, with an extra few days in Devon she might be able to find an excuse to see George again. The morning after their night at the Barton she had been deeply embarrassed at her behaviour. He texted her in the afternoon and their usual banter picked up where it left off, but he hadn't come round again since and she hated to admit she missed him. She was still far too prudish about the whole thing to actually invite him over.

Maybe she could arrange some kind of gathering, a sort of going away dinner or just a few drinks at Newmans.

Gill had assumed Jules was experiencing one of the many waves of anguish they had both experienced since their horses had been taken and not thought anything of her solitude and red-eyes after Boxing Day. Jules had come clean to Gill and Rosie about her Christmas goodbye with Tristan and his departure back to Holland, when Rosie and Matt returned from their family visit.

Rosie and Gill had tried to put a positive spin on it. It was for the best, she could have a clean break, her house was completely hers and she could move back in whenever she liked. She had agreed wholeheartedly with her friends, but it hadn't made it any less painful for her. She had taken Ziggy and spent a few days in Gloucester with her parents. She was due back today and Gill was dreading having to tell her they wouldn't be leaving on Monday as planned.

Rosie had done so much for them both, Gill could hardly deny her some extra time before she took over the running of Newmans again, especially given the reason for her request.

It was Saturday, New Years Day. Gill had spent New Year's Eve with Rosie and Matt in front of the telly. Kelly and her mother had popped over early on in the evening, Kelly clearly excited about the prospect of coming back to work on Monday, after the enforced Christmas holiday Gill had insisted she take.

They hadn't really celebrated the New Year. Too much hung in the balance. Too many things could take a twist for the better or the worst to tempt fate by celebrating a new beginning. For all of them.

Gill was delighted when her phone bleeped and a text came through from Charlie. She hoped it was in response to Gill's suggestion that they see each other before she set off to resume the search for the horses. Charlie's text said she was starting her driving course on Monday, so would be too busy. Gill snapped her phone shut and decided she had better get on with riding Milly.

'Hello, am I speaking to Mr Gillant?' Rosie's voice came out unnaturally high. She had been sat in the office on her own for twenty minutes trying to make the call. She had organised work, she had organised to be away from Newmans, to the detriment of Gill and Jules, at Matt's insistence. She had done everything she needed to do to meet her father, except actually arrange it with him. At the last second, she decided to change tack.

'You certainly are, but I warn you, if you're selling something, you probably won't be speaking to him for long!' The voice was so familiar. He had no real accent to speak of; Received

Pronunciation came back along the line to her. He was jovial, warm even, he made the joke with no malice.

'Hello, Mr Gillant, er, no, I don't want to sell anything to you.' Rosie laughed lightly, aware she sounded nothing like her usual self. Nerves twisted up her vocal chords until her voice tightened unnaturally.

'Then what can I do for you – um – sorry I didn't catch your name?'

Rosie obviously hadn't forgotten her name but the long seconds it took her to articulate it suggested she might have.

'Rosie, sorry it's Rosie.'

'Okay, sorry it's Rosie', that is a bit of an unusual name but we'll work with it!'

Rosie opened her mouth and the awful nervous laugh came out again. She must have been coming across as a complete imbecile, but he was being so patient with her, with a complete stranger, it almost put her at ease.

'Mr Gillant – Eddie – Can I call you Eddie?'

'Certainly, Rosie.'

'I saw your advert in the Horse and County. I have got a horse.'

'Ahh. So, you think I might be able to help you with your horse? If you have seen my ad, you have a good idea of what I can offer?'

'Yes,' Rosie wanted to thank him for making it easier for her. 'Yes I do. I was wondering if we could meet up and talk about him?'

'Sure. I should think so. I don't have my own yard, so I tend to travel to where the horse is. I could come to your yard perhaps?'

'Yes. I mean, no. It's quite a …' Rosie searched frantically for the right word, '… delicate issue. I wonder if we could meet up and talk about how you might be able to help, before you actually come over.'

It was Eddie's turn to pause. He considered the slightly unusual request, but decided he couldn't pass up a potential paid job.

'Well I usually find it helps to meet the horse and see what the issues are first hand, but he's your horse, so we will do whatever you feel comfortable with.'

Relief and apprehension flooded through Rosie in equal measures. She felt awful about fabricating a horse in order to meet him, but she had to meet him and if she told him who she was at this stage, he might refuse to see her. She wasn't lying entirely; she hadn't sat on Red since Christmas Eve.

She offered to buy him breakfast for his trouble and they agreed to meet on Monday morning at a café on the High Street in Reading. On the pretence of being local enough for him to eventually visit her fictitious horse, Rosie pretended to know where he meant.

After she hung up she was proud of herself. She grinned as she googled the café. She might have been a coward about the pretence, but she had an arrangement, she would have breakfast with her father in two days time.

Jules headed over the level crossing and up the lane towards Newmans, she was pleased to be nearing her temporary home. The few days with her mother had done her good. Marianne, although she would never use it as an excuse to be angry at the world, had had a pretty tough life one way or another; a difficult childhood, a battle with cancer, and losing both her parents before she was thirty.

Her experiences gave her a unique way of viewing the world, a kind of peace with what is meant to be and what is for the best.

It made her an excellent counsellor in times of need. Jules would always be grateful for her mother. She was infuriating and exhausting to be with, because of her energy and impatience. A few days was usually enough for Jules, who was more reserved like her father. Her mother had listened, rocked her while she cried and then with firm, but gentle, words had encouraged her to draw out what was in her heart already – that she must grieve for her lost love, but then move on.

It dawned on Jules during her trip, that woe and misery over Tristan was, in the great scheme of things, not worth the effort. She had already got over him once; this brief revisiting of their relationship had really served only as a distraction from the infinitely more painful absence of Romeo.

Ziggy leapt from the back of the car through the gap between the front seats, to sit on the passenger seat beside her. His tail wagged and he barked.

She laughed, not reprimanding him for being in the front of the car. They were so close to home now and on quiet lanes anyway. Thank goodness she still had Ziggy. She lay a hand on the dog's shoulder, Ziggy gazed at her and she consciously tried to absorb the comfort his presence afforded.

She wished it was enough, driving towards her friends and the bosom of a makeshift family. She wished she could look at the Newman's horses and Rosie's, dear Harry, who she had known for so long, without feeling short changed. Instead of the joy she used to exude from being close to equines, she felt a cold disregard, almost anger, because they were not Romeo.

Tears pricked her eyes as she realised she might never be able to derive pleasure from a horse again. If she didn't find Romeo, her lifelong love affair with the horse could end.

'What time do you call this?'

Jules looked up as she got out of her car to the front door where Gill stood brandishing a glass of wine and laughing. Rosie tucked her head over Gill's shoulder from behind.

'Yeah, you bugger – what time do you call this?'

Jules laughed at the sight of her friends, who were both clearly on the road to properly drunk. Ziggy bounded towards them and Gill handed her glass to Rosie so that she could kneel down and hug the dog.

Jules laughed as she retrieved her holdall from the boot, when she got to the door and her friends embraced her from both sides, planting a kiss on each of her cheeks.

'How are you, Ettie? Mum sort you out?' Rosie asked, as Gill handed Jules the glass of wine which had been waiting for her on the table in the hallway.

'Mmm,' Jules nodded, smiling reassurance at Rosie's concerned face. 'What's going on in there?' Jules gestured towards the noise emanating from kitchen. Glasses clinked and laughter rang out.

'We thought we would have a little party! Nothing too special, just a sort of '2013 will be better' get-together. Plus you weren't here for New Year's Eve and it's the last time we will be together for awhile,' Gill enthused.

'Now then,' Rosie shook her head at Gill. 'That's just too many reasons for having a few friends over – almost the sort of crap you would come out with if you were trying to hide the real reason – don't you think Jules?'

Jules eyed Rosie, who was grinning mischievously.

'So what is the real reason?' Jules was intrigued.

'Oh, come on now, why does there have to be a real reason?' Gill tried to shrug it off and motioned they should join the gathering in the kitchen.

Rosie held Jules back and moved in close to speak in hushed

tones. Gill quickly came back and stood with her hands on her hips.

'She arranged this whole thing so she had an excuse to invite George over!' Rosie fell into fits and Jules exclaimed a little too loudly,

'George is here?!'

'Yes,' Gill hissed, 'keep your voice down!'

'Come on, unpack later.' Rosie grabbed Jules' hand and led her towards the kitchen. Gill shook her head and followed, anxious in spite of herself to get back to the tall chef, who had organised cover at the restaurant just to come. He seemed to get more delicious every time she saw him.

'Thanks for asking us, Gill.' Kelly's mother embraced her daughter's boss. Kelly's father had left when Kelly was small and Christmas could be difficult sometimes, just the two of them in their little cottage in the village, she was grateful for the invite.

'See you Monday!' Kelly sparkled at the thought of being back at work again. She only took holiday because Gill made her, she would happily have moved into the horse barn if she thought for a second her mother or Gill would let her.

Gill walked back into the kitchen where George, Rosie, Matt and Jules were making light work of the last of the party nibbles.

It had been a nice evening. Nic and Rob had been their usual comical selves, making everyone laugh with their harmless quips at one another. Mike and Ginny were unusually affectionate with one another and Gill wondered if, after so many years of a casual relationship where independence was retained on both sides, they might be plunging at last into the depths of intimacy.

George didn't leave when the majority of the others left. He was relaxed and fitted in so neatly with the people who were amongst the most important in her life. He retained a maturity though around Rosie and Jules, as though he was careful not to remind Gill he was the same age as the younger women. If Gill hadn't been so concerned with the age difference, so suspicious of his intentions and so frightened of giving herself up emotionally, things would have been going incredibly well. There was an ease about him, a relaxed unassuming confidence which could easily be brought into question and examined. So different, she mused, as their eyes locked across the kitchen, from the arrogance and self-righteousness which never faltered in Alex.

Maybe that was why she liked him. Where Alex was short, tubby and contrived, George was tall and open.

'Why did Kelly say she would see you on Monday? We'll be gone by Monday.' Jules tipped her head back to drop flaky crumbs of left over pastry from the serving dish on the counter into her mouth.

Rosie and Gill looked at each other, a flicker of worry spread across Rosie's face.

'Well, um, we need to talk about that,' Gill said as she saw Jules' disbelief.

'No. No,' Jules folded her arms. 'We are leaving tomorrow. That's what we arranged. We have to leave tomorrow we're not changing it.' Jules voice got louder as she spoke and the small hint of hysteria made and George stand up to leave.

'Right, well, er – Better go.' George held his coat in tight fingers, anxious to leave the women to it.

'Wait,' Gill said to Jules, as she followed George to the door, 'we'll talk about this.'

When they got to the door, Gill looked up at George. He knew about Rosie's extended leave from Newmans and the reaction Jules might have. Gill had confided in him before Jules arrived.

'Don't worry, she'll be all right once she knows it's for Rosie.' George put a tentative hand on Gill's shoulder, ready to retract it if she refuted the physical contact.

Instead, she slid her arms around his waist and pressed her cheek against his chest. He held her gently as they stood in the cold doorway.

She savoured the safety and security of his arms wrapped around her, the comfort of his height. His embrace shielded her from the world in a warm cocoon. She could have stayed there forever.

'Sorry about this,' Gill murmured from the crevice of his coat.

'Don't be silly, you guys need to get things sorted and I don't want to be in the way.'

George kissed the top of Gill's head before finally drawing back.

'Night.' Gill's eyes widened, she focused on his face, absorbing his affection like her heart was dry soil, finally feeling the rain.

'Night. Ring me?'

Gill nodded, not hiding her sadness to part from him. He saw it, and swelled from the bottom of his heart.

'I feel awful now for making such a fuss!' Jules was exclaiming, as Gill walked back into the kitchen.

Rosie sat on a stool looking at the floor.

Jules was having trouble hiding her frustration at not being able to set off until Wednesday. If she was in Exeter, those extra three days meant she should probably go back to work and she didn't want to. She had another month sabbatical agreed and she couldn't face walking into the office, seeing the faces of those who knew about Romeo. Having to explain she was back temporarily and no, not because she had found him. She also felt that, if she was staying, she should go back to her cold, now empty, house in Kysford. She wasn't ready for either and if she and Gill had been leaving tomorrow, she would have had a justified reason not to dip a toe into her new life. Without Romeo at the farm nearby, Kysford itself had lost appeal altogether.

On the other hand, her friend who had found her biological father, was asking for a few days off from a job she hadn't wanted and wasn't being paid for. Jules could hardly make a fuss and disliked the part of herself that wanted to push the issue, to beg Rosie not to go and take the next step in what must have been a painful and all consuming journey to discover her true identity.

'Look. We won't go. I can put Eddie off,' Rosie looked up at Gill as she spoke.

Gill shook her head.

'No, really it's fine. I've waited this long to meet my Dad, I can wait another few months, it's no big deal.' Rosie hopped down from the stool and went to leave the room. Her words were genuine, but she still didn't want to look at either of her friends.

As Rosie walked up the stairs, Gill put the kettle on, she didn't speak to Jules.

'Well, that's okay then. We can set off tomorrow as planned,' Jules said and waited for Gill's reaction.

Gill carried on making herself a cup of tea, her back to Jules.

'She said she didn't mind. She said it wasn't a big deal!'

Gill remained silent.

Jules sighed.

'No right, it is a big deal and she must go.' Jules found herself again.

'Horsewatch are covering the markets for us. It's only a few days and she needs to do this.' Gill finally turned away from the kettle and gave Jules a hug.

Jules made her way up to Rosie and Matt's bedroom, she decided she had survived the unbearable already, a few days at work wouldn't kill her. Going back to her house on the other hand, could wait.

Later, Gill lay in bed with a cup of tea and sighed. Thank heaven Jules had come to her senses. Over the years Rosie had been so good to both of them. She was selfless to the end and to take advantage of that, to allow her to give up a chance to meet Eddie, would not have been on.

She drained the last of her tea and set her book down on the bedside table, reaching up to pull the chord and switch the light off before snuggling into the duvet and wrapping it around her. The warm soft fabric hugged at her back, she drifted off in the memory of George's strong arms.

Rosie sat nervously in a café. The people around her seemed so relaxed, the folk of Reading going about their normal lives, breakfast in a high street café, before a day of normal things like shopping or work. Friends laughed, colleagues' tutted about other colleagues. Even the people who were alone seemed so comfortable in their solitude.

She wished she had allowed Matt to come with her and wait until Eddie arrived. More so in fact, she wished she was just having a day of shopping herself. Not about to have life changing moment that had potential for disaster.

Rosie took out her mobile; she'd already had good luck texts from Gill and Val. She wanted to give herself some armour, to bury herself in writing a text so that when Eddie arrived, she wouldn't be sat there like an idiot, not knowing where to look. Suddenly she couldn't think of who to text or what to say. She briefly considered texting Jimmy, a last minute admission of betrayal, to tell him she was seeking out her alternative Dad.

She didn't feel ready for what was about to happen. She hadn't had enough time from waking up in the twin-bedded room of the local hotel, to now. She was sleep gritty, used to seeing to her horses before the day began properly.

She hadn't spoken much the evening before and Matt had been bored at dinner. He loved her too much to say it, but she knew she had been bad company.

Her phone bleeped in her hand, making her jump. It was from Matt, telling her to look outside. She peered through the window of the café, their car was across the road and Matt waved from the driver's seat. He hadn't left after all; he was sat there giving her silent support, keeping an eye on her.

She stuck her tongue out at him and he laughed. Rosie's smile lit up her face and radiance emitted from her as she showed her teeth, white and slightly crooked in a way that added a character which was lost in stereotypical beauties.

'Rosie?'

Eddie was shorter than Rosie had expected and it threw her. She diverted her eyes to the floor momentarily before she remembered her manners. The metal legs of the plastic chair scraped noisily on the floor as she stood up to shake hands.

'Hi, Eddie.' He took her cold hand in both of his warm palms. Short strong fingers like her own gripped tightly, as he smiled in a way that made her feel at ease.

He sat opposite her and she sat back down, she couldn't help staring at him. She drank in his features, so familiar yet so very distant. She wanted to know every inch of his brown eyes and thick dark hair which curled down over his ears and showed only the smallest touches of grey. But for all the similarities, he was still a stranger.

His initial warmth faded when her silence persisted. She was staring at him in a way which was starting to make him uncomfortable.

'So, shall we talk about your horse?' Eddie reached into the pocket of his worn leather jacket and pulled out a notepad and a pencil. He set them on the table, ready to make notes on the project horse she had asked to meet him about.

'Let's order first, shall we?' Rosie signalled to the waitress and glanced quickly outside. Matt and the car had gone; it was up to her now.

Eddie ordered a bacon sandwich and Rosie asked for a coffee. He didn't question her decision not to eat anything, but continued to wait for her to speak.

Eddie was used to dealing with owners who struggled with the emotional side of having a horse they couldn't train themselves. Even the ones who simply wanted a finished horse, always wanted to over-justify their decision not to deal with their animal alone. He tried not to develop contempt for these women; they were his livelihood, after all. Personally though, he would never have bought a horse and then simply sent it to someone else to turn it into a finished riding animal. He had worked with other people's horses for so long that he no longer felt pride when he turned a horse around. It was like a job rather than a gift these days.

He took pity on Rosie though, something about her extreme nerves, her inability to even begin to speak, softened him.

'I know it's hard sometimes when your relationship with your horse breaks down, but I am here to help, if I can.'

'It's not … I don't know where to start …'

'It's okay, take your time.'

That warming smile again. Rosie took a deep breath. She

couldn't let him leave without telling him.

'Look, Eddie, I need to tell you something.'

Something about the seriousness in Rosie's face made Eddie pause before he took another bite of his sandwich. He set the hunks of white bread back down on his plate and leaned forward.

'There is no horse,' Rosie made eye contact in time to watch Eddie's face fall.

'What do you mean there is no horse? If there is no horse what the hell is this?'

It was Eddie's turn to get nervous.

'I'm sorry, I just had to see you,' Rosie drew her bottom lip up under her front teeth.

'Are you from the Inland Revenue, because I told you people already I don't make enough to pay tax?'

Eddie vigorously wiped his mouth with a napkin and started to stand up.

'Wait!' Rosie reached out and caught his leather clad sleeve. 'Please, I'm not from the tax office, I promise.'

Eddie relaxed a fraction and irritation replaced fear.

'What the hell is this all about?'

Rosie took a deep breath.

'Do you remember Selina Mayhue?'

Rosie watched him carefully, she half expected him not to, expected to see him struggling to recall the name. Instead his anger was direct, almost instant.

'Of course I do.'

'You last saw her twenty-nine years ago.'

'Yes, I suppose it must have been that long … why?'

Rosie felt a bubble of thick, potent emotion rising up towards her throat. She hadn't expected to cry, but a tear found its way from her wide eye and ran down her pale face.

'I'm twenty-nine.'

Neither had any real sense of how long they sat, staring at one another. The silence was broken when the waitress came to ask if she could clear Eddie's plate. He looked down at his half-eaten food and nodded.

'She was cheating on me. I had no idea about you. No idea, none.'

'She was cheating on you? You were the affair!' Rosie shook her head in disbelief, defensive suddenly, for the man who had brought her up, Jimmy was the injured party, and Eddie was the fling – surely?

'We were seeing each other for a few weeks, then I saw her in the supermarket, she was shopping with a man, he had his arm around her. I couldn't bear it; I left my job and everything. I needed a clean break to get over it.' Eddie was still in shock, shaking his head. 'What do you mean I was the affair?'

'The man you saw her with, the man I grew up believing was my Dad – he was her partner, they were seeing each other long before she met you.'

'Are you sure?' Eddie saw the truth in Rosie's eyes. On the way to being lost in renewed grief over Selina, something dawned on Eddie. 'If I was the affair, how do you know I'm your Dad?'

'Jimmy, Dad, he's infertile. And apparently I look like you.'

Eddie looked at the girl sat opposite him, thick wavy brown hair, a nose like his was before a fall from a horse had broken it.

'I don't have very much. I live in a static caravan on a yard where I keep a few youngsters. I suppose they might be worth something one day.'

'I don't want money.'

'But it sounds like you already have a Dad, what do you want from me?'

Rosie considered the question. She hadn't thought about it before.

'I don't know. I just wanted to meet you. I only found out you existed six months ago. Curious maybe? Do you have any other children?'

Eddie shook his head. Rosie couldn't hide her disappointment. She would have loved to have found she had a sibling. Even though she was over the childhood days when a brother or sister to play with would have meant so much, she still longed for that kind of connection with someone else.

'Do you even have a horse?' Eddie asked, laughing.

'Two.'

Rosie began to tell him about Harry, then about Red and the journey she was sharing with the young horse. He listened with enthusiasm when she talked about her training methods. They found an alliance in their understanding of the horse and the importance of seeing the world through their eyes in order to get the best from them.

Then he told her about his life since his encounter with Selina. He spoke of the many yards and different horses he had worked with. He made her laugh with his tales of bad falls and neurotic owners.

He asked her about her job, her friends, and her childhood. She was open with him to a point, but she kept back Selina's alcoholism. The black-eyes and black-days could wait for another time.

'I'm actually looking after an Arab racing yard at the moment. Belongs to my friend Gill. It's hard work but she and Jules need me there at the moment.'

'Never liked Arabs much.' Eddie's eyes twinkled as Rosie nodded and they found another thing in common.

'Too finicky.'

'And sensitive, move your legs too quickly and the bloody thing is off!'

'Oh, I know, that's part of the reason I bought a Quarter Horse. He's nice and solid!'

'I would love to meet him sometime, Rosie.'

'That would be nice,' Rosie smiled; she had underestimated how much they would have in common, how easy it would be after the shock wore off. 'Another coffee?'

Eddie nodded enthusiastically.

When the coffees arrived, they naturally held onto their mugs with their hands forming the same pattern around the porcelain.

'So why are you looking after this Arab yard then?'

Rosie sighed as the question forced her to recall reality and brought her back from the island the café and her new father had created for the past hour.

'Their horses were taken, stolen, in November, from Gill's yard in Exeter. It's so awful, they're beside themselves with worry.'

'Oh, well, that's a shame.'

Rosie was surprised by his response. Based on his obvious passion for horses she had expected outrage, sympathy – it was way beyond being just a shame, it was a complete nightmare.

'I don't know how they will cope if they don't find them. The police and Horsewatch are involved, but so far, no leads. My husband, Matt and I are staying at the yard to run things while they search for the horses. They spent almost a month on the road just driving round looking. It's just awful.'

'What were the horses? I mean, what types?'

'Two Arabs, a mare and a stallion, and a hunter, Irish bred. Romeo, that's the hunter, is such a genuine sort, real gentleman, it breaks my heart.'

'Hm, well,' Eddie looked matter of fact. 'They're probably wasting their time. Those horses will be long gone now. Best they try and get over it and move on, it's very sad, but stolen horses are rarely found these days.'

'I don't think they will ever give up – I mean – would you if it was one of your youngsters?'

'No,' Eddie gave a grim smile, 'I guess I wouldn't.'

Eddie looked at his watch and took a gulp of his coffee.

'It's been wonderful to meet you, Rosie. Having a daughter is going to take some getting my head around. Maybe I can call you soon?' Eddie reached across the table and squeezed Rosie's hand.

'Oh, you're not going?' Rosie looked at the half-finished coffee mug and felt robbed, he couldn't go now, she'd only just found him.

'Sorry, really, I would love to stay and talk to you all day, but I didn't think I would be here this long. I've got appointments with clients and a new horse to see this afternoon.'

'Right, I understand. You probably need some digestion time anyway. Sorry for the way I got you here. I just couldn't tell you on the phone.'

Eddie stood up.

'It's fine, I am glad we met.' He reached over and kissed Rosie's forehead. 'Can't believe how beautiful you are.' He paused as he looked down at her for a moment. 'Will you be okay here, can I give you a lift somewhere?'

'No it's fine,' Rosie tried to smile even though she was gutted, 'my husband is nearby with the car, I'll call him now.'

'Okay. I have your number in my phone now. I'll call – soon.'

With that, he was gone. He hurried out of the café and she watched him walking away along the high street.

Chapter thirteen

Deserted, Rosie looked down at her coffee. It was such a relief when Eddie told her he had been in love with her mother. They had so much in common with their affinity to all things horsey. He had seemed perfect. Too good to be true, even.

In that instant, Rosie knew what she had to do. She hurried to leave sufficient cash on the table and ran out of the café.

She ran up the high street in the direction she had seen Eddie go, fear pushed her heart into the unyielding wall of her rib cage and it throbbed there, heightening her senses and terrifying her all the more.

She was following the father she had only just met. What the heck was she doing? Where the hell was he, he couldn't have gone far already? She bobbed between pedestrians, looking through the crowd, searching for a leather jacket and brown hair.

She nearly fell over a pushchair and as she apologised to the irritated mother she caught sight of him walking 30 paces ahead. She slowed to a walk, eyes glued to his back for the slightest indication he might begin to turn around, which would mean she had to dart into a shop to avoid being seen.

It couldn't have been coincidence – could it? Was she covertly following this poor man for nothing? His reaction when she mentioned the stolen horses, his sudden departure, when five minutes before he had ordered more coffee and seemed like he could happily have stayed talking to her for hours – it didn't add up.

Eddie ducked his head and slipped into a side ally. Rosie reached the corner of the building which bordered the ally and pressed her back against the wall. Before she had time to contemplate following him, she heard the unmistakeable tones of a number being punched into a mobile phone, just around the corner.

'You've got to get them shifted,' Eddie's voice was hard, like he meant business. It was a stark contrast to the soft tone he had used with Rosie and she almost risked a glance into the alley to make sure it was in fact Eddie.

'Never mind why!'

There was a pause and Rosie held her breath, not daring to believe the conversation was actually about the horses, that the suspicion which had caused her to follow him was warranted.

'I don't care how much you get for it, just get it flogged on, today.'

Eddie paused again.

'Well just meet them at the sale and put the other one in the ring.'

Rosie gasped but the sound was lost under the drone of a passing bus. Her brain was working overtime – what sale? What ring?

'I don't give a shit who's running the show. I'm telling you, if you don't want to end up at the nick, get rid of that bloody Arab.'

Rosie heard a snap as the mobile was flipped shut. She quickly pretended to use the cash point in the wall next to her, her head down and her breath held.

Luckily, Eddie darted out of the alley and continued to walk up the high street in the same direction, away from her. When she was sure he was far enough away, she fumbled in her coat pocket for her mobile.

Fingers shaking she struggled to select Matt's number.

'Come and get me – now!'

Rosie knew there was a livestock market to the North of the city. Jules had told her that Horsewatch would be attending it for them, when she had been persuading Rosie to leave Newmans and meet Eddie.

Matt drove at breakneck speed through the town. A kind passer-by had given them directions to the sale. It was already 11am and soon the market would be starting, deals already done in the run up to the first lot.

Matt took his hand from the wheel to squeeze Rosie's.

'Just drive,' Rosie guided his hand back to the steering wheel.

'Rosie, your Dad—'

'We can deal with that later. Right now we have to get the horses back.' Rosie's eyes planted firmly on the road, as she tried to focus on getting to the sale and not on the horrifying discovery that the father she had just found was probably involved in something as low and despicable as organised horse theft.

'What are we going to do when we get there?' Matt started to feel anxious about arriving at the sale and what would happen if they did actually find the horses.

'I don't know.'

'Should we phone the police now?'

'I don't know.'

They continued to drive in silence and Rosie tried to decide if she should telephone Newmans. If the horses weren't at the sale and their hopes were built and dashed, it would be unbearable for both women; however, if the horses were there, they would need to bring passports to claim them. Rosie knew it would take them at least two hours to get to Reading in the horsebox. She had to make a snap decision. So she dialled.

'Gill, you and Jules need to get up here …'

'Hello, Juliette, this is Sheila on reception, there's a lady here to see you.'

Jules replaced the handset and took a sip of coffee. None of her clients could possibly have known she was back in the office for a few days. She was only there to catch up on paperwork and discuss her ongoing cases with the locum. She didn't want to see anyone!

She hiked up suit trousers which were now far too big for her and made her way out of her office. The receptionist was new, she made a mental note to speak to her about taking the details of people who arrived in reception and not committing the solicitor they wanted to see, until she had spoken to them first.

The secretaries at their desks in the open-plan part of the office smiled as she walked between them towards the lift. No one knew how to act around her; she felt so out of it. She was glad most of the other fee-earners, including David, were away on a training course today and she hadn't had to face them.

Jules took a deep breath and put on her most confident smile as she pushed the door open into the plush reception lobby of Hodges and Grath.

'Gill!' Jules exclaimed as she saw her friend, dressed in muddied jeans and muck boots, stood on the marble floor.

'Rosie called me, we have to go to Reading.'

Jules screwed up her face and started to ask why, but Gill took firmly hold of her hand and started making for the exit.

'Now.'

Rosie was out of the car as soon as Matt parked it. The high winds buffeted the horse lorries, which were dotted about the parking area of Reading Livestock Market. The high pitched calls of confused horses, missing their friends and frightened, hit Rosie's ears like cries for help.

Nothing but the prospect of finding the horses could have brought her to a place like this. The white-eyes of the un-handled, terrified youngsters, the sad expressions on the faces of the gentle riding ponies, turned out like worn clothes when their riders got too big for them. Rosie took short sharp breaths and put a hand on her throat to steady herself.

Head down against the thrashing wind, she dashed for the entrance. A short stocky lady caught her before she burst through the doors and into the market.

'You must be Rosie, let's have a chat.' The lady was too calm; didn't she know Romeo, Amber and Monty could be in there?

'No, I have to get inside!' Rosie continued her headlong charge towards the sale ring; any of the horses could be being sold at that moment and led away into one of those horseboxes, while she stood around talking.

Gentle hands stopped her and pressed on her shoulders, a voice spoke softly in her ear.

'It's okay, Rosie, nothing is going to happen for a minute, let's just go around the side there, out of the wind.'

The man who had spoken moved around to face Rosie, he was younger than his voice had suggested, a strong authoritative air exuded from him which didn't match his fresh face. He was dressed in smart-looking jeans and an oversized jumper. He held out his hand. Something about his eyes made Rosie take it.

'I'm Detective North, this is Rebecca Quinn from Horsewatch. Mrs Newman telephoned the Devon coordinator and she got in touch with Miss Quinn who called me.'

'We have to find the horses!' Rosie still didn't understand what all the standing around chatting was for. She was relieved to know the Horsewatch person was there, more so that the police had arrived already, but why didn't they seem to understand the urgency?

Matt reached them and the Detective introduced himself and Rebecca.

'Rosie, it's really important that we don't draw attention to ourselves. Let's move over here?' Detective North gestured again towards the side of the building. Matt rubbed Rosie's arm reassuringly and steered her in the direction of a disused doorway.

Once they were stood in the doorway, Detective North discretely showed them his badge.

'Do you know all of the horses well enough to identify them?' The detective asked Rosie, who made an affirmative noise. She didn't have to think about it, she would know each of them, she was positive.

'If the horses are here, we need to find them all, and then secure them, simultaneously. If we go charging in and try to reclaim one, the person behind this will try to get the others out of the market or just scarper and we don't want that. We want to recover the horses, but we also want to catch the people responsible for taking them. We think there might be a connection between this and a number of other horse thefts.

'We've got an officer and an Animal Health Officer from the Local Trading Standards Department on the front gate, if any horse boxes try to leave in the meantime we're going to stop and search on the pretence of checking horse passports. They've got the details of the horses from Rebecca here and they'll raise the alarm and stop the horse box moving off if there is anything suspicious. There are uniformed officers waiting in a lay-by about half-a-mile from here, on my signal they can be here in less than a minute, but in the meantime, we have to look and act normally. Can you do that Rosie?'

Rosie nodded, trying to take it all in. She was both reassured and frightened by the officer's words. She would give a limb to recover the horses, but it seemed so real now, she was worried she would fall apart if she saw one of them.

'I want you to walk around, if you see one of the horses I want you to make a mental note of the pen number and, when you are a safe distance away from it, find me or text it to me.'

Rosie nodded again. Matt took the Detective's number and saved it into his mobile, before handing it to Rosie.

'Once we have a pen number, I'll ask Rebecca here, or one of the sale stewards, to keep an eye on that horse to make sure it doesn't leave the sale. I'm going to point you out to the market superintendent and stewards on the CCTV in the office while you're walking round, so they know who you are and can let me know if you run into any trouble. In the meantime, Rebecca is going to watch the sale ring in case any of the horses go in for bidding.'

'I'll go with Rebecca,' Matt said suddenly. 'I can help identify them, if one of them is brought in.'

Rosie looked round at Matt's determined face, she was surprised he thought he would know one of the horses, but she supposed he had seen them often enough. Amidst the chaos in Rosie's head, she was momentarily strengthened by pride in her husband.

'Right, most important is finding the horses of course, but you have to stay safe. Don't put yourselves in danger.' Detective North eyed them all, including Rebecca, who nodded eagerly. 'Once today is over, I'm going to need a full statement from you Rosie and you may have to give evidence in any court case that comes of this – is that okay? I understand there is some family connection?' Detective North looked pointedly at Rosie, trying to gauge her reaction.

Rosie's expression changed under his gaze, a flicker of anguish came and went, so that she appeared resolute when she spoke.

'He is not my family. There won't be a problem.'

As the motorway flowed hypnotic beneath the horsebox, Jules and Gill travelled in numbed silence. They'd had false hope before. The lead which had come to nothing at the Yorkshire auction before Christmas had tainted their ability to believe.

Gill hadn't really got the full story from Rosie on the phone, but she had gathered enough to know that Rosie's father had not exactly given her the lead by choice. She wondered how her friend must be feeling.

Jules hadn't really been able to take it in, she could see Romeo so vividly in her head. Rosie's plight was way under her emotional radar. She stared intently at the road ahead, willing each junction of the M5 to pass by more quickly and bring her closer to hope.

Gill glanced quickly across at Jules, wondering if she felt the same sense of dread which was welling up inside her. She should have been positive. As Janet had reminded her on the phone, every lead was a step closer, even if it didn't lead them to the horses right away. Instead, a cold feeling spread from Gill's heart around her body, leaving her torn between wanting to reach the market and dreading her arrival there, and she wasn't sure why.

Rosie walked self-consciously between the rows of pens. She was sure she stuck out like a sore thumb. She might as well have had a sign above her head, any passing horse thieves would surely have known from her face what she was doing there?

She eyed each horse carefully, trying to look as though she

was a serious buyer. Her gaze flickered from left to right. She willed herself to focus on the job in hand, not to see the hollow hindquarters and dull coats of the older ponies that stood quietly, oblivious to their surroundings. They picked at the morsels of hay they had been thrown. They could so easily have been Harry.

The droppings that no one seemed to be collecting carpeted the pens of the more restless horses. Loose fear-filled excrement was trodden into the concrete by panicked hooves, providing an acrid almost unbearable smell. Even the sweat of the most worried animals seemed to be tinged with an unnatural aroma, like it was laced with adrenalin.

Rosie bit her lip and willed herself not to faint. She couldn't bear it.

She reached the fourth aisle of the market's holding area, without warning and sooner than she had dreamed possible, she spotted a chestnut head. She couldn't help but quicken her step. Her determination to look like a horse buyer not forgotten entirely, she refrained from breaking into a run. A man she guessed must have been in his early sixties stood with an elbow over the chestnut's pen. She slowed again as she drew level. The tweedy looking woman he was talking to was crouched, peering at straight strong legs between the bars of the pen. She could hear the man talking about how the horse's young rider was leaving for university and needed to sell him.

'As you can see he is a really good sort. Well-bred and got some go in him, but safe as houses, I'd put my grandkid on him!'

Rosie took in the wide white blaze and hogged mane. The horse's forehead looked so naked and almost clinical with no forelock, but no amount of work with a set of clippers could have put any doubt in her mind, Romeo's eyes stared back at her, as she passed the pen.

She forced herself to look away. Her legs wanted to run to the horse, she wanted to call his name and hear his wonderful whinny, to open the pen door and run with him to the fresh air outside; away from the awful man. But, she carried on walking; she had to stick to the plan. The bubble of excitement within her could have lifted her up to the high ceiling of the agricultural building. She drew out her phone and sent a short text message.

Rosie finished her trawl of the pens and was about to start over again in case she had missed anything, surely if Romeo was here the others must be too. She had heard Eddie mention an Arab on the phone – Amber must be here somewhere?

Rosie hesitated, wondering if she should go to the sale ring and see if Matt had found her. Detective North drew up beside her, gestured for her to walk with him. She fell in step and he linked arms with her.

'Let's pop outside for a minute.'

Back outside in the wind, the Detective ducked his head and drew Rosie to him as they walked, getting close enough to speak over the gale without being heard by any of the sale goers, who were milling around the car park.

'I got your text and Rebecca is stood near the pen keeping an eye-out. The man beside the pen is known to my team. Not for horse theft, but we've had him up for fraud before. Seems he will say anything to anyone to make a buck. No idea he was involved in this kind of thing.

I followed him when he left the pen. Seems the woman he was talking to wanted to buy your friend's horse and he was going to fetch the passport. Rebecca explained the situation to her once he left the holding area.

He's back inside now but he went into a box just down here. The back is open and there's a horse inside, I want you to have a look at it.'

The detective glanced furtively over his shoulder as he steered Rosie between vehicles towards a dark green, five-horse carrier. He stopped for a moment, his arm linked with Rosie's still. He looked at the box and listened. When he was satisfied there was definitely no one inside, they walked to the rear of the box. Rosie's heart was in her mouth. She prayed the horse inside would be Amber. As they rounded the bottom of the open ramp she glanced inside. It wasn't her.

But it was close. Monty's shrill whinny erupted from the horsebox as he swung his head over the partition to look around the car park. The stallion kicked the tattered cladding of the box with a peevish hoof in frustration. Rosie clasped her hand over her mouth. That was all the confirmation the detective needed.

He pulled a penknife from his pocket and stabbed hard at one of the huge tyres before drawing his radio from inside his jumper and giving the 'all go' signal.

'I think we've got enough now.' He nodded to Rosie before striding back towards the market to get his man. Rosie beamed at Monty, unable to believe it had all happened so quickly. She walked up the ramp and cupped his velvet muzzle in both hands.

'Home soon, my darling,' she whispered.

Detective North turned back toward the sale ring and gestured for her to follow him.

'I promise …' she added to the horse before running to catch up.

When they got back to Romeo's pen, Rebecca gestured her head towards the sales office. Rosie trotted after Detective North, who strode confidently towards the office. When they reached the glass windows, Rosie could see the man inside talking to a steward.

Rosie could hear the man asking for Romeo's entry to be withdrawn from the auction. Rosie turned to Detective North on the verge of panic. He spoke quietly.

'It's okay, common practice if you make a sale prior to the auction starting, according to Rebecca. He still thinks the lady is interested and he's made a sale. Rosie, can you confirm for me that this is the man you witnessed attempting to sell the horse you believe to belong to your friend?'

'Yes,' Rosie nodded vigorously, still not sure what was going to happen. She knew the horsebox couldn't leave now with its flat tyre, but she still wanted to get Monty out of it as soon as possible.

'And you'll give evidence to that effect?'

'Yes.'

'My officers will start photographing the horse inside the box shortly, once they have enough you can get him out.' Detective North looked down at a piece of paper he pulled from his pocket. ''Monday's Eclipse' right?'

'Yes.' Rosie bit her lip. She could hear the man wrapping things up in the office, he would be headed towards them any minute. 'What about Amber? The third horse?' Rosie suddenly was terrified, the joy she felt at having found Monty and Romeo was obliterated by the fact that there had been no sign of the chestnut mare. Her heart sank as she recalled Eddie's conversation – he mentioned a horse and one Arab – not two.

If Detective North heard her, he didn't have time to reply. He stepped quickly forward to intercept the man as he left the sales office.

'Mr Farriday, mind if we have a quick word?'

The next few seconds appeared to pass in slow motion. Farriday sidestepped the detective and bolted through the covered area of the market. Rosie was in his path and she hesitated too long, didn't make the decision to move out of the way or try to stop him somehow quickly enough. He collided with her but managed to stay upright, sending her sprawling to the ground while he continued to flee in the direction of the exit.

She pulled her head up just in time to see three uniformed officers burst through the door forming a barrier to Farriday's exit. Farriday hesitated. He tried run again in the opposite direction, but he knew the game was up. He raised his hands and stood still. Detective North caught up with him and told him he was under arrest for handling stolen property. The detective began to read the caution, a uniformed officer placed handcuffs around Farriday's wrists.

Winded, Rosie still hadn't managed to get up and she stayed crouched on the floor as she watched Farriday being led back into the sales office.

Detective North held his hand out to Rosie and gently eased her onto her feet, asking her if she was all right.

'Amber … we have to find Amber … I …' Rosie tried to get the words out between painful breaths.

The Detective helped Rosie to the wall of the office, so that she could lean against it and recover her diaphragm's rhythm again.

'We're going to hold him in the office until the sale is over. I'll ask him a few questions now to try and ascertain the whereabouts of the third horse. And any other missing horses that might be here today. When your friends arrive we'll need to see the passports and take copies for evidence, then the horses can leave. In the meantime the front gates have been shut; no horse will leave here until we have searched every horsebox. If she is here, we'll find her.'

But she wasn't there, Gill's little mare, with her doe-like eyes, masking an intelligence and sensitivity which was all her own.

Rosie begged and pleaded with the officers not to open the

gates of the sale, but every inch of the market grounds had been searched and searched again. Buyers grew impatient as the afternoon wore on, anxious to get their new purchases on the road.

Rosie walked wearily back up the row of now empty pens, towards the last remaining two. Romeo and Monty had been put next to each other were bickering over the metal bars of the pen divider.

Rebecca put an arm around Rosie.

'You did brilliantly today and two out of three is really very good.'

'How am I going to tell her? How do I tell Gill?' Rosie glanced at her watch. It was 3pm and she knew Jules and Gill would arrive soon. She had been putting off phoning and updating the women until all three horses were found. That wasn't going to happen now.

'Let me have her number. I know she doesn't know me, but it's been an emotional day for you,' Rebecca said.

Rosie hesitated, but Matt nodded and reached out his hand to Rosie. Feeling like a traitor, she handed her mobile over. He found Gill's number and gave the phone to Rebecca, who moved away down the aisle as she hit the call button.

'How's your arm?'

Rosie peeled back the sleeve of her jacket. A dark purple bruise spread upwards from her elbow.

Matt drew in a sharp breath and looked concerned, but Rosie put a hand up in protest.

'It actually doesn't hurt.'

A few minutes later Rebecca headed back towards them.

'Gill is okay, she's thrilled about Monty and she knows when Farriday is formally interviewed it may shed some more light on where Amber is.'

'I certainly hope it will,' Detective North came up beside Rosie and gingerly attempted to stroke Monty's nose. Monty put his ears back in disgust at the lack of treats and snapped his teeth together as a warning. Rebecca gently moved the Detective's hand away from the stallion.

'Thanks for your help today, Rosie. We've got your name and address, so I'll send you a draft statement to have a look at and sign soon, based on the notes my officer made with you today.'

Rebecca put her arm around Rosie and said goodbye, promising to keep her ear to the ground for any word of Amber.

Detective North and Rebecca headed away, leaving Rosie and Matt alone.

Rosie eased herself down onto the cold concrete floor and Matt sat beside her. He gathered her into his arms and for the first time all day she was suddenly drained; her real father, the horses. Matt rocked her quietly as she stared blankly ahead, lost in her thoughts.

'ROMEO!' Jules' usual composure deserted her when she saw her horse, his pen flanked by Rosie and Matt; they looked up from their sentry at the sound of Jules' voice. The horse's ears shot upright. He skittered across the washed concrete floor to the side of the pen nearest the sound and fluttered his nostrils, before standing stock still to listen for a reply.

'Oh Romeo …' as Jules spoke, his call to her confirming it was actually, really him, her legs became like jelly. She fell to her knees, immense overwhelming emotion rendering her muscles weak. Her body physically grounded, she smiled and cried, eyes locked onto her horse, not even daring to blink in case, like some epiphanous vision, he disappeared when she opened her eyes. The knees of her suit wicked up the surface water on the freshly hosed walkway, but she didn't care, she would have ruined her entire wardrobe just to go on staring at her horse. A horse she hadn't really believed she would ever see again, until this moment.

Gill passed Jules and headed towards the adjoining pen. Monty had gained so much weight, he was almost unrecognisable as the sleek greyhound he had been three months ago. Surrounded by a thick, tufty winter coat, he barely looked like an Arab any more. But despite his new inches, he was every inch Monty. She sprang over the rail into the pen. Initially Monty shied and backed away, but then he smelled it was Gill. With excited bursts of high pitched whinny, he pushed his nose into her, nudging her over and over again in delight.

Gill threw her arms around the stallion's neck and tried to rejoice in finding him once again, she couldn't stop herself wishing he was her Amber,

'I'm so sorry boy.'

Gill felt Rosie's hand, firm and reassuring rest on her shoulder.

'We found these two, we will find her.'

Gill nodded and continued to bury her face in Monty's sleek black mane; she cried tears of joy at the feel of his strong neck and allowed herself a moment to feel happy, a solitary moment when happiness at finding Monty wouldn't yet be a betrayal to Amber. Suddenly Rosie tensed beside her and drew in a sharp breath. Even Jules, who had pulled herself together enough to reach Romeo's pen and had both arms over his back, sensed the sudden change in atmosphere.

The three women and two horses watched as Rosie's father and Farriday were led through the market towards the exit by three officers in uniform.

Farriday was in handcuffs. Eddie wasn't, but as the men were led past the pens, Rosie could see from the way the officer held his arm, he wasn't exactly free either. Rosie hadn't even known her father was at the sale, her shock was tangible.

Gill recognised Eddie from his photograph on the website and let go of Monty to hold Rosie's arm.

Jules looked with utter disgust at the two men, but feeling Romeo's warm strong body beside her, the joy within her drowned out any hatred which might have made her say something or lash out.

Eddie made eye contact with the daughter he had known so briefly and instead of the anger and recrimination she expected, he spoke with sincerity,

'I'm so sorry.'

Gill woke up the morning after the sale and decided to do the only thing she was able to do, the only thing that seemed right. Look after the horses in her care.

'Kelly, can you bring Marcy in?' Kelly nodded and set off to fetch the outside brood mare, so she could have a day in the stable to let her feet dry out and be rug free for a few hours.

Gill had a hundred things to do, but the only comfort she found was in Monty's stable. She brushed his coat until it became almost reflective like a radiant piece of rayon. She didn't need to brush Monty. He was quite clean already. He was fat and slightly thuggish since his return, having forgotten his manners somewhat, but he certainly wasn't dirty.

Being near Monty was as close as Gill could get to being near Amber. They had shared the same horsebox which had taken them from Newmans two months before. She had no idea how soon they had been separated after that.

In the box next to Monty's was Renashee, the four-year-old that Norah had brought over just before the theft. Gill knew she should be working on him, preparing him for his first racing season in April. Monty nudged her, reminding her she had stopped brushing him. She put her arms around his neck and hugged the big horse. Tears brimmed to the surface, but as quickly as the acute surge of emotion had come, it went again and her eyes remained dry. She wanted a bloody good sob but it never came.

The fact that Monty and Romeo had been recovered, but Amber remaining out there in the ether somewhere, wouldn't quite come to the forefront. She didn't really know how to deal with it. Since the Horsewatch woman had telephoned her from the sale to tell her Amber hadn't been found along with the other two, she had known only numbness. She had sensed what the woman had been going to say, even before she said it. A dread had locked onto her and wouldn't let her go, as though she was closed off from the rest of the world.

'Gill?' Kelly's hand softly rubbed her back.

'I'm okay, Kel,' Gill turned her dry eyes on the girl and let go of Monty, who eagerly nudged both of them, hoping for a titbit.

'No doubt someone was bribed to stay quiet while he was away.' Gill laughed at Monty, who seemed to have developed an unusually persistent approach to getting treats.

'Are you sure, Gill? I miss Amber so much. It must be ten times worse for you.'

Gill nodded at Kelly's concerned face and decided to keep her promise to share more with Kelly.

'You know when something is close to being useless? It's not quite broken, but you know it's getting there and you just wait for the day it finally gives out?'

'Like the kettle in the barn ...?' Kelly said, confused.

'Ha – yes! Well that's a bit like how I feel.'

'You feel like the kettle in the barn?'

'Yes.'

Kelly considered this unusually deep concept.

'Well, we can buy a new kettle. But I can't buy a new you.'

'And I can't buy a new Amber.'

Rosie sat in Newmans' office. She had been staring at the photo of Eddie on his website for a full ten minutes. Why was he involved in stealing horses?

Rosie heard Norah Ranger's voice, loud and confident in the kitchen. She listened as Norah quizzed Gill about how the horses were recovered, wanting to hear the full story, before she went up to the barn to see her horse.

Rosie stood up and closed the office door. Gill would either lie about Rosie's connection, or tell the whole tale with no omissions and Rosie didn't want to listen. She had told the story of her father's involvement herself when Mike and Ginny had come over the day before. She overheard Gill on the phone telling Charlie everything, sparing no details.

She wanted it to go away. She had dared to admire her new father, if only for an hour or so, then discovered he trafficked stolen horses. It would always be irrevocably linked as the grey cloud over the day two of the horses were found.

Rosie wanted to go home. She wanted to go back to work, see Valerie, confide in her in a way the proximity to the situation wouldn't allow her to do with Gill or Jules. Her arm had swollen so much the day after the sale, she had been forced by Matt to go to casualty. Not serious they said, but she must rest it for a few days.

She looked down at her sling. Even if she wanted to go home, it would be sensible to wait until she could move her arm again, just for the sake of the horses being taken care of by Gill for now.

Rosie opened the door of the office quietly. When she was sure

Norah and Gill had gone, she moved through to the kitchen to make herself a coffee. Matt was back at work and Jules had gone for a ride on Romeo. She sprayed water all over the sink and window-sill, as she filled the kettle one handed.

'Let me.' Rosie saw a slender arm reach around her to turn off the gushing tap. She turned around and was surprised when she realised it was Charlie.

With minimal make-up and boot-cut jeans, she didn't look like the slightly slutty teenager Rosie was used to seeing.

'How is your arm?' Charlie spoke kindly as she put her arms around Rosie and kissed her cheek.

'Better, thanks. Charlie you look different?' It wasn't just the lack of brightly coloured eye-shadow and a short skirt, it was the girl's whole manner, as though the fight had gone out of her, but in a good way.

Charlie blushed slightly and laughed.

'Is Mum here?'

'She's up at the barn, Norah is here to see Monty.'

'I had a driving lesson so I got the instructor to drop me off here, Dad can pick me up in a bit. Is she all right?'

'Bit numb really. She is gutted understandably, but I don't think she knows how she feels. It's so sad.'

'Hmm,' Charlie nodded, looking genuinely troubled by her mother's plight.

A coffee and some fairly easy conversation later, and Rosie was still marvelling at the change in Charlie. She had tactfully not mentioned Rosie's Dad, something she probably would have been all over previously, seeing it as good gossip. Instead she was talking maturely about the future of her mother's business.

'Hello, sweetheart!' Gill came in through the kitchen door and lit up to see her daughter.

Rosie noticed Charlie stiffen slightly, a childish grin spread across her face and the confidence Rosie had seen in her wilted away in her mother's presence.

'Hey,' Charlie stepped down from the stool and walked over to kiss her mother's cheek. 'I had a driving lesson, so I thought I would call in.'

'It's so lovely to see you!' Gill's happiness at seeing her daughter was overshadowed by an obvious fear of crowding her, which meshed with Charlie's shyness to create an awkward atmosphere. Rosie was frustrated with them, they both so clearly loved one another, but it just didn't seem to work when they were together.

She poured Gill a coffee as Gill pulled up a stool and sat at the island.

'Norah isn't going to take Monty away,' Gill beamed at Rosie, who put the mug down and hugged Gill, relieved.

'Was she going to then?' Charlie asked, confused.

'Well,' Gill sighed, not wanting to bore Charlie, 'we thought there was a chance she would take him home after everything that's happened.'

Charlie nodded, she seemed to understand what losing Monty would mean to Gill, something Rosie noticed, but Gill didn't seem to.

'But …' Gill turned to Rosie, 'she made it pretty clear she wanted him and Renashee ready for the first race of the season in April.'

Rosie's face fell.

'Which means I would need to get Monty fit and put in some serious hours with Renashee … starting now.'

'Take your mind off things?' Charlie tried to smile brightly.

'But it means I can't leave to search for Amber.' Gill's head fell into her hands. She didn't cry, it was more frustration.

'Maybe it's time to give up now, Mum?'

'How could you say that?!' Gill lifted her head and stared at her daughter, who stared straight back – still believing she was the voice of reason, despite her mother's outraged demand.

'You can still search for her from here and the police are looking, aren't they?'

'I can't just abandon her, Charlie.' Gill tried not to look disgusted in her daughter's apparent flippancy about Amber, she wondered if Charlie knew her at all anymore.

Rosie stepped in.

'You don't have to decide anything now Gill – give yourself a few days.'

Charlie left shortly after. But not before Gill had asked her to move home, when they were alone in the hallway, with Alex beeping the horn from the car outside. She cursed herself almost immediately she had asked the question. The answer was apparent in Charlie's face. Instead of the flat 'no', she might have given her mother a few months ago, Charlie did try to explain why. She had new friends in West Hill, her driving lessons were going well.

Charlie put the shoe on the other foot when she reminded Gill that she probably wouldn't be there either, if she was going to leave again to search for Amber. Gill hadn't known how to answer that. She felt so stupid for asking, but with Norah's assertion that Monty and Renashee had to be started imminently, Gill had clutched at the straw that having Charlie home might have offered a reason to stay.

She knew she couldn't use Charlie to alleviate her guilt about the mere contemplation of giving up the active search for Amber. But, to have her daughter home might have narrowed slightly, the cavernous hole which was just a footstep in front of her.

Gill picked up her mobile and called George. She hadn't replied to his texts since the day of the sale, putting off having to explain how Amber hadn't been found. But now she wanted to hear his voice. Wanted the support he offered, the empathy he was so good at delivering. She could download her anxiety to someone unconnected, someone who would listen without needing to push their own agenda.

She waited for him to answer, squashing down the guilty feeling inside that she was indulging herself in his affection again, without really offering anything in return.

Chapter fourteen

Eddie flinched as the cell doors were locked for the night. Confined to the small bed in the dark, all he could think about was his daughter.

He hadn't called anyone to ask them to pay the bail bond for him. He could probably have scraped together the meagre £500 they were asking for, but the trial would be soon enough and he had little to get out for. He knew he wouldn't be welcome back at the yard where his caravan was pitched, knew word would have spread on the grapevine of his involvement in handling stolen horses. Those he had helped to move the stolen horses around wouldn't come to his aid now either.

He hadn't meant to get involved, but opportunities to earn easy cash had presented themselves over the years and with no one but himself to look out for, there hadn't seemed a good enough reason not to do it. It had cost him a good thing with his old yard in Bristol when the owner had got suspicious about the types he was associating with, but other than that, he had got away with it. Until now.

Two mornings ago everything had changed. Out of the blue he had a daughter, albeit a grown up daughter who already had someone she called Dad, but none the less, his flesh and blood.

She would have to give evidence against him now. If only he hadn't agreed to take the Arab and the hunter on. If only they hadn't been the horses she was searching for.

Eddie laughed at the cruel irony of the situation. The one thing that might have made him turn the corner was now also the thing that would probably see him serving serious time in this hellhole and worse, he knew without doubt Rosie would hate him forever.

'Gill, I don't want to push you, but have you decided what to do?'

Gill continued to mix nuts and chaff together for the evening feeds, she couldn't answer Rosie because she still didn't know. It was a week now since the market. A week since Amber hadn't been found with the boys.

Rosie wanted to know whether Gill was going to continue the search. Gill knew Rosie would stay at Newmans as long as she needed her to run things, but she understood that if she wasn't going to go, Rosie and Matt were anxious to return home. Rosie hadn't had any time for Red since she had been running the yard and Gill could completely understand Rosie's need to get her animals back into their routine. Red was young and bored easily, Gill knew Rosie should be concentrating on him.

What Gill didn't understand was Jules. She hadn't been back to work and appeared to intend to continue her full second month's sabbatical, but she hadn't offered to continue searching for Amber. Gill could kind of appreciate Jules' desire to stay with Romeo. Jules had spent her days going for long rides with her horse and her dog. She was in a kind of trance, she hadn't said anything of real substance since her horse had been found, she just spent every waking moment with him.

Gill kept asking herself whether she would go with Jules if it was the other way around. Of course she would. Jules couldn't drive the horsebox and Rosie would be at Newmans to watch over her horses. But while the shoe was on the other foot, Jules seemed to be quite content to allow Gill to spend further nights cold and alone sleeping in the box at soulless service stations and creepy lay-by's.

'I don't know, Rosie. I don't know what to do.'

Rosie nodded. She understood Gill's indecision. Detective North had given her an update when he had telephoned to check a detail in her statement the day after the sale. Farriday was going, 'no comment' all the way and refused to say anything about the horses, refused even, to Detective North's obvious frustration, to confirm his name or address.

Rosie had asked about Eddie. Detective North told her gently he had arrested Mr Gillant and would probably charge him with handling stolen goods. The yard he kept his caravan on, had apparently confirmed the horses had spent a few weeks there and that alone had been enough to charge him. The phone call Rosie had witnessed proving he knew they were stolen added weight to the evidence, and the admission of guilt Eddie had offered in interview would secure his conviction.

Rosie looked up to see Romeo and Jules coming into the yard.

'What's wrong?' Rosie stood up and watched Romeo's short awkward stride.

'He lost a shoe. His feet are so long, I think they were the same shoes he had on when he was taken.'

Gill put the feed scoop down and walked over to Romeo. She ran her hand down his leg and picked up the bare hoof. She studied the tattered sole, ragged from the nails which had ripped through the long feeble horn when the shoe had come off.

She ran her fingers over his heel and felt the blood before she saw it. A tiny puncture wound from a stray nail was slowly oozing thick blood.

She peered closely at the wound and noticed a flash of

shining metal.

'A bit of the nail is still in his heel. Get him in the stable and get a bucket of warm water, put some salt in it and get him to stand with his hoof in the bucket. I'll call Bob now.'

'Thank you,' Jules caught Gill's arm, as she stood up from Romeo's hoof. Tears began to fall from Jules' face. Gill fought not to get annoyed.

'He's fine, it's way away from the pedal bone and it's gone straight up through the fleshy part of the heel. He will be fine.' Gill went to walk away, regretted how harsh she sounded, but Jules clung on to her arm.

'Thank you. Here you are, helping Romeo and … and Amber …' Jules dropped Romeo's reins to cover her face with her hands as tears overcame her.

Gill looked awkwardly at the ground. She wanted to say it was okay, but it was so far from okay, she wasn't sure she could make the right noise to comfort her friend.

Rosie didn't comfort Jules either, just stood in the barn staring blankly at Romeo's foot.

Jules forced her quivering lips together enough to speak.

'It isn't okay, is it? We haven't found Amber. Rosie, your Dad was involved so you must be feeling … well I don't know how you must be feeling, but it must be dreadful. And here I am, I have got my greatest dream come true.' Jules looked at her friends who were looking at each other. For a moment their hard eyes almost confirmed Jules' paranoia, that they both secretly must hate her. But then Gill's eyes softened. It was out in the open.

'I wouldn't ever take Romeo away from you. Of course, I ask every day why he and Monty were found, but Amber wasn't – but I don't resent you, I'm so pleased you found him, you mustn't think I'm not.'

Rosie stepped forward and sighed.

'Look, it's shit. The whole thing sucks. I don't know how to reconcile being related to someone who could do something as low as steal a horse. I don't know how to comfort Gill in a way that would ever take away what she must be feeling. But – the one good thing in all this is that we did find Romeo and Monty.'

Jules nodded, tears still falling but less violently. She was somewhat comforted, but Rosie was right, it was still going to be shit, no matter how much she tried to avoid Gill's gaze and take Romeo out for long rides so her friend didn't have to look at him.

'Get that foot in a bucket!' Gill pointed to Romeo's hoof, which he was clearly not bearing weight on properly.

Jules caught Gill's arm again as she was leaving to phone the vet.

'If your barefoot trimmer is coming today, will he take Romeo's shoes off?'

'I'm sure he will,' Gill replied.

Jules led her horse towards his stable gently. She smoothed the prickly stubble along his chestnut crest, where his mane used to be, before the thieves had attempted to disguise him by crudely shaving it off.

She hoped Romeo wouldn't be lame for very long. She knew she had to go home to her house sooner rather than later. She hadn't left Newmans, from a mixture of not wanting to desert Gill and not wanting to be alone in her house to miss Tristan. But she had Romeo back, the joy of his warm skin beneath her hand, his solid back beneath the saddle. It would, she decided today out on her ride, be enough to get her through. Plus she didn't want to rub Gill's nose in it any longer.

'Let's ride out together?'

'What?'

‘Come on – my parents had a cob on their farm, I used to ride him quite a lot.’

Gill eyed George, who had his hand on Monty’s nose. She had been about to suggest he move it, before it got nipped.

‘You ride?’ Gill was aghast. George had never mentioned he could ride. She supposed, looking back, he had seemed to know more about horses than you would expect the average chef to know.

‘Well, a bit. Not brilliantly, but I have heard you talk about how good Monty is.’ George smiled up at the black stallion, who had taken pity on George and was nudging his shoulder rather than attempting to remove his fingers in search of a polo.

Gill considered for a second. She wouldn’t usually have allowed someone she hadn’t already seen ride and trusted, onto a client’s horse – let alone one of Norah’s horses. But something about his relaxed attitude to riding intrigued her, a little bit of her wanted to knock his blaze approach down a few pegs. It was Sunday and George had called round to see her. With Kelly off, Jules still in bed and Rosie out for the day with Matt, she decided it would save her a few hours if she could get two horses out together.

Gill tacked up Monty and Milly, while George tried on hats from the collection under the saddle rack. He found one which fitted and Gill tried not to snigger at the sight of him in an old fashioned velvet helmet.

She handed Monty’s reins to George.

‘Lead him outside, I’ll grab Milly then help you get on.’

George nodded and took the stallion’s reins. When he moved forwards, Monty walked with him.

Gill slid her own hat over her blonde hair and opened Milly’s stable door.

By the time she led the mare out into the winter sunshine;

George had already mounted Monty and sat looking uncomfortable with stirrups which were miles too short.

Gill laughed at him until he asked her to stop teasing him and give him a hand. She clipped a rope from the tie up ring on the side of the barn to Milly's noseband and walked over to lengthen the leathers and make George more comfortable.

Once his legs were in a better position, Gill sprang onto Milly and asked George if he was ready. George nodded and swung both legs away from Monty's sides to flap them back against the saddle.

'Stop!' Gill cried just before George's legs made contact with the sensitive Arabian's belly. 'He is not your parent's old cob – you kick him, you'll be off!'

'Oh,' George said, somewhat deflated, he had thought he was about to impress Gill with his masculine control of the big animal.

'Every time you ask him to do something, you need to whisper.'

Gill moved Milly close enough to demonstrate, whilst keeping the mare at enough of a distance not to excite Monty, who was beginning to look slightly bored.

'To ask him to walk on squeeze gently with both legs, only a minimal amount of pressure to keep him at the speed you want him. When you want to stop, relax your legs and squeeze the reins lightly.' Gill demonstrated with Milly, who, to her relief, did stop from a light touch on her bit, instead of fighting.

'Lots of squeezing then!' George laughed and Gill rolled her eyes. They moved off at a steady walk down the drive. Gill couldn't help but be impressed by the natural seat George had, he moved fluidly in time with Monty's walk without having to try too hard. She wondered how he would look dancing. How those fluid hips might feel against her body. She told herself to stop it.

Gill kept off the Killerton Estate and bridle paths and took George on a leisurely hack around the quiet lanes surrounding Stoke Rewe. While she was impressed with his natural ability, she didn't think he was ready for anything faster than a walk, especially not on such a valuable animal. If Gill had been riding Amber instead of Milly she might have been more confident about her ability to rescue George, or Monty, if they got into trouble. Amber always seemed to know when there was a job to do and it made her responsive to Gill on a level which was almost telepathic. Milly, on the other hand would simply get excited and lose her head if Monty were to become out of control. Gill knew she would never find another horse like Amber.

As they rode together, they talked about Gill's dilemma. George offered to get a temporary chef in at the restaurant so he could go with her to continue the search for Amber. She blushed, touched by his offer, but quickly declined. Her brows knitted briefly, thinking that George, a relative stranger, had offered to go with her, but Jules had not.

Gill looked across at George, who had turned his head to look over the hedgerow and across the fields from the vantage point Monty's height offered. She suddenly regretted making George feel silly about his offer by shrugging it off so quickly.

'The trouble is, even if I went, it doesn't solve the problem at the yard. It's my business; it's what pays the bills. I can't allow it to limp along indefinitely. People will start pulling their horses if they don't get the training they are paying for. Even the liveries seem distant, I know they all like Rosie but she isn't there all day like I am. She and Kelly alone can't offer the same level of attention. Even the ones who don't pay for full livery still rely on me if they can't make it to the yard and for the little things I do for the horses without really thinking.'

George turned back to face Gill, his hands resting on Monty's neck, giving him a slack rein to walk along at a relaxed pace.

'If you did stay, worked at the business and kept your customer's happy, would it mean you had to stop looking for Amber altogether?'

Gill had been viewing the dilemma in black and white up until now, but George's words gave her a lifeline, a way to stay at Newmans without drowning in guilt.

'What, you mean stay but still attend some of the bigger sales?'

'Yes. And you can still search on the internet, make regular calls to the police?'

'Hmm,' Gill stared at the lane ahead of them, her view framed by Milly's dainty grey ears. She had known in her heart for a few days that she would have to stay at Newmans and run the business properly. After two months of the bare necessities being done, there was a mountain of work around the barn in addition to the needs of the horses and the looming race season. There was also the matter of the loan from her brother. She knew Mike would never ask her for the five-grand, but that made the guilt she felt owing it to him worse.

Gill smiled at George, he had given her a way to reconcile staying. She would never remove the aching feeling in the pit of her stomach that she was letting Amber down, but she could provide it with a remedy by continuing the search on a smaller scale. It dawned on her momentarily that she had been angry with Charlie for suggesting what was, more or less, the same thing.

'Right!' George shortened Monty's reins and sat up straight. 'I'm ready to find out if I can still rise to the trot!'

'Let's hope so for Monty's sake!'

Jules looked out of her bedroom window to see Gill and a man riding up the drive. Peering through the glass, she realised it was George. She smiled, delighted to see Gill was laughing. Maybe today was a good day to go home.

Romeo's foot was healing well. The vet had removed the small shard of worn nail from the gelding's heel after the portable x-ray machine had confirmed it was not near to any of the delicate bones within the hoof wall and could be extracted manually. She was dressing his hoof with a fresh poultice each day to stave off any infection which could lead to a painful and slow healing abscess. Romeo was sound now and starting to get bored. At least his stable at Maurice's farm overlooked the small field used for the fattening cows and the big open farmyard which was gated and full of calves who were wintering in. She had always appreciated the view from Romeo's stable and she decided it was time they both enjoyed it again.

Jules had already telephoned Maurice, who had readily agreed to modify Romeo's stable door, to accommodate a padlock and agreed he could be turned out with the cows in the secure field, which was overlooked by the farmhouse. He had been more reluctant to agree to chaining the front gates at the bottom of the farm drive shut, due to the inconvenience it would cause when going in and out with the tractor.

Jules decided there was no time like the present. She couldn't stay at Newmans forever. She couldn't put off being at the house alone; she needed to do it now while the bright light of finding Romeo was still shining on her.

Jules walked towards the barn with Ziggy at her feet.

'Hi, Gill.'

Gill stopped explaining about racehorse nutrition to an apparently quite interested George and put down the feed scoop when she saw the serious expression on Jules' face.

'Hi, Jules!' George greeted her.

Jules decided to come straight out with it.

'Romeo is looking much better and … Jules bit her lip and steeled herself to say it, '… and I think it's time for me to go home.'

Gill might have reacted to the news differently first thing this morning, but after her ride with George and the compromise she had reached with herself, she didn't feel angry with Jules.

'You need to start rebuilding your life. I understand. Want me to take him over to the farm now?'

'Would you?' Jules stepped forward and hugged her friend.

Although their embrace was genuine, a warmth that might never return was lacking. Although neither spoke, both were aware of the divide between them.

Gill moved quickly around the kitchen, unpacking the dishwasher and wiping the surfaces with unnecessary vigour. She was very conscious of the fact that, although George had been around quite a lot lately and on the whole she was comfortable with him, this was the first time they had been in the house alone together.

She tried desperately not to make eye contact, or even to look in the direction of the tall man who sat quite still across the kitchen from her. She could feel his eyes on her. It was as though they were making invisible imprints on her skin, which electrified her body against her will.

She knew he had purposely stayed until Jules had left, knew why without asking why. He had helped with Jules' belongings and travelled in the box with Gill. On the pretence of providing some muscle for the move, he provided Gill with support in his quiet persistent way.

Rosie had telephoned shortly after they had returned to

Newmans without Jules, to say she and Matt would be staying away overnight and asking Gill to see to Red and Harry. Gill hadn't asked for details, Rosie needed space at the moment.

She didn't know what to do. His silence was frustrating. He was still here, but he wasn't saying or doing anything and although the thought terrified her, she wished he would just make a move, so she could tell him he was too young and it wasn't going to happen. She wondered if he thought she was a tease, he had put so many hours in. He just never seemed to push it to that inevitable point where she knocked him back.

Gill was experiencing so many things, from an acutely painful mixture of joy at the return of Romeo and Monty and total devastation that Amber had not been recovered. She was lonely without Charlie, and pleased for Jules, now that she had gone home. Somehow though, she thought how foolish it was to get involved with someone so young, how guilty she would feel about allowing her basal desires to rule her actions, but the voice within her just wouldn't quite speak loudly enough in her head to make her ask him to leave.

'Are you going to look at me?' his beautiful voice came softly across the counter.

Gill looked up sharply, surprised at the demand.

She made eye contact with him, brief and charged, before shyly lowering her gaze. She wondered if it was some kind of bet. Had the lads from the village challenged him to pull the old bag who ran the horse yard? He seemed quite different from the relaxed friendly George she had ridden out with and talked about her problems to. He was more intense, more demanding, even in silence.

She sighed; she had indulged in his game long enough.

'What are you doing here, George?' Gill rested her elbows on the table and allowed herself to stare at the exquisite face and deep green eyes, drinking in his masculinity. 'Why exactly are you here all the time?'

'You know.'

'I don't. I know you're eleven years younger than me and I know you are very handsome and could have pretty much any girl you wanted.'

'None of them would compare to you.' George reached his hand across the counter towards her. She didn't take it.

'Look, if you are having some Mrs Robinson episode, go and find some other miserable old woman. I really don't have anything to offer you, George.'

'Why do you assume I want anything from you? Why do you think I need anything more than to be near you?'

'Oh right, so if I said lets jump into bed right now, you would refuse?' Gill felt the slightest tinge of excitement prick up the hairs on the back of her neck.

'I'd hesitate.'

'Oh charming.'

'Because,' George continued speaking as he moved quietly from the stool and around the counter to stand in front of her, 'you miss Amber, Jules has moved out today, you are emotional and if I took advantage of you now it wouldn't mean anything.'

His proximity to her was like a tangible force. Her resolve was weakened as she felt the warmth of his strong body, his breath on her face, the clear need for her which oozed from his every pore, despite his sensible words.

'And what if being taken advantage of is exactly what I need right now?'

George was torn between the overwhelming urge to kiss the beautiful and damaged force of nature before him and the desire to do the right thing.

'What if I need to escape?' Gill stared into his longing eyes and made the decision for him. Stepping so close their bodies touched, she moved her hands to his face, caressing the stubbled cheek and square jaw line she had so often found herself unconsciously contemplating. She stood on tiptoes to meet her lips to his and let the spark of first contact surge through her.

Any control she had in making the first move was instantly lost when his arms wound around her like lightening and his eager lips moved firm around her own, disarming her in terrifying waves.

She allowed herself to be carried in his arms through to living room, where the fire glowed red like a caged animal within the confines of the wood burner. He walked her to the sofa, where he laid her so gently. He kissed her more softly this time, allowing her to explore him.

Gill's inhibitions slipped away as she kissed him. To feel something other than loneliness, other than a sad longing, made her alive again.

Before she had time to remember her usual prudence, she was ripping his T-shirt over his head. She pushed him back from where he knelt beside the sofa and climbed astride him on the floor. With a passion he had not expected, and she had not known was within her, she all but devoured him.

Gill was freezing when she woke. The living room smelled pungently of sex. Clothes were strewn about the floor. The fire had gone out.

She sat up and looked at the naked man beside her. A ripple of pleasure coursed through her, as she drank in the gently tanned taut body.

She reached for her jumper and quickly raked it over her head to cover her breasts. What on earth could he possibly want with her? Their charged writhing encounter had probably been the most exciting and gratifying of her life. He would surely view it simply as another conquest in a long line. He was positively gorgeous and she was so old, how could she be so naive?

'Get up,' she snapped, shoving the defined bicep of his left arm.

He smiled up at her as he awoke and enjoyed the delicious recollection of finally having made love to her. His smile faded fast when he saw the scorn in her eyes. If only he could have known the disgust her downturned mouth portrayed was for herself and not for him, he might not have felt so utterly destroyed.

'Time to go.'

She pulled her jumper down to cover herself as she stood up and left the room, leaving George, bewildered, to dress and make his exit.

Gill lay in the dark, wide-eyes staring for a ceiling she couldn't make out. It was the first time she had been alone at the house. There had always been Charlie, then there had been Jules and then Jules and Rosie and Matt. She missed Ziggy. He would often nose her bedroom door open in the night, long after Jules had fallen sound asleep he would comfort Gill as she laid awake for endless hours tortured by thoughts of Amber. Now everyone had gone. And this was going to be her life.

She crossed her arms over her stomach, hugged her body and desperately tried to fight off the physical memory of George. Her body betrayed her. Warmth spread between her legs and her nipples hardened. She hated herself for crying. Tears slid over her temples and made her shiver, as they wetted her ears and hair. Why had she kicked him out?

On the other side of the large hill, which rose up from Exeter and descended into Kysford, Jules couldn't sleep either. She wandered around the house. The decor and belongings, once so familiar, seemed alien. Tristan had taken his clothes and personal possessions, but the photos of the two of them which hung in each room, were still there. So were the things they had bought together. She couldn't bring herself to sit on the sofa they had argued about the choice of so much. Didn't want to sleep in what had been their bed.

She had stayed with Romeo at the farm for so long she was chilled to the bone and exhausted. She wondered if she could get a baby monitor with a long enough signal range to listen to him in his stable. She had snapped the padlocks tight and tried not to think about the uncapped hinges of the gates, which could easily have been lifted off by a determined thief. She made a mental note to call Janet tomorrow for Horsewatch's advice on security.

Jules stood in the hallway looking at a photo of herself with Tristan at a butterfly sanctuary which they had visited during a holiday in New Zealand. Tristan was laughing as a swarm of bright-blue butterflies landed on her coat. She looked down at Ziggy, who stood beside her, loyally not leaving her side, his eyelids weighed heavily and his paws almost slid out beneath him.

She decided to sleep in the spare room.

The guard looked at Rosie without emotion. He must have seen hundreds of women visiting their lovers, fathers and brothers, with that same desperate look in their eyes.

Rosie had been surprised when Eddie had agreed to see her. She sat on the plastic seat in the waiting room nervously. Her desperation was not for the man she was about to see, it was for the information he might hold.

Matt had driven her to Reading the day before. They had

booked into a small hotel when they had been told the visiting order would take twenty-four hours to process.

They hadn't told anyone where they were going; Rosie hadn't wanted to build Gill's hopes up in case Eddie had refused her application.

Rosie tried to breathe through her mouth. The smell of disinfectant clung in her nostrils, making her want to retch. The large metal doors which locked securely on contact with their solid frames, made her feel trapped. She couldn't imagine having to spend time in a place like this. A wave of fear washed over her.

What would it take? A car accident, you could so easily be driving a long in a hurry, minding your own business, thinking about other things and hit someone. Could so easily end up in a place like this, without even being a conscious criminal. Rosie vowed never to text whilst driving again. She thought back to all those times she had rolled a cigarette in the car, steering with her knees and salivating at the thought of the first drag.

She had allowed herself the occasional roll-up since the sale. Matt must have smelled it on her, but he didn't comment on her guilty secret. The odd one here and there could so easily descend into a full on habit and she cursed her weakness.

'Rosie Hall,' the guard called, not looking up from his paperwork.

He pointed to a door to his left. It made a buzzing noise and clicked open as Rosie took hold of the handle. She walked into a small room and was faced with a grey shell of man.

'Rosie.'

Eddie said her name like the word itself contained an entire universe within its two syllables.

'Rosie, baby, you shouldn't be here. I don't think they can have realised you are a witness in my case or they wouldn't have let you come. You need to go or you could get into trouble.'

Rosie had expected recrimination or anger, perhaps a plea for her not to give evidence against him; she had not expected him to worry about her.

'I need to talk to you first – it's important.'

Rosie sat down and Eddie gingerly held his hand out to her, looking into her eyes praying the hate he dreaded wouldn't be there. Rosie looked at his hand.

'I can't, I am sorry,' said Rosie, colder than she had intended. She was torn between the obvious biological connection they both appeared to feel and the fact that he was a horse thief.

'It's okay, I didn't expect you to. Eddie hung his head. 'I need you to know something Rosie. I need you to know, I didn't steal those horses.'

Rosie raised her eyebrows, as she looked pointedly around the small visiting room of the remand centre.

'Yes, point taken. I only ever looked after horses for short periods. I knew they weren't legit, of course I did, I'm not denying that and I won't deny it in court. But I never set out to steal. I was just trying to make some extra money, however I could. I know it was wrong and if I had any idea I had a daughter out there somewhere, someone else besides me to care about, I would never have done it.'

'How can you know that?' Rosie hadn't intended to get into a discussion about the ins and outs of Eddie's involvement, but his words infuriated her. 'If that was the case, you would have told me in that café. You would have come clean, not slunk away and tried to cover your tracks?'

'I didn't want you to find out. I didn't want to lose you the same day I found you. I know that was selfish now.'

'If you knew me, you would know I would have admired the courage it took. I might have been shocked and angry at first, but I would have seen it for what it was if you had come clean, something brave and honourable. But you don't know me. You don't know me at all.'

'And I won't now, will I?'

It was Rosie's turn to hang her head. She couldn't maintain eye contact with him. She knew he was right, knew the chance for any kind of relationship would forever be lost in the knotted tension of the current situation, however much time passed.

'It's okay, I would hate me too.'

Rosie looked sharply back at Eddie.

'Don't make assumptions about me. I help homeless people, troubled people, even people coming out of prison. I learnt long ago that good people find themselves in bad situations. I'm not some spoilt brat with a closed mind. My mother made sure of that.'

Eddie was taken aback by Rosie's words. He had sensed from their conversation in the café that her childhood had not exactly been a bed of roses, but he had no idea it had been caused by Selina, a woman he had thought himself so unworthy of.

'What did she do, Rosie?' Eddie's face was full of concern.

'It doesn't matter; it's all water under the bridge now. Let's just say her affair with you set her off on a pretty destructive path and leave it at that.'

'Likewise.' Eddie's brown eyes conveyed the meaning of his word.

Rosie grew impatient. She didn't hate him, but she was finding him difficult to look at. The memory of what he had been part of washed away the affection which might have been there otherwise.

'I came to see you today because I wanted to ask you about the other mare.'

Eddie's response was the one she had dreaded, the one which

made her trip and the trouble she could be in for making it, pointless.

'What mare?'

'There was a third horse taken with the stallion and the gelding, my friend Gill's horse. She was an Arab mare, chestnut.'

Eddie's gaze swam loosely around, as he thought. Rosie waited.

'You know I only looked after the horses a few weeks don't you – you do know, I didn't take them?'

'Her name is Amber.' Rosie's eyes hardened. Part of her couldn't have cared less whether he had taken the horses himself or not, knowing, being involved – that was enough.

'Look. Being mixed up in this kind of thing means being mixed up with some pretty dangerous people, you don't ask questions. I don't know much, honestly Rosie, I don't … But I did overhear something, when the two horses were at my yard.'

'Well?'

Rosie looked desperate and Eddie prayed conveying the information wouldn't land him in even more trouble with Farriday. There would be enough when it came out in court that he had led Rosie straight to the horses.

'I heard Farriday talking about a mare. He said she was too high profile, too much of a liability, so he had sold her on quickly and got a bad price. Presumably to someone who would lie low with her. I don't know any more than that.'

'Honestly?' Rosie's eyes challenged him to be truthful.

'Honestly, that's all I know.'

Rosie's head sank and she gripped her forehead with her fingertips, pressing her flesh until it went white beneath the pressure.

'And Farriday has gone completely no comment, so we'll never find her.'

'Never say never, you found the others.' Eddie put a hand out to try and ease Rosie's hands from their grip on her head. Under better circumstances Eddie might have been able to tell her it was a habit he recognised.

Rosie drew back quickly, away from his touch.

'Thank you. Thanks for seeing me.' Rosie slid her chair back from the table. Eddie stood up too and moved towards her.

'Don't go so soon.'

'Don't ask me, to stay.'

Rosie felt so awful, leaving her father in this cage like some animal; she paused, despite herself, to briefly squeeze his arm as she passed him.

He listened to the door being opened behind him, but he couldn't watch her go. He held his arm where she had touched him and stood there, not moving, until a guard came to take him back to his cell.

Chapter fifteen

Gill stared down at her phone.

The blank 'create text' screen, stared back at her, offering no inspiration.

She wanted to text George. Desperately. But what on earth would she say. So sorry I ate you alive and then kicked you out?

She hadn't heard from him and as she waited alone at Newmans for Rosie and Matt to come back from their trip, she realised how much she missed his morning text. She knew after their encounter, there was no chance of him popping in to Newmans as he had often done lately, but that hadn't stopped her having half-an-ear-out for his car all day.

She didn't want to leave things like this. Didn't want him to feel used. So ironic, after months of being convinced he would be the one using her.

He had been nothing but honest and open with her and she needed to afford the same back. She typed out the message and sent it quickly, before she could change her mind.

> Really sorry for acting like a bitch.
> Bit of a mess at the moment

Gill stuffed her mobile back into her pocket, picked up the glass of wine beside her on the kitchen counter and tried to continue reading the Arab Horse Society Newsletter in front of her.

Less than a minute had passed before she got her mobile out again and checked the sent items to make sure the message had gone.

She set the mobile on the counter beside her and continued to try and read an article about racing. She had been delighted when she saw the large advertisement on the back page appealing for information about Monty and Amber. The newsletter had gone to print before there had been time to remove Monty from the advert, but it didn't matter too much, the main thing was that Amber was in there.

Gill was grateful when she heard the front door open. Matt and Rosie came in with their overnight bags and Gill put the kettle on. She was eager to chat to them, hear about their trip, so she could stop watching her phone for a reply that might never come.

'It's okay, Gill, I don't want one. I've got some work to get on with for tomorrow.' Matt said, and headed upstairs.

Gill sensed they were purposely being left alone.

Rosie sat at the counter. Her brown eyes looked unusually puffy.

'What's up Rosie, did you have a bad trip?'

Rosie nodded, her lip quivered.

'Is Jimmy all right?' Gill pulled a stool close to Rosie and laid a reassuring hand on her shoulder.

'I didn't go to see Jimmy.'

'Well, where did you go?'

'Other Dad.'

'Oh, Rosie.' Gill put her arms around her friend as, unusually for Rosie, small dignified tears swam from her eyes.

'I want my Mum,' Rosie whispered. 'Not *my* mum obviously, but if I had a proper mum, I could go to her.'

Gill tightened her embrace and laid a hand on Rosie's curly hair, cradling her head.

'I love you, Rosie. I'm here.'

Rosie drew back suddenly. She reached for the kitchen roll and dragged a wad of the course paper over her sensitive skin, composing herself.

Gill sat back on the stool.

'I went to see him in this remand centre. It was awful. All these men liked caged animals and I had to leave him there, knowing after the trial I probably won't ever see him again because of what he did. Knowing what he's done to you and Jules.'

'Why Rosie – why would you put yourself through that?' Gill brushed Rosie's cheek with the back of her hand. It broke her heart to see someone so logical, someone who was a rock to all that knew her, so distraught. Someone so strong and so just, she would always take the most difficult path, the right path – feeling it her duty. Gill knew the answer before Rosie spoke.

'To ask him where Amber was.'

Gill bit her lip. Gratitude rose up within her. She waited with baited breath for Rosie to continue.

'He doesn't know.' Rosie barely finished her sentence before the tears fell again.

Later, Rosie went to bed, drained and weak from crying. She slept deeply almost instantly, thankfully without dreams.

Gill sat on the stool, which was starting to feel like it had moulded to the shape of her bottom. She just didn't have the heart to go into the living room where the smell of George might linger.

She tried not to think about what Rosie had told her. That Eddie had overheard a conversation which suggested Amber had been sold on cheaply. What did that mean? Would someone who could do that look after a mare? If you hadn't paid much, would you care about the horse?

Gill had told Rosie she had decided to stay at Newmans, so she and Matt could at last go home. Rosie was torn between delight and relief. Gill insisted. Rosie offered to come and stay whenever Gill wanted to go to a sale, or if any more intelligence came to light meaning Gill had somewhere to look.

Gill looked at her phone. Still no reply. She needed to escape from what she had learned about Amber, to escape from the unyielding certainty releasing Rosie had placed on her. She had to stay now; the search was more or less over. She glanced at the clock on the microwave. 11:30pm. George would just be finishing up at the restaurant.

Gill stood behind the Barton Mill. She watched the back door which was illuminated by an outside light. She thought that she must look a mess in her work jeans, army green trainers and a padded coat, which smelled faintly of horse wee. She wished she had changed and tucked further in towards the hedge and the darkness. She didn't even know if he would come out this way. If he went out of the front of the restaurant and headed straight for home, she would miss him.

Minutes passed. Gill grew colder. She was just about to give up and go home, when she heard voices and saw the door open. Suddenly scared at the prospect of seeing George's staff, she pressed herself into the hedge. She hadn't bargained on other people.

She heard George saying goodnight, laughing with the waitresses who hurried away towards their cars. She peered around the hawthorn of the hedge and saw him locking the door and padlocking the security chain. Now was the time. Now was when she should go over to him. Now Gill! The voice screamed in her head. She couldn't do it. She turned to hurry back to her car but the hawthorn snagged at her cheek, making her yelp.

'Whose there?' George called, assertive, alert to an intruder.

Gill put her hand to her face and saw blood on her fingertips; a thorn was embedded in the skin under her eye. She would have to give it up, she heard George's footsteps coming towards her and she moved out in the lane away from the hawthorn into the light.

'It's me,' she tried to sound bright, 'it's Gill.'

George's face fell. She felt sick when she saw the anger in his eyes. Then he noticed her bloodied face and his expression changed.

Without speaking, he guided her back to the restaurant and unlocked the door again. He ushered her inside and sat her down on the sofa in the foyer area and went to fetch the first aid kit.

'I'm fine, George, really,' Gill called after him but he ignored her protest.

He returned and opened the first aid kit on the coffee table in front of her. Using tweezers he gently prized the thorn from her cheek and set about bathing and cleaning her bloodied face.

Gill bit her lip, the alcohol wipe stung. His face was so close to hers as he sat concentrating on her minor wounds. He moved his hand away to discard the wipe and she leaned forward quickly to kiss him. He drew away and glared at her.

'George ... I'm sorry.' Gill's eyes clouded in frustration at his rejection. They weren't married; it wasn't even a proper relationship. Surely he had been relieved to be excused from any mandatory cuddling after the act last night? Most men would be?

'Last night you couldn't get rid of me fast enough and now you're skulking around in the dark outside my restaurant and injuring yourself in the process.'

'I ...' Gill didn't really know what to say.

'Do you have any idea how I feel? You used me.'

'Used?' Gill almost laughed.

'You all but threw yourself at me and when you finished with me you just ejected me from your house! Don't you get it? Don't understand how I feel about you? I'm not in this for sex!'

'Not even really great sex?' Gill's eyes twinkled and she giggled, trying to lighten the mood, not wanting to hear George's proclamations, not yet, she wasn't ready.

For a moment George looked hurt, pain shone from green eyes and she thought he was going to ask her to leave.

'One step at a time George, let's just have fun for a while? I'm not in a good place right now, I don't want us to get serious when I am such a mess, and it wouldn't be fair on either of us? I freaked out last night and it wasn't fair on you.'

George's expression changed at her use of the word serious. He took it as a positive, despite the context.

'So you just want me for really great sex?'

'And your company.'

'For now.'

'Just for the time being.'

Jules glanced up from the letter 'before action' she was drafting on behalf of a client and looked at the photograph of Romeo. She grinned inanely at the chestnut horse's beautiful face staring back at her from the silver frame. Knowing he was at the farm with Maurice and Ziggy. Knowing at 5:30 she would be able to drive home and he would be there, whickering for his dinner. She could touch him, could talk to him. The feeling filled and completed her.

It was a month since Romeo had been returned and there

was still no sign of Amber. Gill was throwing herself into the yard and it seemed she was coping, perhaps even moving on. George was playing a part in her ability to deal with losing her horse. Jules smiled at how happy he made Gill, even though Gill would never admit it and always played things down.

Rosie was working hard with Red and seemed to be dealing with her father's impending trial with a strength Jules knew she couldn't have mustered herself.

The days grew longer and riding after work was on the cards again. She wondered if she could squeeze a quick ride in tonight if she missed the traffic that would save her having to walk Ziggy; they could all go out together for a quick sunset hack across Maurice's sweeping fields. Delight at the prospect of riding, puffed out her heart, there was no one to cook for or rush home to. February was dry, the daylight extended further by clear ice-blue skies.

Jules looked down at her file and realised she'd been in a daydream for about ten minutes. She had a lot to do before the afternoon, when she was due in court.

It was a hearing on a case where her client was suing his ex-business partner. The client ran a stud on Exmoor breeding native ponies and the business partner had mis-sold a number of ponies before leaving the business to pick up the pieces and compensate disgruntled buyers.

Since Romeo had been returned, Jules had become a force to be reckoned with at work once again. She had suggested a specialism in equine related litigation, and David had agreed to her idea with open arms. At the partner's say so, the marketing office had done the rest. Now she had a bank of clients with horse related litigation issues and her knowledge made her a passionate representative. She fought for compensation when a loaned horse was returned to its owner in a terrible condition; she acted for a saddle fitter accused of damaging a horse's back when the fault clearly laid with a negligent yard manager. She still had enough non-equine work to meet her fee targets, which allowed her to choose carefully the cases she took on, acting primarily in the interests of the horses themselves and only taking on just causes, although she didn't admit that to David.

Thankfully, word of mouth alone was now creating lots of new clients and David was talking about hiring a junior solicitor to assist her. She had heard rumours that she would be offered a partnership in the firm next year.

She finished drafting her letter and checked her emails. There was an email from Gill suggesting dinner at Newmans that Friday. Matt would be at conference, so Rosie had already confirmed she would come and they could have a girl's night, just the three of them. Jules replied hastily saying she would love to, before dashing out of the office calling goodbye to her secretary as she went.

'It's still bloody hard.'

Gill stared into the fire. The three women had spent an enjoyable evening, dining on roast chicken. It was really the only thing Gill could cook with any confidence, but earlier that day with George's help, she had added a few additional herbs and a caramelised parsnip accompaniment, which had transformed the meal into something much more special than the usual overcooked carrots and dry meat.

Wine had flowed along with laughter while they ate, but as they curled up on the sofas enjoying the heat from the wood burner, the conversation turned more serious.

'It's bound to be.' Jules smiled sympathetically at her friend, much like the guilt Rosie felt for her father's involvement, the guilt Jules felt about having Romeo back might never fully subside – would always place a strain on the relationship. Jules wondered quietly, if things would ever be the same, no matter how much Gill appeared to be getting over it.

'It's still bloody hard,' Gill said again, 'but it isn't like it was. It's better.'

Rosie was sat beside her and she leant over to kiss her friend on the cheek.

'You're doing really well, Gill. I'm proud of you.'

'I would feel proud too, if I didn't feel so guilty. Every time I have an hour or so where I don't think about Amber, the benefit of not feeling miserable for that time gets cancelled out by how rotten I feel for forgetting her.'

'You'll never forget her. She will always be in your heart,' said Jules.

Gill gave Jules a resigned smile, but a smile nonetheless, before deciding to change the subject. She started talking about Renashee and how he had bucked her and Kelly off in the school that week.

'I can't believe a horse that is so laid back in the field, moves that fast in the school. The first time I sat on him, he walked round like a lamb, didn't bat an eyelid, but now as soon as me or Kelly ask for anything a bit faster than a walk, he goes off like lightening and throws in these whopping great bucks! I think I should have done more lunging with him. I'm going to have to go back to basics and teach the silly bugger the gaits between painfully slow walk and rocket. If you're on him he takes 'trot on' to mean go like hell!'

'Huh,' Rosie sighed impatiently and rolled her eyes.

'What?' Gill exclaimed, making Ziggy wake up and gaze up at her from his position sprawled across her lap. The dog had made a beeline for Gill as soon as she sat down.

'What indeed ...' Rosie shook her head.

'No seriously, what?' Gill was genuinely perplexed by Rosie's displeasure.

'Never mind bloody race horses, we want to hear about George.'

Matt woke to the sound of Rosie dressing frantically, having overslept, and stretched before rolling over to go back to sleep. 'It's good to be back home,' he mumbled.

'It's good, but I seem to have gone straight back to normal.' Rosie pulled on a pair of socks. She felt the cold floor on her heel as she went to leave the bedroom. Seeing a huge hole she tore the socks off in disgust and threw them towards the bin before rummaging in the drawer for a more complete pair. Matt sat up, blurry-eyed.

'Yes, but when we were at Gills' you were tired all the time, and stressed. The horses don't mind waiting a bit longer for breakfast – it's nice you're relaxed enough to sleep in!'

Rosie laughed and sat on the bed next to her husband, giving in to how late she was already. It was Sunday morning. Matt had returned in the small hours the night before, after his conference, exhausted.

Matt put an arm around Rosie, she hugged him back. She took his quiet easy going nature for indifference sometimes, but she understood she was very lucky to have him. His support might not have been vocalised into long discussions about feelings, but it was unwavering and rock solid.

'Matt …'

'Yes, darling.' Matt raised his eyebrows, recognising from the tone Rosie was about to say something more serious than 'get up and put the coffee on'.

'You know how I always said I didn't want to think about

having a family until Red was older and his training was finished and he could afford some time off being ridden. And that we needed to get the cottage redecorated and sorted and save up before we could even think about children?'

'Yes.'

'All this stuff with my Dad and with Jimmy, and even with the horses and now being home, I feel different somehow, about everything, older I guess.'

'Rosie get to the point,' said Matt, and he ruffled his wife's knotted bed-hair, mocking her inability to get to where she was going with the conversation.

'Well maybe, maybe, stuff planning everything to the enth degree. Maybe I want us to have a baby.'

Matt's gaze fell to the duvet covering his legs. His face tightened ever so slightly.

'Are we ready though? Will we be good at it?'

'I don't know – don't think we will know until we take the plunge.'

'I love you and it would be nice to have a child, little version of me and you ... but you have always talked like it was way off in the distance – if at all – I might need some time to get used to the idea.'

'Oh, of course!' Rosie put her arms around him. She had half expected him to say, 'yeah, okay', make jokes about all the sex they would have to have and not really think about it too much, but she was genuinely pleased he was taking it seriously and wanted to be sure.

'What if it's ugly?' Rosie giggled.

'What if it gets on our nerves?'

'I probably won't be that interested until it's old enough to help me pooh pick.'

'Shall we just give it to my mum until it's out of nappies and it can talk?' Matt laughed and Rosie rolled her eyes. Matt's mother had been hinting about grandchildren since their wedding day.

'I'll ring her now shall I – Hi, Joan, we're thinking about having a baby could you bring it up for us?'

'She'll be delighted!' The hilarity faded as their eyes met.

Matt pulled Rosie on top of him and kissed her neck. He pushed his hips upwards so that she could feel his erection through the duvet.

'Let's make it now,' Matt whispered into her ear.

'I thought you wanted to think about it!' Rosie struggled to place her hands on the bed to push herself up but he grabbed her wrists and rolled on top of her.

'Get your jeans off.'

'You are mad!'

'Jeans.'

'I haven't even stopped taking the pill yet.'

'Practice makes perfect, Mrs Hall.'

'My poor horses.'

'I'll be quick!'

It wasn't during one of their passionate love making sessions where she reached heights of pleasure she hadn't dreamed possible. It wasn't when he brought home lovingly prepared food which he called left-over's for her, after he finished a shift, knowing she wasn't sleeping and wouldn't have eaten anything. It wasn't when he sat with her at the kitchen counter and the pleasure he derived simply from watching her eat, shone in those green eyes. It wasn't even when he mucked in with the horses and made Kelly laugh and Gill feel safe. It wasn't any of those things that made her realise she loved him.

It was a morning she woke up and he wasn't beside her. She

could hear him downstairs clattering about in the kitchen, probably preparing something delectable for breakfast. She was content knowing he was down there, not going anywhere. In fact he was decidedly hard to get rid of, even when she thought they were taking things too fast. Gill imagined the cottage without George. She imagined losing him when she could still feel the loss of Amber like an open wound. She imagined not feeling the security of his adoration and the certainty of his persistence to be with her as often as he could be. Gill suddenly felt a desperate need for him to hold her.

'George,' she called, her voice carrying through the open door and down to the kitchen. Something in the way she had said his name saw George running up the stairs full tilt, but he didn't manage to reach her before she started to cry.

He held her and rocked her, not asking questions, making no demands for explanation at her sudden emotional outburst.

Gill took hold of George's shoulders and pushed him back, so that they were face to face.

'I swore. I swore the night Alex left that that was it. I swore I would not let myself go again.'

She gave a snotty sniff, the tirade of emotion caused her blue eyes to shine and brighten, the door to her soul unusually wide open.

'I won't hurt you.'

'No, let me finish,' Gill shook her head resolutely. 'What I am trying to say is it doesn't follow any logic and you're far too young for me and I had decided this was a fling and I was just missing Amber. But it's real isn't it?'

George nodded slowly. A warm rich smile spread across his face, his world completed by the realisation she had finally made.

'Its complete madness, but I love you.'

It was George's turn to feel overcome with emotion. He wrapped his strong arms around her and she returned his embrace. They rocked gently as they clung to each other, both holding on too tightly as though the strength in their locked bodies could solidify their feelings. He drew his head back to plant kisses over her forehead in showers. He had told her he loved her so many times, only to be dismissed with a patronising kiss on the cheek or even laughter. In waves of overwhelming certainty, his love for this remarkable woman was finally requited.

It was hard to part when George had to leave to open up the restaurant later in the morning. They stood holding one another at the front door until George was so late it would cost him customers.

'I'll come back straight after service.'

'Promise?' Where before, Gill would have been off hand, acted like arranging the next time they would see each other was overkill, she looked longingly into his eyes, wishing he didn't have to go at all.

'I promise.' George indulged in one last tender kiss, before dashing towards the gates of Newmans to spring over them and sprint along the lane to his staff, who were probably impatiently waiting outside.

Gill stood at the door until he was out of sight. It felt good giving in at last. She was comfortable with the love running through her veins, thickening her blood and giving meaning to her existence. She had no fear about the prospect of him hurting her. He might, she was fairly convinced his dedication to her meant he wasn't going anywhere, but he might hurt her and she had given him that power. The fear wasn't there though, because she understood for the first time that this feeling – this wonderful feeling she had right now – was worth the risk.

‘Right then horse.’ Rosie straightened Red’s forelock and thought how gorgeous he looked in the English saddle she had bought for him. ‘Let’s go!’

Since the bad ride she and Red had shared at Newmans, Rosie had been leading Red out and ground-working him. She had baulked at the thought of getting astride him in his Western saddle. She was out of her depth. She didn’t even feel like she was a good enough English rider to back and train her horse herself, let alone embark on a brand new discipline after two lessons. She hadn’t felt like she could ask Gill to take Red back to Mel for any more lessons, not yet anyway. Gill was rebuilding her life and her business, she didn’t need to be ferrying Rosie around. There was logic behind that reason. The other reason Rosie tried not to dwell on was that she was a bit scared of her horse.

Yesterday Karen, the local saddler, had arrived with a selection of second-hand English saddles. The third one they tried fitted. When Karen stood back and said she would like to see him move in the saddle, Rosie had lead Red forward. Karen laughed and said she meant with Rosie on top! Pride gave Rosie the courage to mount. She had eased herself gently into the saddle, while Red stood quietly. The familiarity and comfort of an English saddle was like coming home.

Before Karen left, she asked to see Red’s Western saddle. To Rosie’s dismay Karen hadn’t thought it was a particularly good fit for Red. Karen wasn’t an expert, but her conviction that the saddle was too wide grew, as she felt around Red’s back and showed Rosie a pressure point developing in his muscles, which would slowly have led to a back problem. Rosie had read that Western saddles were 'one size fits all' but with Karen there in front of her, showing her, that wasn’t ringing true for Red. She realised how naive it had been to assume an eBay saddle would just fit perfectly.

Karen had agreed to take the saddle away to add flocking, to create a better fit for Red.

Rosie was glad the Western saddle was gone for the time being. She led Red to the mounting block; she could have laughed at herself, always running before she could walk. Trying to back a horse Western when you could barely ride Western!

She decided to ride Red, who looked adorable in the Havana brown general purpose saddle, English, until they were both more confident. Rosie called goodbye to Harry, who booted the stable door in disgust. She always shut him in when she took Red out and he always hated it. He had dropped some weight and grown noticeably stiffer and more arthritic during the two months in sodden fields at Newmans. Now he was back at home and had the option of an open fronted stable to roam in and out of at his leisure and Rosie's undivided attention, he was slowly becoming more like his old-self again. He snorted a short sharp whinny, which sounded distinctly like a reprimand to Red for leaving him behind. Rosie laughed and promised him they would be back soon.

She gently eased herself astride her young horse and was comforted by his grounded, relaxed footsteps leading them forward, the future was beneath her. The brightness of all Red had the potential to achieve, mingled with the daffodils springing up along the banks either side of the lane. The world awakened for the creation of a new era for Rosie. One where the prospect of having a baby at last felt natural and right, and one where the simple joy of walking Red along a quiet lane was enough to make her feel at one with the world again.

Jules was having a less pleasurable Sunday, but one which was not without its upside.

She had arrived at the farm that morning looking forward to a good long hack. Romeo was a bit reluctant when she led him out of the stable to mount. She hadn't thought much of it and soon they were riding across Maurice's fields towards the Northern gate, which led straight from his land onto a forestry track. It was Jules' favourite ride and involved no roadwork, which was ideal for Romeo who was acclimatising to having no shoes on. They climbed towards the precipice of the hill and Jules sang somewhat tunelessly at the blue sky above her.

Suddenly Romeo had stumbled, almost dropping to his knees, pitching Jules off and into the dewy wet grass. She picked herself straight up, concerned for Romeo. She took hold of his reins and he gingerly stepped forward. She walked backwards in front of him and saw that his steps were shorter than they should have been.

Jules immediately turned Romeo for home; walking beside him and encouraging him to make his way slowly back down the hill.

She had telephoned her veterinary practice from her mobile and a shiny 4x4 was parked in the yard by the time they arrived back at Romeo's stable.

'Ahhh, ere she is!' Maurice bellowed, as Ziggy bounded towards the farmer, who was stood with the vet in the yard.

'Hi,' said Jules, and knew she was blushing as the vet stepped forward to shake her gloved hand and introduced himself.

'Hello, I'm Nick. I'm on call today, this must be Romeo.'

Jules was too concerned about Romeo to focus on what a dish he was initially, but once the vet had assured her it was nothing too serious, she relaxed and started chatting to him.

'So, are you new, I don't think we've seen you before?'

'Yes. Just qualified last year and moved down to Devon for

the job. I wanted to specialise in equine practice and there was a vacancy here.'

'Well, you seem to be very good with Romeo.'

The horse was nuzzling the vet's back where he was stooped over, examining the hoof.

'Thanks! Come and look at this,' Nick gestured.

Jules moved around to look at the hoof.

'See that tiny trickle of moisture there?' Nick pointed to a black spot on Romeo's heel, where the nail injury had been.

Jules could see a clear liquid dribbling slowly from the spot. 'Abscess?' She folded her arms, furious. She had been so careful not to let the hole get infected. An abscess could be so painful and take so long to heal properly.

'Yep. Afraid so. Doesn't matter how careful you are with a puncture wound, sometimes they can brew very slowly from just the smallest intrusion of bacteria. Luckily though, he has burst it himself, probably when you were riding. Hot poultice for three days, then a dry one for two, then see how he is looking. I'll give you some antibiotics.' Nick gently released Romeo's hoof, allowing him to place it back onto the concrete of the yard. As he stood up, he patted the big chestnut's strong shoulder.

Jules was embarrassed as she noticed Nick briefly regarding Romeo's mane, which was starting to look like a toilet brush.

'I didn't hog him, it was—'

'When he was stolen, I know.'

'But how?'

'The whole practice is talking about it. It's such a good-news story.' Nick smiled and Jules supposed it was, she had only really thought about how she felt about having Romeo back.

Jules started to blush again, as the young vet continued to smile at her. He was quite short, not much taller than Jules herself and had a sort of barrel shape to his torso, not at all the athletic sinewy type she would normally have found attractive. There was something about his smile though. Something about his brown eyes, which made her feel sexy.

She chatted to him about where he was living and how he liked the area. He said he was renting a room on a farm and had been working so hard he hadn't really had chance to make any friends, outside the practice.

Jules found herself asking him out for a drink.

Gill decided she had wandered aimlessly around the house for long enough.

It was time to get some work done. She was in a daze. She just couldn't wait until tonight, when George would finish up at the restaurant and be back. That was hours and hours away and she had to fill her time somehow. The horses in training often had a day off on a Sunday, but if she got Renashee out now, it would be one less for her and Kelly to work-ride tomorrow.

She stood by the back door, trying to decide whether she needed a coat. She was, she decided, completely useless today! She couldn't stop thinking about how close she and George had unexpectedly become that morning and amazingly, how right it felt. She was never going to heal the scar on her heart which Amber had created. It was as though the void where her horse should have been was permanently sealed off within her, like the scene of an unsolved crime, dusty and uninhabited. George didn't fill the void, but he filled another part of her enough to make the void bearable.

She saw his jumper over the stool at the kitchen counter. She hung her jacket back on the peg and picked up the jumper, pressing it to her face and deeply inhaling the scent of him. She pulled the jumper over her head and pushed her arms into the sleeves, which she rolled up. It was far too big but she didn't care.

Just as she was finally donning her boots, her mobile rang from her pocket. She thought it would be George, but was not disappointed to see that it was Charlie.

'Hello, darling!' she answered.

'Hey, Mum, how are you?'

Gill hesitated, she wanted to say she was bloody fabulous, but she hadn't told Charlie about George and, although she had reconciled the age difference herself, she was embarrassed about revealing the new relationship to her daughter, who might scorn her.

'Good thanks, was just about to ride out, but am very pleased to hear from you darling.'

'Oh … not to worry then …'

'No, no, I have got plenty of time for a chat – what is it? Are you okay?'

'Yes, yes Mum I'm fine. I was going to ask you if you wanted to meet up in Exeter for a coffee?'

'Today?'

'Well, yes, but—'

'No today is fine, what time?'

'An hour?'

Chapter sixteen

Gill burst into the coffee shop on the high street at an ungainly run. She was ten minutes late. She smiled from the bottom of her heart when she saw Charlie, sat by the window with a magazine and a steaming mug of cappuccino. In a royal-blue dress over leggings and black boots, her straight long hair cascaded around her shoulders, she was like a bright light in an otherwise mundane and soulless place.

She looked so grown-up, so familiar yet so changed, she was becoming a woman. Gill would never have predicted that living with Alex could actually have been what Charlie needed, but the serenity about her was noticeable, even from across a crowded café.

'Mum.' Charlie stood up and embraced Gill warmly. Gill promptly burst into tears.

'Oh, Mum, what is it?' Charlie put a hand on her mother's, ready to be sympathetic to whatever tragedy had befallen her.

'Charlie, it's you.'

'Mum, look … I just feel with Dad is where I need to be right now. I love you but—'

'No no, Charlie, you get me all wrong. I'm not going to beg you to come home, really I'm not. I can see the difference in you and I know you're growing and changing. I am so proud of you and I feel like I don't deserve that pride. A few months away from me and you are this, this woman!'

Charlie's grip on her mother's hand tightened.

'Of course you should feel proud. You brought me up! Mostly on your own since I was eleven!'

Gill looked at Charlie, through tears. Charlie had never said anything close to that before and Gill couldn't quite believe she had.

'But mum I needed space to change. I needed some time and independence to find out who I was. I was never going to get that at home with you. I was too close, too used to behaving like the spoilt brat who was jealous of the horses. I had to break the cycle.'

Gill lowered her head. In the deepest buried corner of her heart she had always known Charlie was jealous of the horses. When she poured herself into tending to a sick horse, but roughly told her daughter to pull herself together when she was poorly, she fuelled that jealousy.

'You had a right to be, Charlie. I would always have been there if you needed me, but they take up so much of my energy.'

'I get it now though, Mum. I understand it is your business and you have to be passionate about it. I know it's hard work. I always thought you were just choosing them over me, but I get it now! Living with Dad and seeing the amount of time he spends at the office, the amount of time he's on a work call, even when he's at home. At least you were always at home, even if you were up in the barn!'

Gill leaned forward and held Charlie's hand in both of her own.

'You must know I love you Charlie. More than anything, you are my child and I simply adore you. It's not even conscious, it's like you are a part of me and you are there all the time. I thought you were a teenager and you needed space. I even hated you sometimes, when you were shouting at me or coming in late. The things that can come out of your mouth, but I never stopped loving you!'

'I was a bit of a bitch sometimes.' Charlie smiled, slightly ashamed.

'How did we get so tangled up?'

'Mothers and daughters will fight!'

'Let's not?'

Charlie nodded and Gill reached towards her daughter to caress her cheek and kiss her forehead.

'It's so nice to see you. I love that top.'

'I bought it with the Christmas vouchers!'

'Maybe we could go shopping sometime. I need some new clothes. You can help me pick some out?'

'Definitely.' Charlie grinned and started planning what colours would suit her mother and which of the current fashions could be pulled off with her figure. Charlie didn't want to offend her mother, but if she had just a few outfits that didn't come from charity shops it would be a start.

'Are they going to serve me then?'

'Think you have to go and get it.' Charlie pointed towards the counter, where three teenagers in matching uniforms used the lull in customers the mid-afternoon afforded to gossip and giggle.

'Okay. I'll grab a coffee, and then maybe we can do a bit of window shopping?' Gill stood up, deciding not to mention that she probably wouldn't actually be able to afford to buy anything for some months yet.

While she stood waiting for her latte to be prepared, she glanced at Charlie, who was rummaging in her bag. She wondered whether she had been too hasty in her decision not to mention George. This new more mature Charlie seemed like she might be happy for her mother.

Gill sat back at the table and was about to tut and comment

that she could have made a latte at home in less time, but she noticed printed website pages on the table in front of Charlie.

'What are they?'

Charlie took a deep breath.

'Don't get your hopes up, but I was looking on the internet last night and I saw this.'

Charlie slid the colour printout towards Gill. Gill looked at the page.

It was an advert from a classified site Gill recognised. The advert was headed, 'Great all Rounder' and a photograph of a grey pony filled the mid-section. She skimmed through the long description which assured any prospective buyer that the part-bred Arab pony, Douglas, was great in traffic and 100% to box, shoe and catch. Sadly outgrown by his rider, Douglas was an ideal competition pony for a young teenager to excel with.

'Okay.' Gill was completely confused, she had no idea why Charlie was showing her the advert. Gill had been offering to buy Charlie a pony since she was five but she had never been interested in riding. Surely Charlie didn't now want a grey pony called Douglas?

Gill shook her head and looked questioningly at Charlie.

'I don't get it?'

'Look again.'

Gill looked at the advert again but was still confused.

Charlie pointed to the photograph.

'Look harder, Mum.'

Gill peered at the grainy photograph, unable to grasp what her daughter was talking about. Suddenly she saw what Charlie was showing her.

Behind Douglas, stood on the other side of a post and rail fence, was a chestnut Arab mare.

'Oh my God.'

'That's what I said.'

Gill continued to stare at the printed sheet. She would never have seen it if Charlie hadn't pointed it out.

'Hi there, I'm calling about Douglas,' Charlie was putting on the syrupy voice of a posh girl looking for a pony.

Gill looked up sharply and almost snatched the phone from Charlie, wondering what the hell she was doing.

'Yes I think he would be just perfect. Mummy says she can drive me down to see him tomorrow.'

Gill stopped herself from interrupting just in time and continued to listen, white-faced, as Charlie extracted the information it might have taken the police days to find.

'Ten am is fine. My name is Lucy,' Charlie paused and her eyes sparkled, 'let me just get a pen.' Charlie reached into her bag and poised her pen over the white margin at the side of the advert. 'Churry Tree Stables, Tolvadden, Cambourne,' she repeated, as she wrote the address down. 'Oh – and Mummy says, what's the postcode for the sat nav?'

Gill drove back to Newmans, she still couldn't believe it. She glanced into the rear view mirror, Charlie was behind her in her Peugeot, following. She smiled at her daughter in the rear-view mirror. Charlie had passed her test the week before, first time, and she looked so relaxed already.

Charlie's performance on the phone, the long shot of finding Amber hidden in the background of a classified photo, seeing her driving along behind her in her own car, Gill could have cried with joy. Her daughter, the rebel.

'Come on.' Charlie headed straight for the horsebox, as soon as she had parked the little car.

'Shouldn't we call the police? Mike?'

'Mum, let's just get there.'

'We'll phone once we know it's her,' Gill nodded in agreement. Thankful Charlie was coming with her; she didn't want to do anything to ruin it. She let herself into the barn and grabbed the keys for the two-horse van. She paused briefly, as she passed Monty, to caress his cheek and kiss his nose. She beamed at the horse, who looked at her with pricked ears and an expression which, looking back later, would make her think he knew.

The sun was setting and an orange glow bathed Newmans in a light too beautiful to last very long. Mother and daughter ascended the cab and Gill manoeuvred the small box around to face the driveway. Charlie stared ahead out of the windscreen, with a mixture of determination and sheer excitement.

They drove past the house as George rounded the corner into Newmans and almost collided with them. He jumped out of his car, leaving it blocking their path and jogged towards the driver's side to speak to Gill.

Gill reluctantly wound down the window and he started to introduce himself to who he assumed must be Charlie, but Gill cut him off.

'Charlie found a classified ad, Amber looks like she might be in the photo, we're going to the yard now.'

George looked truly delighted and reached forward through the open window to kiss Gill on the lips, before she had a chance to fend him off. Gill sensed Charlie's eyebrows raise.

'George can you move your car?' Gill asked, politely.

'I should come. Let me come with you?'

'No, me and Charlie are going – sorry, listen, I'll call you as soon as we find her, if we find her – okay?' Gill softened, it was too late; Charlie would be bound to ask about the kiss, being cold to George would be pointless. She caressed his cheek and pressed her forehead to his.

'Go back to the restaurant, finish service, I will call.'

George reluctantly nodded. He smiled briefly at Charlie, before heading back to the black Lexis and reversing back down the drive. Gill waved her gratitude as they passed him.

'According to the GPS, it's going to take us two hours and thirty five minutes to get there, so tell me who that man was!'

Gill pulled onto the A30 westbound and sighed a deep resigned sigh. All the way from Newmans to the dual carriageway Charlie had demanded an explanation of George. Gill had to agree her argument that there wasn't time, didn't stand up.

'All right, but you have to promise not to judge me ... It all started at Christmas....'

By the time they crossed the border into Cornwall, Charlie knew the full story, including George's age, and the only detail Gill spared was how wonderful the sex was. She knew from finding the pill in Charlie's room that her daughter was not a virgin, but she was sure Charlie wouldn't be comfortable hearing about the overwhelming and delicious extent of her mother's new found pleasure!

'I underestimated you, Mum.'

Gill took her eyes off the road and turned to glance at Charlie's face, expecting to see disgust, but Charlie actually looked gleeful.

'You underestimated me?'

'Yeah, pulling a gorgeous toy boy and making him fall in love with you. I am well impressed!' Charlie laughed. Gill laughed too, she should have known.

'Can't wait to see Dad's face!'

Gill realised the old Charlie was still just under the surface.

'Oh, Charlie, don't.'

'Well he deserves it, doesn't he? He cheated on you; he can't expect you to sit around on your own forever?'

Gill peered curiously across at Charlie, one eye still on the road. She couldn't work her out.

'But I thought you and your Dad were really close now?'

'Oh we are. Definitely. I can still see him and you actually, for the human beings you are, the fact you are my Mum and Dad doesn't mean you don't do bad things and make mistakes.'

The old Charlie, plus insight.

'You're a funny girl.'

'Yep.'

The smile faded from Charlie's face.

'Actually, I don't think I had better tell him just now.'

'Why not?' Gill was intrigued, but tried to sound light.

'Him and Megan, not good. I don't know the full facts, but I have a feeling he slept with someone at a conference and she found out. He hasn't been over there for days; he's doing my head in, hanging around all the time.'

Gill imagined she ought to have been happy; he was showing his true colours and getting his comeuppance after all. But actually she felt nothing, except perhaps, sadness for Alex and his inability to hold onto a relationship. Before George, she would have been picking at Charlie for all the gory details, but now she really didn't care.

Gill drew the horsebox slowly up to the turning the GPS told them was their destination. The headlights illuminated the long rutted track, which according to the rusty sign, led to Churry Tree Stud.

'There was a lay-by back along. I'll park up. Better to walk down.'

Charlie nodded.

Gill reversed as quietly as the diesel engine would allow, back to the large lay-by, which doubled the width of the narrow lane. A car, which was coming up the road behind them, waited for her to manoeuvre the lorry out of the way, before driving on.

Gill sat in the cab, trying to compose herself. She wanted to see if the horse in the picture was Amber, she was desperate to get down there. But, on the other hand, she was not in the habit of sneaking around strange yards unannounced looking for a stolen horse in the dark, and was quite scared. What were people, happy to buy a stolen horse, capable of?

She looked over at Charlie in the milky light of the cab, she couldn't tell if her daughter was now worried as well.

'Right,' a surge of courage coursed through her, 'you wait here, if I find her I'll text you and you can call the police.'

'Absolutely not.'

'Charlie.?

'No way. Firstly, I am not being left alone in a creepy lane; secondly, I am not letting you go on your own.'

'Charlie, I am the Mum.'

'I found the advert. You can't stop me being there when we find her.'

'If we find her.'

Gill recognised the determination in Charlie's voice. The maternal instinct inside her told her not to put her child in danger, but Charlie was right, she didn't want to leave her in the cab either.

Gill opened the cab door.

'Right, we stick together.'

They walked in silence, grateful for the full moon above them. They reached the bottom of the track, a yard came into view. Above the yard, to the right, sat a large detached house. Gill could see lights on inside the house and put a finger to her mouth as they passed, signalling to Charlie to stay quiet.

The house was coated in grey pebbledash. The window frames looked old, paint flakes littering the sills. The track dropped into the yard, a hedge rose up between them and the house, obscuring the view. Gill was grateful for the hedge.

They crept towards the first stable in the u-shape block. A horse whickered softly as they approached. The stables were not in a much better condition than the house was, with patched and heavy-looking stable doors between brickwork which had clearly not been re-pointed for many years. But, the horses looked fairly well cared for, with deep beds and shiny coats, making Gill feel hopeful.

They walked silently around the block. When they reached the last stable, Gill peered inside at a bay pony, panic rose within her. None of the horses were Amber, maybe she wasn't here at all, the photo could have been taken months ago. They had seen a grey pony which looked like he was probably Douglas. Charlie had clutched Gill's arm and pointed excitedly, thinking surely it meant Amber would be there too.

Gill stood outside the last box, staring at the bay in the dimpsy light, which made his face looked almost ghostly. Charlie grabbed her arm.

'Come on.'

'Where …' Gill started to whisper back, but Charlie was pulling Gill around the bay's stable. As they rounded the corner behind the stable block, Gill gasped.

The front yard was clearly the show piece. Here, tucked away behind the more valuable horses, was the sourer side of horse dealing. A row of cramped stables fashioned from corrugated iron and sheep hurdles and tied together with bailer twine, housed the horses no one wanted.

Ribs protruded from course winter coats, soiled with the faeces no one had bothered to pick up. Hooves were invisible under inches of muck and rancid straw.

Tears pricked Gill's eyes and for a second she prayed they wouldn't find Amber.

They walked slowly along the row. Some of the horses barely had the energy to lift their weary heads, as the strangers passed them.

Charlie clutched her arm. A 14 hand Palomino pony looked out at them from its filth ridden home. A weeping sore from an ill fitting rug rose up from its withers, the proud flesh shining in the moonlight. Charlie held her hand to her mouth, unable to bear the sight.

Amber wasn't among the stabled horses.

Beyond the desolate row of horses, a sea of paddocks separated by barbed wire, stretched as far as they could see in the semi-darkness.

Gill lifted the wire carefully to allow Charlie to duck underneath. Gill could see horses in the paddock beyond and once she was safety through the wire, she started to walk towards them.

'Wait,' Charlie hissed.

Gill turned to see Charlie, heading towards a dark shadow created by the hay barn, which backed onto the first paddock. Gill's heart pounded as she followed her daughter towards the shape of a horse, which she could barely make out in the darkness.

A hoarse whinny reached Gill's ears like some distant sound

from beyond the realms of possibility.

Charlie put her hand out to the mare when she reached her, but Amber's ears were fixed on Gill, as she floated on air towards her horse. Her heart was rebuilt, but broken almost instantly when she got close enough to see how pitifully thin Amber was. Bloody crusted scabs covered her neck and back. With no rug and the absence of Gill's care, rain scald had eaten away Amber's beautiful copper coat.

Gill silently slid her arms around the mare's neck, she was conscious of how still Amber stood, no fuss or nudging as was her trademark, and it was as though the horse herself could not believe she was back in the arms of her owner at last.

Amber's neck, once proud and thickly muscled, was fey and alien. Gill held on tightly, despite the awfulness of Amber's condition, she gained comfort from the knowledge that she would put her back together as soon as she got her home.

Gill let go of Amber and embraced her daughter with the same compulsion.

'Charlie, you found her … my precious girl, you found her.'

Charlie stiffened.

'What the fuck are you doing on my property?'

Gill turned around, ready to tell the voice exactly what she was doing there, but, as her eyes made sense of the outline of the short rotund man in the moonlight, she instinctively moved in front of Charlie and terror closed her throat.

In his hands he held a double barrelled shotgun.

The shiny metal of the barrels glinted in the moonlight.

Charlie clutched her mother's sides, as she hid behind her.

'Get away from my horse,' the man growled.

But fear locked Gill to the spot, a voice inside her head

screaming, 'Not your horse, my horse. My Horse!'

'I think there's been some kind of misunderstanding here.' Gill held her hands forward, trying to look convincingly innocent.

'Oh yeah? What's that then?' the man sneered. Gill couldn't make out his features, but she heard the scorn in his voice clearly enough.

She didn't know what to say. She tried desperately to think of a reason for them being there, a reason they were sneaking around in the dark, but her brain worked infuriatingly slowly and didn't allow her the chance.

'Thought so, now get away from that horse.' The man thrust the gun towards them, threatening, angry now.

'She isn't your horse, she is ours!' Charlie shrieked from behind Gill, before Gill had a chance to stop her.

The man moved quickly towards them, swift footsteps, no time to run. Gill slid her arms behind, pressing Charlie into her back and ducked her head in readiness for the blow she knew was coming.

Loud, assertive voices echoed around the paddock. The man froze.

Gill realised she was still standing, realised there was no pain.

Flashlights raked across the paddocks until they settled on the pair of them.

'Over here.' An officer ran towards them. The man threw the shotgun down and set off in the opposite direction, running as fast as his short legs would carry him. As he went to go around the side of the hay barn, a well-timed punch in the face sent sprawling to the ground.

George stood over the man, who was groaning in agony and holding his nose. George's eyes lifted to look straight at Gill, his face illuminated by a policeman's torch. She held Charlie while she continued to stare at George, unable to begin to express her gratitude.

The nightmare was over.

It took some persuading but the officer in charge finally agreed to allow Gill to take Amber home without having seen her passport.

She and Charlie had left in such a hurry and with such an unknown ahead of them, Gill hadn't even thought to bring it. Neither had George, who had followed them all the way. He had called the police when he had arrived and seen Gill and Charlie walking down the drive, not wanting to take a risk.

The man had been taken away in an ambulance, accompanied by an officer who would question him, once his nose had been set.

Gill and Charlie were given a fairly stern dressing down about their vigilante antics, but the words of the officer washed over Gill as she cradled Amber's head in her arms. The chaos around her was drowned out by the presence of her horse and she was content to wait until they let her leave and the four of them could return home.

Despite the trauma and relief she had experienced, Charlie remembered the horses in the back yard.

'You have to call an Animal Shelter!' she cried, interrupting the officer, who was taking a statement from George and simultaneously deciding not to charge him with grievous bodily harm.

'Yes,' Gill looked up sharply, 'some of the horses here are in a terrible state.'

The Cornish Horsewatch coordinator, two local Animal Shelter inspectors and the police erupted into action over the following hours.

Horseboxes were arranged to take the worst of the ponies back to the shelter and the man from Horsewatch identified at least two horses he thought resembled those on the stolen horse register.

There was no longer any need for Gill and Amber to stay. The prospect of multiple stolen horses, along with charges for neglect, made the officer in charge less keen for them to hang around. He would be in touch to arrange for Amber's passport to be examined.

Gill didn't have a head collar or lead rope. She gently took hold of the mare's forelock, knowing she would go with Gill willingly. She led her into the box which George had backed into the yard.

George left his car. With all they had been through that night, it only seemed right to travel back together. They could collect it tomorrow.

George drove, Gill and Charlie huddled together beside him.

George's eyes were fixed firmly on the road, concentrating hard, knowing how precious a cargo he carried.

Charlie brought her feet up on the bench seat and Gill cradled her head where it rested on her lap.

Soon she would telephone Kelly and Mike, then Rosie and Jules to give them the miraculous and wonderful news. At that moment though, she just wanted to enjoy the feeling.

She gazed at Amber on the CCTV screen, eyes drinking in the black and white image of her horse. She had everything she could possibly want in the world right now. Gill felt like she was whole again.

Ambition was coming home.

***

The kitchen at Newmans was bathed in a golden July sun which streamed in through the open window. Jules and Rosie were sitting at the kitchen table.

'You absolutely have to marry him,' said Rosie, resolute, arms folded.

'Whatever happened to me taking it slowly and not diving into another relationship?' Jules raised her eyebrows at Rosie, knowing she was talking about Nick the vet.

Gill moved over from the kitchen window towards her friends. She had been watching at Amber in the paddock, the glorious dry summer was healing her back beautifully and Gill felt a delicious anticipation at the thought of the life growing inside of the mare. The foal would be due sometime early next year. They weren't sure when and had no idea who the sire was. The mare had been covered at some point, presumably at hands of the men who had stolen her. She wondered who would arrive first, the baby Rosie had recently found out she was carrying, or Amber's foal. It didn't matter, as long as all were healthy.

Gill put her arm around Jules and rubbed her shoulder.

'Under normal circumstances, I would say you were probably still on the rebound. Normally, I would agree, you should wait and give yourself much longer to get over—'

'Twat face,' Rosie interrupted.

'Yes, thank you Rosie, or to those of us without such a colourful vocabulary, to get over Tristan. But, the man you are seeing is a vet and we simply cannot allow you NOT to marry him.'

'I've only been seeing him for a couple of months, it's very casual!' Jules protested, throwing her hands up with theatrical force, knowing they were teasing her.

'Casual? I think you ought to explain to him just how much we spend on vet's bills between us and I'm sure he will completely understand how essential it is that one of us marries a vet.' Rosie retained a straight face, adding conviction to her quite logical point.

'You think?' Jules stepped off of the stool and put her hands on her hips.

'Absolutely. We need George to cater the wedding, so I can't finish with him.'

'And I'm going to be too fat to pull a vet soon,' Rosie patted her tummy.

'You two have really thought about this then?' Jules shook her head, resigned.

Gill and Rosie nodded in unison.

'If it's okay with you, I'd like to get to know him just a little better first?'

'Please don't take too long Jules, Amber is in foal and Rosie has a baby on the way. All very expensive.' Gill walked towards the kitchen door and started putting her boots on.

'Bit selfish, Jules.' Rosie shook her head in disappointment and followed Gill.

'Can we, at least, go for our ride first?!' Jules protested, as she followed them outside and closed the door behind her.

Gill and Rosie looked at one another and back at Jules. Gill nodded.

'I suppose, I have got three racehorses to get ridden today.'

The three women walked together towards the horse barn. The sun warm about them, each bright at the prospect of being on horseback together. Nothing more important than which way to go for a hack occupied their minds.

Jules looked across at her friend's grins, still wide from teasing her. 'You bitches …'

Indigo Dreams Publishing
24 Forest Houses
Cookworthy Moor
Halwill
Beaworthy
Devon
EX21 5UU

www.indigodreams.co.uk